The Cañon City Chronicles

Books 1, 2 & 3

DAVALYNN SPENCER

The Cañon City Chronicles © 2017 by Davalynn Spencer

Loving the Horseman © 2017 by Davalynn Spencer
Second edition, revised from previously published, *The Cowboy Takes as Wife* © 2014 by Davalynn Spencer

Straight to My Heart © 2017 by Davalynn Spencer
Second edition, revised from previously published, *Branding the Wrangler's Heart* © 2014 by Davalynn Spencer

Romancing the Widow © 2014, 2017 by Davalynn Spencer

Wilson Creek Publishing

Print ISBN 978-0-9989512-1-8

All rights reserved. No portion of this book may be reproduced in any form without prior permission from the author, except as permitted by U.S. copyright law.

Scripture quotations are from the King James Version of the Bible.

The characters and events in this book are fictional, and any resemblance to actual persons or events is coincidental.

Cover design and Book layout by www.ebooklaunch.com

Books by Davalynn Spencer

THE FRONT RANGE BRIDES SERIES
Mail-Order Misfire - Series Prequel
An Improper Proposal - Book 1
An Unexpected Redemption - Book 2
An Impossible Price - Book 3

THE CAÑON CITY CHRONICLES SERIES
Loving the Horseman - Book 1
Straight to My Heart - Book 2
Romancing the Widow - Book 3
A Change of Scenery - Book 4

Novellas
Snow Angel
Just in Time for Christmas
A High-Country Christmas - two-novella collection
The Snowbound Bride
The Wrangler's Woman
As You Are at Christmas
"Taste and See" in *Always a Wedding Planner*

The three books making up *The Cañon City Chronicles* were first released as unrelated titles in 2014. However, I originally wrote them with the intention that they tell the ongoing story of the fictional Hutton family, set against the backdrop of historical Cañon City, Colorado. Now, with fresh edits, *Loving the Horseman, Straight to My Heart,* and *Romancing the Widow* (2015 winner of the **Will Rogers Medallion Award** for inspirational Western fiction), come to you as *The Cañon City Chronicles,* offered for the first time as a complete series under one cover. I'm thrilled to release these stories again, in accordance with my original dream.

Loving the Horseman

Davalynn Spencer

Dedicated to the indomitable spirit of
those who through trial have burnished their faith
to shine brighter than the purest gold.

"For I know the thoughts that I think toward you, saith the Lord, thoughts of peace and not of evil, to give you an expected end."

—*Jeremiah 29:11*

CHAPTER ONE

Omaha, Nebraska
Summer, 1860

Annie Whitaker wrapped her fingers around the arms of the front porch rocking chair rather than her sister's throat.

Of course Edna thought heading for the Rocky Mountains was a bad idea. Everything was a bad idea unless she'd thought of it first.

Perspiration gathered at the nape of Annie's neck. She uncurled her fingers, relaxed her jaw, and in her sweetest voice, shifted the conversation to Edna's favorite topic. "Do you have your eye on any particular fella who's been calling lately?"

Edna stirred the heavy air with her silk fan and lowered her gaze. The porch swing creaked as she toed it back and forth. "Perhaps."

Annie rolled her eyes, grateful that Edna couldn't see out the side of her head like a mule. The comparison brought a smile to Annie's lips and she rubbed her cheek to hide it.

No doubt Jonathan Mitchell topped Edna's list. He was financially successful, well bred, and handsome in a soft sort of way. Annie fully expected Daddy to turn the mercantile over to Mr. Mitchell when he left next month.

No—when *they* left next month.

She planned to be on that stagecoach with her father come hel— She pinched off the forbidden word and glanced at Edna, who always managed to read Annie's improper thoughts.

Why shouldn't she say that word? It was in the Bible. And it certainly applied to Omaha at the moment, hot and heavy as an unbroken fever.

Heat waves rolled over their Aunt Harriet's vast lawn and rippled the distant trees into a surreal horizon. Annie unfastened the top button on her thin blouse. She detested summer—particularly July—almost as much as she disliked Edna's propensity for being coy.

"Annabelle May." Edna glared. "Don't be indecent."

"Don't be absurd." Annie released the second button out of spite. "It's unbearably hot and there's no one to see besides you and Aunt Harriet. And she's half blind." So much for her sweet voice.

"Well, I *never*." Edna's eyelashes whipped up the humidity even more than her fan.

Annie pushed out of the rocker and leaned over the porch railing. Even the copper day lilies bordering the front of the house struggled to hold their heads up.

Edna's brow glistened with perspiration. "A little warmth does not give a lady license for indecency."

Tired of the heat as well as Edna's attitude, Annie spun toward her sister.

"Daddy wants to go to Cañon City and I'm going with him. You can stay here in Omaha with all your beaus and Aunt Harriet if you like, but I'm not letting our father go alone." She reset a loose pin in her unruly hair, then fisted her hands on her hips. "It will be an adventure. 'Pikes Peak or bust,' they say. All those gold seekers need to get their supplies from someone. Why not Daddy?"

"Humph." At fourteen, Edna had begun her wrist-flicking. Now, four years later, she had perfected it to a fine art, and the hand-painted silk fan folded in one swift movement. "That's all you think about—adventure. You and Father both."

She palmed damp ringlets off her pale forehead and flicked the fan open for a fresh attack. "I can't believe he's willing to pull up and take off for those ragged mountains at his age. He should stay here and increase his holdings. The general store is doing quite well. Why start over someplace else and risk losing everything."

Edna fluttered furiously and aimed a guilt-laden glare. "Including his life and yours."

Annie folded her arms. Edna's threat echoed their aunt's petulant scolding. Aunt Harriet was bound by tradition and the social constraints of widowhood, and she fairly dripped resentment over her brother's freedom to do as he pleased.

Well, that was Aunt Harriet's choice, not Annie's. She preferred to experience all she could, even if it meant risking her life in the Rocky Mountains. Zebulon Pike, John C. Fremont, and others had conquered those peaks. Why not Daniel Whitaker and his younger daughter?

"Cañon City isn't even established. It's an upstart supply town, Annie, on Kansas Territory's farthest edge."

Annie rested against the railing and focused on the window's beveled edge behind the swing. "I know what and where it is."

"What it *is* is uncivilized." Edna slowed her silken assault, tempered her tone. "You know what that means. They have no law yet, and probably even less order with all those gold-hungry miners and speculators and wild, drunken cowboys."

"And bank clerks and preachers and store keepers." Annie pressed her open neckline flat against her collar bone. "Be reasonable."

An unreasonable request when it came to her big sister.

Predictably, Edna stiffened and assumed a superior posture. "And Indians. You know wild savages live there, as well as all along the way. Don't forget what the Utes did at Fort Pueblo just six years ago. And on Christmas, no less."

Annie gritted her teeth, barring hateful words that fought for release. She and her sister had waged this verbal war more times than she cared to count. She refused to chew that piece of meat again.

A rare breeze suddenly swept the wide front porch, and Annie imagined mountain air whispering along high canyons. She braced her hands against the railing, closed her eyes, and recalled what she'd read about the Arkansas River falling from the Rockies cold and full-bellied with snowmelt. A marvelously deep gorge squeezed the river into raging white water and shot it onto the high plains through a wedge-shaped valley. And guarding the mountain gateway, that brand new town, Cañon City.

Oh, to be involved with something new and unpredictable. To see that canyon, and hear the water's roar—

Edna's lofty *tsk* interrupted the daydream. "I know the stories too."

Annie's eyes flew open to her sister's shaking head and mirthless lips. Edna read her mind as easily as a dime novel.

"Do you know that at last count, Cañon City had only 720 residents?" Edna said.

Annie raised her chin. "Daddy and I have discussed it."

The fan snapped shut. "Do you know that out of that number, *six hundred* are men?" Edna shuddered.

"They're men, Edna. Not animals."

"Don't be so sure, dear sister. With numbers like that, I dare say those *men* are hard pressed to maintain their humanity."

"This is 1860, not the Dark Ages." Annie stepped away from the railing, tempted to undo a third button just to see how fast Edna could flail her fan. "We are going, and we are leaving in three weeks with or without your approval—or Aunt Harriet's."

She marched into the house and down the hall to the kitchen, where she retrieved the lemonade pitcher from the ice box. No doubt she'd not have such a modern luxury in Cañon City. She poured a glass, let it chill with the cold drink, and then held it against her forehead and neck.

The shocking relief conjured images of clear mountain snowmelt. Goose bumps rippled down her spine. The Arkansas must be delightfully cold, nothing like the Big Muddy slogging along dark and murky on its unhurried journey to the Mississippi.

At nearly a mile high, Cañon City was close to Denver City's famous claim. That in itself had to present a cooler climate. Much more pleasant, even in the summer. Edna didn't know *that*.

Guilt knifed between Annie's thoughts, and she regretted her snippy attitude. But Edna infuriated her so. How had they both come from the same parents?

A familiar ache squeezed Annie's heart. That was one thing Edna did know that Annie did not—their mother's comforting arms.

She doused the pain with a sweetly sour gulp that quite reflected the two Whitaker sisters. Annie thumbed the corners of her mouth, certain that she was not considered the "sweet" one of the mix. She and Edna were no more alike than the dresses they wore.

Edna was polished satin. Annie, plain calico.

Was that the real reason behind her determination to go west with Daddy?

She slumped into a kitchen chair and traced the delicate needlework on the tablecloth. Several eligible young men called on fair-haired Edna. But no one called for the wild-maned Annie.

She pushed a loose strand from her forehead as tears stung her eyes, bunching up for an ambush. Swallowing the dregs of jealousy, she whispered, "Forgive me, Lord. Help me love my sister. Even if I don't like her very much sometimes."

The screen door slapped against its frame, and Edna's full skirts rustled toward the kitchen. Annie rushed to the icebox and filled a second glass with lemonade for her sister, hoping the gesture would ease the tension between them.

It was the least she could do.

CHAPTER TWO

Cañon City, Colorado
Autumn, 1860

 The late October sun bled pink and gold, impaled on a rugged ridgeline. Caleb Hutton stopped at the lip of a bowl-like depression, leaned on his saddle horn, and studied the jagged silhouette. He could just make out a shadowy monolith jutting from the mountain and at its base a narrow green vein that pulsed across the valley floor. To the right, a dozen buildings stood below a craggy granite spine. The faint sounds of hammers, people, and livestock drifted across the valley.
 Cañon City.
 The fledgling town huddled north of the tree-lined Arkansas River where canvas tents, lean-to's, and camp fires sprouted. Approaching from due east, Hutton crossed the valley and rode into town past a livery, corral, and framed-in shops. A white clapboard building stood across from the livery—a schoolhouse or church.
 He stopped at the largest structure, the Fremont Hotel, then dismounted and looped both horses' reins around the hitching rail. Rooster tongued his bit and Sally heaved a sigh. Caleb patted the gelding's neck, slapped dust from his hat, and stepped through the hotel door in need of a room and a bath.
 He found neither.
 Rumors had been right. The burgeoning mine-supply town was full to bursting. Every chair in the hotel's crowded parlor held a man, and laughter and cigar smoke drifted from

the open doorway to the adjoining saloon. Caleb's empty stomach rumbled, and he returned to his horses.

Besides the substantial brick-faced hotel, saloon, and a few other establishments, buildings in varying degrees of completion lined the short, broad street. Fading daylight drew carpenters and masons from their work and into their wagons, but others lingered along the boardwalk. Mostly miners holed up for the winter, Caleb supposed, from the looks of their grimy dungarees and whiskers.

At least he'd beat the snow.

Rooster's head drooped over the rail, eyes closed. Caleb rubbed beneath the red forelock.

"Tired as I am, are you, boy?" He gathered the reins, swung up, and pulled Sally along, turning back the way he had come. The river should be running low and smooth with summer long past, and the cottonwood grove he'd seen on his approach would be hotel enough.

He'd keep the horses with him rather than board them at the livery and sleep somewhere else alone. After three months under the stars with the animals' heavy presence nearby, he doubted he could sleep without them anyway.

Come dark, he'd brave the cold water for a bath.

Near the street's end, a woman swept the boards in front of a narrow storefront. Above her hung a painted wooden sign: *Whitaker's Mercantile*. As he rode nearer, she stooped to reclaim something, and a chunk of chestnut fell over her shoulder. She leaned her broom against the building and twisted the strands into a knot. He didn't realize he was staring until her eyes flashed his way, challenging his steady observation.

As he came even with the store, he touched the brim of his hat. "Evening, ma'am."

She dropped her hands as if caught stealing but held his gaze, nodding briefly before she turned away.

Caleb swallowed a knot in his throat. He reined Rooster toward the river, down the gentle slope to a cottonwood grove, and set his mind on making camp. No point digging up what he'd spent the last three months riding away from.

The horses drank their fill, and he hobbled and tethered them close by. Didn't need some hard case sneaking off with them while he slept.

The breeze danced downstream and shivered through the trees. Caleb's campfire was not the only glow along the river, and he was grateful for its warmth. As he cut open his last can of beans, he counted a half dozen flickering lights scattered up and down the banks.

Beneath his saddle lay his father's old friend, a Dragoon Colt. Good for snakes, his pa had always said. On the backside of Kansas Territory—as anywhere—some of those snakes had two legs and would likely kill to get what they wanted. He would not fall victim.

He sank onto his bedroll, eased back against his saddle, and waited for the stars to show—again. He could nearly chart them from watching them wink into view each night, as constant and familiar as his horses.

Restfulness settled over him for the first time since he'd left St. Joseph. The muscles in his neck and legs relaxed, and tension seeped from his spine as the river chattered like a secret companion just a few feet away.

Three months riding alone had given him plenty of time to think about his life, where he'd been, and where he was going. One more day and he'd be at the Lazy R, where cattle outnumbered people fifty to one.

Suited him just fine.

He pulled off his hat and linked his fingers behind his head.

He knew his way around horses better than most, thanks to his pa, rest his soul. Cows weren't that much different.

At least they wouldn't be sitting in pews waiting for him to say something inspiring.

He snorted at the image, but guilt twisted his gut. He'd tried his hand at people and failed. God must have made a mistake.

Or Caleb had misheard.

A twig snapped, and he slid a hand beneath his saddle. The hammer's click cut through the silence and drew a quick confession.

"Don't shoot, mister. Don't shoot."

Caleb aimed for the voice, considering the scant years that rang out in its tremor.

"Show yourself," he ordered.

Another snap and a boy stepped from between the horses, arms raised stick straight as if he were being hung by his thumbs.

"I ain't stealin' nothin', mister. I swear."

Caleb sat up. "Right there's two things you shouldn't be doing."

Firelight licked the boy's skinny neck, and his Adam's apple bobbed. "Yessir. What's that, sir?"

Caleb eased the hammer back and lowered his gun. "Stealing and swearing. Both will get you into trouble."

He waved the boy over and kept the revolver in his lap. "How old are you, and what are you doing out here by yourself at night? Don't you know you could have been shot?"

"Twelve, huntin' a bush, and yessir."

Caleb held back a chuckle at the nervous answer. "You can put your hands down now."

The youngster dropped his arms fast. Like the woman at the mercantile.

"What's your name?"

"My Christian name is Benjamin, sir, but my folks call me Springer."

"Well, Springer, where *are* your folks?"

The boy pointed upstream. "See that light there in the trees? That there's our camp."

"Aren't you a little far from home for this time of night?"

"Yessir, but like I said, I was huntin' a bush."

A woman's voice called through the dark, quietly at first, then with greater urgency.

"You'd better answer," Caleb said.

"Comin', Ma!"

The boy's voice cracked and Caleb dropped his head and smiled. He poked the fire with a broken branch and sparks licked the sky. "So, Springer, before you head back, I have two questions for you. First, tell me why they call you Springer."

The boy grinned and stuck his thumbs in his suspenders. "That's 'cause I can jump higher 'n anybody."

Life should be so simple.

"Fair enough. Next question. Why were you sneaking up on my horses?"

Springer hung his head, and his hands dropped to his sides. "I just wanted to pet 'em. We had to get rid of our horses, and I miss 'em somethin' fierce."

"Benjamin Springer Smith! I'm gonna tan your hide if you don't get your tail over here right now!"

Caleb laughed. "Off with you, Benjamin Springer Smith, or you won't have a hide left to tan the next time."

"Yessir. Thank you, sir."

The boy crashed through the cottonwoods like a razorback on the run. A high-pitched yelp signaled that his arrival wasn't as quick as his ma expected.

Caleb chuckled, stashed the revolver, and poked the fire again. Embers scattered like Missouri fireflies, and the wood snapped and cracked in surrender to the flames.

The sound punctured his chest, reopened a wound. He shoved the heel of his hand against his breastbone, winded by the unexpected pain.

Once he'd surrendered to a searing flame. Twice, really. Answered a call that proved fruitless and offered his soul to a woman who proved faithless. Both failings twisted into a noose, and he wanted nothing but to rid himself of it.

Inexperience had cost him his life's endeavors—his small pastorate and the affection of the woman he loved. Too young to earn many converts, he thought he'd at least turned Miss Mollie Sullivan's.

He'd turned her, all right. All the way into the arms of the wealthiest man in his congregation. Who also happened to sit on the elders' board.

He grunted and stabbed at the fire again, refusing to let it burn out. He dug for the brightest ember and held the stick against it until the probing wood flamed into a torch.

A similar torch had gutted him, left him ruined for both the ministry and matrimony. He refused to stand in the pulpit, avoiding Miss Sullivan's eyes while he preached God's love and forgiveness. Nor could he call a meeting of the board and explain his sudden departure.

He simply traded his frock coat and collar for a duster and broad brim and tacked a note to the chapel door.

Not exactly Luther's *Ninety-Five Theses.*

A sneer lifted his lip.

He had wanted to smash the elder's smirking, self-righteous face. But then he'd be no better than the thieving scoundrel himself. And what would that tell his parishioners? Turn the first cheek so the parson could punch the second?

He shoved the charred branch into the dirt, stretched out on his bedroll, and folded his arms across his chest. For three months he'd argued with himself about returning to St. Joe and owning up. But he'd already said his piece in the note on the door. Told those gentlefolk they needed a more experienced preacher. Left them the name of his seminary professor.

And if he went back and knocked out one of his congregants with anything other than preacherly conviction, he'd have to apologize all over again. Better leave well enough alone.

He rubbed his chin, scratched at the stubble.

Tomorrow he'd start forgetting. Forget Mollie, the ministry, and everything familiar, including the three people he'd met since riding into Cañon City—an apologetic hotel clerk who didn't have a room for him, a beautiful woman with a broom, and a youngster camping on the river with his family. Two of the three he wouldn't mind seeing again, but that likely wouldn't happen.

Setting his boots aside, he slipped from his clothes and into the shallow water, lowering himself with a harsh gasp as the current wrapped around him. Cold but cleaner, he quickly dressed, stirred the fire, and crawled into his bedroll.

The familiar mix of wood smoke, leather, and dried horse sweat swirled above him, and he stared at the only thing there was to see. A starry band swept across the sky, sparkling a thousand times brighter than it did in St. Joseph. A glittering contrast against the black vault.

Like the shimmer he'd seen in the broom lady's lovely eyes.

Tomorrow. He'd forget all of them tomorrow when he started his new life.

CHAPTER THREE

Annie heard the plop before the smell penetrated the rough wall. Her nose wrinkled and she buried her face in her pillow. Never in all her seventeen years had she dreamed she'd wake up in a barn.

A horse whinnied and pawed, impatient for breakfast. Annie's stomach returned the complaint, but the stench of the fresh deposit warred with her hunger pangs. She pulled the quilt over her head and burrowed into the blankets on her straw-filled pallet.

The Overland Stage had safely carried her and her father across the wide prairie last month, and they'd shared primitive accommodations along the way. But the Planter's House in Denver City and their week-long stay there had led her to believe the rugged Rockies weren't so rugged after all.

Hah. That was Denver, this was not.

What would her sister say if she could see Annie curled up in the Cañon City Livery? A vision of Edna's tightly seamed lips and disapproving fan roused Annie's ire, and the imagined words shot heat through her veins.

I told you so.

Annie tossed the quilts back and reached for the clothing she'd draped over the foot of her pallet. After pulling her arms inside her cotton gown, she traded out the stockings and drawers she'd slept in but kept her chemise. She tugged on a flannel petticoat, topped it with two skirts, then exchanged her gown for a long-sleeved shirt and buttoned on her high-top shoes. She loosened the long braid that hung down her back, and with dexterity born of practice, brushed through the thick strands and deftly twisted them into a knot and pinned it in place. Not that she counted on it to stay. By noon it would be hugging the base of her neck.

She smoothed her quilt top, tucked in the edges all around, and prayed that no mice worried their way into her bed looking for warmth.

A shiver scurried along her spine.

What were their chances of surviving the winter? How would she and her father not freeze to death?

Needing relief, she had no time for fearful thoughts and pulled her heavy cloak about her shoulders for a trip to the necessary.

Since she was always up before her father, she quietly stepped around the curtain they'd hung to separate their pallets and stopped short. He sat at the pallet's edge, galluses drooping off his hunched shoulders, head in his hands.

"Daddy?" she whispered. "Are you all right?"

He raised his head, and worry rimmed his moist eyes. "*We* are not all right, Annie." He spread his hands, palms up. "Look where we are. We sleep in a *barn*. I've brought my beautiful young daughter all the way to the Rocky Mountains to live in a barn."

His head sank to his hands again.

His words burned into the doubts she'd so carefully tucked away, and unladylike thoughts of their new landlord—one Jedediah Cooper—sparked her resolve. "Oh, Daddy, we're going to be fine." She knelt beside him and clasped his arm.

He pulled a white handkerchief from his pocket and wiped his eyes. "We should have stayed in Omaha. My sister and yours were right."

Annie's hackles rose at the idea of Edna being right—*again*. "No, they were not. They simply don't have the adventurous streak that you and I have." She forced her lips into a smile and smoothed his uncombed hair off his forehead. "We'll talk to Mr. Cooper again about giving us the back room in the store. It's just whiskey he's got in there, and he can move it to his saloon. I'll even help."

Her father's eyes latched onto hers and his bushy brows lurched together. "You will not. You don't go near that place of his." He stuffed the handkerchief in his pocket and shook his head. "If we sold the mare, we'd have money against a loan and could build a small cabin. And we'd save on her feed too. She eats as much as the other three horses combined."

Annie stood and brushed off her skirt. It wasn't completely true. Her beloved mare, Nell, didn't eat quite that much. Maybe just as much as two of their other horses, but that wasn't the point.

She buttoned her heart against her father's remark and her cloak against the cold. "I'm going out back and then to the mercantile. You banked the fire last night, so it won't take me long to get the place warmed up." She bent to kiss his snowy head. "That potbellied stove is a blessing. I'll have coffee going in no time."

Her father slapped his hands on his knees and threw back his shoulders. "You've got spunk, Annie girl. Just like your mama."

His words picked at an old scab. The one that always opened anew when he mentioned the mother she had never known.

"I'll feed Nell too, Daddy."

He huffed, wagged his head, and grunted as he pushed to his feet.

Annie opened the stall door and gathered her skirts against her as she pulled it closed. The mare whinnied and hung her massive head over the railing across the alleyway.

"Hungry again, are you, Nell?" Annie scooped an armload of loose hay from a pile and tossed it over the gate. She brushed off her skirt again and picked stubborn pieces from her cloak.

"Take it slow, girl." Reaching over the gate, she stroked the thick yellow neck and hushed her voice to a whisper. "Daddy's going to sell you like the others if you don't quit eating so much."

Nell's ears flicked forward and back as if taking due note.

They'd needed all four draft horses to haul their supplies south from Denver City because Daddy refused to drive mules or pay someone else to do so. But after renting and stocking the mercantile, he'd sold off the other three horses, their harnesses, and the heavy freight wagon. Everything excess had to go, he'd said. She'd fought dearly to keep the big yellow mare.

She checked over her shoulder for unlikely onlookers, then rubbed her backside, remembering how it ached during the jolting ride to Cañon City. Much worse than during the dust-choked miles on the Overland Stage from Leavenworth, though mercifully shorter.

She hurried to the necessary behind the livery, then to the boardwalk, where few people appeared so early—merchants or carpenters or stone masons preparing for the day. At the mercantile door she slid the key in the lock and entered beneath the brass bell's cheerful welcome. The scent of coffee beans, tobacco, and oiled leather soothed her nerves and she drew in a slow, deep breath. Their modest store held everything a person could want—a person with a soul brave enough to head west, that is.

Fine flour and sugar, pearly oats and smooth dried beans, barrels of sour pickles and pale crackers. Bright dress cloth and drab canvas, blue-speckled dishware and cast-iron skillets. Black leather boots and shoes and a few saddles. Strong soaps, wooden toys, a precious sampling of books, and notions like needles and threads and buttons and pins—better than a drummer's wagon.

Peeling off her cloak, she surveyed the cramped, full-to-the-brim space. Aunt Harriet would tell her she had best watch her step, for "pride goeth before destruction." Annie sniffed at the imagined scolding. Of course she was proud. She was useful here, working beside her father, as if what she did mattered. They met people's needs, and that was important. Much more important than sitting on Aunt Harriet's front porch waiting for one of Edna's many beaus to give her a second glance.

To pick her up as second best.

Disappointment clawed at Annie's ribcage, finding her wanting in comparison to her sister. Her unruly hair never stayed put like Edna's flaxen tresses, and her thin chest only half filled Edna's ruffled bodices. But Daddy had called her beautiful this morning. She smiled at his tenderness, though she knew she would never be as fetching as her sister.

So be it.

Her jaw tightened with determination. It was better this way, that she didn't turn the head of every man who saw her. Her father needed help, and she refused to sit by and wait for some man to come along and make her life better when she could do that herself.

She marched to the stove that anchored the long narrow room, bunched her skirt to protect her hand, and opened the door. With a poker she scraped at the ash pile and uncovered a glowing red eye. Perfect. She added a few chunks from the nearby coal bucket and adjusted the damper.

"Lord, you promised you'd meet our needs." She rubbed her hands together and held them open above the squat stove, careful not to let her skirts touch its iron belly. "And you know Daddy and I need a warmer place to stay until we can afford to build a house."

Guilt pointed a grimy finger. Some folks had it worse. How many were camped by the river in canvas tents, cooking over open fires? And hadn't one man died when his gun slipped to a rock and discharged, killing him instantly?

Frustrated that she couldn't build a house with her own two hands, she squirmed inwardly at the doubt behind her pleading prayer.

She left the warm spot and ground fresh coffee, then filled a blue enamel pot with water and set it on the stove. Satisfied with the fire, she closed the damper and arranged several chairs around a braided rug before the stove.

At least she and Daddy could get warm and be out of the crisp fall air. The acknowledgement settled like a thick quilt against her soul, reminding her that small blessings were still blessings.

"Thank you, Lord," she whispered, chastened.

Since her father had agreed to handle the mail for Cañon City, at least a couple hundred people trailed through the mercantile each week. Not everyone had family to write to them, and a few, she'd learned, chose not to have folks know where they were.

Housing a post office, such as it was, her father's store had become a gathering place for several of the town's more respectable residents, as well as a few who weren't—like Jedediah Cooper, their landlord who owned nearly the entire block and acted like he owned his renters too.

She shuddered at the memory of his whiskey-colored gaze.

With everything in order, she hung her wrap on the back wall that separated the mercantile from the small storeroom. Pulling an apron over her head, she dislodged her hair in the process and peeked around the empty door frame.

Anger threatened to get the better of her. That old miser Cooper should have rented them the whole building. What were eight more feet, give or take?

She tied the apron strings and quickly repinned her rebellious strands. Combs. She'd order more combs and hairpins the next chance she got. Other women must have the same problem, and combs might sell along with the gloves and hats they kept on hand.

The bell chirped.

"Smells good in here, Annie."

Relief rushed in with the return of her father's usual cheerfulness. She offered another prayer of thanks and set about greasing a cast-iron skillet. "Coffee's almost ready. Come have a seat and I'll make some pan biscuits."

He pegged his coat and donned an apron. "If the freighters stop in today, I'll mention the mare again. Then you could have a cabin with a real cookstove. Maybe an iron bed too."

Annie swallowed against the dread of losing Nell as she floured the sideboard and rolled out the dough.

The bell rang again, and Duke Deacon and his son, Joseph, stomped in. Annie's heart plopped like a doughy wad. Of course the day's first customers had to be freighters.

By the time she had the biscuits on the stove, the men had taken chairs and coffee. Annie set to making a fresh pot, praying the freighters wouldn't want her Nell.

"Gonna be a long, hard winter, Whitaker," the elder driver said. Blue eyes shone like lights from his weathered face, and his black hair lay slick and flat against his skull. "If there's somethin' you'll be needin' 'fore spring, better order it. I'll be freightin' 'tween storms, so won't be near as regular as it is now. Fact, this is my last trip to Denver City for a spell. When I get back, I'll be stayin' put for a couple weeks."

Her father leaned against a cracker barrel, nursing his own tin cup. "Tell me how you figure on a hard winter."

"Skunk cabbage," Joseph piped, a shorter, smoother version of his coal-haired father. "Higher 'n it's been in a long time, ain't that so, Pa."

Duke nodded and sipped. "That's right. Surprised to see it too. Don't usually get that much snow down here 'long the Arkansas. Not like falls up on the Platte."

Annie caught her father's laughing eyes above his coffee cup. He put no stock in such folklore about cabbage and snowfall and hard winters, and he was more inclined to refer to the almanac he kept under the front counter. Not that he'd say so to his new customers.

The Deacons left with a dozen biscuits in their bellies and an order for ladies' combs and hairpins. All the cabbage talk must have driven Nell from her father's mind, and Annie sighed with relief when the freighters climbed onto their wagon without having bought her beautiful mare.

Strange, the things she'd thanked the Lord for lately.

Perspiring in the cramped space, now that the stove was hot, she rolled her sleeves and wiped her neck with her apron hem. No time to cool herself with a brief walk outdoors. More customers were sure to come.

She plopped a fresh batch of dough onto the floured sideboard sending up a dusty cloud. Rolled and cut and amply greased, a second batch browned on the pot-belly within minutes.

"Believe I'll buy this tin o' molasses to go with those fine biscuits you've got there." Her father stood behind the front counter dusting the tin top with his shirt sleeve. Then he penciled the item on a notepad where he listed their personal purchases.

Annie shook her head. They might freeze to death in the livery, but at least they'd not starve their first winter.

Hefting the black skillet with a towel, she carried it to the sideboard, where she split two biscuits each on two tin plates and drizzled dark molasses over both servings. After adding a fork to each plate, she joined her father already seated and waiting.

Settled and warm with food on her lap and her dear father close by, Annie's brimmed with gratitude as he prayed.

"Thank you, Lord, for feeding us and keeping us safe. And open Cooper's heart, Lord. Before it snows, if possible. Amen."

Refusing to let their stingy landlord's image lay claim to her thoughts, Annie forked off a bite and savored the sweet molasses-covered mouthful. She dabbed at her lips with her apron and eyed her father, who heartily attacked his breakfast.

"You don't believe that nonsense about skunk cabbage do you, Daddy?"

He cut into the second biscuit and sopped it in the pooling molasses. "Nope." Closing his eyes, he chewed slowly and nodded. "Delicious, Annie. Absolutely the best biscuits this side of the Rocky Mountains."

Annie swallowed another bite. "You can't say that anymore."

"And why not?"

"Because now we are *in* the Rocky Mountains."

CHAPTER FOUR

Mollie Sullivan twittered at Caleb's sermon. She chirped again and ducked her pretty blond head as a red-winged blackbird took flight from her Sunday bonnet.

Caleb's eyes flew open, his chest heaving. Palming his face, he took in the pale sky and birdsong. The horses were still tethered, lipping leaves from the cottonwoods and swishing their tails. Rooster looked his way and swiveled an ear.

Caleb sat up, threw back his blanket and canvas, and pulled on his boots. Someone was frying salt pork. Probably Springer Smith's ma, considering the direction from which the savory smell came.

He reached into his saddle bag for his last bit of jerked beef and a biscuit he'd been saving, and laid them on his bedroll. Then he found his razor and soap, turned toward the east, and stopped at the spectacle.

Low clouds slid along the fiery horizon, black and backlit with red and gold and splayed out like the hand of God. Unbidden came the phrase, *Your mercies are new every morning.*

Would he never stop hearing them—words he'd known as a child, handled as a man, turned his back on as a failure?

One more day.

He walked to the water's edge and squatted near an eddy. The first cold dash brought Mollie to mind again. Her image had appeared first thing every morning since leaving St. Joseph, and he dreamed of her almost every night. But this time her features weren't as clear. They were blurred, somehow, by a sorrel-haired woman with a broom.

He huffed. Many a woman he'd seen in towns he'd ridden through, but none had outshone Mollie in his mind's eye. Not when he laid down to sleep or when he rose in the morning. Not until now.

Dousing the vision with another cold splash, he smoothed his hand over his cheeks and checked his fingers for blood. He shook out his razor, folded the wrapper around the shrinking soap bar, and returned them both to the saddle bag, where his hand brushed worn leather.

The familiar rub sent fire up his arm. He pulled out the book, wondering why he'd bothered to bring it, then shoved it back. Old habits were harder to break than an uncut yearling. But he didn't need to open those pages. The words rolled through his mind like living coals.

Two bites finished the hard tack and another the dried beef. He saddled Rooster, tied his bedroll across Sally, and led the horses out of the trees. Laughter drew his gaze upstream, where Springer splashed in the shallows with a small girl. A bit cold to be getting wet so early. Probably fetching water for their mother.

Cottonwood leaves fluttered like paper coins, and the treetops flashed gold as the sun found them. A warning hung in the autumn chill.

Caleb rode toward town and turned onto the main street. Two freighters climbed to their wagon box, and the larger of the men gathered the reins and called to the mules. The wagon creaked in complaint as it rolled away from the mercantile.

Had they slept by the river or under their wagon at the livery yard? Or did they have homes, loving wives, and warm stoves?

Envy jabbed a finger in his gut. *Wrath killeth the foolish man, and envy slayeth the silly one.*

He shook his head to silence the voice, and considered the number of fires at the river, the clusters of tents and canvas lean-tos. Stark witness to the town's greatest need.

Smoke curled a welcome from the stove pipe atop the mercantile. Good a place as any to get directions to the Lazy R. He stopped, flipped his horses' reins around the hitching rail and stepped inside.

The aroma of hot biscuits and fresh coffee nearly bowled him over. The broom lady and an older man sat close to a potbellied stove, plates balanced on their laps. Each looked up at Caleb's entrance, and the man nodded and waved him back.

"Coffee's ready. Annie just made a fresh pot."

Annie.

She watched him without expression, her upswept hair a coppery crown above deep clear eyes.

Caleb removed his hat and kicked one boot against the other to knock the dust from his feet. "Thank you, sir. Coffee sounds good right about now."

The woman watched as he covered the short distance and took the empty chair across from the stove.

"Mornin', ma'am."

Her face came alive and a slight smile tilted her mouth. "Now I remember. You rode by last evening, didn't you?"

"Yes, ma'am." He nodded a thank-you to the man, who handed him a cup.

"I didn't recognize you at first." She quickly scanned his attire and glanced away.

Caleb rubbed his jawline. "I shaved this morning, ma'am. I imagine that made a difference."

She smiled fully then, and it warmed him as much as the hot tin threatening to blister his hands.

"I imagine you'd like some biscuits."

She stood as she spoke and, without waiting for his answer, moved to the back of the room, where she placed two golden mounds on a plate. Turning, she raised a tin. "Molasses?"

"Yes, ma'am. Thank you."

She fetched a fork and presented it to him with the plate and a friendly glance. "I hope you enjoy them."

As a former man of many words come Sunday morning, he found himself nearly mute in her presence. "Thank you, ma'am." *Clever.*

"Name's Daniel Whitaker." The older man extended his hand. "Annie here is my daughter."

Caleb switched the fork to his left hand and returned the greeting. "Caleb Hutton, sir. Nice to meet you." He looked at Annie. "And you, ma'am."

Mahogany eyes flashed his way, then hid beneath dark lashes.

"Where might you be headed so late in the year, Mr. Hutton?" Whitaker sopped a biscuit and filled his mouth.

Caleb quickly swallowed a warm, sweet mouthful. "The Lazy R. In fact, that's why I stopped in, to see if you could tell me how to get there."

"You thinking about signing on?"

"Yes, sir. I hear they're looking for hands."

Whitaker gave Caleb a smooth once-over but kept his appraisal to himself.

Annie leaned in with the coffeepot and refilled the cup he'd set at his feet. Her hair smelled like a summer day, a gentle contrast to the faint coal taste in the room.

"The Lazy R is upstream about eight miles west, but you can't follow the river," Whitaker said. "Once you get to the hot springs at the end of town, take the trail around to the right and on up a long pull. The Lazy R starts at the top. If you keep going, you'll end up in the South Park country, and above that, the gold fields, but that would take a day or so."

Clawing the earth for yellow ore didn't appeal to Caleb, though he knew the lure of easy money had drawn men by the thousands to these mountains. The only gold he'd ever had his eye on fell in ringlets around Mollie Sullivan's face. And he'd gone bust with her as quick as any miner in a cleaned-out claim.

"I'll find it."

Eager to be on his way, he daubed the last of the molasses with a piece of biscuit and stood to take his cup and plate to the back.

Annie reached for his plate. "I'll take those, Mr. Hutton."

"Thank you again." He swallowed hard, looking for the right words. "I imagine you're as good with those dishes as you are with the broom."

A dark look sliced him in half. Her chin jutted higher, and she whirled around and strode to the cupboard at the back.

Feeling the fool, he glanced at the store owner, who wore a peculiar grin.

Caleb cleared his throat. "I meant—"

"No mind, son. We know what you meant." Whitaker pushed out of his chair and walked behind the counter, where he wrote something on a piece of paper.

Caleb plunked his hat on, regretting his woeful attempt at small talk, and dug in his waistcoat for a coin.

"No charge, Mr. Hutton." Whitaker raised an open hand as if forestalling an argument.

At that, Annie spun again, hands fisted at her narrow waist. Fire sparked in her eyes.

Whitaker coughed and wiped a hand across his mouth, extending the other to Caleb.

"Good luck, son. I hope you find what you're looking for."

Caleb nodded and left the store with more questions than answers. Why had Whitaker made such a remark when Caleb had clearly stated his destination? And why had Annie taken such offense at a compliment, ill-put at best?

And why did he want to see more in her eyes than fire at his foolishness?

~

"Daddy." Annie's left foot punctuated her frustration with a sound stomp. "We'll go broke with you giving away breakfast to every saddle tramp that wanders in here."

Her father picked up a feather duster and turned to the shelves behind the counter.

"And how many saddle tramps have we had this week, Miss Annie?"

Even in profile his grin was obvious, and his use of the old childhood endearment only added to her ire. "Quite a few, I'd say."

"And how many did I charge for their food and supplies?" He feathered the top of a liniment tin.

She folded her arms, completely aware of where this was going.

"Well?" Her father glanced her way, a glint in his eye.

"All of them." Her left foot ached for another stomp, but that childish response had prompted him to call her by her childish name. She leaned to the left and imagined pushing her shoe through the plank flooring. "Except him."

"You mean Hutton."

"Hutton. Humph."

Her father tucked the feather duster beneath the counter and rested his hands on his ample middle. "Isn't that what Edna usually says?"

Humiliation flooded her cheeks. Daddy was right. But still. "Didn't you hear what he said to me? That I must be as good at washing dishes as I am at pushing a broom?"

Her father's expression softened, but his eyes twinkled like a Christmas saint. "I think he was trying to pay you a compliment. Just take it at that and nothing more."

Some compliment. The man might have said almost anything else and done no harm. He could have mentioned the coffee, or her fresh biscuits, or ... or ...

Men.

She tugged her apron strings lose and cinched them tighter into a knotted bow. If she had Edna's emerald eyes and yellow hair, that drifter would have found plenty to say. But she kept that indictment to herself, recalling how sad her father had looked this morning hunched over on his pallet.

The memory doused her fury, and she slipped behind the counter and planted a kiss on his cheek. "Never you mind, Daddy. We'll get enough customers to make up for that cowboy."

She hoped. Sometimes her father's generosity outweighed his common sense.

She returned to the back and set a pan of water on the stove for washing their dishes.

That drifter's insult would not have stung so if it had come from a common-looking man. One that didn't carry himself with bridled confidence. One without two dark pools for eyes and the breath of untamed country about him.

She scraped a soap curl into the water and added the plates, forks, and cups. By the time she had the counter cleaned, steam rose from the dishpan. Was it her imagination, or did water boil quicker in Cañon City than in Omaha?

Certainly her emotions seemed to. Just the thought of Hutton's expression as he'd downed her biscuits made her pulse kick up.

How could Daddy be so generous where customers were concerned and so stingy toward Nell?

Flustered, she moved the pan to the back counter, nearly scrubbed the white specs from the blue enamelware, and soaked her apron in the process.

Nell was too big to be a pet, but she was the next best thing. Annie loved the horse's warm breath on her face, the large, kind eyes, and the velvety nose that sniffled her hand for dried apples.

Guilt wiggled under Annie's collar at the purloined apple rings she sneaked into her skirt pockets each evening to treat the ever-hungry mare. Daddy wasn't the only one who gave away food. But if he kept squandering their profits on cowhands like Caleb Hutton, they'd have barely enough to live on and would need to sell the mare for sure. She rubbed angry tears away with the back of her hand at the very thought.

The bell clinked, and she turned to see Martha Bobbins flutter through the door with her customary smile.

"Oh, Daniel dear. I'm so glad to see you're here this morning."

"Daniel dear" shot a nervous glance toward Annie and tugged at his apron straps.

Annie hid her giggle over the dishpan. Martha Bobbins certainly lived up to her name. The woman bobbed in at least once every day to buttonhole Annie's father with a "dire necessity." As the only seamstress in town, she made everything from dresses to dungarees, and she depended upon Whitaker's Mercantile to supply her needs. She even had a foot-treadle sewing machine. Not many people knew about it, but Annie had seen it when she'd delivered several lengths of denim to Martha's tidy cabin.

But the plump little widow came in mostly to see Annie's father, and it didn't bother Annie one bit. Martha's material needs couldn't begin to outweigh her father's need of attention from a woman his own age—someone other than his monopolizing sister, Harriet. Which was the best reason Annie could think of for moving to Cañon City, a town much too uncivilized for the likes of her aunt.

Her conscience twinged.

Yes, Martha Bobbins was more than welcome.

Annie dried her hands on her apron, adjusted the pins slipping from her hair, then joined her father and Martha at the front. Already he blushed as Martha fluttered over the fabric he'd spread across the counter.

This time she fingered a creamy silk.

"I think this will be perfect for the bride, Daniel." Martha snared him with a knowing glance.

He flushed crimson.

"That *is* lovely, isn't it," Annie said, rescuing him from a painful position. She stepped close to his side and patted his back. "We were right to bring it, weren't we, Daddy?"

He cleared his throat and pulled at his mustache. "Thanks to your good judgment, Annie."

She unfolded the fabric, extending a long, smooth swath. "And whose dress are you making, Martha, if I may pry?"

Martha twittered and waved Annie's self-judgment aside. "Hannah Baker. She and the Reverend Robert Hartman are getting married after Christmas. Don't you think that is the most romantic thing you ever heard?"

Daniel slipped away, and Martha's smile weakened.

Annie reached across the silk to touch her arm. "I couldn't agree more."

Disappointment edged the little woman's eyes, and she sighed heavily.

Annie leaned over the counter and whispered, "Give him time. You're making headway."

The comment colored Martha's cheeks with a youthful blush, and a whispery giggle escaped from behind one hand. "You really think so?"

Annie couldn't resist a conspiratorial wink, then returned to safer territory. "So why are Hannah and Pastor Hartman waiting until after Christmas?"

"His brother—also a preacher, you know, from up in Denver with a fancy brick church *and* a steeple—said he couldn't get down to do the ceremony until after all the holiday fuss. Hopefully he won't get snowed in. You know how we always get a heavy storm before the new year."

Annie nodded as she unfolded several more lengths of the luxurious fabric, though really she didn't know. This would be her first winter in Cañon City.

She flicked a glance at the seamstress and considered the possibility of Pastor Hartman's brother performing a simple ceremony for another couple during the same visit.

Inwardly shocked at her presumption, she checked again to see if Martha could read her mind as easily as Edna did. Apparently, Daddy couldn't. Would he figure it out? Of course, if he did, Annie faced a solitary future.

Not a completely foreign thought, given her appearance, her often prickly disposition, and the fact that she had yet to meet a man in Cañon City even close to what she considered eligible, in spite of their numbers.

Caleb Hutton's handsome face worked into her memory with shocking clarity. She shivered.

"Are you all right dear? You haven't caught a chill from sleeping in that drafty old barn, have you?"

Of course the small and sprightly source of local gossip knew about their living arrangements. There was nothing in town that Martha did not know.

"For the time being, we are perfectly fine." Annie lowered her voice. "But I'm hoping to speak to Mr. Cooper later today and convince him to rent us the entire store, not just the front. We could turn the back into a sleeping room of sorts."

Martha tsked and shook her head. "What a leech he is. Pardon me, dear, but it's the gospel truth. He shouldn't ask one penny more than you already pay, the old coot. I've a mind to charge him double for the next apron he orders from me, just to show him."

Annie laughed and folded the fabric into a smooth square. Then she wrapped it in brown paper and tied it with twine.

Martha dug into her reticule for a silver coin and handed it to Annie. "If I had an extra room in my cabin, I'd have you and your father stay there." She stole a quick peek toward the back and pushed an imaginary stray lock beneath her ruffled cap.

"And you're a sweetheart for even thinking of us." Annie made change and wrote out a receipt. "Thank you ever so much, but don't you worry. I'm sure I can talk Mr. Cooper into being a bit more generous before the snows come."

Oh, if merely saying the words out loud would make them true. But she knew better. Cleverness was required when it came to Mr. Cooper. She just didn't know quite how to go about it yet.

CHAPTER FIVE

Caleb followed the river upstream to where it cut through a granite canyon and round a jutting red rock sentinel west of town. Two log cabins squatted in a cottonwood grove. He guessed the mineral springs were at hand, for the Utes he'd heard of camped several hundred paces away against a sheer rock wall. Their fires sent smoke spiraling above a stony ridge.

Surely the river was a certain path to the high country grassland, but Daniel Whitaker had said the banks choked off a few miles in. Caleb didn't have daylight to waste on a hunch, so he turned back and headed north along a narrow valley. It climbed beneath a saw-toothed rim—evidence enough for how these mountains came by their name.

The yellow ridge scraped sky on Caleb's right, and orange sandstone abutments jutted from the hillside like upraised floorboards. To his left, Fremont Peak's lesser points pushed skyward, a prehistoric beast straining against its rocky confines. Strange country, this land that drew cattlemen and gold seekers alike.

Ahead, the trail curved deeper into the mountains toward his longed-for escape. He hoped to make the Lazy R by early afternoon.

Rooster's head bobbed to a steady gait, and the rocking rhythm set Caleb's thoughts to churning. Annie Whitaker's sweet biscuits sure beat the hard tack he'd choked down earlier that morning. Why hadn't he mentioned that instead of how handy she was with a broom?

He touched his boot heels to Rooster's side. The horse quickened its pace but not enough to outdistance thoughts of molasses-colored eyes that warmed Caleb's insides.

A woman like that would make a man's life brighter in this bleak country. Be it laughter or anger, light danced in those eyes. And in her hair. He grabbed a handful of Rooster's mane and pulled his fingers through. Nearly the same color but coarser. Annie's hair must be soft as a baby's whisper.

He jerked his hand back. He must be crazy. After his remark that morning, Annie Whitaker wouldn't give him another biscuit if her life depended on it, much less the opportunity to touch her hair.

Caleb angled his horses west as they climbed between scrubby peaks. Bent and twisted juniper soon gave way to scattered pinion and cedars that stretched against a cloudless blue. Air as fresh and fine as he'd ever breathed filled his lungs with promise. He could start over here. Find his footing again.

By midday, the trail broke into a wide plateau dotted with grazing cattle. Several hundred head, he figured. In the distance, low buildings hugged the base of a steep rise—the Lazy R ranch house and barns.

Caleb touched his heels to Rooster's side, and the gelding eased into a gentle lope. Cool water, a pile of hay, and a new life lay just across the grassland.

He slowed to a trot as he approached a gate with a high crossbeam bearing a leaning "R." As he pulled up, he studied the carver's handiwork, supported by two massive timbers, then rode beneath and took the next quarter mile at a walk. Every clop of Rooster's and Sally's hooves counted out the days that Caleb had spent in the saddle. Anticipation rose in his chest, the payoff for his long trip close at hand.

The main barn shaded two cowboys and a horse. One man stooped beneath the saddled mount's back leg, the sounds of his rasp scraping through the thin air as he smoothed the hoof.

A vaquero held the reins, his leggings trimmed with a line of silver conchos.

The shoer dropped the foot, and both men eyed Caleb and his horses as they stopped at the corral.

Caleb nodded. "Afternoon."

He stepped off Rooster, flipped the reins over the top rail, and offered his hand. "Caleb Hutton. I hear you're looking for ranch hands."

The farrier shook Caleb's hand but cut a glance at the vaquero.

"Where'd you hear that?"

"St. Joseph, Missouri. In the paper there. I saw an ad for the Lazy R."

The man's eyes flicked over Caleb's garb like Daniel Whitaker's had, but this time judgment followed.

"We got all we need. You're too late."

Caleb's heart stumbled. "I'm good with horses. Doctor livestock too."

The vaquero's shaded eyes cut away to the near hills.

The shoer spit a black stream to the side and wiped his mouth on his sleeve.

"No more bunks, son. Sorry, we're full up." He turned away, slid the rasp into a small wooden box, and unbuckled his leather apron.

Caleb couldn't make it back to Missouri before winter. He cleared his throat, pushed through the tightness.

"Are there other ranches around here in need of a hard worker?"

The vaquero swung onto the horse. Sunlight glinted off his long-roweled spur as he reined around and headed for the nearest bunch of cows. The farrier plopped a brown bowler on his head and squinted at Caleb.

"Wrong time o' year. Winter's comin' on, and most spreads are gettin' ready to hunker down. No branding, nothin' that calls for extra help till spring. Come back around then."

"But the ad—"

"There's a lot o' men lookin' for work, son. We filled up quick." A black spot flew from his mouth and darkened the dirt at his feet. "Try the saloon in town. Hotel might have somethin' for you with all the miners comin' down for winter. Or the saw mill."

Reality slapped Caleb, cold and hard. He'd been a fool. Gone off half-cocked on no more than a paper promise. He'd not bunk at the Lazy R tonight or any time soon.

He wanted to rant—holler about the miles he'd ridden, the dust he'd eaten, the new start he had to find. He wanted to preach about turning away the poor and the destitute. But he was no longer a preacher. He had no right.

After he stripped the reins from the fence, he climbed into the saddle. "Thanks anyway."

The first sign of emotion crossed the man's face. "Sorry, son, that's just how it is. Hope you make out." Then he grabbed his shoeing box and walked into the barn.

Caleb reined Rooster back the way they'd come. He wasn't about to ask for a place to sleep for the night or even water for his horses.

He did not beg.

At the high gate, he headed east for Cañon City and heeled Rooster into a lope. The sun pressed toward the peaks behind him, on run from the coming night. It pulled its warmth with it and threw a brassy light on the ridge ahead, where yellow flared through a dark pine blanket.

Caleb had read about the aspen that flecked the mountains—those white-barked trees that bore the gold men didn't hunt, the kind that showed itself year after year as witness to a providential hand.

He snorted. Providence. That was one thing he didn't need.

Providence had drawn him away from his father's wishes and proven livelihood. Providence had left him without a bride, a living, or a place to lay his head. And Providence had led him to the hollow hope of a fresh start.

His gut kicked against the blasphemy, and he kicked Rooster into a dead run. Maybe Providence wasn't to blame.

Maybe he had done all those things to himself.

~

Cooper hadn't been in for his mail and Annie fumed. When she didn't want to see him, he managed to slither in and curl himself around their stove, following her with his glassy eyes. But today he kept his distance.

Well, she wasn't afraid to meet him in his own territory, despite her father's warnings. She'd be in and out in of that saloon like a needle through a quilt and they'd be sleeping warmer because of it.

"Daddy, can you mind the store while I run an errand?" Annie exchanged her apron for her cloak and fastened it up to her neck. She'd not give Cooper and his kind anything to look at.

She reached the door before her father answered, and paused with her hand on the knob, looking over her shoulder for his whereabouts.

"Hurry back." The front counter muffled his reply, and he stood, red-faced from bending over.

Annie's nerves pushed her out the door before he had a chance to ask her destination.

She pulled her hood against her neck and drew deep satisfaction from her heels clacking on the boardwalk. Mr. Jedediah Cooper would agree to her terms or wish he had. How dare he force them to live in the livery stable while his whiskey cases littered the back room.

At the end of the block, she stepped into the dirt street and hurried across to the next walkway that fronted the Fremont Hotel and Saloon. People around here certainly were fond of John C. Fremont. It's a wonder they hadn't named the town after the explorer.

Approaching the saloon, she slowed her steps, well aware that unmarried women were the exception in this town and did not show their faces in drinking establishments unless they, well, weren't good churchgoing women. But she had to talk to Cooper and didn't want to wait for him to slink down to the store for his precious whiskey. She and her father needed a better roof over their heads and they needed it now.

Her left heel involuntarily stomped the boards. Oh—she had to control that childish reflex or Cooper would laugh her out of his saloon.

Stretching to her full height, she raised her chin and opened one of the saloon's double doors, catching her flushed reflection in the oval glass.

Nearly empty this early in the day, the space could easily have passed for a ball room had it not been for the tables and the long mirrored bar against the west wall. Cooper himself stood behind it, his head bent as if ciphering his accounts. The stale scent of tobacco seeped from the red-and-gold-papered walls, and the odor cloaked her like a shroud.

She pulled the door closed and cleared her throat.

Cooper looked up, his frown melting into a lascivious leer as he recognized his caller.

Annie's left hand still held the door knob and her grip tightened.

"Come in, come in, my dear child." Cooper tugged at his brocade waistcoat and made his way from behind the bar, weaving slowly through the empty tables like a python to its prey. "What brings you to the Fremont this fine day?"

Wishing she'd worn gloves, she accepted his moist hand in a brief greeting, then quickly balled her fingers beneath her wrap.

"I want to discuss renting the entire store from you, Mr. Cooper." She held his gluttonous glare, determined to keep up a bold front in his presence.

He gestured to the nearest table and pulled out a curved-back chair. "Please, be seated, Miss Whitaker. Care for a brandy?"

Her throat tightened. "No, thank you. I simply want to discuss the store. If you recall, my father and I rent the front half and more, but there remains a small space behind the dividing wall that we could use." For living quarters, but he didn't need to know that.

His eyes swept her length and back again as if tearing the cloak from her, and then settled on the hand that held the door knob as he stepped closer.

Sensing how she must appear a frightened child, she let go but stood firmly in place. "How much more do you need for the use of all the floor space?"

Cooper shifted his appraisal to the fingers of his right hand. He curled them against his palm as if examining his nails, a ridiculous gesture for a man of his size. "I'm using that space for storage right now."

"I understand, but surely you have room for your whiskey cases here in the saloon." She reviewed her rehearsed argument. "Perhaps behind the bar or in a back room where they would be much handier, don't you think?"

She scanned the room and noted two doors—one near the bar that opened into the hotel, and one at the opposite end of the back wall, closed. "I'm sure my father will be happy to help you relocate the crates."

Cooper's eyes matched his beloved amber liquor. No doubt they hid as much evil in their depths as the corked bottles behind Annie's makeshift kitchen.

"Well, it will inconvenience me, but I suppose we might work out an arrangement."

Her skin chilled at the insinuation in his shadowed gaze. If she and her father didn't need a warmer place to stay this winter, she'd slap that disgusting smirk right off his puffy face.

The door smacked her hard in the back. Both hands flew up as she fell against Cooper's chest. Fighting to regain her balance, she pulled from his clutches and whirled to see who had hit her with the door.

Two men quickly yanked off their hats as they realized what had happened.

"Excuse me, ma'am," one said in a rush. "I'm sorry. I didn't expect anyone to be standing so close to the door. Especially a lady. I should have been more careful." He bobbed his head like a worried goose and fled to the safety of the bar. His companion she recognized as Magistrate Warren, who frowned at Cooper, replaced his hat, and followed.

Cooper's eyes focused on Annie's right cheek, and she quickly reached for the hair knocked loose by the sudden jolt. She tipped her head and repinned the mass, furious that her hair betrayed her when she was bargaining with such a pagan.

He coughed, regained his composure, and waved a hand in dismissal. "It's yours. I'll send someone round to pack up the crates. No need to concern your father."

Startled by the greedy man's sudden change of tune, she also sensed the need to keep a sober face. He wasn't the type to give anything away—unlike Daddy. Unless they came to some financial agreement, Annie didn't trust him to abide by his generosity.

"No, Mr. Cooper, I insist on paying for the space."

A storm gathered in his eyes.

Realizing her blunder, she recanted. "Thank you, Mr. Cooper. We do appreciate your generosity. Would you be so kind as to take a small additional amount each month?"

Distracted, Cooper glanced at Warren and the other man waiting at the bar, then tugged at his waistcoat. He fingered a gold watch, flipped its cover open for a quick reading, and returned it to a shallow pocket.

"Whatever you say, Miss Whitaker. Write up an agreement and give it to my man when he comes for the crates."

He bowed a brief good-bye and left her standing at the open door.

Annie exited the saloon and quietly shut the door. Her heart threatened to leave her there and race ahead as she strode toward the mercantile.

She'd done it.

Or had something else changed Jedediah Cooper's mind and opened his miserly grip?

No matter. She and her father would not freeze this winter or have to slog through the mud and snow to get to the store. *Thank you, Lord.*

The bell above the door announced her return, and she hurried to the back and hung her wrap. Her father sat near the stove, coffee in hand. She hoped he'd forgive her blatant disobedience when he learned of her success with Mr. Cooper.

"What took you out in such a hurry, Annie?"

His dear, trusting face turned her way.

She snugged her apron around her waist, tied the string, and planted a kiss on his cheek. Could they afford the extra rent? And how much should they pay? Enough to keep Cooper from thinking they were robbing him, but not so much that they couldn't get by.

No more free biscuits to passing strangers.

Guilt pressed. And no more dried apples for Nell. Or not as many.

Promising herself that someday she'd have china dishes again, she filled a tin cup with coffee.

"I've made a deal, Daddy, and I need your help." She settled into the chair next to him. "And I need you to promise you won't be angry."

His brow dipped and a cloudy look banished the earlier calm. "What have you done now, Annie?"

She held the cup below her lips and blew across the hot liquid. "I found us a place to stay." His stare bore into her until it melted away all her good intentions. "Now, Daddy, you mustn't be upset. You know we can't spend the winter in the livery. We'd freeze."

"There are no rooms at the Fremont Hotel." His voice was dry and flat. "I check on a regular basis."

"You're right." A hasty sip and she jerked her head back, her lip protesting against the hot coffee.

"Where did you go?"

Lowering the cup to her lap, she straightened her back and focused on the stove. "I spoke with Mr. Cooper, and he agreed to let us rent the entire store space. Now we can live in the back like we talked about." She peeked at her father's face. "Isn't that wonderful?"

Not one to raise his voice—unlike her—Annie's father clamped his lips together. His silence had been worse than any punishment he'd doled out when she was a child, and she hated it just as much now.

They were partners. Equal in this endeavor. He had to stop thinking of her as a mere woman to be protected, and realize that she could help him. *Had* helped him.

She turned in her chair to face him. "Isn't that grand?"

His eyes dulled with disappointment and sadness. "You went to the saloon, didn't you?"

She huffed out a sigh. At least the truth was out.

"Yes, I did. But before you say it's not proper for me to go there, please hear me out. It was nearly deserted so early in the day, and I asked Mr. Cooper how much he wanted for the back room and told him how much handier it would be for him to have all his whiskey close at hand instead of here, and—"

Her father reached over and squeezed her arm. "Oh, my Annie. You torment me so. It's not safe for you to be so bold."

Like a child, she squirmed beneath his rebuke.

His eyes shimmered and his voice softened. "You are so like your mother."

The old ache seeped into her chest. "Please be happy for us," she whispered.

His gray eyes swept her face and he raised one bushy brow. "How much?"

"That's the strangest thing," she said, relaxing. "We were discussing it when Magistrate Warren and another man came in. Mr. Cooper abruptly told me to name my price and give a note to the man he'd send for the whiskey crates."

No need to mention being knocked unceremoniously into the pagan's arms.

Her father rubbed his forehead and kicked at a stray coal chip on the rug. "We can give him what we pay for the livery stall. We can afford that much."

Annie's mind breezed through the figures. "We already rent the store. And you and I both know he should have included the back room to begin with. Let's give him half what we pay for the livery stall."

Her father leaned back in his chair and studied her with a calculating air.

"What?" she said.

"You are *exactly* like your mother." This time he chuckled and stood to refill his cup. "Write the ticket and I'll push all the crates closer to the back door so they'll be handy for whoever comes to get them."

Annie rushed to throw her arms around his neck, jostling his coffee. "Thank you, Daddy. Won't it be wonderful? Almost like a real house."

He cupped one of her shoulders in his big hand and set her at arm's length. "Maybe we could fit a small cookstove in that cramped space."

She hugged him again. "I'm in no hurry." Straightening her apron, she gave him a sideways look. "Besides, I think my potbellied biscuits are quite good, if I do say so."

He laughed and set his cup on the edge of the stove.

"Potbellied, are they now?" He patted his girth with both hands. "I will be too, if I keep eating them like I did this morning."

This morning.

Annie turned away to hide her sudden blush. Others had also savored her biscuits this morning, but thoughts of one man in particular made her heart flutter like Edna's silk fan.

The dark-eyed drifter had managed to do much more than stir her anger.

CHAPTER SIX

Caleb bypassed Main Street and pointed Rooster toward the river. If someone else hadn't beaten him to it, he'd bed down where he'd spent the previous night.

Campfires flickered in the trees along the bank, and cook smoke made his empty stomach groan. Laughter and happy voices floated downstream.

He grunted, begrudging such people their homeless pleasures. Or maybe they weren't homeless. Maybe a campsite by the river was home enough if shared with family—like Springer Smith and his folks.

The Son of Man has nowhere to lay His head.

Like a red-hot coal, the phrase scorched Caleb's thoughts. He didn't miss the irony of having more in common with Christ now than he had all those months at the parsonage. The Women's Society hadn't let him miss many meals.

A moonless night shrouded the river, and he settled for an unfamiliar clearing when he saw that his spot had indeed been taken. He hobbled the horses, tied them together, and looped a lead rope around his saddle horn. At least he'd feel it if someone tried to steal them. Or he'd be trampled to death by his startled mounts.

The open fire warmed his face and feet and offered an odd companionship, another voice to counter that of the river, making him feel not so alone. The remains of his jerked beef teased his stomach into true hunger, and he downed several tin cups of water from the cold river. Glittering stars again filled the sky, reminding him that not many such nights remained before storms gathered against the mighty Rocky Mountains.

Where to now? His stomach knotted at the thought of tending bar. He may not be saving souls anymore—not that he'd had even a single convert—but he couldn't bring himself to encourage men along the road to perdition.

The saw mill was a possibility. The hotel? No. If opportunity didn't show its face tomorrow, he'd return to the mercantile for supplies and ride north to Denver. There'd be a better chance finding work in a more established city.

But cities didn't appeal to him.

He slid into his bedroll and, shunning prayer, rolled to his side and closed his eyes.

Maybe Cañon City had a newspaper. He wrote well enough.

The river's whispering current lulled his weary mind, and soon he saw Annie Whitaker in her long white apron, fresh biscuits in her skillet.

Maybe tomorrow she'd invite him to stay for breakfast.

He grunted. And maybe he'd walk on water. Stroll right across the swirling Arkansas without even getting his boots wet.

The next morning, his stomach twisted with a surly growl, and he sat up and rubbed his face. A jay scolded from a nearby thicket, and the river laughed over rocks and swirled through eddies, mocking his need for food and work.

He palmed his jaw. Just one day's growth, not enough for a razor unless it was Sunday. But it wasn't. And even if it was, that didn't matter anymore.

He pulled on his boots, stirred the fire to dead ash, then saddled Rooster and rode into town.

The Whitakers would be up and around by now, feeding that potbellied stove so they could feed stragglers like him. He imagined Annie rolling out dough and lining her cast-iron skillet with perfect biscuit rounds. And smiling at him like she had yesterday morning before he'd made a fool of himself.

He wondered if he'd ever find his way around words again.

Few people walked the streets, and he gave more notice to the buildings and store fronts. A bank. An assay office. A printing office. He'd check there first.

Right after he ate.

He stopped at a corner and twisted in his saddle to eye the other end of town. A few small cabins huddled this side of the white clapboard building across from the livery.

He snorted. If the clapboard was a church, there sat two callings—or so he'd thought—faced off one against each other. Turning around, he heeled Rooster's side, and let the gelding amble along until they came to the mercantile. The sun was a good half hour above the horizon, and smoke spun from the store's chimney. He stepped off and flipped the reins around the rail, hoping for the same greeting he'd received the previous day but doubting he'd get it.

His mouth watered and his pulse raced. He jingled the few remaining coins in his pocket, figured he had enough for hard tack and a can of beans. Some dried beef, maybe ground coffee.

He caught his reflection in the window. Discouragement stared back, cold and calloused. Swallowing, he opened the door.

The smell hit him full force, just as he'd hoped. Annie Whitaker stood at the back, working at a long counter. Her father sat in his chair near the stove, coffee in hand. He raised his cup in welcome.

"Come on in, son. Didn't expect to see you so soon."

Caleb cleared his throat and removed his hat.

Annie looked up with a question that soured to a frown. He'd apologize if she'd give him the chance.

He nodded at Daniel. "Don't mind if I do."

Whitaker stood, poured a second cup, and handed it to Caleb as he took a chair.

"Thank you kindly." He hung his hat on his knee and smoothed his hair back, knowing he had to look a sight after two nights by the river sleeping in his shirt.

"Thought you'd be cuttin' cows at the Lazy R by now. You change your mind?"

Caleb sucked in a breathy taste of the hot brew, trying not to burn his mouth.

"I didn't, but they did." He glanced toward Annie, who had turned her back. "Other men must have read that ad in the paper and beat me to the job."

"That right?" Whitaker raised his white brows.

"Said they were full up. No room in the bunk house, didn't need any more hands." He tried the coffee again and managed a scalding swallow.

"Hmm." Whitaker scratched his clean-shaven cheek. "So you heading back home?"

Home. If Caleb knew where that was, he'd gladly head that way. When his pa died, the bank took their small acreage, and at that time, Caleb had the church.

Now all he had was a kind look from the storekeep.

He shook his head. "If I find something here in town, I'll stay the winter, then head for Denver come spring. But if nothing turns up by tomorrow, I'll leave the day after."

"Got your sights on gold?" The older man eyed him over his tin mug.

"No, sir. I'm not of a mind to dig for shiny ore. But I'll do just about anything else if it's honest work."

A clear "Ha!" sounded from beyond the potbellied stove, and a grin spread across Whitaker's face.

Caleb glanced from father to daughter. "The foreman suggested I check at the saloon or motel, but I'm not much on pouring whiskey, and I doubt I'd make a very good chamber maid."

This time, a distinct snort rose near the sideboard. Whitaker's stomach bounced as he stifled a laugh, and Caleb couldn't keep a twitch from his lips. Caught in the swift current of gaiety, which he'd not experienced in a very long time, he leaned closer to Whitaker. "Do you need someone to help sweep the front walk?"

Any moment the skillet would fly.

Annie spun in a skirted flurry and stomped to the stove with a batch of freshly cut biscuits. She slammed it down, adjusted the damper, and skewered Caleb with a glare.

"I can handle the sweeping myself, Mr. Hutton, as you so clearly pointed out on your last visit."

Caleb saw his opportunity and stood. "About that, Miss Whitaker. Please accept my apology. It's biscuit making at which you excel. I meant no disrespect."

She balled her fingers on her hips and kept her chin in the air, but her face softened. Dashing a russet strand from her forehead, she mumbled some epithet and whirled away.

Caleb dropped into his chair, realizing it was going to take more than a compliment about biscuits to mend matters with Annie Whitaker.

"What do you *really* do, son?" her father said with a twinkle in his eye. "What did you do back in—where are you from?"

"Missouri. St. Joseph." Caleb fought off the vision of the stone church he'd left behind. "I have a way with horses, sir." But not people. Especially not women.

"Have you inquired at the livery? Henry might put you to work." Whitaker paused, and an idea clearly crossed his ruddy features. "You could bunk there if you don't mind a stall. I happen to know there's one available. It's only a little warmer than where the horses are, but there'd be a roof over your head come winter."

Caleb nodded and eyed the biscuits browning on the stove. "I'll look into that. Thank you."

"And when you get there, look in on the big yellow mare and tell me why she's nearly eating me out of my profits. I'm wanting to sell her"—he glanced at his daughter—"but Annie thinks she's a pet and sneaks dried apples to her every night after we close up."

Annie peeked over her shoulder, worry etching her fine brow.

Fine brow? Since when did Caleb notice a woman's brow? Or call it fine? "I'll do that, first chance I get."

Annie moved to the stove and picked up the skillet. A whiff of fresh bread floated past his nose, and Caleb nearly had to holler to cover his stomach's impatient rumbling. Then she delivered two deep plates with biscuits floating in dark molasses.

One for her father and one for him.

"Thank you, darlin'." Whitaker gave her a tender smile.

Caleb looked into eyes the same color as the sweet molasses and nodded, afraid of what might come out of his mouth if he tried to express his gratitude. "Miss Whitaker."

She met his gaze without anger, false humility, or the coy flutter at which Mollie Sullivan had so excelled. Strong and confident but kind, she returned his look, as if willing to meet him on level ground.

"It's Annie."

His heart curled up like a pup on the hearth. Maybe he'd get a fresh start after all.

~

Annie feared she'd drop the plate if Caleb Hutton didn't take it from her right that instant. His dark scrutiny unsettled her, as if he saw through her bravado, all the way to her quivering insides.

As unexpected as snow in summer, his apology had all but doused her anger. What kind of man apologized to a woman he didn't know? In front of her father, no less.

A good man.

She stepped back, flushed with heat from the stove. Loose hair stuck to her forehead and neck, and she retreated to the counter where her own plate waited. Dare she join the men in her condition?

Turning her back, she stretched her apron hem between her hands and flapped it in front of her face. What she wouldn't give for one of Edna's painted silk fans.

She drew a deep breath, pushed her hair off her neck, and with plate in hand walked calmly to the chair farthest from Caleb Hutton.

"You've outdone yourself again, Annie girl. We should have opened a café instead of the mercantile."

Embarrassed by her father's complement in a stranger's presence, she adjusted the plate on her lap and tamped down her longing for a table. And a house.

"Thank you, Daddy, but I do believe you are prejudiced." She swirled a biscuit bite in molasses.

"He's right," Caleb said between bites. "'Course then there'd be no place to get supplies."

He smiled her way, or as close as he could come to a smile with his mouth full.

She dropped her gaze to her plate and wondered what Edna would say at this point. Oh, she knew what her sister would say. She'd bat her thick lashes, wave the remark away with a milk-white hand, and say, *Oh, you shouldn't carry on so. They're just plain ol' biscuits.*

"Thank you both," Annie managed without looking up.

"If word gets out about your cooking, we may have to set a table in here."

Her father's words sparked hope, but they had no room for a table. Besides, they didn't have a real cookstove yet, and she couldn't do more than biscuits, pan gravy, eggs, or beans and coffee on the old iron hunk they did have.

"Maybe I'll paint a sign—*Annie's Potbellied Biscuits, Five Cents.*" He swept his hand through the air as if displaying the imaginary notice for all to see.

Caleb's mouth curved up on one side. "Potbellied biscuits?"

Annie felt the flush return to her neck. "It's the stove, Mr. Hutton. The potbellied stove, and I dare say I don't think I'd care to spend the day cooking over this boot-warmer."

"Caleb, ma'am." He cast an earnest look her way. "I'd be pleased if you'd call me Caleb."

Her father suddenly stood with his plate and cup and made for the front counter. "I never did sort yesterday's mail," he scolded himself. "I must be getting old and forgetful. You two go on without me. I'll just be killin' two birds with one stone over here."

Forgetful, my eye. Annie speared the last biscuit piece. She'd be having a few words with her father after Caleb Hutton left.

Thankful she hadn't sat next to him, she slid a glance his way and noticed how seriously he consumed his food. As if his life depended on it. Instantly remorseful, she realized that he might very well depend on what she served. Where else in Cañon City would he find a meal, other than the Fremont Hotel, which always had more patrons than tables and chairs?

She laid her fork in her plate. "There's more, Mr. Hut—Caleb. Would you like a couple more biscuits?"

"Thank you." He gave her a sober look and a nearly clean plate. "They really are good."

At the counter, she opened two biscuits, covered them with thick syrup, and for no reason she could name, plucked an apple from a bowl full set aside for a pie. She cored and sliced it with a paring knife and fanned it out next to the biscuits. On her way past the stove, she lifted the coffeepot.

"More coffee?" She held out the plate and watched his reaction.

His eyes found hers. "You sure you can spare this apple?"

"We have plenty. Apple trees grow around here nearly as well as skunk cabbage." She filled his tin cup and, straightening, smoothed her apron with one hand. "If you have everything you need, I'll be in the back room unpacking." Not that it was any of his business.

"Unpacking stores? I can help if you need."

His sincerity gave her pause, but she turned away from his scrutiny. "No. Thank you."

She set the coffeepot on the stove and fled through the doorless opening into what was now her new home. Backing against the dividing wall, she fanned her apron in her face, feeling she'd barely escaped from—what?

She surveyed their few belongings and the scant space. They'd been so eager to leave the livery before Cooper changed his mind that they'd hauled everything to the store before Annie had time to clean the long-neglected room. Dusty cobwebs laced the ceiling corners, and even more dust covered the window sill. The entire room needed a good sweeping and washing down, but she'd not pick up the broom with Caleb Hutton around.

Booted steps headed for the back, and she stooped near a carpet bag. Tin dishes clinked together in the wash pan on the sideboard. A quick glance over her shoulder revealed her father stuffing mail in letter boxes behind the front counter. No one else had come in, so it had to be Caleb washing his plate.

She paused in her hasty riffling through the satchel's contents and imagined him scrubbing the sticky syrup. He must not be married, for surely a man with a wife simply assumed that a woman tended to the dishes. Even her father hadn't helped in the kitchen, always relying on his sister and daughters to complete such mundane chores.

First an apology. Now a helping hand. Who was this Caleb Hutton?

And why did he catch her fancy?

CHAPTER SEVEN

Caleb paid for his breakfast and few supplies, thanked Whitaker again for the tip about the livery, and headed that way. He'd check with the blacksmith before he stopped at the printing office and the sawmill.

If given a choice, he'd take livestock over letters and lumber any day, though his life had been fairly equally divided between the first two.

The sprouting city sang with commotion, the street considerably more crowded than when he'd ridden in that morning. Hammers pounded from inside rising buildings, and freight wagons moaned beneath their burdens. Drivers whistled and cussed at their animals, and people on foot hurried along the boardwalks with apparent purpose.

And his purpose?

It wasn't washing dishes, that was for sure, but evidently some part of him thought otherwise.

He grabbed his horses and led them toward the livery. What would Annie Whitaker think when she returned from unpacking and found the plates and cups drying on the sideboard? Would she see his efforts and wonder what they meant?

He sure enough wondered. Even Mollie Sullivan hadn't had this effect on him.

At the stable, he slapped dust from his hat and turned his back to the building across the road, grabbing hold of the last bit of optimism he could muster.

An oak of a man stood before a brick furnace at the back wall, sleeves rolled above massive forearms. One hand held tongs that gripped a glowing horseshoe atop a stump-mounted anvil, while the other hand wielded a hammer. The man lightly tapped the iron, then raised the shoe to appraise its shape. Another tap, and he dunked the hot shoe in a bucket of water.

Caleb approached. "Mornin'," he offered above the hissing bucket.

The smithy retrieved the dripping shoe, held it to the anvil, and eye-balled Caleb. "Mornin'."

"Name's Caleb Hutton. Might you be Henry? Daniel Whitaker sent me round. Thought you might be needing some help."

The leather-aproned man laid the hammer across the anvil and held out a blackened hand.

"I'm Henry Schultz. You know anything 'bout livery and stock?"

"Yes, sir. Been around horses my whole life. Shod a few, birthed a few, and trained even more."

Henry didn't release Caleb's hand but turned it over. "Looks mighty soft to me. Like a preacher."

At the word, Caleb flinched, and Henry released his grip. Burning as if he'd touched the glowing iron instead of the smithy's hand, Caleb held his gaze. "It's been a while." His jaw tightened. "But I haven't forgotten. Just lost a few callouses."

Henry chuckled. "Well, if Whitaker sent you to me, I'll give you a try. I do my own shoein', but you can clean stalls and feed. Soap and mend the tack, and keep the freight drivers off my back." He jerked a thumb over his bearlike shoulders. "They park their wagons in the yard."

The offer wasn't as alluring as cowboying all day, but it was work.

"Don't pay much 'cause I don't got much."

Caleb was in no position to argue. "Whitaker mentioned a closed stall you lent out to someone else who moved on."

"That would be himself and his daughter."

Caleb hid his surprise. That explained why Annie had refused his help with what he'd thought were stores. Rooms must be harder to come by in Cañon City than he thought if Whitaker was forced to board in a barn. Why hadn't they moved into the store to begin with?

Henry turned to the anvil, raised the hammer, and pinged on the perfectly curved metal. "They just moved into the back of the mercantile. You're welcome to it, but it'll lower your pay by two bits a week."

"I'll take it."

Henry jerked his head toward the front. "First stall on the right. I'll throw in some straw for bedding, and you can put whatever you've got in there. You got a horse?"

"Two. But I can turn them out in your corral for the time being."

"That'll be fine. I'll deduct their feed from your pay, but they probably won't eat as much between the two of them as Whitaker's mare."

Caleb let himself smile. "That's what he told me. Asked if I'd take a look at her."

"Across the alley from your new room. At the end." He dropped the shoe in a wooden box. "You start today?"

"Yes, sir."

"Good. Settle in and start on the stalls. Stock's all been fed this morning. Give them fresh water and hay at dusk. The pump's out by the corral."

Caleb nodded, put his hat on, and left the barn with a lighter step. His eyes lit on the building across the road. For the first time, he saw the cross above the door and nearly uttered a prayer of thanks. It would have been the first in a long time.

He unsaddled the horses and rubbed them down, dumped his tack and bedroll in the box stall, then led the animals around to the pole corral. Rooster trotted through the gate and kicked his heels, then dropped to the ground and rolled. Sally did the same, grateful, Caleb assumed, to get free of their burden.

He came close to the same feeling himself.

Inside the stable, Whitaker's mare watched him over the stall door and stuck her nose in his chest when he reached her.

"Looking for those apples, aren't you, girl." He finger-combed her pale forelock and ran his hand down her thick neck. Stepping inside the stall, he spoke softly as he worked his way around her, picking up each foot to check its condition and taking a discreet look while he was down there.

Her back was smooth and strong, not swayed, but her belly protruded on each side like a barrel. Suspicion urged his hands on, his fingers palpating, feeling for tell-tale bumps.

She slapped her tail and reached back to nip his shoulder.

"It's all right, girl." He straightened. Whitaker wouldn't be too happy with Caleb's findings. The man's yellow mare had about sixty days before she foaled.

By the time he mucked out all the stalls, mended tack, and fed the horses, late afternoon had tucked down behind the western peaks and shadows filled the livery. Tired but grateful for the sense of accomplishment in his aching back, he opened the door to his new home and stopped short.

He hadn't noticed it when he'd tossed in his tack, but the smell wasn't right. Something sweet hung in the air, something that didn't belong in a horse barn. Perfumed soap or ...

He drank in the summery scent of mahogany hair. The Whitakers had lived in this stall long enough to leave their mark.

Annie's mark.

He ignored the tightening in his chest as he felt along the walls for a lantern he'd seen earlier, then pulled a match from his pocket and struck it against the lamp's base. The tiny flame threw shadows into the rafters and hayloft. Lifting the glass globe, he held the match to the wick, then pinched out the flame before dropping the match back in his pocket. A quick adjustment of the wick revealed his lodgings.

A mound of fresh straw lay against the inside wall, and he spread it out and topped it with his bedroll. He hefted his saddle to the hay rack and hung the bridle from the horn. The floor was surprisingly clean for dirt, and he smiled to himself. Annie Whitaker had taken her broom to it.

His stomach cried treason as he plopped onto his bedroll and dug through his saddle bags for a scrap of dried beef. Instead he found his Bible.

The book had once been food for his soul. As he thumbed through the pages, a thin copper casing fell to his lap. Mollie Sullivan's sweet face looked up at him, and his empty stomach plunged to his feet. He slipped the image back between the pages of Jeremiah.

The weeping prophet. An appropriate place to hide the cause of his own sorrows.

He set the Bible next to the lantern as a sudden rap on the stall door sent his hand to the Colt tucked inside his canvas.

"Hutton. You asleep?"

Caleb scrambled to his feet at Daniel Whitaker's voice and drew the door back. "Just settling in." He shoved the pistol in the back of his pants.

Annie held a cloth-covered dish, and a rich aroma curled into Caleb's face. Her father stood behind her.

"Hoped we'd find you here," Daniel said.

Caleb took the plate, and his fingers brushed Annie's warm hands. "Thank you."

A shy smile curved her lips and she smoothed her apron.

"We thought you could use a good meal."

"I appreciate it." More than he could say.

Her smile deepened and she stepped back.

"Looks like you made out all right with Henry." Daniel peered over Caleb's shoulder into the stall.

"Yes, sir, thanks to your recommendation. Work and a roof over my head." He looked up into the open rafters and wondered again why the stable had once housed the Whitakers. But it wasn't any of his business.

"Have a good night, son." Daniel motioned a farewell and turned toward the broad front doors.

Annie threw a side glance at the mare's stall, then followed her father.

I know the thoughts that I think toward you.

The familiar words rose with a wonderful aroma, and a tightness gripped Caleb's chest as he closed the stall door. He eased onto his bed roll, leaned against the wall, and lifted the checkered cloth from the plate.

"Thank you," he said to no one in particular, laying the cloth in his lap. With relish, he grabbed the spoon buried in the thick stew. The first real meal he'd had in weeks.

~

Pleased, though not completely satisfied, Annie stood in the center of the small storeroom, with hands on her hips that evening. Since they now had extra space, she and her father had assembled the two rope beds they'd purchased in Denver and pushed one into each corner behind the dividing wall. In between, Annie had unrolled a large braided rug and topped it with a small table, lamp, and two chairs. A shelf against the back wall held a basin and pitcher and served as storage for their personal effects. And a camel-back trunk hid their extra clothes and blankets and a few items from the hope chest she'd left behind in Omaha.

Meager furnishings, indeed, but the sproutings of home.

"And you'd be thinking what, Annie?" Her father stood in the doorway to the store front, studying her thoughtful mood.

She reached to clasp his hands in hers.

"I'm thinking how much better this is than the stall at the livery." And wondering how Caleb will fare at the barn.

He looked around the room. "Almost like home, isn't it?"

"When we have a bigger table and a real cookstove, *then* it will be closer to home. But this space is too small for all that." A deep sigh escaped her. "Someday we'll have a real house."

He stepped into the room and squeezed her shoulder, then turned to face the doorway. "We'll be needing a curtain here for privacy during the day. But with the stove out front, we should keep this open at night for warmth."

"I'll set out some canvas for Martha when she comes by tomorrow. I'm sure she can make us a curtain in no time with that fancy sewing machine of hers."

Her father coughed and rubbed a hand over his mouth. "What makes you think she'll be in tomorrow?"

"You know very well what." Annie picked up the folded quilt on her straw ticking and shook it out. "She's been in every morning since we got here—ever since she discovered what a handsome and eligible father I have."

His face suddenly reddened. "Confounded woman."

"Don't you mean confound*ing*?" Turning to hide a rising giggle, Annie retrieved two more quilts from the trunk, dropped one on her bed, and handed the other to her father. "That woman is taken with you, and I think you know it."

He huffed at her remark and sank onto his bed with a grunt.

"Don't let her get away, Daddy. She'd be good for you."

He met Annie's look with a worried frown. "Don't you go tryin' to marry me off. I don't need Martha Bobbins making my life more worrisome than it already is."

"Daddy, you've been alone for seventeen years. Don't you think it's time for a companion?"

He fretted with the quilt, and finally tossed it across the foot of his bed. "You're the one who should be looking for a beau, Annie. I've had my turn at life. And the Lord's blessed me with two beautiful daughters and a good business. I've no need for anything else."

His unselfishness touched her deeply, but she knew he enjoyed Martha's attentions.

Annie traced one of the red eight-point stars on her quilt. She expected no man to call on her here in Cañon City—even if they did outnumber women six to one. Most had gold dust in their eyes or whiskey on their breath. Jedediah Cooper's flushed face materialized in her mind, and she shuddered.

"You're cold." Her father reached for her quilt. "I'll stoke the fire and hold this in front of the stove while you get ready for bed."

She handed him the bright quilt, her favorite.

"That Caleb Hutton showed himself a gentleman today, didn't he?"

Stunned by the comment, she stared at her father. "Why do you like him so much? Because he says *sir* and *ma'am* every other breath?"

Flustered for some inexplicable reason, she busied her hands, drawing several pins from her hair. "We don't know anything about him other than they turned him away from the Lazy R. That might be a warning in itself."

Her father's brows raised above an elfish twinkle. "Manners never did anyone any harm. And I believe that boy is honest and good."

"Well, I think he's hiding something. There's more to him than he's telling." She pulled her loose hair over her shoulder and began braiding it. "And he's no boy. He's at least twenty-five."

Annie's left foot twitched as her father chuckled all the way to the stove, but she held it firmly to the floor and unfastened her shoes. After all their travels and finally settling where nary a grass blade grew along the dusty streets, she'd worn the soles desperately thin. She had half a mind to order a pair of men's boots—if she could find them small enough. They were made so much sturdier than the thin-soled shoes women had to choose from.

What would Caleb Hutton think of her if he saw her stomping around Cañon City in men's boots?

And why would it matter what he thought?

She chided herself as she shed her multiple skirts and petticoats and slid beneath the blankets, recalling her room upstairs in Aunt Harriet's home. How often had she complained each summer in the thick, humid air that kept even a simple breeze from whispering through the open windows.

She tugged the blankets to her chin and gritted her teeth, refusing to pine away for that ornate home, even if it did have a lovely fireplace in every bedroom and real bed warmers in the winter …

Sitting up, she looked around the room, her mind assessing each object for one to serve her purpose.

"I thought you'd be tucked in up to your ears by now." Her father draped the warm quilt over her and pushed the edges under the ticking.

Annie laid back and burrowed into its comfort, the smell of warm fabric tickling her nose. "Thank you, Daddy. This is wonderful. But I just remembered the bed warmers at Aunt Harriet's. We didn't think to bring them with us or buy any in Denver."

Her father laid one arm across his stomach and propped his other elbow on it as he rubbed his chin. "I've an idea."

He retrieved his coat from the wall pegs, took the oil lamp from their small table, and strode to the back door. "Be right back."

Within minutes he returned with a brick under one arm and another in hand. He set them both on the table and bolted the door. "I saw these lying next to the building when we were moving in this morning. I'll set them on the stove and, as soon as they heat up, we'll put one at your feet and the other at mine."

His cold-nipped cheeks bloomed as he shot Annie a proud grin. "Sound good to you?"

"It sounds wonderful."

Before long, the warm quilt, a hot brick at her feet, and the long day's labor conspired against her, and she drifted from her storeroom corner into the land of hopes and dreams. But even there, cold, crisp air brushed her face and gold leaves fluttered against a bright blue backdrop.

Bundled against the autumn chill, she walked with a basket of apples on her arm, approaching a stranger who stood before a small white church. He held his hat in his hands and his dark head bent as if in prayer.

She touched the man's shoulder and he looked up. With a start, she gasped at the pain on his face and drew back from the sorrow-filled eyes of Caleb Hutton.

CHAPTER EIGHT

By sunup Caleb had all the stock fed, watered, and blowing their warm, belly-filled breath through the livery, dulling every memory in his brain but that of horseflesh and hay.

His stomach had forgotten the previous night's hot meal, and he swung open the wide stable doors and headed for the mercantile in hopes that Annie Whitaker was making fresh biscuits.

Keeping his eyes from the church across the road, he focused on the smoky finger curling from the mercantile rooftop, beckoning him. His breath clouded before him in the cold air, and he shoved his hands in his coat pockets.

He now had a place to sleep, honest work, and good food—much for which to be thankful. So why did he still feel ... cheated?

He dusted his hat against his leg, then stepped through the mercantile door to the chime of the overhead bell. Annie stood at the back counter, and her father fed the stove. The aroma of fresh coffee vied with coal dust and the merchandise of a fully stocked store. It was a tableau he was beginning to count on more than he wanted to admit.

"Mornin', Caleb." Whitaker grabbed another tin cup.

The bell rang a second time as Caleb closed the door, and Annie looked over her shoulder. Caleb nodded a greeting, and she smiled briefly before returning to her work. The simple gesture set his ears to ringing as loud as that brass bell.

He took the cup Whitaker offered and sat, trying not to look at Annie while he was talking to her father. It was harder than he would have thought.

"I'd say it's all perfect timing." Whitaker took his seat and looked at his daughter. "We moved out of that stall yesterday morning and into the back of the store here—thanks to Annie's insistence that Jedediah Cooper rent the whole blamed place to us, not just the front." One white brow raised in a crook and the other pointed toward his nose. "Not that I approve of her methods."

Looking unusually meek under her father's stern glance, Annie brought a large cast-iron skillet to the stove. It brimmed with thick white gravy.

Caleb jumped up and reached for the skillet, sloshing coffee on his boots. "Let me help you."

"I have it." She turned the skillet from his reach. "No need to go spilling your coffee on account of this gravy. I'm just heating it up. Had to take it off to make room for the biscuits."

He watched her deftly handle the heavy skillet, centering it on the small stove top.

"Smells mighty good, ma'am." He hoped he wasn't as pushy as his charges at the livery had been. Taking a seat, he caught a quiet laugh coming from behind Whitaker's raised tin mug.

Annie straightened and planted her small hands on her hips, but this time her eyes held a friendly glint, unlike the double-edged sword he'd met yesterday morning.

"Do you like sausage gravy, Caleb?" A slight blush colored her cheeks at the use of his given name, and it made her look even prettier, if that was possible.

"I surely do. It's been a while since I had such fine cooking." Not counting last night.

The remark raised her hand to her brow. She returned to the side-board, set out three plates with biscuits and forks, then brought a ladle to the stove and stirred the gravy. "Won't be but a minute now."

After serving, she took the only seat left. Next to him.

"Daddy, don't you think a prayer is in order, seeing as how we all have a place to live and food to eat?"

Caleb choked on the bite already in his mouth.

Annie shot a worried look his way. "You all right?"

He nodded, coughed a couple of times, and jerked beneath Whitaker's vigorous back slap.

"You're not against praying are you, son?" The laughter in his voice assured Caleb that Whitaker was jesting.

"No, sir. Not at all." He pulled a bandana from his back pocket and wiped his mouth.

"Then why don't you do the honors?"

Caleb stared at the man. Did the man see *preacher* written across Caleb's forehead?

Whitaker raised his silvery brows.

"Yes, sir." Caleb swallowed. "Be happy to."

Annie dipped her head and folded her hands. Her father closed his eyes.

Caleb feared his heart would stop any moment and the others would be praying over his dead body instead of the biscuits and gravy. It had been a while since he'd offered up a prayer like this. He sucked in a deep breath and clamped his eyes shut.

"Lord … thank You." A familiar warmth invaded his chest as he aimed his thoughts toward gratitude. "Thank You for this fine cooking and for the Whitaker's hospitality. And thank You for giving us all a roof over our heads and"—his voice bottomed out to a near whisper—"and for sending Your son. Amen."

He opened his eyes to Annie staring at him as if he'd transformed right in front of her.

Which, in a way, he guessed he had.

"Amen to that, son," her father said. "Amen to that."

Caleb couldn't tear his eyes from Annie's, and his throat tightened at the tenderness he saw there. Something he'd never seen in Mollie Sullivan.

Annie scraped the last bit of gravy from her plate into a scrap tin. Her mind kept replaying Caleb Hutton's prayer, and each time it stirred something in her that she shouldn't be feeling.

Not for a man she knew nothing about.

Peeking at him sitting by the stove, she paid little attention as she washed her dish and the skillet. One thing was clear—there was more to this cowboy than he cared to let on, and she was determined to find out what it was. She dried her hands on her apron as her father hurried past without a word and out the back door.

Martha Bobbins rushed in beneath the singing bell. "Good morning to you."

Annie shook her head at the woman's perpetual good nature, stuffed a handful of dried apples in her skirt pocket for later, and greeted Martha at the front counter.

"You're here early." Annie noted how the crisp fall air had rouged Martha's cheeks, brightening her eyes to perfectly match the blue floral print she wore.

"Martha, may I introduce you to Caleb Hutton?"

He stood with his hat in one hand and an empty plate in the other. "Ma'am." He nodded.

"Caleb, this is Martha Bobbins, our dressmaker in town and a good friend."

"Nice to meet you, Caleb." Martha's attention flitted around the store for its older proprietor, and her shoulders dropped the tiniest bit when she failed to find him.

"He's out back," Annie whispered with a conspiratorial grin.

The revelation brought a glow on Martha's already ruddy face, and she began an urgent search through her reticule. "I know my list is in here somewhere."

Caleb slid his plate into the dishpan and retrieved his cup from the stove, where he stood tall and mysterious, sipping his coffee.

Annie's face warmed as she caught his eye, but she turned her thoughts to Martha's visit, pulled a bundle of heavy canvas from the shelves, and unrolled a double length across the counter.

"Oh no, child. I need lace. And buttons for Hannah's wedding dress."

"Yes, and I have some beautiful pearl buttons I'm sure you'll want. But before I fill your order, I have one of my own. I'm glad you came by."

Martha looked up, delight in her eyes.

"See the opening through the back wall, behind the stove? Daddy and I just moved in back there and we need a curtain to draw during the day. I thought that might be an easy task for you with your sewing machine. Nothing fancy, just straight seams."

Martha patted Annie's hand. "Good for you. About time that old fox showed a little generosity." She picked up the canvas, giving Annie a moment to turn away and hide the hot blood that warmed her cheeks.

Fox indeed. Wolf was more like it.

"A nice print would be more attractive, but this heavy canvas will do. I'll measure the opening and get started on it for you later today. Will that be soon enough?"

"Perfect."

Martha moved toward the doorway just as Annie's father appeared.

"Oh, Daniel, dear. I'm so glad to see you," Martha cooed. "Annie tells me you need a privacy curtain here for your new living quarters."

He coughed nervously, and Martha joined him in the back room as if she'd been invited.

Though she couldn't see him, Annie knew exactly how her father looked with his brows dipped to the bridge of his nose and his chin tucked in his chest.

"I know I have a measuring tape in here somewhere," Martha said. "Yes, here it is. Daniel, hold this end for me while I take a measurement."

Caleb's boots sounded against the wood floor and he stopped at the counter. Annie busied herself refolding the fabric, trying to ignore his strong presence. She failed miserably and looked up into dark, worried eyes.

"Is your landlord less than a generous man?"

His voice came low, for her ears only, and she sensed that Caleb's penetrating gaze would eventually pull the truth from her.

"Yes." She raised her chin, determined to hold her own against the likes of Jedediah Cooper. "But he has seen the error of his ways."

A question slid across Caleb's face, but the bell rang and a woman with two children entered. The little girl's eyes lit immediately on the licorice jar on the counter, and the boy, perhaps twelve, assumed a grown-up air until he recognized Caleb.

"Springer Smith." Caleb broke into a broad grin so unlike his earlier worried expression that it took Annie by surprise.

The boy stuck out a hand and pulled off his floppy hat with the other. "Mr. ..."

"Hutton." Caleb gripped the boy's proffered hand. "Caleb Hutton." He looked to the mother. "Mrs. Smith? Springer and I met a couple of evenings ago at the river."

Her concern vanished as she relaxed and cast a scolding eye at her son. "Yes, I do remember Ben mentioning a man camping downstream with his horses."

Caleb's demeanor warmed as he clasped the woman's hand with the slightest bow. "Good day, ma'am. I am sure you will find what you need here at the Whitaker's."

With that, he disappeared through the door, leaving Annie more puzzled than ever.

She wanted to follow the perplexing man and demand that he tell her who and what he was, but a customer awaited her. Gathering her thoughts, she turned with a smile.

"What can I get for you?"

The woman pushed her bonnet back and loosened her cloak. "Have you heard of any rooms or cabins to rent?" Her bright cheeks betrayed a brisk walk, and from the sand that stuck to the girl's buttoned shoes, Annie guessed they were living at the river like so many other folk had during the summer.

"I'm Annie Whitaker." She came from behind the counter.

"Nice to meet you. We're the Smiths. I'm Louisa, this is Emmy, and that's Ben, or Springer, as he prefers, over there eyeing your halters."

"You have a lovely family, Louisa." Annie reached for the licorice jar and lowered her voice. "May I offer a welcome-to-town gift to the children?"

Louisa's lips thinned but quickly curved at Emmy's beseeching expression. "All right, but only one between them, please."

Overhearing the offer, Springer lived up to his name and volunteered to divide the black whip in half.

Annie held the jar toward him, and when he reached for a candy she playfully pulled it back. His startled eyes fastened on hers.

"If you break it in half, then your sister gets first choice."

He reached again, snapped the candy in two, and took a knee in front of his sibling. "You get to pick."

Thrilled at getting to choose first, the child pulled the longest piece from her brother's fingers. "Thank you, Springer." She leaned in to kiss him on the cheek.

"Thank Miss Whitaker too, children," Louisa said with a laugh.

Springer grinned around the piece already in his mouth. "Thank you, ma'am."

"My pleasure." Annie bent toward Emmy. "I'm a younger sister too, so I know we sometimes get the short end of the deal."

Emmy wrinkled her fair brow. "But I took the *long* one."

Springer laughed and returned to the saddles and horse blankets, and Emmy followed, giggling.

Annie straightened and faced Louisa. "There are so few places to live, but the Turk brothers are cutting timber in the Shadow Mountains this month and hauling logs for cabins. They made a trip last week, hoping to bring a sled full back before snowfall. If you'd like to leave them a note, I have paper and pencil here."

The woman looked longingly at the crates of potatoes and apples, then sifted a handful of dried beans through her fingers. "We're more likely to stay in our tent before we raise a cabin. I was hoping there might be an extra one with all the building I hear going on."

Annie's ached at the thought of keeping a family warm all winter in a tent.

Louisa spun slowly to survey the offerings. "Do you have stoves?"

"We have two ordered and they should be in next week. They're small, not really cookstoves. More like the potbelly we have here in the store. But they're wonderfully warm, and if you plan it right, you can cook a good meal on one."

Louisa looked Annie in the eye with a smile. "Anything is an improvement to a campfire."

Relieved to see good humor in the woman's expression, Annie agreed. "How true."

"My William is a stone mason, and he's working for the Fairfax family. With the high demand for housing, he hasn't a moment to spare for cutting and fitting stones for our own home this winter. We'll just have to make do as best we can."

Annie fiddled with the shriveled apple rings in her skirt's seam pocket and thought of the box stall. Would Caleb give it up if the family couldn't find shelter? Dare she ask him? And where would he sleep then?

By the time the Smiths left with their purchases and an order for a few specialty items, Martha and Annie's father sat together near the stove. Relaxed and laughing, her father didn't see Annie studying him from behind the counter she pretended to dust.

She'd been right about them. They needed each other.

And what did she need?

Caleb Hutton's gentle voice settled on her memory like the yellow leaves that fell along the river.

That was what she needed. The river.

Her father and Martha could mind the store and enjoy a few moments alone.

"Martha, do you mind staying for just a bit? I've an errand to run, and I hate to leave Daddy alone in case we're flooded with customers."

Her father stared, his mouth half open.

Martha rose with distinct pride at being needed. "I'd be happy to, dear." She fluttered her fingers toward Annie. "You run right along. We'll be fine."

Biting the inside of her mouth to keep a grin from breaking free, Annie stole a retreating glance at her father, who sat with one brow arched above a cutting glare. A family trait, that flying eye brow. Did she look as humorous when she did the same?

"You're not going back—"

"No, Daddy. I promise." No more visiting the Fremont Saloon. She shivered as if shaking off the notion and again saw Caleb's questioning look. Tearing a strip of brown paper from the large countertop roll, she twisted two licorice pieces inside it, then escaped out the door before her father could say anything more.

Indian summer in Omaha was hot, muggy, and hazy. In Cañon City it was warm, clear, and sharp against a brilliant sky.

Last night she'd shivered in her bed. And though it'd been chilly this morning, the sun was now brassy and warm, melting wintery thoughts and drawing birdsong from the woods. As she lifted her face to a breeze, cottonwood leaves trembled, gossiping as she passed.

Annie strolled along the river on her so-called errand. She'd had little time for a minute alone, and the late morning lull was a perfect opportunity.

A sudden whiff of beans assailed her, and Annie studied a tent cluster huddling in an open space ahead. Someone was baking their evening meal with salt pork no doubt, for the aroma nudged her stomach into a whimper even though she wasn't hungry.

Rather than intrude on the tent settlement, she turned downstream. Immediately the temperature changed, and she stopped and faced the mountains again. A draft definitely followed the river eastward, tickling her face, nipping her ears. Turning around, she continued with the breeze at her back and walked along the water's edge, mildly disappointed that it merely chattered over rocky places. Where was the roaring whitewater of the mighty Arkansas? Where was the impassable raging river that gouged the Rocky Mountains?

A quick toss of her stockings and a hitch of her skirt, and she could wade right across without getting her knees wet. She paused and rolled the temptation around on her tongue, imagining what it would taste like to tell Edna she'd done such a thing.

Childish laughter caught her ear and she looked upstream. Springer and Emmy ran through the shallows near the tents, giggling and splashing water on each other.

Annie and her sister had never played like that. Edna had always been so proper, so ladylike, that her attitude goaded Annie to be as different as possible. And look where it had gotten her.

Alone in Kansas Territory—though the townsfolk insisted on calling it Jefferson Territory. Regardless, Cañon City lay at the farthest edge, and her father was on the verge of finding companionship while she had few friends as of yet. But that was no different than before. She'd had few friends in Omaha.

Caleb's image rose in her mind, and her father's words slipped in beneath the water's happy murmur. *I believe that boy is honest and good.* What did Daddy know about Caleb? He was no boy, that was for sure. Good? Well, his prayer had sounded a chord in her spirit that both pleased and disturbed her, which made her doubt his honesty. She'd keep her own counsel on that one until she knew more about the brooding horse handler.

Last night's dream had only added to the mystery, as did his remarkable way with the Smith family today.

She stepped over smooth river rocks and up onto a small ledge that testified to higher water. Perhaps in the spring when the snowmelt ran down the mountain's face she'd hear the water's roar.

A sudden honk and a splashing lifted her gaze. Two Canada geese rose from a sandbar where others rested. She had come upon the gaggle without noticing them sunning on the midstream isle. Oh, the down ticking she could make from their soft undersides.

With a cautious glance around and a deeper scrutiny of the woods across the river, she leaned against a large boulder, stripped off her shoes and stockings, and gathered her skirts. The water's icy caress pulled the breath from her lungs, and dozens of brown, black-necked geese rose at her gasping intrusion, honking in protest.

No matter. They would return when she finished gleaning their shed feathers, and she'd ask a special blessing on their goslings when she snuggled beneath a new warm cover this winter.

After gathering a meager start for a feather ticking, she waded back through the icy river, clambered up the smooth granite boulder, and stretched her legs in the sun. A perfect place to warm her face and dry her toes.

Truly this was a land of extremes. Cold as snow one moment, warm and cozy the next. She must visit the mineral hot springs she'd heard so much about, but they were at the town's west end near a Ute encampment. Oh, Edna would faint dead away.

Annie wiggled her feet into her stockings and shoes and tied the downy feathers into her handkerchief.

As she approached Main Street, Jedediah Cooper exited the mercantile. She ducked back into the cross street and pressed against the barber shop wall, hoping he hadn't spotted her. Her hair would surely give her away. Why hadn't she worn a hat or scarf?

She shuddered. The saloon owner made her ill. He was not to be trusted, particularly by a woman alone, of that she was certain.

Peeking around the clapboard building's corner, she watched Cooper walk toward the saloon. Swagger, really, his bowler tipped to one side as if he owned all Cañon City and everyone should be grateful for it.

On her right stood the church building and directly across from it the livery. With a deep breath, she stepped from behind the building and crossed the wide street, praying Jedediah Cooper would not see her running for refuge.

CHAPTER NINE

Henry's hammer sang on the anvil as Caleb tossed straw into the yellow mare's stall. She'd cleaned her hay rack by the time he'd returned from breakfast, and now she slipped through the fresh bedding for stray oats in the mix. He needed to tell Daniel Whitaker about the horse's condition, but he suspected the storekeep would be less than thrilled.

Caleb leaned the pitchfork against the stall, stepped inside, and kicked the straw around to spread it. "You need a few carrots from the mercantile, don't you, girl." He let her smell his hands and then rubbed them gently along her shoulders, back, and distended belly. "You going to make it to Christmas?"

As if in response to his question, a sudden kick pushed against his hand. The little hoof lay low toward the mare's hind quarters. Concern pulsed in Caleb's temple as certain as the foal resisting his hand, and he answered his own question, soothing himself as much as the mare with his low, easy comments.

"Too early to say, Mama. That baby could turn round head first in no time." With an arm over the mare's rump, he walked around her back legs and along her right side. "We'll just have to pray for the right presentation, won't we?"

He surprised himself with the suggestion, but there it was again—an old habit. This morning's prayer at breakfast had widened the hairline fissure, let something leak through. Resentment was draining away as sure as the green from the cottonwood leaves along the river.

"Forgive me, Lord," he whispered. He tipped his forehead against the mare's neck and pulled his fingers through her mane. "I'm stubborn and hard-hearted. I deserve less than a bed in a barn."

A scuffling step jerked his head up. Annie Whitaker stood watching him, her face flushed, eyes wide. As she approached, her expression softened and warmed. Her lips parted as if to speak, but instead curved slightly as she slid a hand over the stall gate and let the mare lip her open palm.

Caleb ducked beneath the horse's neck, and when Annie stepped back, he exited the stall.

"I knew she'd be missing the apples."

He stood close to her, against the closed gate, and her hair, mere inches from his face, enticed him with its sweet fragrance.

She dug in her pocket again and this time offered Caleb the wrapped licorice whips.

He grinned. "Why, thank you, ma'am."

Her brows pulled together. "I told you, it's Annie. You make me feel like an old woman every time you say *ma'am*."

His fingers brushed against her palm. "Annie." Just a passing touch, but with power to warm him all over. He popped a licorice piece into his mouth and offered one to her.

She shook her head, and he could smell the sunshine in her hair again. "Those are for you. I have my own."

"Deep pockets," he said.

Catching the jest in his voice, she laughed. "Only for apples and penny candy."

"So you're barely making it, like everyone else around here, I expect." He bit into another strip. "Except maybe the owner of the Fremont Hotel and Saloon."

She stiffened at his remark, and he faced her straight on. "What's wrong, Annie?"

The rose in her cheeks had all but faded, and she pushed at the loose hair falling so appealingly against her neck. "What do you think of Nell?"

Her sudden change in tone and subject convinced him that he was right—that there was a problem with Cooper—but her lovely eyes focused on the bulging mare.

"So her name's Nell?"

"Mm-hm." Annie nodded and rubbed the horse's head.

"You were right about her eating more than the others." He broached the delicate subject the best way he knew how.

"Do you know why?"

His hand ached to touch Annie's cheek, finger her russet hair. Instead he gripped the gate and watched the horse that stood half dozing under the loving attention. "Yes, I believe I do."

Annie raised her beautiful eyes to him, wide with the question for his answer.

He cleared his throat. One hand rubbed the back of his neck. "Well, uh ..."

His hesitation tugged her questioning look into a frown, and worry darted across her face.

"Is Nell all right?" She laid her hand atop his on the rail. "Is something the matter with her? We didn't take care of our horses in Omaha, someone else did. Have we done something wrong here?"

"No, nothing's *wrong*." How should he put it? And how could he speak calmly with her hand on his in such an earnest, trusting gesture?

He squeezed the rail and took a deep breath. "She's eating a lot because she's not the only one getting her food." He watched to see if Annie gathered his meaning.

Her eyes flicked from his face to the mare and back again, and he saw the exact moment realization settled. With a gasp, she jerked her hand from his and covered her mouth.

"You mean …"

He nodded. "My guess is sometime around Christmas. You didn't know?"

Light danced in her eyes and her mouth bowed into a perfect circle. "Oh—that's wonderful!" She leaned over the half door and kissed Nell on the nose. "You old darling. What a Christmas surprise you've brought us."

Relief spilled out with Caleb's pent-up breath. "At least your father will be surprised."

His comment triggered her frown. "You are right about that." She turned her back to the stall and leaned against it, folding her arms across her waist.

Caleb knew conspiracy when he saw it.

"We can't tell him." She gave him a threatening look. "Promise me you won't let him know. He'll sell her for sure, and it just wouldn't be fair, not when she's … she's …" A becoming flush appeared on her cheeks, and she pushed away from the stall and paced the alleyway.

"It's not going to be a secret for very much longer. If he comes down here, he's bound to figure it out."

She stopped and studied Henry at his fire in the back of the barn, then whirled on Caleb.

"Are you a veterinarian?"

Annie Whitaker didn't sashay around the point. If he wasn't careful, she'd drag every ounce of his past right up through his gullet.

"No." He reached for the pitchfork.

"Then what are you?"

Returning to the straw pile, he forked a load, stalling for time and a decent answer. He wasn't about to start lying, but he wasn't ready to admit he'd turned from his calling, either.

"I told you. I'm good with horses." He tossed the straw into the stall farthest from his inquisitor and stabbed the tines in the ground at his feet. Then he crossed his own arms and waited, daring her to press the issue further.

~

Annie narrowed her eyes. She'd heard Caleb Hutton asking forgiveness for something, so what was it? Was he hiding some terrible deed and lying to them? One thing she knew for sure—he was as stubborn as Edna ever had been. By his rigid chin and the wide stance of his feet, she guessed he had a passel of younger brothers and sisters and knew all the tricks to avoiding a direct question when he didn't want to give the answer.

His broad shoulders and steady gaze nearly weakened her determination, but she averted her eyes just in time. There were more important things to consider than his disarming looks. Like a veterinarian for Nell, or at least someone who knew what to do when the time came.

He might not be an animal doctor, but Caleb Hutton knew more than he was letting on. Much more than a livery hand, or horse handler, or whatever he chose to say about himself.

Still water runs deep, Daddy had said a hundred times.

If that was true, she was squared off against a bottomless ravine.

Nell stomped, pulling Annie's attention from the infuriating man in the alleyway. How did he know so much about horses? And what was his connection to the sorrowful Caleb in her dream? Suddenly, she wasn't quite sure who she was talking to, and suspicion rose again.

Annie scoured her pockets and found two more apple rings. Nell lipped them from her palm, then nuzzled Annie's shoulder. "You poor dear. Don't you worry. We'll find someone to help you."

"I don't think she's worried."

As if in reply to Caleb's low murmur, Nell tossed her head, nudging Annie off balance. She stumbled back into a hard chest and strong hands—the second time in as many days she'd found herself thrust into a man's arms.

Only this time, she had to admit, was much more pleasant, and the realization threatened to unbalance her even more.

"Whoa, there." Laughter edged his voice as he gently braced her arms.

She gathered her footing and her pride and moved away. "Thank you, but I'm perfectly capable of standing on my own."

His expression quivered with mirth.

Her left foot itched to stomp the hard-packed dirt, but she held it firm. "I need to get back to the store. Daddy will worry if I'm gone too long."

Stepping around him, she refused to look up until she reached the livery door.

"You won't tell him?" she asked over her shoulder.

"No, I won't tell him." His mouth knit up in a ridiculous lopsided grin. "But Nell will, eventually."

Annie huffed and jerked her head around, dislodging her hair. A thick strand fell over her shoulder and she hurried through the wide doorway, refusing to stoop for the traitorous pins.

Once she made it past the corral, she glanced back to see Caleb bent over, picking up something from the dirt. He caught her eyes before she looked away and escaped to the boardwalk.

By the time she reached the mercantile, Annie had fretted up enough steam to wilt an entire garden of Aunt Harriet's daylilies. The door slammed harder than she intended, and her father and Martha's shocked expressions warned her to calm her billowing emotions.

Caleb Hutton's stubbornness was stouter than her father's coffee. She paused, looked out through the door glass, and drew in a slow deep breath. Nell's secret must not be found out. Not yet.

"I must be going, Daniel." Endearment flavored Martha's tone. "Thank you for the coffee and company. You've done my heart a world of good."

Annie forced herself to walk calmly toward the back. Her father offered Martha his hand and smiled as the little woman stood and faced him.

"You are a dear." She gathered the folded canvas and her reticule, and addressed Annie.

"I didn't get my lace and buttons, but I'll be back tomorrow with your curtain."

Guilt wedged under Annie's festering irritation, and she burned with chagrin. "I apologize. I shouldn't have been gone so long."

Martha fluttered her fingers over her shoulder on her way to the door. "I shall return, dear." She paused and sent a secret look to Annie's father. "For more of that coffee, Daniel. I may even find some cinnamon rolls while I'm rummaging around in my kitchen."

The bell sang much more sweetly upon Martha's departure than it had at Annie's arrival. She regarded her father's changed countenance. What had transpired while she was gone? He was as peaceful as she was agitated.

"Daddy?"

He stood with his hands clasped behind his back, rocking onto his toes, deep in thought.

"Daddy?" She moved closer and touched his arm.

"Annie girl, you may have been right after all."

Fear skipped from her stomach into her throat. She wasn't ready for her father to make any sudden changes—in spite of what she'd said earlier. Wasn't it enough that they'd uprooted and moved to Cañon City?

"Daddy, what happened here?"

His eyes twinkled with a secret, and Annie's pulse quickened. One secret between them was enough, especially when it was *her* secret.

She planted her hands on her hips and assumed her most commanding posture. "Daddy, what's going on between you and Martha?"

Exactly like Caleb had earlier, her father turned his back on her. He reached into the coal bucket, opened the stove door, and planted two small pieces inside. It wasn't even cold in the store.

After closing the door and adjusting the damper, he addressed her with controlled grace. "I enjoy her company, that's all."

He walked purposefully to the front counter. "She's a fine woman, that Martha. A fine woman."

Yesterday, Martha Bobbins had been a "confounded woman." Today she was "fine."

That left Annie as the confounded one—confounded over her father as well as the feelings growing within her for one mysterious horseman.

CHAPTER TEN

Caleb shoved the pitchfork beneath a soiled straw pile and tossed it onto the wheelbarrow. A pungent scent rose from the heap.

November nights had been considerably colder, but by sunup each day he worked up a sweat cleaning stalls and tossing hay from the loft. And if Henry had the fire stoked and blowing, it felt like near summer in the livery by noon.

The last time he'd been to the river, he'd found ice forming along the banks and Springer Smith treading dangerously close to it. He hoped the family had better shelter by now, something more than a camp fire and a tent. Wintering along the Arkansas would be unbearable.

Cañon City needed a boardinghouse, someplace where families or single men could afford to stay.

Like himself.

He moved to the next stall, raked out what needed to be raked, and added it to the wheelbarrow. *Thank you, Lord, for warmth and work and good food each morning at Whitaker's Mercantile.*

Annie's image came to mind, as it did so often now. It seemed everything brought her to mind. Just the thought of her drew him like a bear to a bee hive—a dangerous delight. No matter what he did, he envisioned Annie Whitaker with her flaming hair and luminous eyes and persistent questions about his past.

The woman pressed in where she had no right to go.

He dug into the pile of fresh straw in the alleyway and sent a heaving pitch against the far wall and all over one of Deacon's draft horses. Caleb shook his head and jabbed the fork in the dirt, then climbed in to brush off the big gray.

So why didn't he simply tell Annie the truth?

Because it was none of her business.

The gray stood calmly as Caleb dusted its broad back and pulled straw pieces from its mane. The irony of his work set his teeth on edge. Sunday or not, the animals required care and their needs came before his.

He stepped through the gate and looked to Henry's furnace staring from the end of alleyway, cold and empty. The anvil lay dutifully quiet on this day of rest for everyone except the former preacher.

The last two weeks Caleb had slipped into church after the singing and stood near the door, ready to bolt if confronted. Pastor Hartman was near his own age, and his straightforward sermons rang a familiar note. Almost a comfort.

Both Sundays Caleb had left during the closing prayer and managed to avoid Hartman, the Whitakers, and Martha Bobbins who clung to Daniel's arm like a foxtail to a dog. But today he planned to stay and face the fire.

The fire of repentance or the fire that burned for Annie Whitaker, he wasn't sure which.

He hung the pitchfork on the wall and hauled in water from the hand pump. His new basin and pitcher rested on an upturned crate in his stall, and he washed his hands and face. He changed into his clean pants and shirt, thankful that he'd stopped by the barber's the day before for a haircut.

If he wasn't careful, gratitude might become a habit.

He reached for his Bible and found the passage he'd read last night by lamplight. *Whither shall I go from thy spirit? or whither shall I flee from thy presence?*

An honest question that Caleb hadn't been willing to answer.

But he couldn't hide from God forever. Not even in Cañon City at the edge of nowhere. It'd be a long winter if he kept running from the church folk in town, especially since he wanted to get a lot closer to one in particular.

Clattering hooves, creaking buggy wheels, and the curious snorts of his stablemates told him people were gathering across the road. His gut twisted, anticipating Annie Whitaker fresh as a spring flower in her Sunday dress and bonnet.

He buttoned his waistcoat, dusted off his hat, and walked the line for one last check. Nell dozed with a back leg cocked forward, her distended belly looking painfully tight. There could be two inside—double the problem if Annie was right and her father wanted nothing to do with another horse to feed.

Satisfied that no one had kicked over a water bucket, he slid the front door back and left it open a few inches. He brushed off his shirt sleeves and wished he had a nicer overcoat than his slicker. The chill nipped clean through his thin shirt, but he couldn't wear his work coat to the meeting house. They'd run him off for sure.

A woman's clear laughter sang from the boardwalk. *Annie?*

He hurried out to spot the source of the melodic sound, something deep within him insisting it must be her.

She walked beside her father, her head tilted back in an unguarded moment. Daniel wore a grin beneath his white mustache and Martha Bobbins on his arm.

The threesome stepped into the street and Annie hitched up her deep green skirt as they crossed, revealing high buttoned shoes and a glimpse of dark stockings.

Warmth flashed in Caleb's chest and his need for a coat vanished.

"Mornin'." Henry Schultz's hearty welcome caught Caleb staring.

"Henry." Caleb pulled on his hat brim. "Mrs. Schultz, ma'am."

He fell in with the couple as they made their way up the steps, then waited behind them when they stopped before the pastor.

Hartman stood at the door greeting each congregant individually, and he offered his hand to both Henry and his wife.

"Good to see you this morning. Bertha, don't you look lovely." An honest smile accompanied his words, and he shared one with Caleb as well. "You're early." Laughter sparked in the parson's gray eyes.

Caleb pulled off his hat and took the pastor's hand. "Thought I'd sit in on the whole service this morning."

Hartman slapped Caleb's arm. "I'm glad to hear I haven't driven you off."

Henry offered seating at their usual bench, but Caleb begged off on pretense of keeping an eye on the stable and stopped at the back row. He wasn't quite ready to be so close to the pulpit.

And the view was better from back here.

Henry leaned toward Caleb and lowered his voice. "I do believe you're keeping an eye on more than the livery."

Bertha pulled on Henry's arm and Caleb pulled on his collar, surprised that the chapel's woodstove put out so much heat.

~

Annie had seen Caleb exit the livery. She'd wanted to cross to him right then and there and tell him that she knew there was something he wasn't saying, and it had nothing to do with their secret about Nell.

But ladies did not run after men in public—or anywhere, for that matter.

She clutched her Bible and continued toward the church, failing miserably at ignoring how handsome Caleb looked this morning. With his long confident stride, clean white shirt, and low, tilted hat, he seemed so unlike the stubborn man who had refused to answer her questions.

She paused at the steps to let her father and Martha go ahead. Once inside, she angled away from the door, and fussed with her reticule as she listened for a certain deep voice.

The warm timbre sent shivers up her back as Caleb spoke to Pastor Hartman. She stepped in behind a young couple heading down the aisle and took the empty spot on the bench next to her father.

During the sermon, it took all her concentration to focus on the message. Not that she dared look Caleb's way, but her mind wandered. She kept stumbling over who and what he could be, and the possibilities scattered themselves throughout Reverend Hartman's sermon on the parable of the sower.

A hired gun? He wore no holster.

A grieving widower? He wore no ring.

A swindler, a bank robber, a gambler?

She snickered, and her father cocked an eyebrow her way.

Quickly she seamed her lips and rubbed her cheek, a trick she'd often used when hiding a joke from Edna. But it wasn't enough to keep her mind from Caleb. He piqued her curiosity with his mysterious avoidance of anything to do with his past.

The man had all but finished off an entire apple pie on his last visit to the store. He ate more than she and her father put together. Perhaps he was a farmer, missing his fields and family back home. Had he come for a share of fertile land in the Arkansas River Valley and been robbed? Was he a miner who'd had his claim jumped? No, his clothing and mannerisms said otherwise.

Everyone stood, and Annie jerked to her feet, a flush rising to her face. The closing song drew her attention to the blessed tie that binds, but during the prayer she finally gave in and peeked over her shoulder. She couldn't make out Caleb through all the bowed heads. Either his was also bowed or he'd slipped out already. The binding tie pulled to a disappointed knot.

Annie drifted out the chapel door, a single drop in the human stream, her ears dull to the chatting voices until Martha Bobbins broke through.

"You must come for dinner, dear." The woman took hold of Annie's elbow. "I've made a chicken pie and a lovely rice pudding for desert."

Annie looked to her father, whose eyes fairly brimmed with longing for both, she guessed.

Laughing, she linked her arm with the little woman. "Of course we'll come. Can we bring anything from the mercantile? Tea or coffee?"

"No, I have everything. But we'll need to hurry. I left the pie on the back of the stove to keep warm."

Hannah Baker, Cañon City's bride-to-be, caught Martha's eye as they descended the front steps.

So much for hurrying.

Wanting her heart's soil to be fertile and not futile, Annie resisted the tug of envy. Fair Hannah could not be more than sixteen, yet here she was, engaged to be married to Pastor Hartman. An Abraham and Sarah romance, no doubt. Or was romance even involved?

Annie watched the animated girl describe to Martha the precise placement of seed pearls that she wanted on her gown. Her flushed cheeks and the urgency in her voice betrayed a deep and earnest passion.

Envy took a step closer, but Annie backed away.

While Hannah bombarded Martha, Annie's father ambled over to visit with Henry and Mrs. Schultz. Annie's breath froze in her chest.

What if Henry mentioned Nell's condition?

She couldn't bear to sell the mare now, not like this. Not with winter coming on and long dark nights ahead. *O Lord, please.*

"He won't say anything."

She whirled to face the man who had read her thoughts and answered her unspoken prayer.

Reaching for her breath, she fingered her ruffled collar.

"Are you sure?" she whispered, clutching her Bible to her chest.

One side of his mouth twitched as if he fought a smile.

"He might not even know." Caleb dipped his head, holding her with his eyes. "He doesn't pay the horses much mind. Seems to trust my care of them."

Annie ordered her pulse to stop pounding. Was it fear of discovery or the intimacy of Caleb's rich voice that left her light-headed? Such a voice should not be wasted on livestock.

"Oh, I pray so."

A muscle flexed in his jaw, and his eyes swept her face. She dipped her head and touched the small hat clinging desperately to her hair. Where was the anger that she'd last felt in his presence?

He held out his opened hand, revealing two hairpins. "Looking for these?"

Meeting his gaze, she found nothing but gentleness there. No mockery, no criticism. She reached for the pins and as her fingers brushed his palm he clasped her hand in his.

"Truce?"

His query drew the breath from her. Or was it the touch of his strong hand?

She nodded, helpless to do more, and he released her fingers as quickly as he had closed upon them.

"Come along, dear," Martha piped. "And you too, young man. There's chicken pie a plenty to go round. You know what they say: the more the merrier."

Annie's Sunday suit squeezed tightly as she fought for a steadying breath. Now she must face much more than a truce with Caleb Hutton. And not just casual biscuits around a potbellied stove, but an intimate meal with Martha and her father.

~

Caleb offered his arm. For three beats of his heart, he watched indecision cloud Annie's eyes. When she finally rested her fingers in the crook of his elbow, his pulse nearly broke and ran. With one hand, she again lifted her skirt as they crossed the dusty street, and he fought the urge to sweep her into his arms and carry her across.

They walked behind Daniel and Martha, and once on the boardwalk, Annie withdrew her hand and stopped at the mercantile.

"I'm going to drop off my Bible, Daddy. I'll only be a moment."

Martha kept her place on Daniel's arm, and while they waited, the couple peppered their quiet words with youthful laughter. Caleb moved away to study the new stoves displayed in the window, envisioning a small pot belly in the box stall's outside corner.

True to her word, Annie returned before he could plan an argument for Henry about the stove, and the foursome continued along the boardwalk toward the west end. He offered his arm and Annie accepted.

As they passed the Fremont Saloon, she tensed, raised her chin, and stared straight ahead. The others walked by the ornate doors with no indication of concern. What had Jedediah

Cooper done to make Annie react so strongly to even the man's establishment?

At the next corner they strolled north, and Martha led them to a rock-lined path and a small cabin with a stone chimney. White lace curtains peeked through the front window, clinging to their place against the rough logs and chink that framed them.

"Come in, come in." Martha held the door wide with a smile to match.

The aroma of baked chicken and pie crust set Caleb's mouth to watering. The amply set table in the center of the room vied with church dinners he'd long forgotten.

An unusual contraption hugged one wall, draped in long silky folds with silver pins along an unsewn edge. Must be Martha's latest project.

A large braided rug covered the tiny cabin's floor, but by Caleb's living standards, the homey room was a palace.

He hung his hat on a peg by the door and noted that Martha had set the table for three in expectation of the Whitakers. She whisked an additional plate and utensils from a shelf, quickly balanced the small round table for four, and insisted everyone be seated.

Following Daniel's prayer, Martha served each guest from the Dutch oven dominating the table's center.

"Thank you, ma'am," Caleb said. "I'm hungry as a horse."

A frown notched Annie's brow.

"Speaking of horses, Caleb,"—Daniel leaned over his dish and breathed deeply—"have you noticed anything unusual about our mare that would keep someone from buying her?"

Annie sucked in her breath and choked on the morsel in her mouth.

Caleb flinched at the barbed looked she threw him over her napkin. So much for their truce. Her heart would break if her father sold Nell, especially with the foal on the way. And she would blame him.

He rested his hand at the table's edge. "Why sell her, sir?"

Daniel harrumphed around a mouthful, then swallowed. "Well, I imagine by this point, you've seen how much she eats."

Caleb glanced from Daniel to Annie's warning glare and back.

"I expect it'd be hard to sell her now, so close to the snow coming. You might get a better price if you wait until spring."

Daniel chewed on Martha's chicken and Caleb's reply, his white brows pulling together. "Duke Deacon said he'd think on buying her."

Annie's head snapped toward her father. "We can't sell her." Apparently startled by her own abruptness, she dabbed her mouth with her napkin and softened her tone. "Did the freighters really say they wanted her?"

Daniel's tender glance at his daughter eased the creases at his eyes. He shook his head. "I know you love her, though why, I'll never understand. But she's too expensive a pet, Annie girl. And she's built for pulling a load."

Martha eyed her guests and diverted the approaching storm. "Wasn't that a most uplifting sermon this morning?" She winked at Caleb. "What do you think, Daniel?"

The man's countenance softened further as his eyes met Martha's. "Indeed it was. Love your neighbor as yourself."

"That wasn't it at all." Annie balled her napkin. "It was the parable of the sower."

Daniel laughed and his belly bumped the table's edge. "So it was, Annie. So it was."

Martha flushed pink and worried a chicken piece on her plate. Things had definitely changed between Annie's father and the seamstress, and Caleb wondered if Martha would be changing her name as easily as she'd changed the topic of discussion.

His gaze shifted to Annie, who stared at a spot on the white tablecloth above her plate. Her fitted green jacket set off her hair in flaming contrast, and two tortoiseshell combs held it off her face, exposing the tender skin at her temples. Maybe the pins he'd returned to her weren't as important as he'd thought.

"There's plenty more." Martha lifted Daniel's empty plate, heaped on creamy chicken and vegetables, then reached for Annie's.

"No, thank you," she said, returning from her reverie. "It was wonderful. Really quite good, but I cannot eat another bite." She pressed one hand against her narrow waist and tucked her napkin beneath her plate. "It's so nice outdoors, I think I'll walk through the garden while you and Daddy finish."

Martha waved a hand. "Oh, it's hardly a garden. Just a few rose bushes that attract more deer than honeybees."

Annie scooted her chair back and took her plate to the sideboard.

Daniel missed the brooding in his daughter's eyes. Caleb did not. He was the reason for their somber expression.

"Believe I'll do the same." He sensed a rare opportunity to talk to Annie alone. "Again, thank you, ma'am. This was a fine feast."

Martha tilted her head modestly, but her fingers had already found their way to Daniel's free hand lying conveniently near her on the table.

Caleb set his plate atop Annie's in the dishpan and quickly followed her outside, eager to apologize to her once again.

CHAPTER ELEVEN

Annie looked up from a fading rose at the cabin's corner to see Caleb making his way toward her, a sober look on his face.

"I'm sorry."

She shook her head and turned back to the rose, plucking at the dying petals. "It's not your fault." Her finger snagged on a thorn and she jerked her hand back. A red bead formed on her fingertip. Squeezing it, she commanded the tears that pricked her eyes to hold their place.

Caleb reached for her hand, unpocketed a blue bandana, and held it against the wound.

Feeling foolish for such a careless act, she tried to pull away but he held her fast—firmly yet gently. His eyes roamed her brow, her cheeks, her lips, as if charting every inch of her face. A flutter caught in her throat and she feared that she echoed the rose's once deep pink.

"I could have said *bear*."

Curious, she tipped her head.

"I could have said I was hungry as a bear."

Laughter eased the tightness in her shoulders, and she relaxed her hand in his. He continued to hold it after the bleeding had stopped.

"It's not your fault. Daddy has wanted to be rid of Nell ever since I talked him out of selling her in the first place. But I don't want to let her go. I love her soft breath on my face, the way she nuzzles me for the apples …"

Catching herself, she withdrew her hand and looked away. What was it about Caleb Hutton that made her want to trust him with such personal details? Feeling exposed, she regretted leaving her hat indoors and nervously fingered the new combs in her hair.

"We left everything familiar back home, and when we bought the horses in Denver, it was as if our traveling family expanded. I had more to care for than just myself and my father."

Her mouth was running away with her but she couldn't stop herself.

She clasped her hands at her waist. "How could I have known that she was ..."

Embarrassment warmed her face and rushed into her hairline.

"I'll talk to those freighters the next time they come to the wagon yard. Spring is the time for buying a horse. They're not looking to make as many trips out until then anyway."

She peeked at his face, looking for the truth to support his words and found it lying quietly in his dark eyes.

He stuffed the bandana back in his pocket and, offering his arm, gestured toward the narrow lane that bordered other cabins. "Care to walk?"

Hooking her fingers in his elbow she allowed him to lead her away from the roses.

They strolled up the lane, where transplanted cottonwoods marshalled the path, their falling leaves laying an amber carpet. Wood smoke painted the breeze, and Caleb cleared his throat and threw her a sidelong glance. "Which is worse?" he asked. "Telling your father about the coming foal before it arrives or waiting until it gets here?"

A heavy sigh slipped out. "I've asked myself the same thing a hundred times. I'm just afraid."

He stopped abruptly, surprise and doubt mingling in his scrutiny. "I find that hard to believe, oh you of the broom and the biscuits."

His boldness startled a laugh where once it would have elicited a scowl. "You are taking a fearsome chance with that remark, Mr. Hutton. A fearsome chance."

Placing his free hand atop hers, he resumed their stroll. "I can't imagine you afraid of anything on this earth, Annie Whitaker. I've seen a fire in your eyes that I'm certain lies deeply banked within your spirit."

Poetry? Annie doubted her sister's beaus spun words as charming as this horseman at her side.

Though he wasn't a beau. At least not hers.

Befuddled, she studied the ground ahead. Her right hand burned hotter than her left, covered as it was by his calloused fingers. Strength flowed from him—steadily, faithfully, as if he drew upon some hidden source. His prayer so long ago at the mercantile suggested an intimate knowledge of God. Did he share her faith?

Each time they were together, something new came to her attention—his humility, candor, humor. What *was* he? Saddle tramps didn't talk like that—or pray like that. This man had a way with more than just horses. So what was he hiding?

"Have you been upstream?"

Caught in her puzzlement, she took a moment to reorient. "Upstream?" She cocked her head to look up at him. "As in upriver?"

Amusement pulled his mouth on one side. "Yes, upriver. Have you ridden up the river, into the canyon above town?"

"Not yet." Disappointment pinched. The very thing she'd dreamed of in Nebraska still hadn't occurred. As far as she knew, the Arkansas River didn't roar any more than the lazy Mississippi, at least not near town.

"I plan to take some time off tomorrow—if we don't get any new freighters—and ride up past the Ute encampment. Take a look at the canyon the town is named for."

Envy danced across her mind. "Daddy says the canyon narrows down to the width of the river. At least that's what someone told him." Again, someone else—a man— doing what *she* wanted to do.

Her responsibilities at the mercantile had given her little free time before dark, and only a fool ventured out at night. But even during the day, who would go with her into the canyon? Daddy would never let her ride unattended, but neither would he take time off from the store to ogle the scenery.

Caleb cast a questioning look her way. Evidently her hidden frustration was not so hidden.

A pump handle squeaked behind one of the cabins, mocking a whine that she struggled to reach her throat. "When you get back, you'll have to tell me all about it."

"I'd be happy to." He brushed her with a lingering glance. "If it's not too treacherous, I'll take you up for a look. That is, if your father doesn't mind."

His comment warred against her earlier resolve. She'd not come to Cañon City to have her head turned by a wandering cowboy with no home or livelihood. But she *had* come to hear the mighty river roar.

Lifting her chin to a dignified angle, she skimmed every eager note from her voice and aimed for detached and demure. "How delightful, but I'd have to wait until after Nell ..."

Annie allowed her remark to fade into the breeze and pinned her eyes on the razorback ridge stretching against the sky to their left.

Caleb stopped and faced her. "You could ride Sally."

"Excuse me?" She eased her hand from his arm and hid it safely in the folds of her skirt.

"My other horse." Amusement lit his eyes. "She's a gentle old girl and would serve you well."

"Oh." Uncertain how she felt about him practically laughing at her and fighting her instinctive reaction to accept his offer, she turned back the way they had come.

In one long stride, he fell in beside her. "I've had Sally since I was a boy. My pa gave her to me, and she's been a faithful mount. Never bucked or bit, and fared better on the trip here than I had hoped."

Unpredictable didn't begin to describe Caleb Hutton. Now the tight-lipped loaner was spilling history with a schoolteacher's flair.

She stopped and faced him, determined that he would not be the only one full of surprises. "Thank you for your kind offer to ride Sally on a river excursion. I think it is a splendid idea."

~

That night Caleb lay with his hands linked beneath his head, his lamp trimmed low, the light thinning into darkness where overhead framework faded into the haymow. The barn cat begged outside the stall door.

He mulled over the pastor's morning message, picking through the seeds he'd sown in the last five years. Not much had sprung from his meager plantings, and yet the quiet walk with Annie had set his dreams to spinning. But what did he have to offer a beautiful woman with mahogany eyes? A box stall in a livery stable?

Again he saw the warm parsonage he'd left in Missouri. And Mollie Sullivan—far from warm as he compared her now to Annie. He'd had a calling and a home when he lost Mollie to someone of greater means. He was a fool to think Annie would give him a second thought when he had nothing.

A scratching sound lifted his attention to the rafters, where a black-and-white feline walked the crossbeam like a high-wire performer. Without a sound, it leaped to the railing along the wall and dropped to the floor.

He chuckled as it neared his bedroll.

"Won't the horses let you sleep with them?"

The cat purred against him and pressed its head into his rough blanket, adding warmth from its small body. He missed the heavy quilts back in the parsonage, the colorful spreads pieced together by the Women's Society. He'd never properly thanked them for their labors—another shortsighted sin.

He'd thought only of himself in St. Joseph. Of marrying the prettiest girl in the congregation, of listing converts beneath his name, of counting the people who sat in the walnut pews of his sanctuary.

His sanctuary. Not the Lord's.

He grimaced at his arrogance.

When had he fallen from serving God to serving himself?

The cat curled into a ball at his side and wrapped its tail around its face. He stroked its smooth back, ran his fingers through the soft hair.

"Tell me what to do," he murmured. "Not just for a warm hearth and a woman's love, but for You. I'll stay in this barn if it's what You want. Just show me what to do, how to get back to the place I should be."

He trimmed the lamp on the crate until the wick smoked out, then rolled to his side. His eyes closed and soon he drifted across a ripening wheat field with golden heads bent beneath a scuttling breeze. He saw himself running through the field—running toward an aging man who stood open-armed, tears streaming down his face and into his beard.

Caleb fell at the man's feet but was lifted upright and embraced. Enfolded, Caleb let go of his remorse and resentment. Exchanged them for peace. And found the deep restful sleep of one who is forgiven.

By the time Caleb broke ice on the water trough, fed the horses, and made his way to the mercantile the next morning, a crowd had already gathered around the potbellied stove. He removed his hat and stepped into the boisterous group helping themselves to fresh cinnamon rolls and arguing the merits of the recently elected president. Had he been in the states and not on the frontier, Caleb would have cast his vote as a citizen ought.

"Lincoln won by a landslide," boasted Jeb Hancock, a tall freighter from Illinois. His chest swelled more than the last time he'd been in the livery, and if Caleb had been a betting man, he would bet his week's wages it had everything to do with the election.

"Yesiree, got us a good 'un this time," Hancock boasted.

A stumpy miner jostled to the front and grabbed two rolls. His crumpled hat and ragged canvas coat bore witness to a played-out claim.

"It's the end, I tell ya, the end." He shoved one roll in his mouth and the other in his pocket and headed for the door.

"Good riddance," Hancock called over those who crowded the stove. "Naysayer." He swiped his buckskin sleeve across his mouth and downed his coffee dregs.

Annie stood at the back counter watching the commotion with concern. When Caleb caught her eyes, she brightened and seemed to relax. Or was his imagination showing him what he wanted to see?

It certainly wouldn't be the first time.

Caleb edged his way closer to the old stove. "Mornin'."

"Good morning." She retrieved a covered plate from the sideboard and handed it to him. "You almost didn't make it in time. Martha brought only two pans of cinnamon rolls."

Her welcome soothed like a beloved hymn. "You saved this for me?"

She took his hat and hung it on the peg holding her cloak. "I think half the town followed their noses in here this morning."

A sliver of hope wedged into Caleb's chest as he pulled the checkered napkin from the plate. The spicy aroma set his mouth to watering, and he accepted the fork she offered.

"I kindly thank you, Annie."

Blushing, she busied herself smoothing the creases from her apron. "You'll have to stand, I'm afraid, but it shouldn't be long. Milner, the editor, will no doubt be leaving soon since the newspaper comes out today. As will Karl and Kristof Turk, Hobson the barber, and Mr. Smith, who, I understand, has finally hired the Turk brothers to raise a cabin for his family."

Caleb remained at the group's edge, inhaling Martha Bobbins's handiwork and Whitaker's coffee. The men talked politics and claim jumpers, comparing both to an upcoming turkey hunt competition sponsored by Jedediah Cooper. The saloon owner snagged a roll, waved it above his head, and vowed a twenty-dollar gold piece to the man who shot the biggest wild bird.

"More than a hundred men have already laid out the two-dollar entry fee," Cooper boasted. "But any of you could be the winner. Don't be left out."

"Not in here." Daniel Whitaker raised his voice above the cheers. "You'll not be doing your business in the mercantile. Take it elsewhere."

Caleb caught Annie's pained expression and glanced at Cooper. Something had happened, something unpleasant. The room's temperature spiked.

God help Jedediah Cooper if he'd been inappropriate with her.

"Caleb?"

Her tone pulled him from morbid thoughts. She was staring at the fork gripped in his hand like a weapon.

He relaxed his fingers a bit and cut another bite from the frosted, cinnamon-laced coil as big as a horse's hoof. Turning the other cheek was a worthy rule to follow, but not where a woman was concerned. If Cooper offended Annie, Caleb would not be turning a cheek or an eye away from him, regardless of how ingenious the man appeared to be.

"Is something the matter?" She touched his arm as lightly as her voice touched his ear.

The gesture fired through his body like heat roaring from Henry's forge. Sweat beaded at his hairline.

Martha's bubbling laughter drew Annie's attention, and Caleb silently thanked the woman for her timely rescue. He moved back, as far as possible from the stove, afraid that he'd already filled the cramped room with stable perfume.

Chairs scooted across the floor, some snagging on the braided rug. Tin plates clattered into a dishpan on the stove, and Daniel Whitaker met his customers at the front counter where he accepted their coins and thanks and wished them a good day. Martha busied herself with the dishes, and Annie ground coffee beans and filled the pot with fresh water.

Caleb pulled a low-back captain's chair away from the stove. His vengeful thoughts about Jedediah Cooper surprised him, but he stopped short of repentance. No man dared lay an unwanted hand on Annie Whitaker, and he didn't mind being the one to ensure that.

He didn't mind at all.

Because he was losing his good sense to the spirited young woman, even though he'd sworn never to let such a thing happen again.

The brass bell sang out as the last customer left, and Daniel returned to the stove, where he chucked in a black lump from the coal bucket and adjusted the damper. He sat with a hefty sigh, rubbed his hands across his aproned girth, and shook his head.

"Martha, you'll make a fat man of me yet."

Martha laughed and splashed at the sideboard, dunking plates in the rinsing pan and handing them to Annie who dried them and stacked them on a shelf.

"Oh, Daniel, you are good for my heart."

Caleb glanced up from his disappearing breakfast and caught a boyish grin on the older man's face. He winked at Caleb and smoothed his mustache.

Three bites finished Caleb's cinnamon roll, and his plate had barely emptied when Annie's hand entered his view, open and waiting.

His first thought was to take it and kiss her fingers, but with her father watching and his lips sticky from the frosting, he settled for a smile.

Her eyes lingered. Oh, Lord, how could he bear to see her every day, knowing he had nothing to give her but a broken heart and broken vows?

The bold truth sobered the warmth right out of him. He wrapped both hands around his cup, planted his elbows on his knees, and stared at the braided rug beneath his feet. His eyes followed a red strand that wove through the pattern and circled halfway around the rug before giving way to a dark brown. Maybe he needed to give way himself, leave now rather than wait until spring. Denver was a three-day journey, and he'd saved enough to stake himself for a few weeks.

"You joining the hunt?"

The question brought Caleb back to the moment, and he caught Whitaker watching him over a tin mug.

"No, sir. I don't own a rifle."

Whitaker's mustache twitched and his eyes narrowed. "A cowboy like you with no gun?"

Too late Caleb recognized his blunder. The man had more on his mind than a turkey shoot.

"I have a side arm, for snakes and such. But I've never been a hunter."

Whitaker leaned on his knees, as much as his belly allowed, and threw a cautious glance toward the women. Then he lowered his voice and looked Caleb dead in the eye.

"What *do* you do? And don't tell me you're good with horses. You're hiding something, son, and if you're taking an interest in my Annie—which I can see that you are—you'd best be telling me now rather than later."

CHAPTER TWELVE

Whitaker's stare burned like hot iron.

Caleb cleared his throat. He hadn't hidden his affection for Annie any better than he'd hidden himself from the Lord.

He could simply leave. Like he'd left his church in St. Joseph. Or he could take his chances and come clean. Annie and her father deserved that much and more, after all they'd done for him.

"I was a preacher."

The confession set Whitaker back in his chair, but he never took his eyes off Caleb. One white brow cocked like a pistol hammer. "That explains it."

Exposed, Caleb started to rise.

Whitaker stopped him with a quick hand. "You've got a way with words as well as horses. I heard it when you prayed over breakfast that day, and I hear it when you talk to Annie." He looked up as the women went into the back room, then he refilled his coffee cup and offered more to Caleb. "What happened?"

Caleb breathed easier with Annie and Martha out of earshot. He thought of the old man in his dream who looked nothing like Daniel Whitaker, but maybe there was a connection. Maybe confession was a stop on the journey home.

"I pastored a small church back in St. Joseph, on the edge of town. About forty people." He pulled the hot coffee through his lips, uneasy at talking about himself. "I wasn't any good. No converts. Just the same people every Sunday, living the same lives." He cut a look toward Whitaker. "Except one."

Might as well spill it all.

"She wasn't living the life I thought she was. Then she accepted a wealthy banker's proposal—a man who also happened to be on the deacon board."

Whitaker reached for the coal bucket and added another piece to the stove. "Over yours, I take it."

Caleb cringed, feeling the fool again.

"So you left."

Whitaker's look was more compassionate than judgmental, but Caleb didn't want the man's pity. He wanted the man's daughter, and that was becoming more unlikely by the minute.

"I figured those people needed a real pastor. Someone older with more experience. I sent word to the seminary, and I'm sure they've replaced me by now."

Whitaker leaned back in his chair, balancing his cup against one leg. "So who called you to preach?"

There it was—the question Caleb had dodged for half a year until recently. The question for which he knew the answer but not the reason it hadn't worked out.

He met Whitaker's eyes and caught Annie's fire in them.

"God called me."

"And do you suppose God changes His mind about that sort of thing?"

Seminary lectures scrolled through Caleb's memory, but Whitaker's question made them personal. "No, sir."

"You're familiar with the eighth chapter of Romans, the twenty-eighth verse?"

He was. It lay like a banked ember awaiting rediscovery. "We know that all things work together for good to them that love God, to them who are the called according to his purpose."

The called.

The words scorched Caleb's soul.

"You can't outrun God, son. I'm no preacher, but I for sure know that much."

Annie came in from the back room, and the flame in Caleb's chest burned deeper. Her eyes lit on his with a smile. What would she think if she knew the truth?

He shoved his hat on. It wouldn't be long until she did. He needed distance. Perspective. Air.

He set his cup to the dishpan. "Thank you, ladies." He turned to Whitaker. "And you, sir." Then he left the store before he crumbled to ash in front of them.

Cold air slapped his face and bit through his shirt as he made his way back to the livery. He shoved through the door and the temperature rose noticeably. Fire blazed in Henry's brick furnace against the hiss and tap of the blacksmith's work. Everywhere—extremes.

Caleb grabbed the pitchfork as he walked up the alleyway. "Mornin'."

Henry's hammer paused in its dance against the anvil and he looked at Caleb. "And a good one it is."

For some.

"After I finish the stalls, I'll be heading out for a while. Be in this evening."

Henry took a step back and craned his neck toward the spare harnesses and tack hanging against the last stall.

"Everything is mended and soaped," Caleb said. "Finished Saturday night. The Turk brothers and Hancock are already gone."

Henry took to his work. No frown, no affirmation. "Fine by me."

Caleb reached for the wheelbarrow and pushed it into the alleyway. He could never tell what Henry was thinking unless the man came right out and said it plain.

Caleb should take lessons.

Nell whiffled a low greeting as he opened her stall door. "Missing Annie, are you?" The bulging mare tossed her head as if she understood and rumbled deep in her chest.

He knew the feeling.

By noon the stalls were cleaned with fresh bedding laid for all fifteen horses and mules inside. He saddled Rooster and hand-fed Sally a fistful of oats. "Maybe next time, ol' girl." He rubbed the bay mare's shoulder, truly hoping for a next time. "If the way is easy and Annie doesn't change her mind, we just might be taking another ride before the big snows fly."

Or he might be riding on out of town alone, snow or not. He hoped to have some direction after his trek today.

He buttoned his waistcoat and turned up his duster collar against the cold, then mounted the gelding and rode through town half expecting Annie to be sweeping the boardwalk in front of the mercantile. As he passed by, he saw her busy inside with a customer. Just as well.

The river ran low and easy enough to cross, but he kept to the north side and Rooster took quick to the trail. Slate blue clouds hunched over the distant ridges, threatening a storm. A soaking might be part and parcel of his day. He needed a good drenching, something to wash away his indecision and wring out the uncertainty in his soul.

He skirted the brick-colored granite guarding the canyon across from the Indian encampment. Mountain Utes, he'd been told, wintering near hot springs that seeped close by and living off deer that fed along the river.

Beyond the red monolith, the canyon tightened to a narrow green valley that hugged the river with cottonwood clusters, bushy grass, and spiny fingerlike cacti. A wide creek spilled from cedar-scattered hills on the south side and joined the river in liquid laughter.

A merry heart doeth good like a medicine. He'd give all his earnings for merriment or at least the understanding of what was weighing him down.

The dream had unsettled him and it hung with him still, especially after today's inquisition by Daniel Whitaker. He didn't begrudge the man's watchful eye for his daughter, but he'd cut near to the quick.

It didn't take a seer to know the dream dealt with a kind of homecoming. Trouble was, Caleb didn't know where home was because he didn't have one. Hadn't had one since he left his parents' place for school and the ministry.

The farther he rode, the more carefully Rooster chose his footing on the roughening trail. An occasional piñon pushed up through the rocky soil, holding its own in the rugged landscape.

The hills pulled themselves into straight-walled battlements, red rock layers jutting out like planks at a saw mill. Scrub oak and juniper jammed rocky crevices.

An unforgiving land, it seemed.

Perfect for an unforgiving heart.

Was that it? Had he not forgiven Mollie and the deacon? Himself? God?

The canyon suddenly narrowed. Granite walls rose hundreds of feet in shades of pink and gray and ochre, and beside him the river raised its voice, complaining loudly where boulders blocked its path.

Just like him.

His complaints were silent, but they were complaints nonetheless, shouting in his soul, drowning out his meager gratitude.

He startled at a sudden movement and yanked Rooster to a stop. Had the four deer not been leaping up the barren rock face, he would not have seen them—three does and a young buck. Stunned, he watched them climb the tawny granite on unseen footholds, loosening bits of gravel and bounding up to the treeless rim rock and out of sight.

Effortlessly.

He maketh my feet like hinds' feet, and setteth me upon my high places.

Those live coals kept falling into his mind, like a glowing, burning rockslide. Everywhere he looked, he saw Scripture played out before him. Had the Lord hobbled him in one spot so all Caleb could see was what He wanted him to see?

The realization struck him like a blow. He'd always believed those lofty places to be forested hilltops, lush with knee-high grass and gentle streams. He looked up again at the forbidding rock wall, almost doubting he'd seen the deer scale its face and leap to the top.

Almost.

"*He* makes my feet like hinds' feet." Rooster swiveled his ears at Caleb's voice, pulled at the reins, and reached for a grassy cluster struggling through the smooth river rocks.

"It's *Your* work, isn't it?"

Caleb laughed at the sudden clarity. It was all God's work—the spiritual condition of his former parishioners, his calling, his climb through imposing circumstances. All he had to do was surrender. Come home.

His eyes stung and the rushing river blurred before him as he pulled Rooster around and headed back downstream.

The sunlight thinned, and he looked behind him to a roiling gray cloud clambering over the canyon walls. A feathery flake settled on his hand, another on his leg. A sudden gust funneled through the canyon and tugged at his hat. He screwed it down tighter and touched his heels to Rooster's side, urging him along the rocky path.

By the time he made the cottonwood clearing, the cloud had dropped and dusted the trees and grass in a sugar-fine powder. Only on the river did the snow melt and mix with the silver water.

At the edge of town, Caleb quickened Rooster to a lope on the empty street. He dismounted at the stable, led Rooster inside, and stripped the saddle. Then he ran the gelding into the corral where Sally sheltered beneath the livery's long eaves. Rooster joined his trail partner and together they stood slack-eared, rumps against the building, watching the snow. Silence blanketed the town, the stock pens. All lay still beneath the settling white.

Grateful for his accommodations, Caleb went inside.

He'd spend the next few days listening. Not complaining. Not licking his wounds, but looking to the wounds of his Lord and listening for His voice.

~

As she did every morning, Annie rolled the pin across the floured dough, cut eight large biscuits with a baking powder can, and laid them in a greased skillet. Gathering the leftover dough to roll again, she looked for the third time over her shoulder at the front door.

Where was he?

Caleb hadn't been back for breakfast since Martha Bobbins brought cinnamon rolls, and that was days ago. Was he waiting for more of the same? Were Annie's "potbellied" biscuits no longer good enough?

Had he been toying with her when he mentioned taking her to ride up the river?

Had he left town?

Tears pooled against her lashes, and she swiped the drops away with a floured hand. She'd been too busy to visit Nell—and thus see about Caleb. It seemed there were always several customers in the store at once, laying up for the coming holidays. And by the time her father closed each evening, it was dark and cold and she couldn't bring herself to make the trip to the livery alone.

She recalled the Sunday stroll near Martha's home, that gloriously golden day that left her thinking more frequently of Caleb, reminding her that there was so very much she didn't know about him.

Edna would say Annie had lost her grip falling for a man of no means. What future could she possibly have with someone she knew so little about? But oh, the gentleness with which he'd tended her thorn-pricked finger and tucked her hand inside his arm.

A tear escaped and spotted the flour-dusted board. Again she swiped her face, irritated that a man would make her cry. Despite her resolve, she stomped her left foot hard against the floorboards. Her heart tore just as her finger had, but no one stood by to stop the bleeding.

The brass bell sang, and hope flashed only to die at a lilting voice.

"Good morning, dears." Martha pushed her bonnet back and bustled to the stove, where Annie's father prodded coal chunks with a long poker, settling them just so on last night's banked coals. She laid a hand against his bent shoulder and a kiss upon his cheek. The blood rushed to his face, and he glanced at Annie as if caught committing the unspeakable.

Annie gave her father a sly wink before turning away to stifle yet another onslaught of tears bent on escape.

She'd soon be the only unwed Whitaker in her family, other than Aunt Harriet. Edna's last letter had announced her engagement to Jonathan Mitchell, just as Annie had expected. And she'd wager her last speck of baking powder that her father and Martha would be announcing a similar pledge. Some things were simply too clear to ignore.

"Annie, your coffee smells heavenly. Might I have a cup?"

Before she could answer, her father snatched a mug from the sideboard, filled it with the hot brew, and added sugar from a covered bowl. The spoon pinged against the sides as he stirred the coffee. Obviously smitten, he tapped the spoon on the edge and handed the cup to Martha with open adoration.

Annie pounded the extra dough and squeezed it through her fists, guaranteeing it to be tough and heavy. She would not cry. Why shouldn't her father show such affection for the seamstress? Martha had brightened his life in a way that Annie and her sister had never been able to, even though he loved them dearly. And Annie had wanted this for him since the moment she'd first realized Martha had feelings for him. His happiness should be her first concern.

"Where is your young man?"

Martha's unexpected question sent a stinging dart through Annie's chest. She blinked hard, mashed the final biscuits into the skillet, and carried it to the stove. Her young man? Hardly. For all she knew he had settled into a fancy Denver hotel, or found work on another cattle spread between here and there.

Or been robbed and murdered.

She sucked in a breath at the wicked thought and caught Martha's questioning gaze.

"Are you all right, dear?"

"Quite." Annie s's spine stiffened. "I have no young man. But if you might be referring to Mr. Hutton, I've no idea where he is."

"Oh my." Martha's sweet face sobered. "I'm so sorry to have upset you."

"I'm not upset." The sharp edge to her voice prodded her to face Martha with a more peaceful explanation. Taking the chair next to the kindest woman she'd ever met, she folded her apron around her hands to hide her agitation.

"He hasn't been back since the day you brought your wonderful cinnamon rolls."

Martha's emotions warred visibly—pleasure over Annie's compliment and regret over news. She looked to Daniel. "Do you think he's left?"

Annie's father stroked his mustache, dipped his brows, and looked everywhere except at Annie—a sure sign that he was thinking how best to answer.

Did he know something she did not?

She sat straighter and held him with an unwavering glare.

"I imagine he's just been busy at the livery." He raised his cup to his lips and peeked at Annie above the rim as if giving her a secret message.

No one need tell her twice.

She jumped to her feet and hurried into their private quarters, where she yanked the star quilt from her bed and rolled it into a tight bundle. Then she grabbed her scarf and mittens, pulled on her woolen cloak, and paused by the stove.

"Martha, do you mind watching the biscuits for me? I have an errand that I must run immediately before business picks up and I can't get away."

Martha's eyes darted from Annie to her father and a rosy tint warmed her cheeks. "I would be happy to, dear. Take your time. Daniel and I can handle everything." She reached over and patted his arm. "Isn't that so?"

He coughed and shifted in his chair. "Of course we can." Then he followed Annie to the door.

"Be careful, Annie girl." He patted the quilt and leaned nearer. "And listen with your heart."

She had half a mind to ask him exactly what it was that he knew, but she didn't. "I will, Daddy."

Then she bolted out the door.

The boardwalk rang beneath her heels as she strode toward the livery. What if Caleb wasn't there? What if he really had left? And what would people think of her carrying a quilt to the stable?

She glanced about at the few people out so early, all men. Those who caught her eye nodded or touched their hat brims in a respectful greeting. Most were businessmen on their way to work. A few were miners down from the camps for the winter. But since when did she care what others thought?

Squeezing the bundle against her waist, she hurried on. The boardwalk ended at the bank building, and she hiked her skirt as she stepped down to the dirt. No dust blew in the street today, just the dry cold that was so unlike Omaha's damp winters. Her breath advanced ahead in a cloudy puff.

Five horses occupied the corral at the livery, their breath rising white from soft muzzles to vanish above their ears. Her steps slowed as she approached the wide doors opened only inches. Delivering a quilt had seemed like a good idea back in the mercantile. Now she wasn't so sure. What would she say?

She stopped and tugged her scarf higher against her chin. Then gripping one door's edge, she pulled it open and slipped into the stable.

A smoky tang struck her lungs, and for a moment fear clutched her throat. But the steady ping, ping, ping of metal on metal reminded her that Henry's blacksmith shop filled the back of the stable. As her eyes adjusted to the dim interior, she saw him at the anvil with his back to her, just beyond the last stall. Her shoulders relaxed, and she faced the box stall where she and her father had once lived. The door was swung wide, and she stopped on the threshold. A black-and-white cat curled tightly on a bedroll lying atop a thick layer of straw. A Bible lay close by. In the near corner stood an upturned crate with a basin, pitcher, and oil lamp, and on one wall hung a saddle, blankets, and bridle.

It might all be Caleb's. Nothing betrayed the owner, other than the plain white pitcher and basin he had bought from the mercantile. But if he'd left, he'd leave those behind.

Hope sank. No hat or coat lay about that she recognized, but it still could all be his, sparse as it was. Her gaze lit on the Bible. Did he have one?

"Looking for someone?"

The deep voice sent her off balance and she stumbled forward into the stall. A strong hand caught her arm and steadied her, and she turned to see a bearded man with dark laughing eyes.

Gathering her wits and clinging madly to the quilt, she took a deep breath. "Caleb."

One corner of his mouth twitched. "You were looking for someone else?"

"No! I mean… No."

What would Edna do in this situation?

Annie pulled her overly warm scarf away from her throat. Never mind Edna.

"Where have you been?"

His sudden grin made her wish she'd not been so bold. He leaned against the door frame and folded his arms across his chest. A two-week growth hugged his jawline and gave him a rugged, almost dangerous look. "You were worried?"

Frustrated, she lifted her foot for a good stomp but thought better of it. Easing it back to the straw-covered floor, she thrust the rolled quilt at him.

"Here. Maybe you can use this."

He caught the bundle before it fell and his expression shifted to surprise. "Thank you."

She stepped forward as if to pass, but he remained in the doorway. "Excuse me, but I came to check on Nell." Annie held her ground, inches from him, close enough to feel his warmth.

His gaze traveled to her lips before returning to her eyes, and his breath dusted her face.

What would she do if he kissed her?

What would she do if he didn't?

"Thank you," he repeated softly. He leaned closer.

Her breath caught.

"Nell is doing just fine."

Heat flooded Annie's cheeks, and she hurried past, gratefully turning her back on Caleb as she made for the mare's stall. A soft nicker greeted her, and she regretted having no treat for the mother-to-be. She'd left the mercantile in such a hurry that she hadn't thought to bring dried apples or a few carrots.

Annie held her cheek against the mare's warm head and stroked her thick neck. "You poor dear. Just look at you."

The horse's belly hung like a bulging grain sack, distended and heavy with promise. Yet for all her size and distortion, Nell seemed calm and unconcerned.

Footsteps whispered behind Annie, and she sensed Caleb's closeness.

"I owe you an explanation." His voice was low and rough as ground coffee.

He moved closer, leaned over the stall gate and combed his fingers through Nell's mane.

Annie's pulse quickened as she remembered her father's words: *Listen with your heart.* She swallowed. Listening with your heart meant opening your heart. Was she ready to open her heart to Caleb Hutton?

Or had she already done so without realizing it?

CHAPTER THIRTEEN

Lilacs bloomed in winter with Annie so close that Caleb could bury his face in her hair. The desire nearly overwhelmed him, but he concentrated on what he needed to say rather than on what he yearned to do.

"I'm not who you think I am."

She looked at him, doubt and expectation dueling for dominance. "And who do I think you are, other than what you've led me to believe?"

She wasn't going to make it easy, but then she wouldn't be Annie if she did.

"I left out some things." He uttered a silent prayer for clarity. "I'm a preacher. Or at least I was."

A short intake through her nose. Her eyes rounded and she turned to the mare.

He leaned against the stall gate. Nell flicked her tail and craned her neck over the railing toward Annie's coat pocket.

"No apples today, girl." Annie's gentle tone shot hope through Caleb's chest that she'd show him as much kindness, even though he didn't deserve it. She kept her eyes on the mare as she stroked the broad head. "Why did you say you were good with horses, a ranch hand?"

A fair question. He propped his right arm across the stall door and angled himself to see her reaction. "Remember when Abraham told Pharaoh that Sarah was his sister?"

Annie's fine brow creased at the bridge of her nose.

"It was true," he continued. "Sarah *was* Abraham's sister. But it was only half the truth."

"So you're saying that you told my father and me only half the truth."

"Yes."

"Why?"

He cleared his throat and pushed from the door, facing her squarely. No more hedging. He'd run from a broken heart and broken a vow in the process. If he wasn't man enough to tell Annie Whitaker the whole truth, face-to-face, then he wasn't man enough for anything.

"My father was a veterinarian and wanted me to follow in his profession. Taught me much of it as I was growing up." He rubbed the back of his neck, as tight as a barrel band. "But I believed, at the time, that I was called to preach the gospel. My father conceded and helped pay my way through seminary."

"So you really *do* have a way with horses."

The scent of leather, fresh hay, and horses hung in the barn's still air, stirring images from his youth. His tension eased a bit, and he gave her a brief nod.

"My first and only church was in St. Joseph, Missouri. A small congregation. No new converts, but good people. Faithful. Except for one."

Her reaction offered no clue to her thoughts, but he pressed on.

"I offered myself to a woman who later chose a wealthy deacon instead. Rather than stay and face them from the pulpit, I convinced myself that the congregation needed an older pastor, one with more experience and wisdom."

He paused, dread curdling in his stomach. "I left. Turned my back on God and preaching and headed west to cowboy on the Lazy R."

With this final confession, the tension in his neck and shoulders escaped like air from the smithy's bellows.

Annie had removed her mittens and threaded the fringe from her loosened scarf in and out between her fingers. Her eyes met his, free of scorn or derision. "And like Jonah, you ended up where you didn't want to be."

Her comparison surprised him, but he was grateful she hadn't called him a coward and stomped out of the barn.

"Why didn't you go home to your father?"

"My parents are no longer living. The next best thing was a ranch out west."

Annie reached for the dozing mare's forelock. "Do you still plan to leave here too? Come spring, like you mentioned earlier?"

Not if she'd give him reason to stay. But he couldn't tell her that. Not now, not yet. What did he have to offer? Life as a laborer's wife?

"I'll look for another church and start over. Maybe take up a circuit and preach in the gold camps."

"Not another ranch?"

She had him there, and he was framing an answer when she spoke again.

"I saw the Bible on your bedroll. Have you made your peace with God?"

He hooked his thumbs in his waistband. "You make it sound like I'm about to bite the dust."

Her laughter warmed his insides, melted the dread that had frozen in his chest. "In a way, you already have. You've died to yourself if you're brave enough to try again."

He would not call himself brave, but the clear sense of her words breathed hope into him. Fanned the belief that God had indeed forgiven him and offered him a second chance.

But would she?

Annie pulled her mittens on, stepped back from the stall. "You haven't answered my question."

Confused, he waited for her to continue.

"Where have you been the last two weeks? We've missed you at breakfast." A slight blush tinted her cheeks, and she moved toward the barn doors.

"I had to 'make my peace with God,' as you put it. Clear my head, get things straight."

"And you couldn't do that at the mercantile?"

Not when he thought only of her when he was there.

Silhouetted in the open stable door, she stopped and spoke over her shoulder. "I was afraid you didn't like my potbellied biscuits anymore."

The air cleared at her teasing tone, and he shook his head and held one hand against his stomach. "I've sorely missed them. But I'll be back if you'll have me."

Her luminous eyes caught him unaware. "And why wouldn't I? You promised me a ride up the river."

As she walked out the door, he leaned against the stall and scrubbed his hands over his face and thickening beard. Back home he'd always stayed clean shaven. But here in the dry, colder climate, the beard kept him warmer.

Warmer. He rushed into what he'd come to think of as his room and lifted the rolled quilt. Clutching it in his arms, he buried his face in a bright red star, inhaling Annie's scent.

Thank you, Lord.

The cat rubbed against his leg and offered its sleepy opinion.

"There's hope." He stooped to run his hand along its arched back. "Today I've been given hope."

He'd take Annie on that ride as soon as possible—if it didn't snow. Because come spring, he'd be riding out on his own. The prospect pulled his gut in the opposite direction, but he'd known for several days that he was to return to the ministry. Would Annie wait for him if he rode a mining camp circuit? Or join him if he found another church far from Cañon City?

Would her father let her?

He laid the quilt on his bedroll and walked down the alleyway to where he'd earlier left his slicker and hat on a nail. The print shop had paper. He'd write to his seminary professors, see if the gold camps or other towns farther north needed a preacher.

Maybe they'd give him another go.

~

She *knew* it.

Only she hadn't.

Annie hugged her cloak tighter. Caleb Hutton had been hiding something all right, but she hadn't pegged him as a preacher. Her fingers tingled in her mittens—not from the cold December morning but from excitement.

Excitement? Over the fact that Caleb was a minister?

No, that wasn't it. But what?

She tucked her hands beneath her arms and slowed her pace.

He didn't strike her as a clergyman. But as she gave the idea greater consideration, what should a preacher look like, act like? Quiet, intelligent, gentle. She laughed. Her pastoral characterization fit Nell better than Reverend Hartman. He was intelligent and gentle, but she'd never classify him as quiet. The man exuded energy, joked with his small congregation, and flirted unashamedly with Hannah Baker, his bride-to-be.

Come to think of it, Annie's pastor from back home met all three qualities, but he was, well, boring.

Caleb Hutton was anything but boring.

The mercantile door opened to welcoming warmth. Her father and Martha sat by the stove chatting while Karl Turk picked through a notions box on the counter.

Did her father even know the man was in the store?

"Can I help you, Mr. Turk?" Annie stuffed her mittens and scarf behind the counter, laid her wrap over a crate, and scowled at her father. Either he was going deaf or he was so hopelessly smitten with Martha Bobbins that he had ears for no one but the seamstress.

Turk grumbled and poked through the box.

"Are you looking for something in particular?" Annie's voice raised on the last word, and she tied on an apron as she watched the lumberman's thick fingers fail to catch on any item.

"A razor," he mumbled. "But I can't find one in all these do-dads and baubles."

"Oh, the razors are over here." Turning to the shelf behind her, she threw one last glance at her father. He caught it and erupted from his chair as if burned by spilt coffee.

Red-faced, he hurried to Annie's side. "Razors, you say. I got a fine assortment in on the last shipment." He winked at Annie and pulled a long box from the shelf.

She frowned as if scolding a spoiled child, but there was no use staying mad at her jovial parent. It was impossible. Besides, her own spirits were so light she fairly skimmed across the rough floorboards.

Gathering her cloak, scarf, and mittens, she headed toward Martha who was washing her cup in the dishpan.

"You don't need to wash your dishes here."

"Oh yes, I do." Martha clicked her tongue and shook her head. "If Daniel hadn't been so caught up in our conversation, he would have known Mr. Turk was here." She dried the cup, set it aside, and pushed a few stray hairs beneath her cap. Looking at Annie like a shy school girl, she blushed. "I didn't even hear the bell myself."

Annie laughed and hugged the little woman's rounded shoulders. "Never you mind. It all worked out." She poured herself some coffee and added sugar. "I think he's quite taken with you, Martha."

The seamstress blushed even more and pulled at an invisible thread on her skirt. "Do you mind, dear?"

"Not at all." The older woman's nervousness was endearing. "I think it's wonderful. My father has been alone far too long—even with me and my sister." As she uttered the words, her soul trembled at the thought of living by herself in the storeroom, but she stuffed the worry down.

Martha held her in a knowing gaze. "Did you find your young man?"

Annie's lips pulled at the corners. "I gave him the quilt." Dare she share her secret with Martha, tell her that she was losing her heart to a wayward preacher-turned-cowboy?

"I really must be going." Martha lifted her wrap from a chair and snugged it around her shoulders.

Annie followed her to the door in time to hear Mr. Turk mention Christmas trees.

"I brought several down from my last trip to the Greenhorns. They're out behind my place by the river. If you don't mind spreadin' the word, I'm sellin' 'em for two bits a piece."

People would sell anything. Imagine, charging money for a sapling or cut tree top. Yet how splendid to have a tree for Christmas, festooned in popcorn garland and round red cranberries. Well, maybe black choke cherries here in the Rocky Mountains.

"I'll take one, Mr. Turk." Martha turned to Annie's father and softened her voice. "Could you drive my buckboard down and pick it up for me?"

"I'd love to have one for the store window too." Annie watched her father calculating the tree's cost against the opportunity to visit his sweetheart. She turned to Martha. "Will two trees fit on your wagon?"

"I believe they would." Martha dug a coin from her reticule and handed it to Karl. "Twenty-five cents, paid in advance."

He smiled and tipped his hat. "Thank you, ma'am. I'll set one out as soon as I get home."

"Well?" Annie eyed her father and caught the glint in his eye as he dug in his pocket for a coin.

"Make that two trees, Turk. I'll be by after I walk Miss Bobbins home and stop at the livery for her buckboard."

Annie almost envied her father. She hadn't ridden in a buggy or even a buckboard since their arrival in town last summer. And she had so wanted to visit the great canyon upriver with Caleb. Maybe it wasn't too late.

"I'll mind the store while you're gone, but don't dally." She gave her father a playful pat on his shoulder as he shrugged into his coat.

"I managed to get the mail out, so that's one less worry for you. I'll be back shortly."

That wasn't likely, but she'd not begrudge him a change of pace after the daylight-to-dark hours he put in.

As soon as he opened the door, Martha tucked her hand in his arm and together they headed up the boardwalk.

Annie checked the fire, added a chunk of coal, and set about clearing the window display to make room for the tree.

She removed lamps and basins and dry goods from the heavy oak table and set them on the counter. As she leaned into the table to shove it against the far wall, a shadow paused at the window and she looked up.

Jedediah Cooper hovered like a hawk ready to sweep down on its prey.

Her blood chilled.

He moved to the door before she could lock it. The bell tolled ominously, and she hurried behind the counter and reached for the broom.

"I was afraid the mercantile was closed when I saw your father stepping out with the widow Bobbins." Cooper's voice slid around the words like snake oil as he closed the door and loosened the muffler from his neck.

Annie's fingers tightened on the broom handle and she raised her chin. "How can I help you, Mr. Cooper?"

His lips curled in a sly smile, and he raked a hungry leer across her bodice. "Don't be so formal, Annie. By all means, call me Jed." With great aplomb, he pulled the gloves from his hands one finger at a time. "You may *help* me, Annie, by considering an update of our arrangement for your occupation of the back portion of this fine establishment."

Annie's chilled blood heated to a boil. She drew a slow breath, hoping to prevent red anger from surging into her face. "We already reached an agreement, Mr. Cooper. You agreed to our offer before my father and I took over the storeroom six weeks ago."

Cooper laid his gloves on the counter and slowly made his way around the end, where he breached her sanctuary. She backed away, never taking her eyes from him, mentally measuring the distance to her escape.

"All agreements are subject to change, Annie. Didn't I mention that?"

He lunged for her. She shoved the broom in his face, but he fended it off, sending it over the counter.

Annie bolted for the door. Her fingers gripped the knob and turned. He grabbed her from behind, one arm cinching her waist, a hand over her mouth. As he whirled her around, her hand swung the door open, clanging the bell.

"Not so fast," he breathed against her neck. Stale tobacco from his coat sleeve vied with his whiskey-laced breath. Her stomach lurched.

"We're meant to be, Annie. I knew it when you fell into my arms that day at the Fremont. So soft and warm." He spread his fingers to crush her nose as well. She kicked at his legs, striking his shins with her boot heels, and dug her fingers into his smothering hand.

Was that what he intended? Cut off her air until she passed out and then—

His throaty laugh twisted through her. "And a fighter you are. That's good. I like my women feisty."

Reaching up, she groped for his face and dug her nails into his cheek. He swore and twisted away, hefting her up like a sack of flour. Past the counter, the chairs. At the stove, she flailed for the coffeepot, but knocked it to the floor.

"You must show me what you've done with the back room, Annie. Have you made it more *comfortable?*"

She clawed at his beefy fingers. *O God, help me!* Her lungs screamed for air and her vision blurred, darkening at the edges.

Keep fighting.

Squeezed against him, she felt the growl deep in his chest before she heard it. Before he pushed through the curtain and into the darkened storeroom.

With a final shove, she twisted until his ear brushed her face and then bit down as hard as she could.

He screamed and slugged blindly at her, hitting her in the temple. He threw her on her bed, her head at the foot, and followed her down, pinning her with his weight. Another inch, and her skull would have cracked on the brick lying beneath the bedclothes. If she could reach it, pull it from the blankets, she'd have a weapon.

As if reading her mind, he crushed both her wrists together in one meaty hand and licked his lips.

CHAPTER FOURTEEN

Caleb thanked Milner, the *Cañon City Times* editor, whom he left sifting through notes on a cluttered corner desk. He tucked a folded weekly and extra note paper into his waistcoat and exited the print shop.

Across the street in the next block, Jedediah Cooper stood on the boardwalk in front of Whitaker's Mercantile. The dandy pulled at his cuffs, looked both ways along the street, and walked into the store.

Caleb's neck prickled as if lightning were about to strike. He didn't want that man anywhere near Annie, landlord or no. Maybe he should pay a visit to the mercantile himself. Come to think of it, he hadn't told Annie about his ride up the river. And he was running short on supplies. Needed a cake of soap. Crackers, canned peaches. A needle and thread.

Rubbing his left elbow, he jabbed a finger through the thinning material. A new shirt. Might as well get one now.

He adjusted his hat and stepped off the boardwalk. A couple strolled past the Fremont Saloon and Hotel, and Caleb held them in his gaze. He'd walked behind that miniature woman and her burly escort a few weeks ago.

What were Martha Bobbins and Daniel Whitaker doing out on the town so early in the day?

The pin pricks worked from Caleb's neck up into his scalp.

Without looking, he rushed into the path of an oncoming buckboard. The horse reared, the driver pulled up and hollered.

Caleb reached for the startled animal's bridle and offered a gentle word as he rubbed the horse's neck. "Sorry about that," he told the driver.

"Watch where you're going."

Caleb stepped back as the angry farmer drove on, then ran across to the opposite boardwalk. The mercantile's door stood open.

He thought of his Colt revolver tucked beneath his bedroll as he stepped inside.

Annie's broom had fallen in front of the counter. He leaned it against the edge near a pair of men's gray gloves. No one sat at the stove, but the coffeepot lay on the floor, its contents spilled. His gut galloped into his throat.

He softened his steps and crossed the worn floorboards as if approaching a wounded animal. A scuffling behind the curtain drew a vow that if Annie was in harm, Caleb would be wounding whatever animal he found there—man or beast.

His fingers curled into fists.

Annie would not invite a man into her sleeping quarters, especially with her father gone. A flash of Mollie Sullivan on her beau's arm stabbed at Caleb's memory, and he clenched his jaw. Annie was not Mollie, but he readied himself to find either of two equally horrifying possibilities and pulled the curtain aside.

Like a giant slug, Cooper's body covered Annie. One hand held her wrists above her head, the other pressed against her mouth. Fear screamed from her rounded eyes, louder than Caleb's hammering heart.

He'd never wanted to kill another human being. Until now.

Cooper must have seen Annie's eyes lock on Caleb, for the man glanced over his shoulder. Caleb jerked him to his feet, spun him around, and smashed his fist into Jedediah Cooper's sputtering explanation. Blood spurted from the man's nose with the first hit. The second opened a dark gash above his lip. The third dropped him to the floor, out cold.

Annie pushed up on her elbows, gasping for breath, her face ashen.

Caleb's chest heaved with murderous emotion, his fists opening and closing. He held Annie's eyes with his own until she flung herself into his arms. Pressing her to his chest, he buried his hands in the thick hair tumbling down her back. His voice climbed from a deep, dark place, nearly unrecognizable. "Did he hurt you?"

She shook her head, fighting to control her sobs.

"No," she whispered. "But if you hadn't come …"

Bile rose in his throat.

With a steadying breath, she relaxed somewhat. "I begged God to help me." Tears welled anew and spilled into rivulets down her reddened cheeks. With a trembling hand, she swiped them away. "I never dreamed He'd send you."

A breath convulsed suddenly in her chest. "How did you know?"

Hesitant to let her go, Caleb guided her through the curtain to the chairs at the stove and settled her into the closest one. "Give me a minute."

He cut two lengths of twine at the counter, tied the curtain back with the shorter one to keep an eye on Cooper, and bound the man's wrists with the other. Then he pulled another chair close to Annie and reached for her hands.

"I was at the printing office. On my way out, I saw Cooper walk in here. Then I saw your father and Martha on the boardwalk. It didn't set right with me."

She clutched his hand like a drowning woman grasping a rope. "Daddy will never forgive himself for leaving me alone. It could spoil everything for him."

Puzzled, Caleb studied her face, looking for explanation, waiting for her to voice it.

"Daddy and Martha." Letting out a deep sigh, she pulled her hands away and twisted her hair into a knot at her neck. "I fully expect them to ..." Her gaze fell away. "They haven't yet made a declaration, but Mr. Cooper said ..."

Her voice trailed off as she held her hair with one hand, searching through the folds of her skirt with the other.

Her combs.

He stepped over Cooper's unconscious hulk and rage churned again. On Annie's bed he found the combs where they'd worked loose, and he returned them to her, pressing them into her hand.

"Thank you," she whispered. "Again."

He might as well be the one drowning, the way her eyes drew him through deep water.

"Annie, I have to ask you a question." He wrestled with his desire for vengeance, shoved his fervor down. "Has Cooper ever tried anything like this before today?"

Her face blanched. She shook her head, swallowed. "But the day I asked him about renting the storeroom, I was pushed into him."

Caleb waited for more.

"I went to the saloon to talk to him, but I went no farther than just inside the door. As I stood there, someone outside pushed it from behind. I lost my balance and fell against him."

She glanced at Cooper's still form and shuddered.

"Did he hurt you then?" Revenge skirted Caleb's thoughts, goading him to finish what he'd started with the no-good lecher.

She shook her head again. "No. But I was humiliated. The way he looked at me ..."

"He'll not try it again, I assure you."

Again he encased her hands in his. "You were going to tell me something, something he said. What was it?"

Fresh tears formed against her lashes. "Today—before you got here—he said if I told Daddy, he'd kick us out of the mercantile."

His jaw tight, Caleb drew both air and hatred in through his nose. God help him, he wanted to do a whole lot more than just hate Jedediah Cooper.

"That won't happen. I'll be speaking with the magistrate as soon as your father returns, and I intend to tell him the whole story."

"I'm so ashamed." The chin that usually took every assault from a lofty perch drooped against her chest.

"No, Annie." Gently, he tilted her face to meet his eyes. "You have nothing to be ashamed of. Nothing at all."

He longed to tell her how he felt, but now wasn't the time. She was too vulnerable. Declaring himself, even in an honorable way, would have to wait.

Heavy footsteps fell across the threshold, and Daniel Whitaker's voice boomed into the store. "Did you see me coming with this monstrosity and leave the door open?"

Whitaker held the cut end of a large evergreen as he dragged it through the door. Both Caleb and Annie rose to help him.

One look at Annie's disheveled appearance, and Daniel dropped the tree and reached for his daughter.

"Caleb Hutton!" he thundered.

"Daddy, it's not what you think." Annie ran to her father and threw her arms around his bulk. "He came just in time."

A moan from the back room drew their attention to the man on the floor. Caleb strode to Cooper and dragged him to his feet. Blood stained the man's shirtfront and brocade vest, and he lifted his bound hands to his swelling nose.

Caleb grabbed his arm and shoved him past the stove toward the store front. "Tell Whitaker what happened, Cooper, or I will."

Red-faced and stammering, the man's eyes darted between Annie, her father, and escape. Caleb stepped around him and soundly shut the door.

~

Annie stood with her arm linked through her father's as they watched Caleb usher Jedediah Cooper, none too gently, to Magistrate Warren's office.

"Annie, girl, I never would have forgiven myself if that man had hurt you."

She hugged his arm and looked into his guilt-reddened eyes. "I shouldn't have gone to the saloon, Daddy. I should have listened to you. You were right."

He pulled her into a fatherly embrace and cupped her head in his big hand. "I've been thinking too much about myself lately, and not enough about you."

Stepping back, she gave him a scolding look. "Nonsense, Daddy. You've been happy, and that makes me happy."

He blustered and hugged her again. "I'm just glad you're all right."

Still shaken from the ordeal, she willed her nerves to calm, determined to cling to their simple holiday cheer. They had to keep moving forward.

"Have you delivered Martha's tree yet?"

He huffed. "Don't know that I'll ever view a Christmas tree the same after today."

Brushing aside her father's comment, she reached for the aromatic tree that lay across their floor. "I'm not letting that varmint spoil my Christmas."

The less-than-ladylike term rolled off her tongue with delicious precision. Bless the freighters and their colorful language. Well, some of their language. "And neither should you."

If they quaked at every horrible thing that *might* have happened, they'd cower themselves into an early grave, and that she refused to do.

She closed her eyes and held her face near the tree's branches. "This smells so good. Help me set it in the window."

"Let's lean it against the wall. Turk showed me how to make a cross and nail it to the tree bottom so it'll stand by itself."

Her father set the tree's peaked top between two saddles hanging on the wall opposite the front counter. "I've got an old box out back that I can bust up and use. Be right back."

He stopped to pick up the coffeepot and pegged her with a warning. "You holler if anyone comes in and I'll be here faster than you can blink."

Her ragged nerves quivered at his protectiveness and she resisted the urge to follow him outside. "I'll be fine, Daddy. Besides, I can just topple this blue spruce on anyone who is less than gentlemanly."

He set the pot on the stove and headed for the back, wagging his head.

Drinking in the sweet woodsy scent, Annie's thoughts wandered to her other protector. A shiver coursed through her body as she recalled the chilling anger in Caleb's eyes when he'd found her pinned beneath Cooper.

Held in two men's arms in less than ten minutes' time, yet each with such different intent. She fingered her swollen lower lip and winced at the taste of Cooper's brutality.

Leaning again into the evergreen branches, she imagined they were Caleb's strong, protective arms. The thought fanned a fire in her belly as sure as the open flu pulled sparks from coal.

Thank you, Lord, for sending Caleb.

The back door shut, and her father stomped his feet before coming up front.

"It's snowing."

Annie turned toward the window. Penny-size flakes fell from the gray sky and settled on the boardwalk. Dry and crisp, they held their starry shapes instead of melting like the first snows in Omaha.

"Oh, Daddy, it's beautiful."

"It's also cold." He brushed the white dust from his shoulders. "Let's get this tree set and I'll stoke the fire. It's going to be a cold one tonight."

Grateful to be in the store and not the livery, Annie prayed that Caleb would be warm and dry in the box stall. Maybe she should take him another quilt. With the down from their Christmas goose, plus what she'd gathered at the river, she could start a feather cover for him. She'd let Martha know too, and maybe barter for enough down to finish one this winter.

Such a thought for a single woman to have.

Her father laid the tree flat on the floor, held a squared wooden cross against the cut edge, and positioned a large nail in the center.

With two swift hammer hits, he drove the nail head flush to the wood, and repeated the process with a second nail.

"Imagine," she wondered aloud. "A cross and nails at Christmas holding everything together."

Box slats did not resemble Calvary's cruel tree. Then again, maybe they did—a sober foreshadowing of the Lord's calling from manger crib to cross.

Caleb's confession came to mind with a bitter-sweet recognition that he must follow God's leading—even if it took him away from Cañon City.

Away from her.

Her father raised the tree to stand straight and tall.

Annie slipped an arm around his waist. "Thank you."

"We'd better get some corn popping so you can start on a garland for the tree. That is, if you're feeling up to it, Annie." His gaze fell to her bruised mouth.

"I'm fine, Daddy. Truly."

Not as fine as she wanted to be, and her lip stung where it had cut on her teeth. She still felt Cooper's weight pressing her down, and if she could, she'd strip off the dress she wore and burn it in the stove. Burn away the memory of his sour breath, of her helplessness.

She wasn't sure which was worse, but right now, she needed to put on a good face for her father.

The bell clanged and the Smiths poured through the door, bundled and stomping and laughing. The children's eyes glittered like Christmas candles when they saw the stately spruce.

"Oh, Mama. It smells so pretty. Can we have a tree?" Emmy Smith tugged at her mother's skirt. "Can you buy one from Mr. Whicker for us?"

Louisa Smith laughed and knelt beside her daughter. "Where would we put a tree in our tiny cabin? Maybe we can just come visitin' and enjoy this one."

Emmy's lower lip quivered and her blue eyes pooled with enough tears to set Annie's father astir.

"I know just where you can get a tree for your new home." He threw an exaggerated wink at Springer, who stood behind his mother and sister, failing to hide the yearning in his own eyes.

"Just this morning I saw one that could sit on a table top. Just right for a pint like you." He patted Emmy's head.

She tucked her chin. "I ain't no pint."

"You *aren't* a pint," Louisa corrected.

Emmy stomped her little foot. "That's what I said."

Annie stifled a laugh and moved behind the counter. Did she look like that when she stomped her foot?

Her father drew something from his pocket and slipped it to Springer with a whisper and a nod.

An oversized grin spread across the boy's face, and he tugged his hat and addressed his mother. "I'll be right back. Got an errand to run."

"Well, hurry. I want to be home in this storm, not out stuck somewhere in a snow drift."

Louisa pegged Annie's father with a merry frown that twitched her lips into a smile. "You're going to spoil us all, Mr. Whitaker."

Annie pulled a letter from the Smith's mail slot. "I have something here for you, Louisa. It's postmarked Kansas City."

"Land sakes." The woman snatched the envelope from Annie's fingers with something a kin to hunger. "It's from my sister Emma." She slid a finger beneath the flap, glanced at her audience, then tucked the letter in her cloak. "Pardon me. How rude. It can wait."

Annie knew full well what it meant to get a letter from home brimming with news of everything familiar. Suddenly she missed her sister. Even Aunt Harriet a little.

Louisa shuttled Emmy to a table to look through a button box, then returned to the counter and lowered her voice. "I'd like to see your calico, please."

Annie laid a length of sky-blue cotton on the counter. A dress for Emmy, no doubt. Aunt Harriet wouldn't be fingering calico this Christmas, nor would Edna. In fact, her sister was probably up to her ringlets in ruffles and lace, planning the perfect dress for her spring wedding.

Louisa held up one finger, silently noting how many dress lengths. With a deep sigh, Annie rolled out the fabric and cut it with shears.

"Her doll gets a new dress too," Louisa whispered. "And give me three lengths of that light wool there, please. Springer and Ben need shirts."

And there it was. Family.

Annie would gladly take calico and wool over satin and lace any day, unless it was *her* wedding day, of course. With no warning, she saw herself in a beautiful dress with Caleb awaiting her in the church, but the startling image fled as suddenly as it had appeared. Such an event didn't even peek over the far horizon's edge.

"Looks like you'll be mighty busy." Annie dragged her morose thoughts back to the task at hand, folded the fabric, and added it to the Smith's purchases. Despite her resolve, her mind wandered to the traditional Christmas preparations for her aunt's ornate home. Glass ornaments and tinsel for the tree. Candles, star-shaped cookies …

"Annie?"

Startled from her daydream, she focused again on her customer. "I'm sorry. I was just thinking about … your cabin. You mentioned a cabin. So you are out of the tent in time for winter?"

Louisa sighed and her eyes gentled with adoration. "My William worked so hard to get it completed, and the Turk brothers helped, bless their souls. It's not big, but it's so much warmer with the fireplace and solid walls."

Annie stooped behind the counter and brought out a large tin. She lifted the lid for Louisa to peek inside.

"Oh," Louisa whispered. "Wrap several of those for me, please." Her blue eyes sparkled like her little girl's. "Just tuck them into the fabric bundle."

Annie giggled. "I couldn't resist these when we put in our last order. I knew the few children we have around here would be delighted."

She chose six white candy canes, wrapped them in brown paper, and laid them on top of the calico. "And if you have heavy shears, you can cut stars from empty tins and tie them to the tree. That will add a little shine to Emmy's Christmas surprise."

"That is a wonderful idea," Louisa said.

"What's a wonderful idea, Mama?" Emmy skipped to her mother's side and eyed the large container on the counter.

Annie returned it to its hiding place with a wink.

"You have too many questions for this time of year." Louisa pulled her daughter into a quick hug.

The bell over the door rang out, and Emmy's two small hands clapped her cheeks, her mouth a rosebud O.

Springer held a perfect little sapling in his hands. "Just right, don't you think, Ma?"

Annie reached for a skein of red yarn, snipped off a generous length, and rolled and tucked it inside the Smith's package.

"For hanging the stars," she whispered to Louisa.

As Annie watched the family hurry through the falling snow, she couldn't help herself. She couldn't keep from wondering what it would be like to hurry home with a certain horse-handling preacher for a husband.

CHAPTER FIFTEEN

Caleb shoved Cooper through the magistrate's door and waited for Frank Warren to draw his long, lean body out of the chair by the woodstove. More cabin than jail, the room housed a single stout cell in the back.

A frown creased the magistrate's brow as he gave the saloon owner a quick once-over, pausing on the man's blood-stained brocade vest.

"I found him taking liberties at Whitaker's Mercantile that were completely unacceptable." Caleb stepped back, distancing himself from the no-account before giving into the urge for further action.

"And what were you doin' at the mercantile, Cooper?" Warren folded his arms and sat on the edge of his desk.

"Can't a man make a friendly call on the local shopkeeper?"

Caleb took a step forward, and Warren stopped him with a glare.

"And that shopkeeper would be Daniel Whitaker?"

Cooper mumbled something about the Whitaker woman being excessively unfriendly.

Caleb didn't know if he could control himself.

Warren ambled across the open space and escorted the bloodied saloon owner to the back corner.

Cooper twisted in the magistrate's grip, shouting at Caleb, "I'll see you pay for this."

"Keep your threats to yourself, Cooper." Warren locked the iron door and pocketed the key. Three long strides returned him to the stove's warmth, where he lowered his voice. "Those liberties happen to involve a Miss Annie Whitaker?"

Caleb's blood surged. "I figured murder was a hanging offense even this far west, so I brought him to you instead."

Warren's sweeping mustache quirked with apparent appreciation of Caleb's self-restraint. "The People's Court meets day after tomorrow. We'll hold the old cuss here until then." He crossed the room, took a seat behind his broad oak desk, and opened a ledger. "This isn't the first report we've had of him taking a shine to the single womenfolk, but you're the first witness we've had to the offense other than the women themselves."

"Will there be a trial?"

"More likely an informal hearing." Warren's gaze shifted from the ledger to Caleb's reddened knuckles. "I take it you're the one responsible for the bloodletting?"

"Yes, sir." Caleb flexed his fingers, swollen now from the force of Cooper's face coming to blows with his fist.

"Any other witnesses?"

"Just myself and Ann—Miss Whitaker, but I saw to it that Cooper apologized to her father, who returned to the store not long after the incident."

Warren grunted his approval. "Good. A confession. That will speed things right along. I'd just as soon get Cooper out of these parts, and this might do it. Time he sold out to somebody else and moved on." He laid his pen down and leaned back in the squeaky chair. "In fact, I think I know someone who might be interested in buying the Fremont Hotel and Saloon. Give Cooper a stake to leave and clean up the town all at the same time."

Caleb reset his hat. "I work at the livery. I'd appreciate a word about the hearing before it takes place."

"Oh, you'll hear. Court meets in Cooper's building, upstairs above the saloon. You might even be called on to testify."

Caleb nodded his thanks and opened the door.

The chair creaked. "Good timing."

Pausing, Caleb looked over his shoulder into the magistrate's coal-chip eyes.

"Good thing you happened by the mercantile when you did."

A tight throat and tighter chest prevented Caleb from speaking before he stepped onto the boardwalk and closed the door.

In spite of the drop in temperature, he smoldered with the closest he'd ever come to righteous anger. *Lord, vengeance is Yours, You say …*

A sudden wind whipped down the street, swirling giant snowflakes into his face. He screwed his hat down, turned up his collar, and shoved his hands in his pockets. His need to see Annie was as stinging as the wind. He had to make sure she was all right, let her know Cooper was locked up until a hearing.

Scouting both ways along Main Street, he bent his head against the wind and crossed the frozen roadway. A large evergreen filled the mercantile's front window, and a dozen such trees from his childhood paraded across his memory. As he reached for the knob, the door flew open and Springer Smith darted out with a miniature tree, his sister chasing close behind. Caleb stepped back and tugged his hat brim to Springer's mother, who quickly followed, arms heaped high with wrapped bundles.

"Can I help you, Mrs. Smith?"

Tired but smiling blue eyes met his for a moment before latching onto running children. "Thank you, but I've got help aplenty—if I can just catch it."

The woman dashed down the boardwalk as if a child herself. Springer had already tossed the little tree in a nearby buckboard and was lifting his giggling sister in. He relieved his mother of her armload, then helped her to the seat before climbing in and gathering the reins.

The family scene clutched at Caleb. Would he ever know such blessings?

"Well, are you coming in or are you going to stand there until you look like a snowman?" Annie stood in the doorway, hands on her hips.

He stomped his boots on the walk and stepped inside, wondering which he was more grateful for—the inviting atmosphere of the mercantile or the beautiful woman who worked there.

Slapping the snow from his hat, he smiled into gold-flecked eyes. "Don't mind if I do."

Her gaze dropped to his knuckles and she reached for his arm. "Your hand."

Her touch stalled his speech for a moment. "No need to worry, Annie. It's you I'm concerned about."

Daniel Whitaker tossed two coal chunks in the stove and clapped black dust off his hands. "Looks like we're about to have the first good storm of the season."

Responsibility pulled Caleb's attention to the windows. Snowfall had thickened in a matter of moments and blanketed the boardwalk. From what he'd heard of Rocky Mountain blizzards, he should leave now for the livery and check the stock before the storm worsened.

"Surely you'll stay and have a bite with us, won't you, Caleb? I'm sure my father is as eager as I to hear what happened with the magistrate."

A slight flush replaced her pallor from that morning, and he ached to pull her into his arms again. Torn between duty and desire, he chose the latter, convincing himself that a quick meal, hot cup, and good company would give him the sustenance he'd need to weather the storm in a stable.

"Let me take your hat while you warm yourself at the stove. And I'll have the stew ready in no time."

He followed her with his eyes and watched her assign his worn felt to a peg on the back wall. Her father filled a tin mug and raised it in Caleb's direction.

"Coffee's hot, son. Come have a cup."

Caleb took the mug and a chair and felt as naked as a jay under the storekeeper's scrutiny. He glanced at the tree. "That's quite a spruce you've got there, Mr. Whitaker."

"That it is." The man lifted his gaze to the tall evergreen at the window." Sorrow slid across his features, landing briefly in his eyes.

"That blamed tree nearly cost me the most precious thing in my world." He blinked a time or two and rubbed the back of his hand beneath his nose.

"Daddy, such language." Annie tightened her apron sash and gathered tin plates from the cupboard. "We've the good Lord to thank and Caleb here." She shot a bright look his way and her eyes settled on his fingers worrying the hole in his sleeve.

He jerked his hand away.

"Daddy, didn't we get a ready-made wool shirt or two in our last shipment?" A look passed between father and daughter that Caleb didn't quite understand.

Daniel pushed out of the chair with a grunt. "I've got a wool shirt that might just fit you, son."

Caleb set his cup beneath his chair and followed Whitaker to the front. The storekeeper reached under the counter and pulled out two waistcoats, heavy socks, and a deep blue wool shirt that probably cost half the wages Caleb had managed to save.

Fingering the dark wool, he weighed the promise of warmth and knew he'd be a fool not to buy it. He set it aside and pulled the notepaper and *Cañon City Times* from his waistcoat and laid them on top. Then he unbuttoned a heavier tweed waistcoat that looked like it fit, and exchanged it for the lighter one he wore. Already he felt better.

"I'll take this waistcoat and the shirt." He dug his money from the old waistcoat pocket. "And a soap bar if you've got it."

Whitaker pulled a box from a shelf behind him. "If you need it, we've got it." Then he tore a large square of brown paper from a roll on the counter, laid the shirt and Caleb's old waistcoat in the center, and topped it with a soap cake and two pairs of heavy socks before wrapping it all together with twine.

"That'll be two dollars." A cocked brow and sober eyes dared him to quibble with the storekeeper's generous assessment.

Caleb laid his money on the counter, fully aware that Daniel Whitaker was giving him five dollars' worth of merchandise, at least by Missouri standards. It was all worth a lot more out here, but he'd not assault the man's dignity—or his tender show of gratitude—by arguing.

"Thank you."

Whitaker's mustache twitched and his eyes watered, and Caleb thought of Saint Nicholas, though a sadder saint than usual.

"I'll leave this here until I go."

"Go?" Annie's question floated to him on a meaty current, chased by the smell of warm, buttery biscuits. "We've got a tree to decorate, and I can use all the help I can get stringing choke cherries and popcorn."

She stood before the stove, a plate in each hand, loose hair curling against her neck. The most beautiful site Caleb had set eyes on in his entire life.

"You hear that?" Whitaker blew his nose and returned the handkerchief to his pocket. "You'll not get away without poking a hole in every one of your fingers."

Caleb laughed but glanced out the window at the steadily falling snow. He'd stay just long enough to eat and then get back to the livery.

Returning to his chair, he accepted the heaped plate Annie offered and waited until she had seated herself between her father and him.

Whitaker bowed his head and began nearly before his daughter settled.

"Thank you, Lord, for protecting my Annie." His voice cracked, and he paused to clear his throat. "And thank you for sending Caleb when you did, and for this food and the strong roof over our heads. Amen."

The memory of Annie pinned beneath Cooper pushed itself unwelcomed into Caleb's mind. He turned his thoughts instead to the stately spruce in the store window and last year's tree in the parsonage decorated by the Women's Society. Glittering guilt tried to top the pine, but he doggedly knocked it away and replaced it with gratitude.

Cañon City might just be where he belonged. For what reason he wasn't yet sure yet, but he hoped it had something to do with the storekeeper and his auburn-haired daughter.

~

Annie pushed hard against the door after Caleb left. Thin powder drifted through a gap at the bottom and swirled against her shoes. She hugged her arms across her chest and watched until he disappeared into the blowing snow. Without his duster, he'd be frozen solid by the time he made it to the livery. Thank goodness she'd given him another quilt before he left.

Shivering, she retreated to the stove. Her father sat sipping his coffee and staring at the potbelly. She had to get his mind off the Cooper incident—for her sake as well as his. They'd both go crazy this winter if she didn't.

Caleb had assured them that the People's Court would meet soon to deal with Cooper. At least that was what Magistrate Warren had said.

Annie had made the acquaintance of several men who served on the court—upstanding citizens who often visited when they came for their mail or shared coffee round the stove. Edna had been right about one thing: there was no law in Cañon City. At least not like they had in Omaha. No sheriff or marshal yet, but these men didn't seem to brook much nonsense. She'd already seen a couple of scoundrels run out of town, and she prayed the same fate would befall Jedediah Cooper.

She filled the dishpan from a crock by the wall and set it on the stove. Gazing at the beautiful spruce in the window, she shifted her thoughts to Christmas, which was only two weeks away. Oh, for the delicate ornaments that adorned Aunt Harriet's tree, and the crèche that held the highest honor on the mantle. All the way from France it had come, Mary, Joseph, and baby Jesus tucked into the stable—

With a jolt, Annie thought of the livery and Nell. She hadn't checked on the mare in weeks, and she'd not thought to ask Caleb about her condition.

She rubbed her forehead with the back of her hand. It was just as well she hadn't brought up the subject, because Daddy still didn't know. But what if Nell foaled during the storm? Alone? And needed help?

Caleb was there.

Relief nestled in her thoughts. He knew what to do.

Warmth threaded through her arms, and she doubted it came from the stove or the water bubbling in the dishpan. She shaved in soap curls and from the corner of her eye noted her father's pensive mood.

"As soon as this weather lets up, we could invite Martha and Caleb and the Smiths over for a tree trimming. What do you think?"

Her father let out a deep sigh, drained his coffee, then stood and added his cup to the dishpan. "I think that's a fine idea, Annie girl. A fine idea." He planted a kiss on her cheek and twisted the end of his mustache.

Turning his back to the stove, he clasped both hands behind him and looked through the front windows. "I doubt we'll have any more customers today."

Nerves fluttering like a sparrow, she pressed on. "I've been meaning to tell you, but Nell's in a …"

Waiting for the right word to form on her lips, Annie gathered her skirt in her hands and lifted the dishpan from the stove and set it on the back counter.

"In a what? A stall? 'Course she is, and I still don't think it's worth what I'm paying to board her. Can't sell her now, but come spring, I'm sure the Turks or Deacons will offer a good price."

Annie's pulse quickened. "She's in a family way, Daddy. She's carrying a foal."

His gasp sucked the air from the back of the store, and Annie clamped her mouth tight to guard her own desperate breath.

"How long have you known?"

She glanced over her shoulder. Surprise, rather than anger, rimmed his eyes, and she heaved the breath out as quickly as she had grabbed it.

"Caleb told me. I'd thought she was just getting a hay belly, but he expects her to foal sometime around Christmas."

If she phrased it right, things might still turn around. She shook her hands over the dishpan and rubbed them against her apron before joining her father at the stove.

"Isn't it wonderful, Daddy? A Christmas foal. A new little life in the stable, just like—"

He pulled her into hug and kissed the top of her head. "I feel you twisting me around your finger, Annie Whitaker."

He chuckled and the laughter shook her as he held her close. "But I guess it's as Martha says—the more the merrier."

Brimming with gratitude, Annie inched back from her father's embrace. "Speaking of Martha, is there anything you'd like to tell me?"

Her father harrumphed and sputtered and flushed from his collar to his snowy crown. But his eyes took on a mischievous gleam and he pinched Annie's chin like he had when she was little.

"Don't avoid the subject, Daddy. Will there be a wedding this spring instead of a horse sale?"

His full-bellied laugh bounced Annie from his arm, and she sent a silent thank-you heavenward.

"How did you know?"

"I'd have to be blind and deaf not to." Annie returned to the dishpan, dunked the plates and spoons in the rinse water, and set them upside down on a towel to dry on the sideboard. She'd worry about details later—like living alone in the back room once her father moved into Martha's home. Right now she wanted to simply share in his good news.

"I'm not blind either, Annie girl."

She looked up from the water.

"What'd you learn at the livery that day you took Caleb the quilt?"

Resting her hands on the edge of the dishpan, she studied his smug expression. He knew. "When did you figure it out?"

He smoothed his mustache and sat down. "I didn't. He told me a couple of weeks ago, but I had my suspicions. Remember the morning I asked him to offer thanks? A prayer like that comes from a man who's on a first-name basis with the Lord."

She picked up a plate and absently rubbed a cloth against its clean surface. "I think he'll be returning to his calling." Sadness gripped her belly, followed by regret that she would react so, rather than be happy for Caleb—happy that he'd found his way back to the Lord and his life's purpose.

The front door rattled in a sudden forceful gust, and concern needled into Annie's mood. Snow drifts climbed the windows. She looked to the halfempty coal bucket and through the storeroom entrance to the back to the door, where a fine white powder swirled in eddies along the floor.

Her father shrugged into his coat and gloves and headed toward the back with the coal bucket. "Find towels for the doors and I'll bring in more coal. We'll probably need a full fire going all day and night."

Annie followed him and kept the door from blowing clear open, filling their makeshift home with snow. In a moment he returned, stomping in like a wooly white bear.

"At least it's dry." His words huffed out on a white cloud. "Tend to the front door and I'll take care of this one."

She knelt at the trunk and withdrew blankets and fine linens intended for the table, not the floor. But they had no table and staying warm was a priority. Aunt Harriet would be appalled.

At the thought of her proud and proper relative, Annie's heart squeezed with longing for her sister. And though she missed her sibling desperately, for the first time in her life she was grateful for their satin and calico differences. Grateful that she didn't panic before a howling blizzard and the possibility of being snowbound for days. Grateful that God had brought her and her father safely to Cañon City, to people like the Smith family and Martha Bobbins and …

And Caleb Hutton.

With this wind, snow would easily penetrate the slatted stable walls. Nell wasn't the only one she prayed would be safe and dry and warm during the storm.

She tossed the extra blankets on the beds, gave her father a length of toweling, and took two finely stitched dish towels to the front, where she weighted them against the door with flat irons. After she carried two new skillets to the back, her father shoved them against the door and the toweling he'd wedged along the threshold.

Not exactly the way she'd planned to use those embroidered pieces from her hope chest, but at least she had them to use.

Small blessings were still blessings.

Indeed. It was the smaller blessings they needed to stave off the cold—linens and coal chunks, unglamorous amenities in Omaha and her aunt's fine home. But Annie would not trade this narrow store and potbelly stove for all the finery and wealthy beaus Omaha could offer. Here she belonged.

And here she would stay.

~

Caleb dropped his bundle by the stable doors and ran to bring Rooster and Sally inside. Shouldering his weight against the broad panels, he managed to close them against the wind before too much snow blew into the alleyway.

He led his horses to the last two empty stalls and tossed them each an armful of hay. Unsettled by the creaking rafters and whistling walls, a few of his other charges blew and stamped nervously. Rooster, Sally, and two of the mules seemed unconcerned. Nell dozed in the ruckus, one back leg cocked at the knee and her eyes half closed.

Caleb heaved a heavy sigh. At least there'd be no delivery tonight.

He pitched his bundle and the new quilt onto the bedroll, rousing the cat from a tight curl. It blinked once, stretched its toothy mouth in a wide yawn, and recoiled itself against the quilt.

Annie's quilt.

He knew because he'd held it to his face all the way back from the mercantile and her scent had nearly driven him mad. Did she really care that much about his well-being, that he was warm during the storm?

Henry had a fire in his forge, bless him, but he must have gone home to ride out the storm with his wife. The thought set a yearning inside Caleb stout enough to push him out into the wind and back to the mercantile. But what would he say? *Marry me, Annie. Come live in a barn and be my wife.*

The sheer audacity of such a proposal disgusted him. He'd not ask her to share his life until he knew where and what that life would be. It'd be a long while before he shared anything more than a simple meal with Annie Whitaker.

He unwrapped his bundle, tucked the soap in his pocket, and took his water bucket to Henry's furnace along with his new shirt. In the fire's radiant warmth, he stripped down and washed, then exchanged his thin cotton shirt for the new dark wool, grateful for the comfort and fit. Whitaker had judged right.

Back in his stall, Caleb lit the lamp and unfolded the *Times*. Milner was quite the writer, setting his opinion in plain view of the paying townsfolk. Touting the rise and economic progression of Cañon City, he reviewed how it had weathered bad reports of disheartened gold seekers following "prominent discoveries lying in a northerly direction."

Caleb huffed. Those prominent discoveries had resulted in Fairplay, Oro City, and a half dozen other mining camps.

He read on concerning the "sunny side of Pike's Peak," and rubbed his head, still damp from a good scrubbing. Maybe he should have tried the newspaper office before the livery.

Milner's account spoke of business houses doing an enviable trade, a town population near eight hundred, and one hundred and fifty finished buildings—twenty of them stone.

Caleb snorted at mention of a three-story hotel. He hadn't seen any work on such an establishment. Maybe Milner knew something he didn't. Though he had certainly heard enough of what the editor called the "fall of the hammer, the click of the trowel, and the blast of the stone quarry."

It all looked good in the newspaper, but seven hundred people sure didn't fit in those hundred and fifty finished buildings. Milner didn't mention the tents clustered along the river.

Caleb set the paper aside and lay back on his bedroll. Gold seekers weren't the only disheartened souls who had sought out this far Kansas Territory. And if Milner was right and the place continued to grow, Cañon City might soon be as big as Denver City or Santa Fe.

He reached for his Bible and let it fall open. Jeremiah again, the weeping prophet, and Mollie Sullivan's picture. He studied the image. Pretty, yes. Beguiling, certainly. A woman after his heart? Not at all. She never had been, he realized now.

He took his Bible to Henry's forge, where the fire lay dying in a cooling bank. With no malice or ill thoughts, he laid Mollie's picture against a fading coal. "Bless her, Lord. And may she and her husband serve you."

The copper-edged image curled and shriveled to ash as he watched, and he sensed a small flame purging a place deep in his soul. Then he found the twenty-ninth chapter of Jeremiah, dimly illuminated by the fire's thin glow. But he didn't need the light, for the words had taken up residence in his memory.

"For I know the thoughts that I think toward you, saith the Lord, thoughts of peace and not of evil, to give you an expected end."

The promised peace settled upon him like a warm cloak. Outside the wind beat against the livery, and the building groaned in the onslaught. He wrapped his arms across his chest and held the book within them. Finally, after months of running, here in a barn, he could rest in God's expected end. Not what he, Caleb, had expected, but what the Lord had planned.

With a deep sense of surrender, Caleb returned to the box stall, snuffed out the lamp, and crawled beneath his canvas tarp, Annie's quilts, and the enduring grace of a loving God.

CHAPTER SIXTEEN

A blue china sky greeted Annie Sunday morning, the air as crisp and cold as deep well water. White drifts leaned against the Main Street buildings, and the roadway was a frozen, mudless track. In Omaha, a storm like yesterday's would have her sister and their aunt soaking dirty skirt hems after church for sure. Not to mention their fine cloth shoes.

She snugged her scarf closer and waited on the boardwalk for her father.

Only the Lord's Day could still the perpetual hammering of the city's rising. Though the community stretched and fussed with growing pains, life was simpler in this bare-bones mountain supply town. The simplicity of hard work left her feeling lighter, with fewer cares and worries, knowing she didn't have to compete with Edna's fashionable clothing or cringe beneath Aunt Harriet's glaring judgment of unruly hair.

Annie knew she fell short of her aunt's expectations, particularly where men were concerned. Not that Cañon City was teaming with eligible bachelors worth even a second glance. Most were lonely miners who drank too much, dusty cowboys in need of a bath, or entrepreneurs who knew a good investment when they saw one.

Or a gentle horse handler who continued to occupy her thoughts. She took a forceful breath to clear her mind. So sharp was the air, it nearly cut through her lungs.

"Ready, Annie girl?"

Her father shut the mercantile door and offered his arm. Grateful for the short walk to the church house, she curved her fingers inside his elbow. Buggies and buckboards lined the street beyond the church, and a few horses stood loosely tied to the livery's hitching rail across the way, a location upon which her eyes so easily settled.

The big front doors were parted just enough for a peek into the shadowy stable. At the thought of Caleb wrapped beneath her quilts, she banished the vision with a quick prayer that he'd been warm and safe through the storm.

Annie hiked her skirt to mount the church steps. Hannah Baker was not at her usual post at the door with her soon-to-be husband, Pastor Hartman. Surely a brisk winter storm had not been too much for the rancher's daughter, always cheerful as a meadowlark, greeting everyone with her melodic voice and bright smile.

Annie hurried inside. Hannah sat slump-shouldered halfway to the front, wilting beneath a woolen scarf and dabbing at her cheeks, cloistered by her family. Annie and her father took the bench behind Hannah, and she cringed at the young woman's whispered explanation.

"My dear Robert remains in the pulpit and I remain with my family."

By the time Pastor Hartman finished his closing announcements that morning, everyone knew why Hannah couldn't stop crying.

The couple's pending marriage the week after Christmas had been postponed indefinitely. Hartman's brother, Reverend Justice Hartman of Denver, had broken his leg in a buggy accident earlier in the month and word had just arrived that he dare not make the trip south to perform the ceremony.

In fact, he'd sent for Robert to officiate over Christmas festivities in Denver.

What arrogance. Annie sucked in her cheek to keep her thoughts to herself in Hannah's presence. How dare the elder brother presume upon his sibling and this fledgling community. Just because Justice Hartman's congregation had a fine brick building with a bell tower didn't mean he could drag Cañon City's beloved pastor from his flock.

But clearly, blood was indeed thicker than water—even at Christmas. No wedding before the new year. And unless someone stepped forward, no Christmas Eve services for the town's small congregation of merchants and miners and ranchers. The pastor's tone made it clear that he had bowed to his brother's wishes and would be leaving that very afternoon.

Annie nearly cried herself as she filed out with others after the service. This was not the Christmas she'd hoped for. Truth be told, she wasn't sure what she'd hoped for in the first place. There would be no traditional trimmings she'd grown up with, no Edna or Harriet, no festivities at all—other than what she cobbled together at the mercantile. And now, no Christmas Eve service with carol singing and warm wishes from friends and …

Oh, it just wasn't fair.

Her foot ached to stomp, and she held it to the wooden step and leaned her weight into it. She hadn't even had the small pleasure of speaking with Caleb.

Was he worried over Nell?

Annie's father spoke quietly in Pastor Hartman's ear, and both men stared at the livery.

Of course.

She snugged her cloak tighter and looked around for Martha. The seamstress stood commiserating with Hannah, and guilt's cold fingers clutched Annie's conscience for thinking only of herself and her own disappointment.

She approached with an outstretched hand. "I'm so sorry Hannah." A squeeze of the young woman's arm brought fresh tears. "I'm sure things will work out. He'll be back as soon as he can. You know he will."

If it didn't snow three feet between Christmas and January like every freighter said it always did.

Turning to Martha, Annie lowered her voice. "Please tell Daddy I'll be along directly. I'm going to stop at the livery and check on Nell."

Martha's sorrowful eyes transformed. "You tell that young Caleb that we expect him for Sunday dinner. I've already set a place for him at the table."

Annie planted a kiss on Martha's cheek, squeezed Hannah's soggy handkerchief-wrapped fingers one more time, and hurried across the road.

The perfume of hay and horse flesh wafted from the stable as she squeezed between the doors. Had Christ's birthplace smelled like this? She'd never considered the possibility since every holiday season in her aunt's home summoned the scents of baking and spices and candles and greenery. But here, in the shadowy stalls and open livery rafters, she felt somehow closer to the essence of the first gentle Christmas.

Well, maybe not so gentle.

Caleb's low voice sounded from Nell's stall and sent shivers up Annie's arms. She moved closer, watching him work his way behind the mare, his deep tone as comforting as a mother's lullaby. Annie held a hand to her mouth, afraid for even the quietest word to disturb the moment.

Caleb had rolled up his shirtsleeves, and his muscled forearms bore evidence of hard work. Annie knew the strength in those arms, but his hands smoothed along Nell's swelling body as gently as a whisper. She knew that touch as well, and it stirred something deep within her.

The memory of his rescue flooded in and she shivered, drawing his attention outside the stall.

"It won't be long," he said softly, not changing the meter or volume from his earlier murmurs. "Could be any day now."

Apparently satisfied with his charge's condition, he ducked beneath Nell's neck and slowly slipped through the stall door. Standing close in the alleyway, he rolled down his sleeves and searched Annie's face in the most disarming way.

She loosened her scarf, grateful to be in shadow. "You might want to pray that she foals soon, because I think you're about to be asked to fill in for Pastor Hartman at the Christmas Eve service."

Caleb's expression sobered. "What makes you say that?"

"The pastor's brother in Denver was injured and won't be coming down to perform the wedding. Instead, he's asked Pastor Harman to come to Denver and take over duties there for Christmas. Not only will there not be a wedding here, there won't be a Christmas Eve service either."

Annie's sense of injustice had twisted the scarf she fingered into a knot.

Caleb stared at her.

Clearly, he hadn't made the connection.

"I believe Daddy told the pastor of your previous calling."

Caleb buttoned his cuffs and reached for his hat. A sharp downward pull hid his eyes, and Annie took a step closer seeking their depths. "You'll do it if they ask you, won't you?"

His embattled expression gave her pause and she drew back. He stopped her with a hand at her waist and closed the distance between them.

Annie's pulse danced at her temple and in her throat. How dark his eyes, as if he warred against some inner torment. She clutched the ends of her scarf in one hand and laid the other against his chest. His heartbeat ran as hard as her own. "Do you doubt that you can do it?"

With his free hand, he touched her hair, then smoothed the back of his fingers against her cheek.

"You are beautiful, Annie Whitaker. Beautiful in spirit and in form."

She commanded her breath to come evenly, steadily. It wouldn't do to swoon in his arms right there in the livery. Lowering her gaze, she studied the texture of his new waistcoat, at a loss for words the first time in her life.

Caleb lifted her hand from his chest and pressed her fingers against his lips before putting a safer distance between them. "I can do it if He calls me."

Annie's hopes hitched. "Pastor Hartman?"

He smiled at her confusion. "If God calls me, He'll enable me."

"But didn't He already call you?" Regret followed immediately upon her remark, for sadness washed over his face. Without thinking, she reached to smooth it away.

He caught her hand. "Will you be there?"

"Yes." Would breath ever come again without her heart racing like a runaway horse?

His smile returned, and he squeezed her hand and released it. "If God wants me to stand in His pulpit again, He'll make it clear to me and present the opportunity Himself."

Stunned by his humility and flushed with emotion, Annie coiled her scarf around her suddenly empty hands and moved toward the door, seeking the clarity of cold air. "Martha is expecting you for dinner. She's already set a place for you at the table."

His features softened, and he lifted his duster from a nail on the wall. "Then we'd best be going, hadn't we?"

~

Caleb took one last look at his charges, then closed the livery doors against the cold. He offered his arm to Annie, and she rewarded him by tucking her small hand into the crook of his elbow. Without hesitation.

A week and a half until Christmas Eve, with a Sunday service before that. Annie's news had simply confirmed his recent commitment. He'd already told the Lord He'd go where he was called.

Clattering hooves drew his attention to a cloaked rider approaching with hat pulled low. Annie's fingers tightened on his arm.

"Caleb." Robert Hartman reined up beside them. "Annie." He touched his hat and his gray mount blew its smoky breath and stomped impatiently, invigorated by the cold and anticipating a run.

"Pastor Hartman." Caleb offered his hand. "We'll miss you at Christmas, but our prayers go with you for a safe trip to Denver."

"Thank you." Hartman yanked unnecessarily on the reins, sending the horse dancing backward.

Caleb stepped forward and took the headstall, mumbling low.

"Annie's father tells me you're a preacher," Hartman said.

"Yes, sir. Spent a year or so at a small church in Missouri, then came west." With the flat of his hand he rubbed the horse's face while reading Hartman's expression. No need to go into reasons and regrets.

"Wish I'd known sooner. We could have visited, compared notes. But as you know, I'm on my way to my brother's and need someone to hold the Christmas Eve service that people are counting on. Not to mention next Sunday, and maybe more after that, depending. Are you willing?"

The gray startled forward at Hartman's clumsy kick, and the man jerked back on the reins again.

"Easy," Caleb murmured. Hartman's eagerness to leave transmitted to the horse. Caleb stepped aside. "I'd be happy to. Thank you for your trust."

The gray reared slightly and tossed its head. "I'll be back as soon as I can, and will send a letter to Hannah telling her when to expect my return."

Hartman looked at Annie. "Thank your father for me. I feel better knowing someone will be here in my absence."

He nodded to Caleb. "I'll be praying for you."

"And I for you." Caleb's concern for Hartman's safety rose as the gray tiptoed on the frozen roadway. "Let up on the reins and watch your heels and he'll be easier to handle."

Hartman grinned. "Thank you. I might say the same about our unique congregants. Merry Christmas."

Winning the struggle, the gray wheeled and charged east out of town. Caleb snugged Annie's arm close against him, confident that he already knew the text for his Christmas message.

As they passed the magistrate's office, Annie tensed.

"It's all right." He covered her gloved hand with his own. "Cooper's locked in a cell at the back of the building. Saw it myself."

His little fighter wasn't as calm as she tried to appear, and the look she gave him drew every ounce of protectiveness up through his veins. He wanted to keep her safe, warm, close.

God help him.

Two blocks west and they stepped off the boardwalk and turned north toward Martha's home. The dry snow squeaked beneath Caleb's boots, and powdery crystals swirled in a light crosswind. Annie tucked her scarf against her chin.

Martha's walkway had been swept clear, and smoke curled from the chimney. Caleb stomped his feet and opened the door for Annie, and his mouth watered at the aroma that welcomed them. The small cabin swelled with good will and good food.

He'd gladly live in a cabin like this if Annie shared it with him.

He took her cloak from her stiff shoulders, wishing he could wrap her in his arms until she relaxed against him. "Don't think about tomorrow," he said quietly. "Just enjoy this time, here, now."

Sufficient unto the day is the evil thereof. A good thing to remember.

Tomorrow would indeed have enough worries of its own.

~

Monday morning, the hall above the Fremont Saloon overflowed with people for Cooper's hearing. Word got around fast.

Caleb stood against the back wall, a position that gave him a clear view of Cooper, Magistrate Warren, and Annie seated with her father toward the front.

The saloon owner wasn't as cocky as he'd been the day Caleb dragged him to the jail. He was probably sober—a frightening condition for a man given to liquor and license.

Caleb wished there was some other way to go about justice that didn't require Annie's public testimony, but she held her head high and spoke clearly and unemotionally.

Cooper squirmed in his seat, and the truth was apparent, if the murmurs and nods rippling through the crowd were any indication. Warren must have been right. It seemed that Cooper was overdue for his comeuppance.

After a brief discussion, the court members told Cooper that if he sold his property and left town immediately, they'd let him go. Otherwise, he'd serve time in jail and be required to pay a heavy fine. Caleb felt they were letting the man off too easy, but one look at Annie reminded him that Cooper's absence was what she really wanted.

A keen sense of protectiveness surged through his blood again. Whatever it took.

The gavel sounded and Cooper was led away to turn over the deed to his hotel and saloon and ride out of town.

It was done. Now Caleb could spend a few days preparing for his next public challenge. His return to the pulpit.

CHAPTER SEVENTEEN

Caleb started a fire in the woodstove, lit the lamps, and set out extra tapers for the evening service. Then he swept the front steps and carried in the heap of pine boughs Karl Turk had earlier dropped by from his cuttings. Several branches still bore cones, and their sweet pitch filled the clapboard building with a familiar Christmas promise.

Fresh hope. A future. God's expected end.

Caleb longed for all three.

His first Sunday had gone well. People had not stayed away simply because their pastor was gone and his fill-in was a stable hand.

Humbled by Pastor Hartman's willingness to leave his flock in Caleb's care, and the congregation's willingness to give him the opportunity, he checked the fire again and adjusted the damper. The small building should be warm by the time people arrived for the evening's service.

But rather than stay and go over his brief sermon, Caleb answered his instincts that called him back to the livery. He'd learned a long time ago to follow that call where animals were concerned. He just hadn't paid it as much heed with people.

Scanning the room and pleased with his preparations, he softly closed the door and hurried to the livery.

Thank God, he'd listened.

Nell flattened her ears as Caleb entered the stall—not her usual easygoing welcome. Her rounded belly had a more angular look, and she swished her tail and stomped a back foot. Caleb's gut twisted at the signs. *Not now.*

Agitated and twitchy, Nell's discomfort sent her head reaching back toward her sides, blowing and whiffling. Caleb had no way to predict how soon or how quickly she would foal, and he couldn't be two places at once—in the livery with Nell and across the street at the Christmas Eve service.

He'd assured Pastor Hartman he'd care for the congregation—the brave souls who'd left the comforts and customs of home to start a new life in the Rockies. Maybe he could leave Nell to her own devices. How many times had he been surprised, as a boy, to walk in on a spindly legged foal nuzzling a carefree mama who had delivered without anyone's help?

But one never knew for sure. And Nell was Annie's joy. There was more to this delivery than simply another foal.

With divided loyalty tearing at his gut, he grabbed his duster and set out for the mercantile. The sliver of daylight above Fremont Peak told him folks would soon be arriving at the church. He'd ask Annie and her father to watch Nell while he greeted people, and to let him know if she was in distress

Annie stood bundled at the stove, ready to leave, while her father banked the fire and set the lid. The bell pulled her toward the door, and her eyes warmed with welcome until she saw what lay behind Caleb's own.

Hurrying to him, her voice rose tight and worried. "What is it? Is something wrong at the church house?"

He clasped both her hands in his, regretting the tension he'd set in her brow. "It's Nell. She's close to her time."

He looked over Annie's head to her father tugging on his overcoat and scarf.

"I'm here to ask if you'll stay with her while I start the service and let the people know what's happening."

"Of course we will. Let's go." Daniel stormed out the door as if he'd put all his life and soul into that mare rather than bemoaned her appetite.

The lantern Caleb had hung outside Nell's stall pooled a yellow light in the alleyway and deepened the shadows beyond. Nell whinnied at the intrusion, and flattened her ears in warning.

"Don't go in," Caleb warned. "No matter what happens, do not go in the stall."

Annie and Daniel leaned against the railing, looking as if they'd never seen a horse in all their lives. Maybe this wasn't such a good idea.

"Promise me." Caleb laid his hand on Annie's shoulder, pressing until she looked at him.

"I promise," she said.

Nell paced as much as the cramped box allowed, and Caleb wished he had a larger space for her. In her irritable condition, any unwelcomed intruder could be hurt. Or killed.

"It's very likely she'll deliver without any problem. She may lie down and get up again. She may kick or moan. Whatever she does, do not go in there."

"What should we look for if we need to come for you?" Daniel's steady voice and calm expression restored Caleb's confidence in his choice of guardian.

"Two hooves and a nose is what we want to come first." His discomfort at mentioning such intimate details in Annie's presence subsided as he studied her unflustered profile. "If anything else presents instead, come and get me."

She touched his arm. "Daddy will come and get us. I am going with you." Her fingers pressed into his sleeve, and she lowered her voice. "I'll be praying for you as well as for Nell."

Caleb's heart hammered into his throat. With a final glance at the mare and then at the lovely woman who believed in him more than he deserved, he took her hand and they walked out the livery doors and across the street.

~

Hannah and her parents had driven in from their ranch, and Caleb gratefully acknowledged the young woman's tending of the lanterns and candles. The little church glowed with goodwill, and people chose benches closer to the front this evening, either to join in the festive Christmas spirit or to avoid the dropping temperature that lurked beyond the back door.

Caleb stepped up on the rough-hewn platform to lead the first carol.

No organ or piano accompanied the rich vocal mix of miner and merchant. But all knew the tune, and those who were braver broke into harmony. The few children's angelic voices joined the chorus, and Caleb's spirit rose on the sound. The very angels who declared the Lord's birth could not have announced it more majestically than the simple folk of this little mountain town.

His eyes settled on Annie, seated with the Smith family. She caught his look and held it with what appeared to be a promise. Could she someday be his?

Warmed by the fire and the people crowded into the tiny church, the air simmered with paraffin, lamp oil, and fresh pine. Bible in hand, Caleb stood next to the simple pulpit, wanting nothing between him and the people this night.

"As you all know, I care for the stock at the livery—a skill I learned many years before my seminary training. I stand here this evening to extend to you your pastor's heartfelt Christmas blessings, to rejoice with you in our Lord's priceless gift, and also to explain the situation at hand."

People settled in their places, women removed gloves, and men balanced hats on their laps.

Caleb cleared his throat and took a small step forward. "The Whitaker's mare has chosen this night to birth her foal, and if I'm needed—I apologize—but I'll be stepping out."

A few women ducked their heads at mention of such a thing in public and murmurs hummed across the room, but no one left. A good sign.

A deep breath loosened his chest and the familiarity of God's Word in his hand strengthened his stance. "The Scriptures tell us that our faith is more valuable than gold. We know something about that around here, don't we? *Gold.*"

His emphasis of the word set heads to wagging and eyes to glittering.

"Consider the gifts the Christ child received from the Eastern kings: frankincense, myrrh, gold. A king's gold, pure and refined and weighty, nothing like what men scrabble for in the creek beds and canyons of these Rocky Mountains."

A few chuckles rippled across the room as men cast knowing glances among themselves and women *tsked.*

"So what kind of treasure do we bring to the Babe this Christmas? Refined, pure gold or crusty ore mixed with pebbles and dirt?"

The question sobered his listeners, and he lifted his Bible to read from First Peter. "Wherein ye greatly rejoice, though now for a season, if need be, ye are in heaviness through manifold temptations."

He looked up from the page and into the eyes of those seated on the benches and standing against the back wall. "We have manifold temptations represented here this evening. I personally have enough to pass among you with plenty left over. But I confess that I haven't greatly rejoiced in them."

Again he lifted the book and read from it. "That the trial of your faith, being much more precious than of gold that perisheth, though it be tried with fire, might be found unto praise and honor and glory at the appearing of Jesus Christ."

A chilly gust swept in, and Caleb looked up to see Daniel at the door, worry tightening his brow. Annie looked toward the back and straightened, as if ready to stand.

He was nearly finished with his message. "Prospectors and speculators will tell you there is no gold in Cañon City. Show them otherwise. Let the trial in your life—whatever that trial may be—purify your faith to a burning, burnished gold, worthy of the King who was the Child, so that something more valuable than mined mountain ore will shine for Him here."

He closed his Bible and looked over the celebrants. "With Mr. Whitaker's sudden arrival, it appears that I am needed at the stable."

Low voices buzzed, and most turned toward the entrance.

"I apologize for cutting this celebration short, but I wish you all a blessed Christmas, and pray for your safe journey home and warm memories of your first such event in the great canyon's guardian city."

Hannah rose to attend to the candles and lanterns, and Caleb thanked her as he grabbed his hat and duster and hurried out, Annie at his side.

The few lines that Annie heard Caleb speak revealed a side of him that she longed to know more of. But right now, she needed the horseman, because Nell must be having a tough go of it.

Caleb stripped off his hat and coat as he entered the barn, gave them to Annie, and rolled up his sleeves. Nell remained on her side, and great rolling contractions rippled across her belly. Caleb eased into the stall, sending his rich, warm voice ahead. Nell's ears flicked his way and back again.

His gentle confidence stilled Annie's pounding heart, and she linked her arm through her father's. Within moments Caleb caught two tiny hooves in one hand and a white nose in the other. With one final heave, Nell pushed a miracle into his arms.

The mare lay still, exhausted and breathing hard. Annie feared she had no strength left at all when the horse raised her head and curled back around to sniff and nicker a motherly welcome. Finally, she pulled herself up and turned to stand over the leggy infant, licking and rumbling deep in her chest.

Annie stood enthralled by what she saw, so much so that she hadn't heard the great livery doors open and a small crowd approach. When a child's voice broke the stillness, she looked around to see a dozen people pressing into the alleyway, craning their necks for a look at the newborn.

"Welcome to Cañon City, little fella." Emmy Smith peeked through the stall slats at the wobbly foal whose spindly legs fought for purchase.

"I think you mean little *filly*," Caleb corrected with a smile in his voice.

Laughter rippled through the onlookers, and Emmy tucked her chin and poked out her lip.

"They're not laughing at you, they're laughing with you." Springer knelt beside his sister. "It's a little girl. *Filly* means girl."

"Like me?" Emmy's bright eyes searched her papa's face, where he stood with an arm tight about her mama's shoulders.

"That's right, darlin'. Just like you."

"Guess you knew what you were talkin' about, Hutton." The crusty voice rose from behind the crowd, and heads turned to identify the speaker.

Magistrate Warren cleared his throat and tugged at his hat. "There's more gold here in these hills than the kind that glitters."

The yellow filly hobbled forward and nuzzled its mother, and people jostled and bid Merry Christmas on their way out of the stable.

At last, only Annie, her father, and Caleb stood at the gate watching Nell and her foal. Annie slipped an arm through that of each man standing beside her and pulled them closer. "Imagine, spending Christmas Eve in a barn. What would Aunt Harriet think?"

Her father coughed out a laugh that startled the filly, and he clamped a hand over his mouth and stepped back.

Annie giggled and looked to Caleb, whose eyes held such love that she wanted to melt into his arms right then and there.

"I'd best be getting to the mercantile." Her father's face fairly glowed. "Martha's there with a Christmas pudding waiting on us all to string popcorn for the tree."

Annie hugged his girth and planted a kiss on his ruddy cheek.

"You did a fine job tonight, son. A fine job." He slapped Caleb on the shoulder and headed for the door. "I'm going on. You both come along when you're finished here." At the door, he paused. "You know you're invited, Caleb. We wouldn't have it any other way. The more the merrier."

Annie caught the twinkle in her father's eyes and swore she saw his mustache twitch.

Caleb retrieved a water bucket and towel from his living quarters, then washed his arms and hands in the lantern's light. Annie looked away, warmth flooding her neck and cheeks. Such intimate moments they'd shared this day, and they weren't even courting. What would Edna say?

Her left foot gave a small stomp. She didn't care what Edna would say. Annie had found more in Cañon City than she'd ever dreamed. And she wasn't about to let proprieties take that from her.

With new resolve, she turned to see Caleb watching her, pulling on his duster and settling his hat on his head. An odd smirk played on his lips.

"What?" Suddenly fidgety, she swirled her scarf around her neck and dug in her cloak pocket for her mittens.

As he moved toward her, her feet grew roots. She couldn't have fled if she wanted to. But she didn't want to. His dark eyes drank her in. Her hair, her temples, her lips, disarming her until her insides went limp.

He stopped just beyond her tightly clutched hands, so close his breath touched her face, as did the scent of him—wool and leather, his canvas duster. He slipped one hand around her waist and pulled her into him, brushing her mouth with his eyes and then his lips.

She flattened both hands against his chest and felt again his heart beating a rhythm in time with her own.

"I love you, Annie Whitaker. Will you wait for me?"

What's to wait for?

Searching for her voice, she found it snagged on a question. "Wait?" she whispered.

"Until I have something to offer you. A home. A livelihood. Something besides a stable boy's pay and a box stall."

Her voice fled again and tears pushed behind her eyes. She swiped at them, determined not to be a silly twit like her sister. With a shaky breath, she yanked her voice back from its hiding place.

"On two conditions."

His jaw flexed at her counter and he pressed her closer. "And what might they be?"

"That you take me riding up the river as soon as the snow and ice melt."

A slow smile pulled his mouth on one side. "And your second condition?"

"That you kiss me again right now before Daddy and Martha come looking for us."

EPILOGUE

Annie fussed with the black trim on the bodice of her blue silk dress and reset her hair combs for the hundredth time.

"Let me." Martha shooed Annie's hands away from her head. "Be still now. You look absolutely divine. I tell you, that young man of yours won't know his head from his hat when he sees you in this blue taffeta. I knew I'd have a need for it someday, and with your hair shining like a kiln fire, how will he ever concentrate enough to officiate over Hannah and Robert?"

Annie wrapped the seamstress in a quick hug, then allowed her to fuss with the folds of her skirt. Hannah watched them both with a nervous twitch that set her bouquet to quivering against her cream-colored gown.

"Oh, Hannah, you're not frightened, are you?" Annie held a hand out to the girl, who looked as if she might faint any moment.

"I'm just so nervous," Hannah whispered as if sharing a secret. "I want everything to go right and be done with—before we have another storm or someone else breaks his leg. Tell me again how this is going to work."

"We're all going to be *Mrs.* to our dear husbands, child." Martha bloomed like a rose in her garden as she gave Annie's hair a final pat and turned to the youngest of the three brides. "You will lead us between the bench rows at the church house, followed by Annie and then myself. Your Robert, Annie's Caleb, and my Daniel will be waiting for us at the front."

"Then Caleb will take you and Robert through your vows." Annie fluffed Hannah's full sleeves. "He's going to kiss you in front of everyone." She couldn't resist teasing.

Hannah went white. "Caleb is going to kiss me?"

Martha burst into laughter and Annie colored with guilty delight. "No, silly. *Robert* is going to kiss you. After Caleb marries the two of you."

"Then you will step back, Robert will step forward, and Caleb will take his place beside Annie for their vows," Martha explained.

Annie's pulse threatened to burst her tight neckline.

"Who will marry you and Daniel?" Hannah asked Martha, the flowers steadier in her hand with so many questions on her mind.

"Robert," Annie said. "He is the most senior pastor, and as his last duty here—at least for a while—he will have the honor of joining my father and Martha."

She slipped her arm around the seamstress's waist and gave her a quick hug. "Thanks to you and your talents, we make three lovely brides. Who would have thought you could fashion winter roses from ribbon and lace and fabric scraps?"

Martha blushed and waved away the remark, her cheeks nearly matching the deep burgundy of her simple but finely pleated dress.

Annie walked to the mercantile door. It looked as if the entire town was trying to squeeze into the clapboard church house. Three brides and their grooms would not be the only people standing for the ceremony.

Winter had calmed its blustery self just long enough for Pastor Hartman to return for his bride the week after Christmas as originally planned. Annie prayed for it to hold until their safe return to Denver, where Hartman would take over for his still recovering brother.

How suddenly circumstances had changed. Gratitude swelled within her for God's mysterious plans unfolding so perfectly. She and Caleb planned to live in the parsonage, her father would move in with Martha, and Springer Smith had already taken over at the livery under Caleb's watchful eye—at least until the boy learned to handle the horses. Oh, how Springer's face had lit when Caleb asked if he'd be willing.

Louisa Smith stepped off the church steps and headed up the street. "She's coming," Annie said, her breath suddenly shallow and quick. She looked to her fellow brides. "Are we ready?"

Both ladies straightened and raised their chins as if marching into a parade. What an affair this wedding promised to be—better than any Saturday night dance Cañon City would ever see.

"Here we go." Annie opened the door and set the bell to ringing.

"Like I always say,"—Martha linked her arm with Hannah and winked at Annie as they filed out to the boardwalk—"the more the merrier."

Annie fought the urge to hike her shimmering skirts and run to the church and into Caleb's arms. The effort consumed a good deal of her composure until they mounted the swept church steps and she peered through the doorway into the small sanctuary.

Caleb stood at the head of the crowded room in a new white shirt and borrowed frock coat, a string tie at his throat and a groom at each elbow.

His dark eyes locked on hers and drew her to the end of the terribly long aisle where she stopped before him, anticipation spinning through her. Their gaze broke when Robert moved to Hannah's side and Caleb looked away to officiate over the eager couple.

Annie's own bouquet quivered like Hannah's, but against the easy rhythm of Caleb's warm voice, the trembling soon settled and her mind wandered back over the past five months.

She had dared to venture west with her father. And in the doing, she had found much more she could have dreamed—a vast and magnificent land and a wealth of love far greater than all the gold the Rocky Mountains could offer.

And every ounce of it shone in the invitation of the horseman who now held out his hand to her. "Annie."

With the surety of love and the promise of a shared future, she entwined her fingers in his and took her place beside him. The next great journey was about to begin.

The Cañon City Chronicles

Straight to My Heart

Davalynn Spencer

For all those who entrust their hearts to God's unfailing love.

"Trust in the Lord with all thine heart;
and lean not unto thine own understanding."

—*Proverbs 3:5*

CHAPTER ONE

Fremont County, Colorado
Spring, 1879

Whit Hutton eyed the rimrock. His buckskin's ears swiveled toward a deep fissure, nostrils flaring for scent.

No padded foot dislodged loose shale. No yellow eye glinted from the shadows, no tail whipped in the cool predawn. But she was there.

He heeled Oro up the ledge that hugged the cliff face, let the gelding pick his way along the incline at a cautious clip. More bighorn mountain sheep than horse, Oro took them higher while Whit kept his eyes on the rimrock and one hand at the ready.

His father's Colt lay holstered on his right hip, and a Winchester rested easy in the saddle scabbard. Trouble was, Whit didn't know what he'd need. If he spotted her from a distance, he'd use the rifle. But if he rode up on its lair, he'd do better with the handgun.

And if the cat got the jump on him, it'd be too late for either one.

The hair on his neck stood. Feline eyes were watching.

Two calf carcasses in as many weeks proved an old lion stalked the herd—one too slow for a swift pronghorn or mule deer. It needed easy pickin's, and Hubert Baker's cow-calf operation appeared to be the chosen chuck wagon.

Oro heaved them up and over the edge and Whit reined around for a view of Wilson Creek bottom. The sleeping Bar-

HB covered the stream-fed valley and several thousand acres of unseen park, timber ridges, and rocky ravines. Baker, Whit, and the Perkins brothers called it home. Along with three hundred cow-calf pairs.

Lately, so did Baker's granddaughter, Olivia Hartman.

Whit turned his head toward a distant, rhythmic *ping*, not surprised that the echo carried so far on the clear air this early. Train barons were fighting for the narrow right-of-way up the Arkansas River canyon, and crews with both the Denver and Rio Grande and the Atchison, Topeka and Santa Fe were racing to lay track through the gorge. Only one railway would fit where sheer granite shot a thousand feet straight up from the river. And that rail owner would benefit mightily from the lucrative Leadville silver strikes.

While rich men pawed the earth and lawyers bandied, ranchers like Hubert Baker were still driving their cattle to mining camps a few at a time or in herds to Pueblo or the Denver railhead. Ten days of dust-eating trail, that one.

He shifted, squeaking the saddle leather in tribute to riding drag. No more, since Baker crippled himself and put Whit in charge. Which meant Buck and Jody Perkins ate dirt on the drives like Whit had when he was an upstart. With no ma or pa of their own, the towheaded Perkins boys were happy enough to get chuck and a bed in the bunkhouse.

At least they hadn't lit out after easy money laying track for the feuding railroad companies.

The sun broke free, climbed Whit's back, and jumped into the valley. He looked over his shoulder, dipped his brim against the new light, and turned Oro toward the ranch house and breakfast. The cat had eaten. Now it was his turn.

His stomach snarled and he hoped Baker's granddaughter had whipped up some of her white gravy. She'd come to the ranch after her grandmother's death a month previous, and the little gal could fix up biscuits and gravy better than anything

Whit had ever tasted. 'Cept his ma's cooking, of course. Couldn't beat her potbelly biscuits, as his preacher pa called them.

Guilt snagged a rib as Whit tied Oro at the house rail and walked around back to the washstand. He hadn't been home in three months, and he suspected his parents and little sister held it against him. But he had responsibilities now. He couldn't be traipsin' off to Cañon City whenever he wanted.

His spurs jangled against the kitchen floor and he continued through to the dining room, where the Perkins brothers were already elbow deep in steak and eggs. Baker insisted his hired hands eat at the house since his beloved Ruth passed. The old rancher was lonely. Whit could see it in his eyes when he looked at Livvy, a younger image of her mother, Hannah, Baker's only child. Whit used to tease the pig-tailed girl at church picnics when her family visited from Denver. But he hadn't figured on scrawny Olivia Hartman growing up to be such a good cook. And a beauty to boot.

"You wash?" She leveled her blue eyes at him, ready to fire if he gave the wrong answer.

"Yes, ma'am. Right out back at the washstand. Even used soap this time."

Jody grunted but didn't stop chewing to comment.

"Hands." She leaned slightly forward, demanding he lift his calloused fingers to her pretty little nose.

He pulled a wounded look across his face. "You don't believe me."

His mouth must have twitched, for she straightened to take the plate back to the kitchen. He jerked his hands out, palms up, and stepped as close as he could and still be the gentleman his parents raised.

Livvy sniffed, and her eyes smiled if her lips didn't. "Good." She set the plate on the table to the right of Baker, who sat at the head, and retreated to the kitchen.

Whit watched her disappear through the doorway. Someday he'd be sharing his meals in private with a woman like that.

"See any tracks?" Baker cut into a biscuit and sopped it in gravy.

Whit hung his hat on the chair back and took his seat. "No, sir. Too much shale in those bluffs to leave track. But I found her latest kill in the cottonwoods, half covered with leaves and brush."

He gulped his coffee, welcomed the kick. "But she was up there this morning. I could feel her."

Buck snorted. "You'll feel her, all right. Just as soon as she leaps down on that buckskin o' yours and snaps your neck in two."

"Won't happen." Whit cut his steak and met Buck's jab with a poker face. "She's waitin' for a corn-fed one. Like you."

Jody choked on a piece of meat and grabbed his coffee, sloshing most of it onto his plate in the process.

Baker didn't join the fun like he usually did, and his soberness dampened the younger men's humor. Whit laid down his fork and took up his coffee. The boss had something on his mind and Whit would just as soon hear it straight-out.

~

Livvy stood at the stove and wiped her hands on her apron. Pop wasn't his jovial self this morning. She had hoped the men could wheedle him into a better humor, but their good-natured bantering wasn't breaking through the dour mood he'd carried home from town yesterday.

She stirred the gravy in wide slow circles, listening for Pop's voice. It came low and tense, and she stilled the spoon to concentrate on his words.

"I'm sure you all know about the feuding that's been going on over the railway the last couple of years."

Knives and forks scraped against her grandmother's Staffordshire china, and a coffee cup clinked on its saucer. No one spoke, and she imagined the others nodding somberly.

"I don't want my men getting mixed up in any rail war." Pop's voice carried an edge. "This blasted railroad business is going to get someone killed, and it better not be any of you."

Someone cleared his throat. Whit, she guessed, who usually spoke for all the hired hands.

"We're too busy," Whit said. "Gathering starts today, and I figure we'll be branding for two or three days. We don't have the time or notion to be riding up that canyon taking pot shots at our neighbors."

Pop cursed and Livvy clapped a hand over her mouth.

"That's the problem," he said. "Those train barons have called in outside guns and they're offering money to any man that will sign on with them."

"Which side?"

The heavy silence meant Pop was staring a hole through young Jody, the only one foolish enough to ask such a question.

"Not that I'm thinkin' on joining them, mind you. I was just curious, that's all."

"Both sides."

A cup slammed into its saucer and Livvy flinched. She had only eight of the original twelve left, and the way Pop and these cowhands treated her grandmother's lovely blue-and-white china, she'd have no unchipped cups by summer's end. Tin suited them better, but at the dining table Pop insisted on the "good dishes." A tribute to his beloved Ruthie.

Chair legs combed the carpet as someone stood.

"You can count on us," Whit said. "We work for this outfit, not some railroad company."

Buck and Jody quickly agreed and flatware clattered against plates.

Livvy hurried to the sink, filled a dishpan, and set it on the stove, grateful again that her grandfather had the convenience of an indoor hand pump.

Pop and the boys made their way through the kitchen, thanking her as always. Whit went out the front. She checked the other water pan already on the stove and returned to the dining room for the rest of the dishes. Through the lace curtain she saw Whit at the hitching rail, adjusting Oro's cinch. A few steps closer, and she could watch him unnoticed—something she did too often of late. Comfortable in the knowledge that he couldn't see her through the lacework, she wrapped her arms around her waist and studied his dark, angular profile.

Jaw shadowed with stubble, he was still lean but no longer the gangly boy who had chased her in the church yard. So different, yet so much the same.

How did he see her now? As the skinny little girl who'd begged him to push her in the swing and cried when he teased her? Or as a woman who had lost that child's heart to hero worship years ago?

He looked at the window. Livvy sucked in a breath and tightened her arms, holding her place, lest movement give her away. A slow easy smile tipped his mouth and he nodded once. Then he gathered the reins, swung into the saddle, and touched his hat brim before riding away.

Her vision darkened and she swayed. Reaching for a ladder-back chair, she gasped for air, her temples throbbing. This had to stop. She couldn't spend all summer holding her breath every time Whit Hutton looked at her.

She finished clearing the table, set a small leftover steak on the sideboard, and covered it with a napkin. Then she carefully placed the china in the dishpan and checked through the kitchen window for the men's whereabouts. Satisfied that they were busy elsewhere, she grabbed a sharp knife and went out the front door.

An overgrown lilac bush billowed with deep purple blooms beside the dining room window. Carefully she cut three bunches and held them to her nose as she walked to the hitching rail. Glancing at the barn and bunkhouse, she turned to face the window. The lace curtains blocked her view of the chair where she had stood. Convinced that Whit could not have seen her through the sheer fabric, she went inside to search for a vase among her grandmother's crystal.

The heavy oak door opened right into the dining room with no formal entry hall. The ranch house had grown out each end of the original square-log cabin, spreading into a comfortable home. A small porch announced the entrance, but Mama Ruth had never bemoaned the informality. She had directed her British ancestral convention to more important things.

Like décor.

The Bar-HB might be a working cattle ranch, but Ruth Baker had swept a generous hand through her house where furniture and carpets, crystal and china were concerned. Livvy chose a lovely hand-painted vase from an ornate curio cabinet. She fussed with the heady blooms, slicing off the bottom of one bunch so its heart-shaped leaves cupped over the vase's lip. Several four-point blossoms dropped to the tablecloth and the rich perfume filled the room.

Mama Ruth loved lilacs, and every window in the rambling house had a bush nearby that bloomed profusely from late spring into early summer—gentle lavender, brilliant white, or deep purple. Even the dainty detail that edged the vase replicated the delicate blooms.

Livvy removed the soiled cloth to reveal the fine cherry wood table, then stepped back to view the lilacs.

Whit could not possibly have seen her. So why did he act as if he knew she was there? How full of himself he was—just as he'd always been—assuming she stood at the window. That arrogant air had not changed one bit since their childhood.

She glanced down at the simple bodice of her blue calico and the full white apron that covered her skirt. Had it shown through the curtain?

Or had he *felt* her eyes on him?

CHAPTER TWO

Whit reined Oro in behind the barn, jumped down, and hurried through the side door to watch from the barn's shadowed innards. Sure enough, Livvy came outside and set to cutting purple flowers off the bush by the dining room window.

He laughed under his breath as she held the blooms to her nose and walked to the hitching rail only to turn and face the house.

She didn't think he could see her through those frilly curtains. And he wouldn't have if she hadn't been wearing that white apron. It stood out like a bright square patch against the dark room. He hadn't been able to see her face, or even a faint outline of her form. But he'd seen the apron, and who else wore one at the ranch?

His chest swelled against his work shirt and he chuckled as he returned to Oro.

Miss Olivia Hartman had her sights on him.

Which brought to mind the lion on the rimrock and all the work that needed tending to. He didn't have time to be thinking about grown-up Livvy with her yellow hair and sky-filled eyes. Three hundred mamas and their calves were grazing this spread, and he and Buck and Jody had to gather them for branding. And they needed to get it done quick enough to keep Baker from joining them and bustin' himself up even more.

The man never had said exactly what happened, but by the way he favored his right leg, Whit guessed he'd tried to peel one too many broncs.

That's what the younger fellas were for.

Whit turned Oro for the nearest draw, where he'd told Buck and Jody to start. They'd hunt for pairs and drive those they found into the lower corral. Working their way into the rough country, they'd gather in bunches and cut and brand as they went.

He set his heels to Oro, and they clipped along a stream bed and turned off toward a red rock patch jutting from the valley floor. Just ahead, Buck and Jody flanked a juniper cluster, hollering and slapping coiled ropes against their chaps. Whit circled behind them, took down his rope, and jumped the old cow out of the thicket. Two calves followed close on her tail.

Buck whirled his mount away as the cow swung her wide horns. Jody took in after her at a trot, and Whit joined the brothers as they pushed the threesome to the corrals.

"That was close." Too close for Whit's liking.

Buck grinned. "She's a snorty one for sure. Glad I was watchin' her. Don't need a gutted horse or a hole in my leg."

Exactly why Whit didn't want Baker gathering stock. A good cowman through and through was Hubert Baker, except when it came to admitting his age and his bum leg. Grief over his wife's death was also carving a notch in him, and now he had a bur under his saddle over the train war. Rarely had Whit heard him swear, and doing so at the table—with Livvy in earshot—was even more of a puzzle. The stubby little man's mind wouldn't be on the work out here, and Buck wasn't the only cowboy who didn't need to take a hookin' this summer.

The home-bound parade drew a bellow at the red rock patch, and Jody loped off to pick up two more head and their calves. By the time Whit and the Perkins boys closed in on the outlying pens, they'd flushed twelve cows from the near canyon. Only one was barren. Pretty good return.

By noon, twenty head were branded and turned out from the holding pens at the windmill. Whit dismounted, left his hat on his saddle horn, and stuck his head under the trough pump. Cold mountain water gushed out over his neck and shoulders. He scrubbed his face and hands and flung his hair back. Wiping his face on his shirt sleeve, he turned in time to see Livvy driving up in the buckboard, a sun bonnet hiding her best features.

Buck and Jody took their turns at the pump and got in a shoving match. Suited Whit just fine. Gave him more time alone with Livvy.

Drying his hands on his pants, he hurried to the wagon to help her down. She wrapped the reins around the brake handle and gathered her skirt in one hand, then took Whit's with the other as she climbed down the front wheel. He thought about grabbing her narrow waist and lifting her down, but if he knew Livvy Hartman, she'd wallop him good with both fists while he was at it. The idea quirked his mouth and he frowned to cover his thoughts.

"What now, Whittaker Caleb Hutton?" Two daring eyes challenged him from inside the shadowed bonnet.

Full given names, was it? "Watch your step there, Olivia Hannah Hartman."

She glared at him and he glared back. How often had she beat him at a staring match when they were children?

"Did you bring dinner?" Jody sauntered over. "I'm so hungry I could eat my saddle blanket."

"Then go to it, brother. Leaves more for the rest of us." Buck jerked Jody's hat over his eyes as he walked by.

The bantering snatched Livvy's attention. If Whit didn't need the Perkinses' help with the branding, he'd thrash both boys into a stupor.

A midday meal during roundup was a treat. Usually they worked clear through and didn't eat again until evening.

Livvy walked to the end of the wagon where she dropped the back into a make-shift sideboard and pulled out two baskets and a covered crock. From one basket she withdrew forks and tin plates and cups. The other basket held fried chicken that licked Whit's nose as soon as Livvy folded back the checkered cloth.

She heaped three plates with crisp chicken, potato salad, and molasses cookies, and then dipped lemonade from the crock into three tin mugs. Whit waited for her to help herself to the meal, but she didn't.

"You eating?"

She dusted her hands on the ever-present apron. "Don't worry about me. Just have at it. I'll be fine."

Livvy Hartman was fine, all right, but she'd picked up a bur like her granddad. She turned and walked off toward a pine and aspen cluster, leaving Whit and the brothers to enjoy her handiwork alone.

"What'd you do now?" Jody shoved the meat end of a drumstick in his mouth and pulled out the bone.

Whit resisted the urge to punch him. If the kid choked on a hunk of chicken, they'd be short-handed.

~

A blue patch at the clearing's edge caught Livvy's eye, and she hiked her skirt to walk through the ankle-deep grass. Whit Hutton made her want to say what Pop had said at breakfast, and her mother would have a fit for sure if she knew it. He was more irritating as a man than he'd ever been as a boy. Could she last six months isolated in these mountains with no one to talk to but her grieving grandfather and his sassy-mouthed foreman who was too big for his britches?

She stooped to cup a blossom in her hand and peeked back at the wagon. Whit leaned against the buckboard drinking lemonade. His britches fit him just fine. Blood rushed to her cheeks, from bending over no doubt, so she knelt before the patch and focused on the delicate petals.

The flowers weren't blue at all but more lavender, like Mama Ruth's lilacs. She'd not seen anything like them in Denver, but living in the city offered little opportunity to ride into the high country. Up until now, school work, helping her mother at the parsonage, and playing the organ for Daddy's congregation had filled most of her days. She'd jumped at the offer to escape to Pop's ranch—without any thought of what awaited her.

"How beautiful," she whispered as she leaned over to breathe in their fragrance.

"They're columbines."

Catching herself before she tumbled onto her face, she looked back to see Whit towering over her. A grin lifted his mouth and his hat perched on his head like the comb of a cocky rooster. Peeved that he had walked up on her while her backside was in the air, she dropped to the ground and assumed a more dignified arrangement.

Whit laughed.

"And tell me, please, what you find so humorous."

He took his hat off and sank smoothly to a cross-legged position. "No need to worry, Miss Hartman. Only a memory that tickled my funny bone." His dark eyes snapped.

Livvy curled her fingers in the grass. She made to stand, and he reached for her arm. The smirk vanished and remorse took its place.

"Don't go."

Surprised by his candor, she sank down. She pushed her bonnet back and let it hang on the wide strings tied beneath her chin.

"I just thought you might like to know what these flowers are called," he said. "I've seen 'em all white like snow, higher up in the mountains."

She relaxed and looked again at the wildflowers. Each one bore a white face, yellow center, and long claw-like growths that tapered from the bottom of every lavender petal.

Whit picked one and twirled it slowly in front of her. "See these long tubes? They're called spurs and they hold the nectar that draws humming birds and bees."

How did a cowboy know about flowers? She shot a quick glance his way and caught him squinting at the ridge above them.

"Spurs, you say?"

Her remark brought his gaze back to her and his features softened. "Yes, ma'am. Kinda like us cowboys." For a moment he looked exactly like she remembered him from her previous visits, before he worked for her grandfather. But now he was somehow more…handsome?

"Well, that's very nice." She fussed with her skirt, making sure it covered her ankles.

He offered her the flower.

She took it and raised it to her nose. Perhaps the taste attracted the hummingbirds rather than the scent. "So you could call it a cowboy flower, I suppose."

"*You* could call it anything you want."

This time she succeeded in standing before he stopped her. With one hand she shook out her skirt and smoothed her apron. "If you and the others are finished, I'll be heading back to the house."

He stood with an inscrutable expression, his jaw set like stone, his eyes flat. "Suit yourself."

Livvy cradled the fragile flower in her palm. The velvety spurs pricked her conscience, and she rebuffed the guilty stab.

She was simply being proper. She and Whit were no longer children who played hide and seek and—

She whirled on him and fought the impulse to shove him off his feet. "You...you...*scoundrel.*"

Stunned and rooted in his tracks, he stared at her, clearly befuddled. "Pardon?"

"You scoundrel! I know what you were laughing at. I remember now—the day we were playing at the church house in Cañon City and I bent over the horse trough."

A slow smile pulled at his mouth and his eyes came to life. "I do believe I have never seen anyone madder."

She burned from the inside out. How dare he make light of her humiliation. Why had she ever forgiven him? "You pushed me."

"I was nine."

"I was humiliated."

He coughed to cover a full-blown laugh. "I'm sorry."

"You are not. And you were not sorry then either."

Choking back his laughter, he grabbed her upper arm. "Please, Livvy, I'm sorry. We were children and I couldn't resist the temptation of...of..."

With cheeks flaming, she fisted her fingers. "I could have drowned."

"But I saved you." Humor and regret battled across his features, and the former was winning.

Jerking away, she marched to the wagon.

Buck and Jody saw her coming and ran to their horses.

She threw the dishes in a basket, slammed the drop board against the wagon railing, and locked it in place.

"Livvy—wait."

She would rather die. Lifting her skirt with one hand, she gripped the bench seat with the other and climbed up the wheel spokes.

Whit ran to the horse and grabbed its bridle. "Livvy, that was nearly ten years ago. We were children. Can't we start over?"

The only thing she wanted to start over was his foot. With a hard yank, she slapped the reins on the horse's rump and nearly got her wish as the wagon lurched ahead. Whit jumped out of the way.

Expecting to see an impish grin plastered on his face, she frowned at the pain gripping his features. Maybe she *had* run over his foot. She pulled on the reins, but the barn-soured horse would not be deterred and continued forward.

It was just as well, for stinging regret watered her eyes and blurred her vision, and she would not let Whit Hutton see her cry.

After a jostling quarter-mile ride, Livvy pulled around to the kitchen entrance and carried the baskets inside, making a second trip for the heavy crock. As she unloaded the dishes and set them in the sink, the crushed columbine fell to the floor.

She must have dropped it on a plate when she packed up.

She stooped to retrieve the bruised and broken flower, so delicate and once so lovely. Holding it against her breast, she closed her eyes and let childish frustration and grown-up disappointment slip down her cheeks.

CHAPTER THREE

Whit Hutton did not swear. Most of the time.

"Not by heaven or earth," his preacher pa had drilled into him. But he sure enough knew a few colorful phrases he could let fly to fit the situation.

He gathered Oro's reins and swung into the saddle, looking for which way the Perkins boys had fled. He hadn't even told them which draw to work next. Livvy had driven every logical thought and plan right out of his head.

Exasperating woman.

Scanning the ground, he spotted a print of the bar shoe on the back right of Buck's mount and followed the tracks. The brothers were riding toward the next canyon, running scared from the storming fury of Miss Olivia Hartman.

He kicked Oro into a lope. Livvy was as bad as his sister, Marti, who still saw him as bothersome. What did he have to do to show Livvy he'd grown up and was as much a man as the next fella?

Stop teasing her.

He snorted. That'd be harder than jumping a maverick steer and not near as much fun. He should forget about Livvy, leave her uppity little self alone.

Priscilla Stockton came to mind. Now there was a more appreciating gal. She sure enough paid him heed the last Sunday he was at church—three months back. He was due for another trip to town, but not until after branding.

He eased Oro into a walk as they skirted a cholla cactus patch, and the hair on the back of his neck raised like a porcupine's quills. Peering up at the rimrock, he tried to see into the shallow caves tucked under the top layer. His right hand slid to the Colt, and Oro tensed beneath his legs, feeling Whit's apprehension. One ear swiveled to the right and one pointed straight ahead.

A lion attack in broad daylight was rare. Whit yanked that truth to the front of his mind and focused on the cattle they were hunting.

A strangled bawl caught his ear, and he gave the gelding its head.

Jody had himself a stubborn one. He held his rope dallied around the saddle horn and the taut line stretched over the butt of his horse as he tried to drag the cow. Buck was slapping his chaps behind her but she choked down. Her eyes rolled white and her tongue hung out as she bellowed at her calf.

"Let up," Whit called as he neared the standoff. "Give her some air before that rope snaps and takes off the side of your face."

Apparently stunned by the idea, Jody eased his horse back. The cow lowered her head and sucked air, and the calf made for dinner, taking a kick for it from its frustrated mother.

They pushed the pair out of the canyon, and on the way to the corrals Whit found a couple more. At this rate, it'd take a month to get the cattle in.

"You need a different horse, Jody. The mare's too small. It's a wonder that cow didn't drag you all the way to the top of Eight Mile Mountain."

Jody looked like his feelings were hurt. Better his feelings than his neck. "You and Buck ride to the upper park and cut out one of the bigger geldings."

After bunching and branding a few more out in the open, the brothers took off into the hills.

By the time the sun tucked in, Whit had driven a dozen pairs to the holding pens. In the morning, they'd brand and cut what they had, then head for the higher bunch grounds and start gathering there.

He unsaddled Oro, rubbed him down, and turned him out in the pasture behind the house. The buckskin had earned his keep today. So had Whit, but Livvy Hartman's angry scowl sat sour on his gut. He had half a mind to turn in early and skip supper.

He slapped his hat against his leg. Baker would hunt him down if he didn't show, that was for certain, and the man didn't need any more worries on his mind.

How could one little blue-eyed gal stir up such a storm in Whit's belly? Even when they were children she'd needled him, drove him into fits with her pestering. Then if he got her good, she'd turn those tear-filled blues on him and he'd feel like a mangy cur. As he had today when she remembered him dunking her in the horse trough.

He chuckled in spite of himself. Served her right, trying to see her reflection in the still water. He just didn't expect the prank to dog him the rest of his days. One little shove, and she hated him for life.

He had apologized, thanks to his ma nearly twisting his ear off. And Livvy had accepted, right there in the church yard, her soaked dress clinging to her skinny legs, two yellow braids dripping water.

Without realizing it, he'd walked to the washstand on the wide back porch. The kitchen window framed Livvy working at the table, peeling the root-cellar spuds he'd brought in yesterday morning.

The lamp on the table cast a yellow light against her hair, setting it to gold. His insides twisted at the thought of touching it—not yanking it like he had as a boy, but filling his hands with it, burying his face in its softness.

Confounded woman had him all in a knot. One minute he regretted knowing her, and the next he wanted to take her in his arms.

He hung his hat on a nail, rolled up his sleeves, and splashed cold water over his head, trying to wash away the image of Olivia Hartman. Lord, what was he going to do? The woman made him loco.

Livvy skinned the small potatoes and sliced them into a bowl. When she had it filled, she took it to the stove and dumped the slices into hot bacon grease in the big iron skillet. They spit and spattered and she set a lid half on and returned to the table. The peelings went into the chicken-scrap tin, which she set on the back windowsill.

Outside, a man bent over the washstand, splashing water on his face. With a gasp she jerked back. *Whit.*

She hurried to the stove, where she wouldn't have to face him when he came inside. Hopefully, he'd go straight to the dining room without stopping to make small talk or apologize. As if Whit Hutton would apologize.

The door opened and shut softly. Spurred boots crossed the bare kitchen floor and stopped a few feet away. Her breath tucked tightly inside, she bunched her apron in hand and lifted the lid on the potatoes, feigning distraction over supper. The boots continued into the dining room, their steps muffling against her grandmother's imported carpet.

Livvy heaved a sigh and returned to the kitchen table, where she fell into a chair. Oh, Lord, she couldn't live all summer like this, tensing up every time Whit came around. Maybe she should leave, go back to Denver, and carry on with her normal, boring life. And abandon Pop?

Never. She slapped her hands on her apron. Those no-account cowboys didn't cook or tend a garden or pick eggs or feed the chickens. They barely kept the firewood stacked and the cow milked.

She pushed her hair off her forehead and stood with new resolve. The men had cleaned up every scrap of dinner today, so she sliced the leftover breakfast steak into the fried potatoes. Good thing she hadn't taken her canned-peach pie out to the bunch grounds, or they'd have nothing to go with their coffee tonight.

Later, she and Pop and Whit took their usual seats at the dining table, and Buck and Jody's absence hung like a cold lantern among them. She held out her right hand to Pop, buried her left one in her lap, and jerked her head down without looking across at Whit. Beneath her lashes she saw him withdraw his hand from the table where he had reached across for hers.

Pop cleared his throat. "Lord, we thank you for all you've blessed us with, this food and this ranch, and the work you've given us to do. Watch over us tonight, Lord. And bring the boys back safely. Amen."

"Amen." Livvy's quiet agreement matched Whit's exactly and she sensed him watching her. Reaching for Pop's plate, she filled it with steak and potatoes and set it before him. She then fixed her attention on the knot in Whit's gray neckerchief and held her hand out, waiting for him to give her his plate. When embarrassment forced her eyes to his face, he was staring at her without smirk or smile. Without anything. He handed her his plate and her heart plopped to her stomach as the potatoes hit the floral scene on Mama Ruth's blue-and-white china.

If she didn't eat, Pop would question her and she'd have to answer. But what would she say? She spooned out a small helping of potatoes. "Where *are* the boys, Pop?"

Baker looked to Whit, who picked up his fork and pinned an elbow on the table. "I sent them to the high park to cut out a gelding for Jody. He got himself lined out with a cow that was bigger than that little mare he rides. I'm afraid he's going to get himself hurt."

Pop grunted and nodded his head as he herded sliced potatoes and steak around on his plate. "When was that?"

Whit set down his fork and reached for his coffee. "Late afternoon." He took a sip. "I probably should have had him wait until tomorrow, given them all day to get up to the herd."

"Do you think they'll cut out for the railroad?"

Livvy's fork stuck on her plate, and she looked straight at Whit, who was staring at his food.

"Before today I would have said no for certain. Now I'm prayin' they don't."

Since when did Whit Hutton pray? Even if his father *was* a preacher.

"There's a few wild head in with that herd, you know."

"I know." Whit frowned and stabbed his steak. "I should have gone with them."

"You can *should-have* yourself into the grave, son. Don't do it. I do enough for both of us."

Livvy's heart squeezed at her grandfather's confession, and she blinked rapidly to keep from tearing up at the table. He insisted almost daily that if he'd ridden for the doctor sooner, Mama Ruth might still be alive.

Might. Only God knew for certain.

A clatter at the kitchen door jerked Livvy to her feet. The Perkins brothers charged in stomping and slapping and laughing, two young giants dusting themselves off in the kitchen rather than outside.

"You march right back out and wash up." Livvy straight-armed them both with a sharp turn of their shoulders and shoved them toward the door. Thank God they weren't dead, or dragging along at the end of their ropes over rocks and down washes in the wake of those running horses.

"And don't you dare be stomping your dirty boots in this kitchen."

She returned to the dining room, filled two plates, and poured coffee before taking her seat. Whit's stare burned her cheeks until she met it with her own.

"Couldn't you even ask them if they were all right?"

Anger curled her fingers in her lap and she jutted her chin. "They are all right or they wouldn't be making such a ruckus. And they might as well learn now to clean up outside before they come in. We are not barbarians."

"Do you even know what that word means?"

Pop coughed and held a napkin to his mouth.

Certain that she'd fall off her chair if she didn't breathe, Livvy inhaled through her nose and held Whit's glare. How dare he.

The back door opened again, and two quieter young men came through the kitchen and into the dining room. They nodded first at Livvy, then at Baker and Whit before taking their seats.

"This smells mighty good, Miss Olivia." Jody plunged into his food, and Buck kicked him under the table and jerked his head at the napkin beside Jody's plate. The younger brother snatched it to his lap and cut a side glance at Livvy before returning to his meal.

Their antics drew everyone's attention, and Livvy couldn't decide who had given in and looked away first: Whit or her.

"Did you find a mount?" Whit held his cup in his hands, both elbows on the table.

Livvy held her tongue.

"Sure did," Buck said with his mouth full.

Livvy shook her head. The Perkin's boys had no manners at all.

"A real nice black with a white blaze."

"That'd be Shade." Pop forked a piece of steak. "Good horse if you take the hump out of him every morning."

Jody looked up with his mouth open and his fork poised in mid-air. "Huh?"

Whit quirked a half grin. "I'll start him for you tomorrow, and in a couple of days he'll get used to you. Either that or you'll get used to the ground."

Pop grunted a near laugh, and Livvy almost wanted to thank Whit for lightening the moment.

"What took you so long?" Whit set his empty cup in the saucer and glanced at Livvy, the dregs of good humor in his eyes.

She filled his cup and Pop's, then went to the kitchen for the pie.

"Them horses can run," Buck said between bites. Took us all afternoon to cut the black out. Rode back in near dark, and by the time we got him in the corral and watered it was well past."

More grunts from Pop, and Livvy whispered a prayer of thanks. Those crazy Perkins brothers were worth her trouble if they could help keep her grandfather from grieving his life away. Pie server in hand, she paused before the doorway and peeked at Whit from the safety of the kitchen. Maybe she should cut him some slack, as she'd heard her grandfather say. Give him the chance he'd asked for today.

She picked up the pie and entered the dining room just as the back door flew open.

CHAPTER FOUR

"Please, can you help us?"

Whit leaped from his chair at the panicked request and almost trampled Livvy in his hurry.

Delores Overton stood against the night, struggling to hold up her near-grown son. Pale and unconscious, the youth sagged against her. On his left shoulder, a hoof-sized blood stain oozed around a small hole in his shirt. Too small for a cow horn.

Whit took the boy.

"He's been shot." She began to sob and covered her face with her hands. Livvy wrapped her arms around the woman.

"Bring me some chairs," Whit hollered.

Pop shoved his chair through the dining room door and angled it beneath the limp body as Whit sat the boy in it.

Buck and Jody stood gaping, slack-jawed.

"Chairs," Whit demanded.

Jumping at the clipped order, they delivered chairs and stepped back as Baker and Whit stretched Tad Overton across the three seats. Livvy gave Delores a reassuring hug, then gathered clean rags and towels. She poured warm kettle water into a crockery bowl and dipped a rag in it.

Delores swayed on her feet, and Whit caught her. "Mr. Baker, please take Mrs. Overton to the dining room and have her sit down on the settee."

After she left the room, Whit opened Tad's shirt and peeled it off his left shoulder. Livvy applied the warm rag to his wound without hesitation. Her face showed only compassion and clear thinking. No panic, no revulsion.

Whit was not surprised.

"Someone needs to ride for the doctor," Livvy said.

Buck stepped forward. "I will."

"No." Pop came back to the kitchen, and everyone looked at him with the same question.

"We need to take him to the doctor. It will be faster." Pop turned to the Perkins boys. "Buck, you harness Bess to the buckboard and fill the back with straw. Jody, take care of Mrs. Overton's horse or wagon or whatever she's got out there. Whit, take the quilt off my bed. You'll find blankets in the chest by my door. We'll make him as comfortable as possible for the trip."

Whit hadn't seen his boss come this alive since before Ruth died.

Livvy continued with the compresses.

Whit laid a hand on her shoulder. "Thank you."

The look she gave him made him weak in the knees.

"I'll go with you," she said. "All that jostling is liable to make him bleed more."

Baker stoked the cook stove, brought the coffee pot from the dining room, and set it on the fire. "Hurry," he said to Whit. "Delores and I will stay here."

As Whit passed by, Pop grabbed his arm. "Take it as fast as you can. It'll be a long ten miles in that wagon." He lowered his voice. "But it'd be harder on him horseback across open country."

"We'll make it," Whit said, offering a promise he didn't know if he could keep.

Tad moaned, and Livvy smoothed back his tousled hair. Something in her manner stirred Whit. He turned away and hurried through the rambling house to the bedroom at the far end.

He recognized the log cabin pattern in the quilt on Baker's oak bed, thanks to his ma's handiwork, and wasted no time stripping it off. Then he lifted the trunk lid and found extra blankets and other linens a woman kept on hand. He took three blankets, set the lid down, and headed outside.

Buck and Jody were pitching straw in the back of the buckboard, and Whit stretched two blankets across the top. "Wait here so you can help me get him in the wagon."

Delores had returned to the kitchen and sat on a stool pulled close to her son's head. She stroked his brow and murmured low as Livvy finished knotting a strip around the boy's shoulder.

"Looks like you've done this before." Whit watched her, waited for her reply.

She picked up the remaining towels, stuffed them in a satchel, and gathered her cloak from a peg by the door. "You could say that."

He wanted to know more, but now was not the time.

Stooping to slip his arms beneath Tad, he lifted him and flinched as the boy's head lobbed back. At least he felt no pain.

Whit stopped at the door and faced Delores. "How long ago did he come home?"

"Just after dark." A sudden sob caught her voice and she held a hand to her mouth. "At first he wouldn't tell me what happened, but I guessed it." She looked into Whit's eyes, searching for hope. "He was up at Texas Creek, on the rail bed. The Santa Fe is paying three dollars a day to lay track. He said it was quicker money than waiting to sell our steers this fall."

Her voice broke on the last word and she covered her face.

Pop swore under his breath, opened the door for Whit, and stopped Livvy on her way out. "Keep your seat, because he'll be runnin' that horse. But you'll be safe with Whit. I'd trust him with my life."

Baker's words tightened Whit's throat as he lifted Tad to the Perkins boys, who each grabbed an end. He hopped into the wagon bed and tucked a blanket and the quilt tight around the Tad. Then he held out his hand to Livvy as she climbed up the back wheel.

"Will you be warm enough with that light wrap?"

Her mouth curved in a gentle smile and she laid a hand on his arm. "I'll be fine, Whit. You just give Bess what-for and get us to Doc's."

He covered her hand with his and squeezed, then shoved his hat down tighter and stepped over the bench.

The Perkins boys stood like orphaned calves watching the herd leave them behind.

"No gathering till I get back," Whit told them. "You can ride to Overtons' and check on things for the widow." He slapped the reins and then pulled up and pegged Buck with a solemn stare.

"You're in charge. If anything goes wrong while we're gone, I'll blame you."

Even in the faint light from the kitchen window, he could see Buck's face tighten.

"You can count on us." The boy stretched to his full height, all sixteen years of it.

Whit looked over his shoulder to be certain Livvy was seated, and she offered him another smile. He flicked the reins and Bess clopped forward.

~

Livvy pulled back the quilt's top corner and blanket and checked Tad's bandage. Not as much blood had seeped through as she'd expected. She tucked another folded rag beneath the toweling strip and pressed it in place.

"Hold on," Whit yelled over his shoulder. At the barn, he turned onto the ranch road, slapped the reins, and hollered at Bess.

The wagon lurched ahead, nearly throwing Livvy on her back. She reached for the seat and pulled herself forward. Turning, she leaned against the low board behind the bench, still close to her patient with his head at her knees. Thank goodness the boy was unconscious.

And a boy he was. Couldn't be more than fifteen. She ran the back of her fingers across his downy cheeks where no razor had ever traveled.

Moonlight full as near day spilled across Tad's features as well as the countryside—the rimrock ledges and pastures and close hills, all colorless in the gray light but clear to the eye. A coyote yipped in the distance. Livvy shivered and pulled her cloak tighter.

Whit had questioned her comfort—an uncharacteristically gallant thing for him to do since he'd spent most of their childhood time together making her miserable. And how quickly he'd responded tonight. Even her grandfather had sparked to life, issuing orders and taking charge. Did personal regret push him to insist they take Tad into town rather than wait for the doctor?

The boy moaned and thrashed his legs.

She stroked his cheek, felt the fever. "Hush now," she whispered close to his ear. "You rest and we'll be at Doc Mason's before you know it." Her grandmother's pantry no doubt held laudanum or even whiskey, but Tad's unconscious state had pushed such ministrations from her mind. Doc Mason would soon take over, though even at this breakneck pace, soon wasn't soon enough.

The wagon hit a hole and she bounced hard, falling across Tad. She was ready to give Whit a piece of her mind, but her ire vanished at the sight of his shirt stretched tight across his tense back and shoulders. He worked to keep them on the road and in one piece, but had not thought to bring himself a coat.

Livvy retucked the loosened quilt and settled herself against the board.

I'd trust him with my life. Pop's weathered face had reflected his need to assure her, adding weight to his words.

Pop and Mama Ruth never had a son—only a daughter, her mother, Hannah. Other cattlemen had tried to buy Pop out over the years, but he'd held on through good markets and lean. Yet now, who would take over the Bar-HB? Livvy's mother had grown up in these remote hills and certainly knew what to do. But her place was with her husband, and Daddy didn't know the first thing about running a cattle ranch. Besides, he'd never leave his Denver pastorate, unless of course, the Lord called him elsewhere.

A new doubt crept in. What if God called Daddy to another church? The thought of leaving what had always been home clenched her stomach. She could never live anywhere else, except maybe…

Pushing the notion aside, she touched Tad's face again. Hot. Drawing back the quilt, she felt the heat in his shoulder as well, and left a single blanket to cover him. Lord, let him live to care for his widowed mother.

Pop had told Livvy how Delores Overton's husband had died from a fall shortly after homesteading beneath Eight Mile Mountain. Determined to make a go of her dead husband's dream, she'd refused to leave even though Pop had offered to buy her 160-acre claim and her few cows.

What choice would she have now if she lost her only son?

Livvy tilted her head back and considered her own options if she found herself in a similar predicament. What would she do in such a place as Cañon City? And to whom would she turn?

Another bounce, and she grabbed for the side rail. How much longer could Tad Overton take such a beating?

Vague visions of an unpredictable future pulled her into a shallow sleep, but a faster gait on a smoother surface woke her with a start. She straightened and looked around. They'd made the turn at the hogbacks and were on the west end of the road into Cañon City. Doc Mason's place was ahead on the right.

Whit slowed Bess to a walk and stopped before a small two-story house with dark shutters and fenced yard. Livvy felt Tad's forehead and looked up to see Whit watching her.

"I'm going to wake the doctor, then I'll be back for the boy."

She nodded, amazed at the gentleness in Whit's voice. "The boy" was not that much younger than she and Whit.

Loud and prolonged knocking garnered an eventual light in an upstairs window, and soon Whit was climbing into the wagon. Doc Mason lowered the back, his unshouldered suspenders hanging from his trousers.

Whit knelt on Tad's opposite side. "Grab the blanket beneath him and help me turn him sideways and drag him to the back."

Livvy complied, and they managed to lay Tad along the edge, where earlier in the day she had laid dinner. Whit jumped down. She hiked her skirts to climb down but stopped at the sight of Whit's uplifted hands. Maybe it was the seriousness in his dark eyes that prompted her to lean over and place her hands on his shoulders as he encircled her waist and deftly set her on the ground. He held her eyes for a moment longer, then turned to cradle Tad in his arms and carry him through the front gate and into Doc Mason's home.

Flustered by Whit's conduct, she brushed the straw off her skirt, raised and locked the back rail, and checked to see if Whit had set the brake. Of course he had, and Bess's reins lay loosely around the handle.

In the shadowy yard, she paused to let her hair down. After recoiling and pinning it against her neck, she smoothed the sides and shook out her skirt. The front door stood ajar, and she pushed it farther open and stepped into what appeared to be a waiting area. Closing the door softly behind her, she took in the simple furnishings, obviously bachelor's décor. No fine cabinet held crystal and china, and no imported floral carpet covered the plank floor. Instead, a large braided rug was framed by mismatched chairs hugging every wall. An empty fireplace yawned at one end and a small table and unlit lamp posed at the other.

For as long as Livvy could remember, Doc Mason had lived at this end of town, caring faithfully for its residents and those from outlying ranches. He'd brought babes into this world and escorted the dying to the next. She clasped her hands. He'd been at her grandmother's side as well, but not soon enough in her grandfather's opinion.

Through an open doorway, she watched shadows move against a papered wall, heard low voices discuss Tad's condition. Her nose flared at the smell of fresh blood. Funny she hadn't noticed it at the ranch house.

Tad lay on a long narrow table. Doc bent over his shoulder, and Whit held a glass lamp close. He must have sensed her presence, for he looked at her and nodded. No sly grin hitched his mouth, no teasing words crossed his lips. A thick line ran around his dark hair where his hat had permanently creased it, and the yellow light cut deep grooves between his brows.

Livvy clenched her hands against the sudden urge to smooth away the worry and trail her fingertips along his roughening beard.

The telltale narrowing of her vision warned that she was holding her breath again. She inhaled deeply through her nose and rubbed her temples. *Breathtaking* was a word she'd not used much before coming to help her grandfather this summer, but his foreman was bringing it more and more to her mind in a most personal way.

Pop's quilt and blanket crumpled against a chair in the corner. For something to do, she gathered them and took them out to the parlor, where she picked off the straw and tossed it into the cold fireplace. Then she folded the blanket and quilt into orderly squares.

Why couldn't she do the same with her emotions where Whit Hutton was concerned?

CHAPTER FIVE

"Thank you, Doc. We'll square up with you when we come back for him, if that's all right." Whit shoved his hat on and shook the doctor's hand. He figured Baker would cover for the widow. If not, Whit had enough stashed in the bottom of his bedroll. There was no way he'd let Delores Overton pay for what her fool-headed son had done.

"That will be fine, Whit, but what are you going to do tonight?" He dried his hands and arms on a towel and hung it over a rod on the washstand. "It's a couple hours till daylight. I have an extra room upstairs, but only one, and with Miss Hartman ..."

"Thank you kindly. I do appreciate it. But I'm taking Livvy, er, Miss Hartman to my folks' place. They'll have room at the parsonage, and I can always sleep in the barn."

Mason rolled down his sleeves and shot a doubtful look over the top of his wire-rim spectacles.

Whit laughed. "Rest easy, Doc. The hay loft is only a little softer than Baker's bunkhouse."

Mason shook his head and rechecked the new dressing around Tad Overton's shoulder. "This is the first gunshot wound I've seen from the railway war they're fightin' in the canyon. I sure hope this is the worst of it."

"Me too. Doc." Whit moved to the door. Blamed kid should have known better than to get mixed up in somebody else's fight, but money could turn a fella's head. Whit gritted his teeth. If the Perkins boys got dragged into it, he'd wear out their sorry hides.

On his way out of the surgery, he stopped in the doorway. Livvy slumped in a chair across the room, her head tipped back and her mouth open. He could get her lathered up over that—but he wouldn't. He'd spent enough of his life riding her about every little thing. He hadn't known any other way to get her attention when they were kids.

Things were different now. He was grown and so was she. It was time to be thinking like a man, and the first thing a man needed was a—

Livvy startled and sat upright. She clamped her jaw and narrowed her eyes. Her reaction put a hitch in his mouth even though he knew it would get her back up.

"Don't you dare laugh at me, Whitaker Hutton."

He frowned and screwed his hat down. "I am not laughing at you." He made for the front door, put gravel in his voice. "Come on. We're going to my folk's place. They'll put you up in the spare room, and we'll go back to the ranch tomorrow. Doc wants Overton to stay here a day or two so he can keep an eye on him."

He opened the door and waited.

Livvy stood and smoothed out her skirt.

"Where's your wrap?"

"In the wagon."

"I'll get it."

She marched past him. "That will not be necessary, thank you. I can get it myself."

She circled round the buckboard, lifted her cloak from the back, and shook out the straw. Then she draped the light wool over her shoulders, clambered up the wheel, and scooted to the far end of the seat before he could climb aboard.

Infuriating woman.

Taking the seat, he reached for the reins. He should have left her behind and brought Jody. But that half-broke bronc would have made a poor nurse. And he'd never smell as sweet as Livvy did right now. He cut a glance to the side and found her stiff-necked as a sulled-up filly. Why couldn't she be more even tempered, like a seasoned gelding?

He coughed, covering a laugh that escaped at the outrageous comparison. Miss Olivia Hartman would whack him good if she knew he'd compared her to a horse.

Bess's hooves clopped against the hard-packed street and echoed off the sleeping store fronts. Whitaker's Mercantile had a new sign painted since he'd last been in town. His grandfather was getting up in years like Baker. He and his wife, Martha, had been running the store all Whit's life, and had often hinted at Whit taking it over.

He loved his grandparents dearly, but the thought of working everyday indoors made his chest hurt. He had to be outside, in a saddle, free to cast his eye over the mountains and timber and parks the good Lord made.

He shuddered, and from the corner of his eye, saw Livvy glance at him. What made her switch so sudden? Sweet one minute and sour the next. Was it him? Was he doing something to set her off?

Near the opposite end of town, he turned into a lane next to a white clapboard church and continued on past the parsonage to a small barn behind it. Two apple trees in the yard had leafed out since he was home last, and even in the falling moonlight, his ma's roses looked about to bloom.

Livvy reached back for the satchel. Whit jumped down and offered his hand. She took it with a quiet "thank you" and stepped to the ground. When he didn't let go of her fingers, she looked up at him with the old challenge.

Her hair caught the moon and shimmered nearly white. Without thinking, he touched it lightly with his free hand. Her breath hitched.

If he kissed her, she'd either slap him or kick him or, worse yet, despise him. He ached.

"Thank you for coming with me."

She didn't pull away. Her challenging glare softened and her lips parted. Could she tell he was looking at them? He forced his eyes back to hers and let go of her hand. "I couldn't have gotten him here safely without your help."

She looked away—the second time that night, and the second time in her life that she'd not won a stare-down between them. "I couldn't let him lie there alone, bouncing all the way into town." Wrapping her arms around the satchel, she held it against her chest like a barrier between them.

Softer, as if admitting a secret sin, she said, "I couldn't let you go alone."

His knees threatened to buckle and he shifted his weight to hide the fact. If he looked her in the eye again, he was liable to haul off and do something uncalled for. Instead, he focused on the shadowed row of columbines his ma had transplanted against the back porch.

"They usually leave the door unlocked. Let's go see."

Without another word, Livvy marched to the parsonage and up the porch steps, leaving him by the wagon.

He'd done it again, though he didn't know what.

~

Breathe, Livvy, breathe. Fine thing it would be to faint and have Whit carrying her into his parents' parlor. She gripped the satchel and stood stock still in the Hutton's small kitchen. Whit lit a lamp, set it on the table, and pulled a chair out for her.

"Have a seat and I'll go check on the spare room."

"And who are you talking to down there, Whitaker Hutton?" His mother descended the stairs holding a kerosene lamp and clutching a wrapper to her chest. "Oh, Livvy. Welcome."

A sense of home swept into the room with Annie Hutton's warm smile and welcoming arm around Livvy's shoulders. "Whatever brings you to town in the middle of the night?" Sudden alarm replaced her welcome with a motherly scowl aimed at Whit.

He'd already removed his hat and was hanging it on a peg by the door. "Tad Overton got himself shot up on the railbed in the canyon. His ma brought him to the ranch, and Livvy helped me haul him to Doc Mason's. We just finished there."

He took a chair at the table, heaving a great sigh and weary at best.

Livvy had the oddest inclination to pull him into her arms and hold him.

Hold him? She prayed the dim lamp light hid her sudden flush from Mrs. Hutton.

"What a dear you are, Livvy. The boy's in good care at Doc's, but you must be beyond tired. Come with me and I'll show you to our spare room."

Livvy glanced at Whit, and he gave her a brief nod. Fatigue and the last vestiges of worry made him look older. Twenty or more. She must look a sight herself.

Mrs. Hutton had already mounted the stairs, and Livvy followed. At the landing, Whit's mother turned to the right and pushed open a door. From the room across the way, a muffled flutter rose. Livvy smiled to herself. The pastor snored.

But so did her father. Maybe it came with the calling.

"Thank you, Mrs. Hutton. I—"

"Please, call me Annie. It's bad enough everyone in town still calls me Mrs. Hutton, even after all these years. Makes me feel old." She set the lamp on a table beside the bed, turned back a beautiful quilt, and fluffed the pillow.

"Thank you, Annie. I do appreciate this, with no notice or anything."

Annie folded her arms against her wrapper and tipped her head to the side. "How long has it been since you and your folks visited? Three years? You've grown up quite a bit since the last time I saw you at a church picnic."

She took Livvy's satchel and set it on a trunk at the foot of the bed. "You helped my Whit and rode all that way in a rough buckboard. You are a dear for doing such an unselfish thing, and I am more than happy to let you rest here tonight."

"Thank you again. You're very kind."

"I'll fetch you some warm water in the morning. I imagine you're too tired tonight to bathe."

Livvy dropped to the bed and hiked up her skirt to remove her boots. She hadn't realized how her back and feet ached until she sank into the soft feather ticking.

"This was Whit's room when he lived at home," Annie said, looking around at the furniture. "I've tried to do it up a bit nicer so it's not so boyish. I hope it suits you."

Livvy gulped most unladylike. "It's lovely." She smoothed a wrinkle in the eight-point star quilt. "Did you make this yourself?"

Annie smiled through a yawn. "Oh, pardon me. Yes, I did. Years ago, before I was married."

Affectionately, she bent to touch a star. "I've always been partial to these red stars. So was Whit when he was a boy, though they're not as bright as they once were." She turned for the door and paused there. "You sleep as long as you want. I'll keep a plate warm for your breakfast." With that, she softly closed the door behind her.

Whit's bedroom. Whit's bed.

Whit's longing look in the moonlight.

Livvy stepped out of her simple dress and petticoat, and shivered. He'd touched her hair. Gently, tentatively, as if...Oh, she didn't know what. Shaking off the memory, she took in the iron bed from head to foot. A common enough piece of furniture found in most households. Surely the ticking and pillow had not been Whit's. But the quilt?

She slipped beneath the covers, muddled in heart and mind by the disconcerting man. One minute he was a childish tease and the next a perfect, caring gentleman. How could he be both at the same time, stirring such opposing reactions in her breast—tenderness and anger?

Perhaps tomorrow would offer fresh light on the subject. Right now, all she wanted was to sleep, surrender to the soft warmth around her. She pulled the quilt higher, tucked it under her chin, and closed her eyes.

~

Livvy pulled her legs up and snuggled deeper into the feather ticking, away from a teasing light. Squinting one eye open, she gasped and bolted upright. An unfamiliar room, a strange bed. Her gaze landed on her satchel, then flew to the four red stars that topped the bed's quilt. Her shoulders relaxed as the facts aligned themselves. Whit's bed.

Clutching the quilt to her throat, she looked around the room. No sign of anyone but her. Bright sunlight poured in the window—it must be mid-morning. She tossed the covers aside.

At the washstand, warm water greeted her fingers, evidence of Annie Hutton's thoughtfulness. If Livvy couldn't have clean clothes, at least she'd have a freshened body.

In no time she was booted, buttoned, and combed out. Standing before the mirror, she pulled her hair over her shoulder, plaiting it into a long braid. She twisted it low on her neck and pinned it in place, wanting instead to let it hang down her back on the ride home.

The thought fanned a tiny flame in her stomach, and she turned to look at the quilt. Quickly she straightened it, propped up the pillow, gathered her satchel, and rushed into the hall. The sooner she was out of Whit Hutton's bedroom, the better.

A door at the landing's end stood open, one she had not noticed the night before. Another fine quilt topped a bed there, and a china-faced dolled perched against a pink pillow. Whit's sister's room. The girl was two or three years younger, if Livvy remembered correctly. She must be about fifteen now.

Women's voices drew her to the stairway, and she hurried down and into the kitchen. A grown-up Martha Mae Hutton stood next to her mother at the counter, her auburn hair as vivid as Livvy remembered. Fresh biscuits veiled the room with a homey scent. Both women turned at Livvy's arrival.

"Good morning!" Annie rubbed her hands against her apron and met Livvy with a brief hug. "I hope you slept well. You seemed to be when I slipped in earlier with the hot water."

Livvy ducked her head at being caught asleep so late. "Thank you. I—I don't usually sleep so long."

"Well, you did arrive well past midnight, so you were quite in need of the rest." Annie turned back to her work. "You remember Martha, don't you? Marti, this is Ruth and Hubert Baker's granddaughter, Olivia Hartman."

A smile as bright as her mother's and terrifyingly close to her brother's spread across the girl's face as she extended her hand. "It's nice to see you again, Olivia. I think the last time was at the church picnic three or four years ago."

"Livvy, please. Call me Livvy." She took the girl's hand, smooth with flour. "Looks like I caught you in the middle of making bread."

Marti pulled a plate from the warmer and set it at the kitchen table. "This is for you. We barely had enough to hold for you after Daddy and Whit finished breakfast. My brother eats like a horse now that he's up at your grandfather's place."

41

"Really, Marti." Annie poured coffee, set the cup before Livvy, and bumped her daughter with her hip, a playful move that forced a laugh from Livvy.

Marti lightly bumped her mother in return. "I'm not being mean, Mama. Just speaking the truth, that's all."

A bank of windows topped the counter and sink all along the east wall, and bright yellow curtains drew back at each end, matching the checked cloth on the table. Livvy seated herself and whispered a quick prayer over the eggs and bacon and biscuits. She was hungrier than she thought.

"It's not often lately that I eat something I haven't cooked myself. This looks—and smells—wonderful."

The back door opened, and Whit interrupted the cheerful exchange. "You ready?"

His question landed on Livvy's plate like a blob of cold grease. She looked at him, at her breakfast, and then back to his creased brow.

"I need to get back to the ranch."

CHAPTER SIX

"Stop fussing, Whit, and sit down and have some coffee." His ma set two cups on the table. "We've hardly had a good visit and here you want to rush off already. Can't you stay for dinner?"

She filled the cups, returned the coffeepot to the stove, and took a seat across the table. Her gentle scolding reminded Whit that no other preacher's kids could have had it as good as he and Marti did growing up, but this wasn't a social call. He had calves to brand.

He hung his hat on the chair back rather than the peg by the door, determined that he and Livvy were not staying. Lord knew the trouble Buck and Jody Perkins could wrangle before noon. But the hungry look in Livvy's blue eyes set him back, and he swallowed what he was about to say. It wasn't eggs and biscuits she was longing for. His impatience settled and he scooted to the table, gentled his voice. "Go ahead and eat, Livvy. We have time."

His ma cocked an eyebrow in that way she had. Made him want to duck every time. She could always tell what he was thinking. He raised the heavy mug to his lips and sipped the black brew. Good cowboy coffee. Amazing what a delicate little preacher's wife could concoct.

"Did you check on Tad?" Livvy spread apple butter on a biscuit, and looked up as she took a bite.

He waited. Waited for the surprise to hit.

She turned to his mother. "This is wonderful, Mrs. Hu—Annie. I'd love to get your recipe."

Livvy couldn't have said anything better.

Ma beamed. "You'll have to come down this fall when Marti and I pick apples and you can make a batch with us." She slid Whit a bold look. "Of course, we'd love to see you before then too."

Clearing his throat, he swirled his coffee even though he had no sugar or cream in it to swirl. He was definitely outnumbered in the kitchen with three women, though Marti hadn't lit into him yet. She plopped a mound of yeast dough in a crockery bowl, covered it with a towel, and then poured herself some coffee. Taking a chair, she tossed her red curls—her long-standing attempt at appearing casual.

"So, is this Tad you speak of Tad Overton?" Marti spooned sugar into her coffee and added a cow's worth of cream.

"Yes," Livvy said, finishing her eggs. "Do you know him?"

Whit stiffened.

Marti turned her coffee mug around so the handle was on the left side. "We went to school together before he and his folks moved to Eight Mile." A slight blush colored her cheeks.

"He's a no-account fool."

Whit's comment deepened the blush. Marti speared him with a pointed glare.

"What an unkind thing to say, Whit." His ma's reprimand didn't carry her usual fire. It didn't need to. Marti's ire heated the room.

Whit gulped his coffee, waited for his throat to stop burning. "He had no business getting mixed up in the train war. Now he's got himself shot and his ma will have to do all the chores until he heals up. Not only that, he took me away from the roundup, and the Perkins brothers are sitting on their thumbs at the ranch waiting for me to get back." He drained the cup. "At least they better be."

Livvy's eyes rounded as if she'd never seen him before.

His ma frowned. "Maybe one of them can help Mrs. Overton until Tad is well enough."

Whit shot her a glance. "They're doin' that too."

Livvy stood and took her plate to the sink. "I'd be glad to help you clean up."

"Thank you, but you're in a hurry and we are not." His ma went into a small room off the kitchen and came back with two jars. She tied them into a dish towel and gave them to Livvy.

"Take these with you. If you don't serve it every meal to those hungry cowboys, it might last you a couple of weeks before you and Whit get back down." She snagged Whit with a motherly smile that hobbled him to a commitment.

Livvy hugged her. "Thank you again for letting us stay on such short notice."

"Think nothing of it, dear. This is home, you know."

No surprise to Whit that his ma embraced Livvy with her hospitality. Maybe someday Livvy would share more than the apple butter recipe, but they best be on their way before Marti busted a cinch. He chanced a side-long look her way. She had a tight rein on her coffee and was still scowling.

He grabbed his hat off the chair and Livvy's cloak from a peg, then opened the door and stepped back for her to exit. Beneath his brim he peeked at his ma and caught her approval. He had to get back to Eight Mile before all these women got him so flustered he didn't know bronc from broke.

"I'll tell your father you'll be back down after branding."

How could he argue with that? "Thanks for breakfast. And the apple butter." He planted a kiss on her cheek and looked over her shoulder through the open kitchen door. Marti stuck her tongue out at him.

His ma patted his cheek and leaned closer. "She's a real sweet girl, Whit."

He met her eyes for a moment—like looking in a mirror—but held his thoughts in check.

"Oh, Whit, look. Columbines." Livvy fingered the lavender fringe bordering the porch. "They're just like those we saw near the corrals."

"Aren't they lovely?" His ma descended the steps and stooped beside Livvy. "Caleb helped me dig these from the hills and transplant them our first spring here in the parsonage. I was in the family way with Whit at the time."

Embarrassed by her casual reference to such a subject, he made for the wagon. Bess stood patiently where he'd left her an hour ago, dozing in the traces. Livvy followed and gathered her skirts. He offered his hand, and she took it without hesitation and climbed into the seat. Joining her, he tipped his hat to his ma, then turned Bess in the yard and up the lane.

~

Livvy set her satchel on the bench between herself and Whit. She'd have liked to spend the day with Annie and Marti comparing recipes, discussing flowers, even helping them with the bread. But she understood Whit's insistence that they get back to the ranch. Pop needed them both. Promising herself she'd return to Cañon City as soon as the apple butter ran out, she focused on the busy Main Street.

How much it had changed since she and her parents last visited. Or maybe it was she who had changed, noticing more now than what a younger girl saw. A distinguished three-story hotel claimed an entire block, with Fremont Bank taking up one corner. Meat markets, a haberdashery, several general stores, a pharmacy. The boardwalk was more crowded than she remembered, and finely dressed ladies with parasols strolled in groups or on gentlemen's arms.

She glanced down at her plain day dress. Not exactly what a young woman wore to town. Fingering her twisted braid, she rued not bringing a hat or bonnet, but their hasty departure last night had not been for a social visit. At least no one in town knew her, other than the Huttons. Slight balm for her sudden discomfort.

A man on horseback loped down the street kicking up dust and pebbles. Empty freight wagons rumbled by, returning from the mining camps and on their way to the livery. Buggy wheels creaked, reins slapped, children hollered. Noise and movement rose around her like a blustery storm. During the last few weeks at Pop's, Livvy had grown accustomed to the serene mountain setting. She'd nearly forgotten the clutter and commotion of city life.

Pretending to look across the street, she peeked at Whit. His face was a study in stone. Unreadable. His jaw clenched so tight that a muscle bulged just below his ear. That should tell her something, but she didn't know what.

In all their growing up days, she'd not seen him as angry as he'd been today when his sister mentioned Tad Overton. Marti was obviously fond of the young patient, and Livvy had no doubt that she'd be paying the boy a visit while he recuperated at Doc Mason's.

Well, Whit better not find out about it.

For a moment, Livvy was glad she didn't have a brother telling her what to do. Not that Whit wouldn't try the same tact on her. He was arrogant enough to assume guardianship on this trip, in light of her grandfather's absence.

But she certainly didn't see Whit Hutton in a brotherly light.

Her pulse jumped into rhythm with the mare's pace.

Drawing a deep, calming breath, Livvy peered past her bench partner and through the trees across the river. She caught the top of the Hot Springs Bath House before Whit took the curve at the west end of town.

Bess slowed a bit on the gently sloping road, and Whit relaxed. He'd been tense the entire time they were in Cañon City—except for last night when he'd thanked her for coming with him. Her insides warmed at the memory.

In addition to that unique moment between them, he hadn't teased her once, not that she missed it, but it was so uncharacteristic. Was she getting a glimpse into what he might be like as a man?

And man he was, of that she was keenly aware. His legs stretched a good three inches past hers where they sat on the bench, and his hands were sure with the reins. Calloused and tanned. Strong yet gentle too. She smoothed back her hair where he had touched it the night before.

He looked at her. She jerked her hand down and tucked it into the folds of her skirt.

"You thinking about something?" The familiar smirk tipped his mouth.

So much for grown-up Whit Hutton.

She straightened, pressing her spine against the hard seat back. "And exactly what should I be thinking about?"

He made that scoffing sound in his throat that she hated. The vision of his tenderness splintered.

She looked to her right, following the jagged skyline that sliced high above the road. A rock-layer rainbow of ochre and red and green stepped down the abutment in wide bands. Such a history the stone must tell, if only she knew how to read it.

"Livvy."

She flinched at his strangled moan, doubting it was her name she'd heard. Which layer of temperament would he present this time?

He turned Bess off the road and pulled to a stop. The horse immediately bent her head to the bunch grass poking through the rocky landscape. Whit twisted halfway on the bench, pinning Livvy in place with dark, inscrutable eyes.

"What?" She lifted her chin, pressed her shoulders back.

"We're too old to carry on like children."

She breathed in through her nose. Breathed out. "Whatever do you mean?"

His eyes had aged since driving Tad into town last night. The earlier smirk and his throaty huff were the only vestiges of boyhood.

"You are like fire and ice."

She splashed him with a scalding look.

"See, that's just what I mean. One minute you are sweet and smooth as my ma's apple butter, the next you're as snorty and mean as an unbroke colt."

Livvy stared straight ahead, focused on drawing air into her lungs. She clasped her hands in her lap and struggled to maintain her composure after being compared to a horse. A *horse*.

"Don't you think we should be on our way?"

He dropped the reins to the floor of the buckboard and leaned closer. "What I think is if we don't clear the air right now, I'll leave you here beside the road."

Her head jerked around, and his face was so close that she nearly brushed his nose with her own. "You wouldn't."

One eyebrow reared. "Oh, but I would."

Angry tears marshaled in her throat, clawing their way upward, and she dug her nails into her hands. He could easily pick her up and toss her off the wagon. Or she could salvage her pride by stepping down voluntarily. Then he'd be forced to tell her grandfather that he was so rude and unkind she'd refused to ride home with him.

It wasn't that far back to the Hutton's parsonage. Wouldn't he regret that—her showing up in his mother's kitchen, alone and dust-covered from walking.

Too old to carry on like children.
Her shoulders eased a bit.
Clear the air, he'd said. She couldn't even clear her thoughts. *Oh, Lord, give me words. Give me a way out. Give me*—
Peace. That's what Whit was requesting. Peace between them. Well, it took two to make peace, and she had a few demands of her own. The realization strengthened her, calmed her swirling emotions.

"Very well. Let us *clear the air,* as you put it." She turned to face him full on, scooting back a bit to add a small distance between them. Thank goodness for the satchel. "You are not exactly the finest stallion in the herd, you know." Poor choice of words, but the first that came to mind.

His mouth twitched. He was laughing at her on the inside.

Her finger flew up like a pointed gun and she leveled it at his nose. "See what I mean. You laugh at me. You mock me. You treat me like I am an eight-year-old with freckles and pigtails."

"Sometimes you are." His mouth rippled, losing ground against the urge to grin.

"You are doing it right this minute."

"And so are you. You're acting like a child, all huff and hooves at the slightest little thing that isn't how you expect it to be. Life is not like that, Livvy. Life is full of badger holes and rock slides. You have to learn how to ride around them or ride through them and pray you don't break your neck while you're at it."

"You pray?" Immediately she regretted the stinging words and covered her mouth as if she could stop the pain that shot across his face. "I'm sorry," she whispered. "I didn't mean that."

His eyes hardened into obsidian.

Bess stepped forward in her grazing and the wagon jerked. A hawk screeched above them, and some small creature in a hidden crevice sent pebbles trailing down the rock face. Livvy felt as hard and heartless as those tumbling stones.

At once she saw the truth in his earlier words—and hers. She'd not deny them either. But he was right. She was not living as she'd been raised. And how long had it been since *she* had truly prayed, asked for the Lord's guidance in her choices?

She laid her hand on Whit's arm. "Please, forgive me."

His eyes softened—slightly—but his lips and his muscled arm remained a hard defense.

"You're right. I am fire and ice." She withdrew her hand. "But so are you. You can be tender and caring and turn right around and tease me in the next breath. I don't like it."

He scanned the ridge above them, worked his jaw, squinted as if peering into the deepest fissures.

"I'll work on it." The words chipped out like flint, but his gaze returned to her face and he reached for her hand, swallowed it with his own. "Truce?"

He'd asked this in the meadow. His eyes had pleaded last night behind the parsonage. She had granted him the slack her grandfather spoke of and then yanked it back. Unyielding. Unbending. Unforgiving.

His rough hand warmed her, promised protection, help. She'd rather have him as a friend than an enemy. "Truce."

CHAPTER SEVEN

The air wasn't exactly clear, but it was tolerable. Whit wanted clean and pure, like the morning after a summer rain. Instead he got cloudy and rushing, like Wilson Creek after a gully washer. At least the water was flowing.

At least there was water.

Turning Bess back into the road, he flicked the ribbons against her rump. She clopped onto the hardened surface, and the wagon wheels found their way into the ruts. Livvy sat more relaxed beside him, as if spent after her storm. He felt the same.

Her comment about prayer bit the hardest, most likely because it was true. He had pretty much followed his own head, not asked the Lord what he should be doing. The family wanted him to take over the mercantile, and his pa had hinted at college. But the idea of books and papers and professors made him want to kick and buck. He'd never be a preacher or any other kind of man who made his living indoors. Ever since that first summer he worked for Hubert Baker during roundup, he'd wanted to cowboy, learn to ranch, someday own his own spread.

It was *in* him.

Ma had often talked about his father having a way with horses. Whit believed he had the same, plus a good head for cows.

He'd even sketched out a brand—a H beneath an inverted V like a mountain peak. He planned to register it as soon as he got a chance.

Today would have been the chance if not for Baker and the Perkins boys waiting on his return. He'd have to make another trip to town, an event sure to please the preacher's wife. A smirk tugged his lips.

She liked Livvy. So did he. But he had to get that hump out of Livvy's back before they could get along—just like a green-broke colt. They had to come to some kind of an understanding.

It took every ounce of grit he had not to look at her sitting beside him all sweet-smelling and proper. And even more not to toss that satchel in the back, reach around her waist and pull her closer. She'd sure enough scared the fire out of him when she didn't even flinch at his threat to leave her behind. He'd thought she was gonna call his bluff and jump right off the wagon. But he'd been right in his guess about what set her off—his teasing. He had to break that habit or get her to see it was all in good fun.

He snorted. As fun as Oro tossing him in the dirt after Whit stuck his spurs to him. A lesson learned.

At the turnoff to the ranch road, Bess picked up her pace without Whit's coaxing, knowing that home lay ahead. But he kept her speed in check. Didn't want her running at it like she had on the way to town. They'd nearly rattled the buckboard apart. He could feel the give in the seat and hear a few extra knocks. He'd check it out at the barn, make sure the under rigging was still in good shape.

Livvy wiped her forehead with the back of her hand. Unlike him, she had no hat to shield her eyes or protect her pale skin from the sun. Would she take his if he offered?

He'd better not press his luck.

They'd left last night in such a hurry that she hadn't brought a bonnet. She'd thought only about Tad and him, not herself. A warm spot spread in his belly like a hot meal on a cold night. He could get used to that.

"You acted like you knew what you were doing last night." He slid her a glance, hoping she'd know that was a compliment.

"Doctor Patterson's place is next door to ours. I've helped him some." She turned her hands palm up and studied them a moment. "He tried to get me to go to nursing school. Said I had the touch. But I don't want to be a full-time nurse."

"What *do* you want to do?"

Her fingers closed and she turned her head toward the ridge line that snaked around the valley and flattened into bluffs at the end. "The same thing most women want, I suppose."

He chuckled. "Pretty dresses and a bunch of beaux calling?"

She shot him a warning look.

He waited for the steam to burn off and tried again. "A big spread in the high parks and cow-calf pairs as far as the eye can see?"

This time she didn't look at him, kept her eyes straight ahead. Had he said the wrong thing already?

"That sounds rather nice."

Her soft answer sent a jolt through him that bounced off his ribs and then settled easy in his chest.

"You do work for my grandfather, you know." Her voice strengthened. "My mother grew up here, and I learned to ride here. It's not like I don't know my way around livestock."

He couldn't argue with that. Didn't want to argue with that. Maybe he could fit another H beneath that mountain peak brand. But he was getting way ahead of himself.

The ranch road skirted the creek bottom, leaving the thick, deep grass unmarred by wagon wheels and horse hooves. He spotted several head he could have easily pushed to the corrals. They watched the buckboard without reaction.

"Why were you so mad at your sister?"

If Olivia Hutton could jump a maverick steer as quick as she asked a straight question, he'd have her riding on the roundup.

"What makes you think I was mad at her?"

Livvy branded him with a blue glare. "Now who's playing games?"

He frowned and flicked Bess into a hard trot. "She has no business getting tangled up with Tad Overton. He's not to be trusted."

"And you know this how?"

Whit bristled against her push into his family's personal affairs. A final turn into the main yard and he stopped Bess at the house. "I just do."

She snickered under her breath. Pretty pleased with herself, she was, as she snatched up the satchel and her wrap and then held him with a taunting look. "Well?"

"Well, what?"

"Are you going to help me down or not?"

He clamped his teeth, wrapped the reins around the brake handle, and jumped down.

Infuriating woman.

He handed her down and watched her stop at the purple bush by the front door and bury her face in it before going inside. She didn't look behind her, just stepped through the door and closed it.

But she did not slam it.

He reset his hat, took up the reins, and clucked Bess to the barn. A skittish hope danced around him and the future began to unfurl itself.

While he unhitched Bess and brushed her down, he calculated how much money he'd saved and considered asking Baker if he could run a few of his own cows in with the ranch herd. But he'd need to register a brand first.

Next trip, he promised himself, pleased at the prospect of doing business as well as visiting his family. Two birds with one stone. Yes, the future was looking better all the time.

He led Bess into the fenced pasture behind the barn and pulled off her bridle. As he closed the gate on his way out, he scanned the green bottom land for the other saddle horses Baker kept close. There should be six. He counted three, including Bess.

He strode to the barn and pushed open the tack room door. Baker's saddle and tack were gone. So were Buck's and Jody's. Whit jerked his hat off, slapped it on his leg, and shoved it back on. He grabbed his outfit and took it to the pasture where he hung his saddle and blanket on the fence and whistled for Oro.

The gelding raised his head and looked Whit's way. His tawny coat gleamed against the meadow's green, and he trotted to the fence and greeted Whit with a deep-chested rumble.

"You saw them leave, didn't you." Whit mumbled his complaint to the horse as he bridled and saddled him. Then he swung up, rode through the gate, latched it, and headed for the farthest canyon. "Let's go find them."

~

Delores Overton was gone. Livvy looked in the bedrooms, the parlor, Pop's study, the dining room and kitchen, even the root cellar out back, though no reason came to mind for the woman to be there. She returned to the kitchen for the egg basket and scrap can and went out to the garden and coop. No Delores.

And no Pop.

She hushed her rampant thoughts. Pop often went for a ride to look over things. Surely he was fine. Out counting his cows. Hopefully not every single one this afternoon. That's what he had Whit and Buck and Jody for.

She tossed the scraps and entered the coop while the chickens fought over the best pieces. Fourteen eggs this morning, or rather afternoon. Enough to bake a pound cake and have a few to boil. She could almost taste Annie Hutton's apple butter melting into a golden slice of warm cake. Her mouth watered.

Buck and Jody would make quick work of the fruity spread. Where were those boys anyway? It was too late in the day to be at Overton's doing chores. And there was enough to be done around here to keep them busy all summer in addition to checking cattle. The fence around the garden plot needed mending, and the wood pile shrank a little every day.

She hooked the basket on her arm, shielded her eyes against the westerly sun, and looked out to the pasture, counting the horses. Her chest tightened as she scoured the green meadow for a buckskin and her grandfather's stocky gray. Bess and another dark horse grazed unhurriedly. No gray. Delores Overton wasn't the only one missing.

Livvy and Whit hadn't been home a half hour and already he was gone.

She hurried from the coop, careful to latch the gate. She didn't need coyotes nosing their way in due to her carelessness. With the egg basket on her arm, she hiked her skirts and ran to the house. Where was everyone?

The kitchen hugged the north edge of the ranch house, shaded behind a big pine on the west end that kept it cooler than any other room in the summer. But it wasn't bright like the Hutton's. How cheerful yellow curtains would be against the dark wood walls.

She washed the eggs and laid them out on a tea towel as her earlier words floated by with tempting appeal.

I learned to ride here.

And she'd done it without a side saddle. No place for such a contraption on a cattle spread. She huffed. Impossible to keep one's seat chasing cows without two feet in the stirrups.

Everyone had ridden astride, even her mother and Mama Ruth. The three of them had often trailed up to the bluffs, where they sat gazing down at the creek bottom and the ranch buildings.

Dusty memories of horseflesh and leather tugged her to her grandfather's bedroom where she knelt before the chest by the door. She had long since outgrown her riding skirt, but Mama Ruth had worn denims, and often said she didn't care what her high-brow English relatives thought. This was America and she'd do as she pleased. Livvy cherished the tender ache the memory pressed.

She lifted the lid on the trunk, tipped it back against the wall, then carefully dug through the linens and dresses that had been Mama Ruth's. Pausing, she leaned out and looked into the dining room. Heaven forbid that Pop come in and find her snooping. Maybe she should wait and ask his permission. Would he allow what she was thinking?

Brushing hesitation aside, she returned to her search and found what she wanted at the trunk's bottom. Denims, just like Whit and Pop wore, only smaller. A boy's size—her grandmother's size. Livvy stood and held them at her waist. Looking at herself in the glass over Mama Ruth's dressing table, she pulled a grin. With a hat and her hair tucked up, she could pass for a hired hand.

Excitement burned through her like a fast fuse. She returned everything else to its neat order and closed the trunk. Then she borrowed one of Pop's old work hats from the back of a bent-wood rack in the corner, clutched the denims to her chest, and ran to her room.

Quietly she closed her door and draped her treasure over the brass footboard. Her movements reflected in the glass across the room that also caught her flushed cheeks beneath Pop's hat. She pulled it forward, low over her right eye like Whit wore his. Perfect. But she'd have to line the hat band with newsprint to keep the old Stetson from flying off.

The back door closed.

Livvy choked and snatched off the hat. She rolled the denims and shoved them under the bed. The hat followed, and she fluffed out the dust ruffle. Did it always stick out or should it be kicked back a little?

She licked both palms and smoothed her mussed hair on the sides, giggling at the childish trick she hadn't used in years.

She opened the door and walked as elegantly as possible into the dining room and toward the kitchen. No other sounds had followed the door's closing, so she had no idea who had entered.

At the doorway she stopped.

He sat at the work table beneath the kitchen window, hat lying next to his propped elbows, head braced in both hands. Looking so alone.

She ached to reach out to him, to be a comfort, a companion. But they were only beginning to be friends, working out their stubborn differences, working together on her grandfather's ranch. Nothing more.

He raised his head and looked straight into her eyes. And as suddenly as that, she knew that Whit Hutton could not only see through the dining room curtains. He could see into her very soul.

CHAPTER EIGHT

Whit stared at Livvy standing in the doorway, her lips parted as if to speak. If he wasn't so angry, he'd kiss her soundly. As it was, his head pounded and it had nothing to do with courting.

"Jody's gone."

"Gone?" Livvy's brow wrinkled as she came to the table. "What about Pop and Buck? Are they okay? Is Pop all right?"

Of course she'd worry for her grandfather. He should have mentioned Baker first. The knots in his shoulders tightened. "Your grandfather is fine. He and Buck are out in the barn unsaddling their horses."

Visibly relieved, Livvy went to the stove and opened the flue. "I'll make some coffee."

She pumped water into the coffee pot and set it over the fire.

He watched mutely as she scooped out beans and added them to the mill. The grinding matched his churning thoughts, but the aroma soothed him. Maybe that was all he needed. Hot, strong coffee.

His stomach growled. Annie smiled and threw him a sidelong glance. "I know you had eggs this morning, but that's all I've got. Want some to go with the coffee?"

He heaved out a heavy breath, rolled his shoulders, and leaned back in the chair. "That sounds good."

He'd not watched a woman work—work for his comfort—for any length of time. It touched something inside him, brought to mind the way his father watched his mother.

Livvy moved smoothly between tasks, wasting no effort. He rubbed the stiffness in his neck and studied her mannerisms, the soft curves her dress failed to conceal, the hair working lose from her coiled braid.

She added the ground coffee to the pot and more wood to the stove. Then she spooned bacon grease into an iron skillet and gathered three eggs from the counter's far corner. At the cabinet she drew out a loaf of bread, cut two thick slices, and laid one on each of two plates.

He could get used to this set up, sitting in the kitchen, enjoying female company. Livvy's company. "You going to share that apple butter with me?"

He winced at his tone. He couldn't seem to say anything that wasn't a borderline jab.

But she must have been worried about Baker, because she didn't goad him back or get all worked up.

"No, I am not. I'm saving it to have with pound cake. You will have to wait." She buttered the bread and set his plate before him, then started breaking eggs into the skillet.

"Thank you." He bit off the corner. "But I don't smell pound cake."

Her cheeks colored. Couldn't be the stove—she'd just stirred the fire.

"I haven't gotten to it yet." She pushed at her escaping hair. "I had other things to do when we got back." Fingering the same strands again, she looked around as if searching for something. "Gathered eggs, fed the chickens. Hunted for Mrs. Overton."

She looked at him then, worry clouding her eyes. "She's not here either."

"I know. Buck said he sent Jody with her early this morning. She wanted to go home, and Jody took her so he could help with chores." Whit shoved the rest of the bread in his mouth and chewed like he wanted to chew on the boy. "He never came back."

Livvy flipped the eggs over, the way he liked, then came to the table and took his plate. "More bread?" She served the eggs with cracked peppercorns and paused at the counter, waiting for his answer.

He could look at her all day and never come up with the right words, so he nodded.

She added a fork to his plate and set the food before him, then took the other chair.

He shoved his back. "I need to wash."

She stopped him with a hand on his arm. "It's all right." A smile hinted and she scooted closer to the table. "Just don't tell Buck and Jody."

He sat. The day wasn't all bad. He was eating in private with Miss Olivia Hartman.

Until the kitchen door banged open and Baker and Buck walked in.

Buck stopped, took one look at Livvy, then ran back out. Splashing sounds carried into the kitchen.

Baker pumped water at the sink, washed, and dried his hands on a towel that Livvy kept on a nail for his use. His ranch, his house. He could wash where ever he pleased.

Livvy whisked away her plate and checked on the coffee. She added grease and several more eggs to the skillet, and soon offered two more plates filled with fried eggs and buttered bread. Baker brought two chairs from the dining room and motioned for Livvy to join them.

The coffee smelled ready and Livvy must have agreed, for she bunched her apron and brought the pot to the table. Baker set three stoneware mugs and a china cup and saucer on the smooth wood surface and took the farthest seat against the west wall with his right leg angled out from the table. He had a clear view of the kitchen, the window, and the back door.

Buck joined them, as did Livvy. She lifted her brows at the mixed dishes on the table and eyed her grandfather.

Baker read her query. "In here I like a mug. Less formal. Your grandmother didn't mind."

"Makes the coffee better, I think." Buck shoveled into his eggs, and Baker watched him fill his face. Withering under the close examination, the boy swallowed, laid his fork down, and bowed his head.

Silence stood at the table as Baker gathered his thoughts. "Thank you, Lord, for this food and for bringing Livvy and Whit home safely. Thank you for bringing Tad and his ma here so we could help." He paused and cleared his throat. "Save him, Lord. Amen."

Baker sure enough knew how things stood. Whit wasn't sure if the saving had to do with Tad Overton's body or soul, but it really didn't matter. God always seemed to take both into account.

⁓

Livvy bit into her bread and sipped coffee from the tea cup. What an old softy Pop was, knowing she liked the colorful china better than the heavy stoneware.

From the way Buck finished off his eggs, she wondered what the men and Mrs. Overton had for breakfast. If they'd had anything. Livvy glanced at the pie safe, remembering last night's interrupted dessert. She had a second pie tucked away, if it hadn't disappeared too.

"What did Doc Mason say about Tad?" Pop sheared off half his bread and gulped his coffee.

Whit shook his head in disgust, a signal Livvy recognized all too well. "He wants to keep him for a few days, keep an eye on him."

"Keep him out of trouble, more likely." Pop's bread disappeared beneath his silvery mustache, and he chewed as if the bread were a week old and tough.

"I told Doc we'd take care of the bill. Can't see the widow havin' enough to pay for what her fool son did."

Buck studied his plate and kept his head down. The men stopped eating and stared at him. In the silence, the boy must have sensed their scrutiny, for he peeked out from under his pale brows and frowned.

"I know what you're thinkin'."

"And just what are we thinkin'?" Whit's eyes narrowed into skewers.

"That it's all my fault."

"How's that?" Pop said.

Buck cut a glance at Whit and blanched as if he'd seen a Ute warrior, spear in hand. "Whit said I was in charge and if anything went wrong, he'd blame me."

Pop grunted, gulped another mouthful of coffee, and eyed his foreman. "I was here too. Can't be entirely your fault."

Color returned to Buck's face and he sat a little straighter.

"Though he is your brother, not mine."

Whit's mouth quirked on one side and he picked up his coffee. "Where do you think he went after Overtons'?" He held Buck with a you'd-better-tell-me stare.

Buck stalled.

The boy was about to become the next entrée.

Livvy regretted having nothing else to feed the men. Gone one night, and here they were near starving. And now they'd cleaned out her eggs too. She'd never get to sneak off and ride with a day's worth of baking and cooking ahead.

She stood and walked to the pie safe.

Safe, indeed.

"He's a good boy," Buck said. "I'm sure he helped Mrs. Overton with her chores like I told him to."

"That's not what I asked you." Whit's eyes flicked a warning.

Livvy set the canned-peach pie on the table near Whit and sliced a fat piece for him. "Look what I found."

He ignored her.

Buck fidgeted with his fork and then laid it on the table with a defeated sigh. "I think he went upriver toward Fort DeRemer at Texas Creek."

"Fort what?" Whit's expression hardened.

"DeRemer," Pop said. "Named after a man who fought in the Civil War. Just a rock wall, but the Denver and Rio Grande men are building them at strategic points along the river and firing on the Santa Fe workers. Heard about it when I was in town last week." He mumbled something into his coffee. "It's all gonna bust out like a full-bellied storm caught in a canyon."

Buck watched the pie-cutting. "Jody wanted to hire on to lay track for the Santa Fe company. He ain't a good-enough shot to hole up behind those rock forts with the Denver fellas. But I didn't think he was serious, 'specially since we got all them cows to gather and calves to brand."

Livvy's hand stopped above the oozing pie as an idea sliced through her mind. Buck noticed and looked as if he wasn't going to get any of the juicy dessert. She caught herself, cut him a bigger piece, and set it before him.

"Thank you, Miss Livvy."

"You are welcome." At least the boy was learning something.

"I'll admit, we talked on it some," Buck said around a mouthful. "Fact is, Jody thought they'd want you for a hired gun, Whit, being's you're such a crack shot and all. Figured they'd be after you for sure since you know the country."

Whit's hand tightened around his fork, and Livvy feared he might stab Buck right there in front of God and everyone. Instead he nailed the boy to his chair with an icy glare.

Pop snorted. "Whit's too smart for that, son. He knows which side his bread's buttered on."

Buck frowned but didn't ask, and Livvy wasn't about to tell him what it meant. This was not her conversation. Plus she had something on her mind that required all her concentration to frame exactly right, and now might be the perfect time to bring it up.

She served Pop and then herself and took her seat. A quarter of the pie remained.

Whit attacked his serving. "My guns are for snakes, coyotes, and cougars, not taking pot shots at men laying a railroad that we need through these mountains. Regardless whose name is on the train."

Pop grunted again. Seemed like he did that more and more since Mama Ruth was gone. She'd always insisted he speak in complete sentences.

"I'll ride over to Cunninghams' early tomorrow." Whit finished off his pie and pushed his plate back. "See if their boys can help us with the branding."

"Won't be necessary." Pop leaned his arms on the table, tilted his head over his plate. "I can still ride. But I'd be more help on the ground. You and Buck can drive them off the mountain to the bunch grounds. You rope 'em, and Buck and I can hold 'em down."

"Who will brand?"

Pop cut a look at Livvy without raising his head.

Her breathe stuck in her throat. Did her grandfather really have that much faith in her? Did he remember all those years she and her mother and Mama Ruth had horsebacked through these hills?

"No." Whit's jaw tightened and the muscle below his ear bulged. Pop's gaze shifted to his foreman. "Are you questioning my judgment?"

Livvy pulled air through her nose as she watched the battle in Whit's eyes—his desire to please and respect his boss, and his apprehension at taking a woman on a roundup. He wouldn't meet her gaze and she was glad. She couldn't stand to have him look down on her. Not now. Not after the truce they'd reached today.

But she wasn't going to sit quietly by and let them discuss her as if she wasn't there. "I can do it, Pop. Mama Ruth and Mother and I rode all over this ranch when I was growing up."

"I know you did. They were good teachers." He smiled and his mustache quivered. "All the Baker women can horseback. But it's the branding I'm thinkin' on. Can you handle that?"

"Yes." Not that she ever had, but why not? She'd wrung chickens' necks and cleaned fish and patched up bloody men like Tad Overton. How hard could it be?

"You listen to what Whit tells you. He'll show you how on a couple and then turn it over to you."

Not willingly, he wouldn't. A side glance at Whit revealed the battle still raging. Not only was his boss taking the reins back, he was telling him how to do his job and bringing a woman into the mix. She sat straighter, determined not to disappoint him.

"You'll be needin' your grandmother's denims." Pop stood and grabbed his plate.

Fear leaped up and Livvy followed it. "I know right where they are." Should she have said that? "I'll get them from the trunk right now."

She dashed out of the kitchen, through the dining room, and into Pop's bedroom, where she opened the trunk for a moment, then dropped the lid and peeked around the doorframe. Chairs scraped against the kitchen floor. If she hurried she could make it to her room unseen.

How wicked she was, deceiving her grandfather into thinking she was pure and honest. Guilt sat heavy on her formerly light spirit. She must confess. But not yet. Not until after she proved that she could ride and brand as well as any cowhand on the ranches of Eight Mile Mountain.

And brand she would.

CHAPTER NINE

The muscles in Whit's neck clamped like a farrier's clincher. His wild-hare comparison of Livvy jumping maverick steers was about to come to life. That was just what he needed—a girl and her crippled grandfather traipsing off into the thick brush. Blasted Jody Perkins. If Whit got his hands on him before the boy got himself shot, Perkins'd wish he'd never heard of the railroad.

Livvy had lit out of the kitchen quick as lightning. He took his plate and cup to the sink and told Buck to do the same. Baker had already gone to the barn.

What happened to the peaceful afternoon of watching a beautiful woman do what she was good at? Now he had to spend two or three days—maybe longer—watching her do what she'd never done before.

It could be worse. But not much.

Riding leisurely along smooth trails and open meadows was not even close to chasing a wild cow without getting hooked. Or breaking a horse's leg in a badger hole. Or getting raked off the saddle in thick timber. Lord have mercy on them all.

As he reached for his hat, she returned to the kitchen, cheeks flushed and near bustin' with excitement. He didn't need excitement—he needed level-headed cow sense, a strong back, and a sure hand. Speaking of hands ...

"I thought you were gone." She pumped water into a dishpan, then set it on the stove before pulling out the flour bin.

He left his hat on the chair back, spread his feet squarely beneath him, and crossed his arms at his chest. "Do you have gloves?"

The question stopped her forward motion. "Excuse me?"

"Gloves. You know, those things you put on your hands." Irritation called up the worst in him, and he almost regretted the sarcasm.

She planted her fists on her hips and faced him. "What has your back up, Mr. Hutton? Or do you not like the idea of a woman on roundup?"

He stood his ground. "What I don't like is you dodging my question."

"Hmm." She turned back to the counter and set out a large crockery bowl. "Let me see now. I have some lovely pine-green gloves I wear with my traveling suit, white gloves I save for church, and a very nice pair of kid leather gloves for riding." With a tin cup she scooped flour from the bin into the bowl. "Yes, I have gloves."

His neck muscles tightened even more. This was exactly what he didn't need.

In two strides he was beside her and grabbed her hand, relieving it of the cup. He forced her fingers against his own, palm to palm. Hardened and rough, his fingers topped hers by two knuckles.

He leaned in. "Feel that?" He pressed her hand between both of his. The racing pulse in her bare wrist beat against his arm, and her eyes widened with surprise. "Feel those callouses? The hard, cracked skin? Is that what you want for yourself?"

She didn't pull away. Just stared at their hands flattened against each other like two hotcake griddles.

He dropped her hand. "Your nice kid leather won't last through one morning. And neither will your skin without work gloves. You'll be branded as sure as the calves Baker is so all-fired certain you can handle."

"I know that. I have watched brandings."

"Watching is not the same as doing."

An internal fire flared her eyes to sapphires, and the flame jumped to his heart like a wild ember. Anger or protectiveness, he didn't know which pressed him harder, but either one would cloud his judgment and he could not afford that. He took a step back, grabbed his hat, and shoved it on with a stony stare.

"I am sure Pop has something I can use." Her hands balled around her bunched apron and her chin hitched up. Determined as an old steer on the fight.

He growled, irritated that he couldn't scare her off. "We leave at sunup."

He slammed the door on his way out. Infuriating woman.

Storming into the bunkhouse, he went straight to his warbag and found the gloves he'd worn when he started for Baker four years ago. He'd grown a might since then. Like skunk cabbage in a wet summer, his pa had said.

He held a glove against his hand and his fingers topped it by two knuckles. No holes. Stiff, but still good protection. They'd do. He shoved them under his bedroll and headed for the barn, working on a strategy for Baker.

~

Livvy dragged in air and braced herself against the counter. Whit Hutton had more gall than any man she had ever known. How dare he compare the two of them. Why, that was like comparing gingham and leather. She looked at the hand he'd held, felt again the heat in his fingers and the way it made her pulse pound.

No, that wasn't it at all. He'd simply taken her by surprise. Caught her off guard the way he always did. What happened to their short-lived truce? Why couldn't he let her be who she was? *Accept* her for who she was.

She mixed yeast and warm water in a small bowl and set it aside. Then she carried the now-boiling dishpan to the sink, dunked the day's dishes, and shaved in a few soap curls with a paring knife.

After washing the dishes, she turned to baking bread—the perfect activity for taking out her frustration. Adding flour by the cupful, she worked the dough into a sizeable mound, punching out the air and knots, picturing Whit as she kneaded.

Her mind played with the word and brought up *needed.* Humph. She pounded the dough again, tucked it under into a smooth ball, and threw it in the bread bowl to rise. She needed Whit Hutton like she needed a third leg.

The afternoon flew by with baking, and packing plates and flatware in an old flour sack she planned to tie on her saddle horn. But after considering the clanking of tin against her horse's shoulder, she unpacked everything. Instead she'd get up early and slice meat and bread and stack it together. The men could eat with their hands. So could she.

They weren't taking a wagon. No lemonade. Surely Pop had an extra canteen. She'd rather die of thirst than ask Whit for one.

Working the Bar-HB and the fringes of neighboring ranches for strays, they'd be back each night to sleep. As happy as she was about riding with the men, she knew she'd be dog tired at day's end. She also knew the others depended on her to keep them fed whether she was helping jump strays or not.

She put a roast in the Dutch oven, added water, salt, pepper, onions, and the lid, and shoved it to the back of the oven to cook overnight.

Preparations continued in her bedroom, where she hunted for a blouse or shirtwaist to wear with Mama Ruth's denims. Maybe Pop had an old shirt she could borrow. And gloves too. Rubbing her hands together, she recalled Whit's rough forcefulness—so unlike that day in the columbines.

At least she'd had enough sense to bring her own boots for summer on the ranch.

Gathering up Pop's hat, she headed for his study, where she found a stack of old *Cañon City Times* newspapers he kept for fire starters in the winter. She pulled one from the bottom, and a headline caught her eye. Tucking a leg beneath her, she settled into the leather-covered desk chair to read:

> The United States Supreme Court on April 21 granted the primary right of way through the narrow gorge above Cañon City to the Denver & Rio Grande Western Railroad. The ruling should put to rest the ongoing Royal Gorge Railroad War between D&RG and the Atchison, Topeka and Santa Fe Railway.

Livvy let the paper flop back. The article was nearly two months old. If the Supreme Court had ruled, then why were Santa Fe crews laying track? No wonder the Denver men were sabotaging the railbed. But must they shoot at mere boys like Tad Overton?

She spread the paper across the desk and folded back the edge. Then she turned the broad sheet over and folded the new edge back, continuing to alternate the folds front and back until she had a large fan-like strip. Pressing the folds together, she flattened them, then tucked the strip under the sweat band inside Pop's old hat. *John B. Stetson* was stamped into the leather in gold letters.

She tried it on and it slid down over her eyes. Tipping it back, she looked through the stack of papers for other interesting stories.

"School Superintendent Unearths More Fossil Remains." Livvy shuddered. Who wanted to go around digging up old dead animals on purpose?

That sheet became another long fan, and three pages later, her grandfather's Stetson stayed put. Rising to go look in her mirror, she stopped short. Whit leaned inside the doorway, arms folded against his chest, one booted foot crossed over the other.

She jerked off the hat. "How long have you been standing there?"

"Long enough to know you look like a toadstool with that thing on."

Hot blood rushed into her face and her jaw clenched. He'd better be on his horse when she got that stamp iron in her hands.

Uninvited, he sauntered to the desk, picked up the hat and shoved it back on her head. She couldn't move. Nor could she see him, he stood so tall above her and so close. Mindful of her tendencies, she focused on breathing.

He bent to the side and peeked under the brim. A distinct ripple twisted his mouth before he straightened and shoved the hat down farther until it pinched her ears. "You want it screwed down good and tight so it doesn't fly off if you get to running."

Her feet ignored her command to walk away.

He snorted like the horse that he was, but she refused to raise her head and look at him.

He waited. Well, he could wait all day. She watched his boots. One moved as he shifted his weight, accompanied by a sharp brush against fabric. A pair of thick leather gloves appeared within her view, and he lifted her hat brim and looked her in the eye.

"These are for you."

She took the gloves, and before she could form words, he turned and walked out of the study, across the dining room carpet, into the kitchen, and out the back door.

Slumping into her grandfather's chair, she pulled the hat off her stinging ears.

"Thank you."

~

That evening at supper, Jody's dining room chair sat glaringly empty. Buck shoveled his food like he always did, and Whit ate quickly and left.

Livvy had stared at her plate during most of the meal—anything other than catching Whit's eye and blushing with anger or humiliation. A fine line ran between those two emotions at the best of times, and tonight the delineation was even narrower.

"You ready to leave early?" Pop studied her over the coffee-filled tea cup he held before his lips.

"Yes." She straightened, assuming her role as fellow cowhand and cook. "I'll have biscuits, coffee, and bacon ready for anyone who wants to eat before we leave."

Buck grinned at her, and Pop grunted.

"I also have food for us at midday."

Her grandfather nodded and placed the delicate cup on its saucer. "We're not taking the wagon, you know."

"I have a sack of food, and if everyone has a canteen, that will do." She laid her flatware across her plate and topped it with her napkin. "Do you have an extra canteen I could use?"

"Sure do. I'll bring it up from the barn along with mine to rinse out tonight." He looked at Buck. "You might want to do the same."

Buck nodded and wiped his mouth.

"Why don't you go to the barn and get 'em all right now?"

Buck glanced between Pop and the remaining sausages and potatoes on the serving platter, clearly struggling with his boss's request.

"Now."

"Yes, sir." Buck scooted from the table and lifted his plate. "I can take these to the kitchen if you'd like, Miss Livvy." He reached for the platter.

"Leave it."

At Pop's quick command, Buck snatched his hand back with a grimace.

"If there's any left when you get back with the canteens, you can have 'em."

Livvy prayed that Buck wouldn't toss her grandmother's china in the dishpan on his way out, and sighed in relief as the back door opened and closed without a preliminary clatter of plate against metal. Her shoulders relaxed and the day's activity and drama seeped from her arms, leaving her empty and tired.

Pop reached for her hand. "You'll do fine tomorrow, Livvy. I know you will. You've got Baker blood in you."

She drank in his confidence and affection. "Thanks, Pop. I won't let you down."

"I'm not worried about that." He patted her fingers with his other leathered hand. "But I want you to be safe. That's why I want you to ride Ranger."

Shocked, Livvy met her grandfather's solemn gaze. "But he's your horse, Pop."

"That he is, but he's a good, sure-footed mount, and that's what you'll be needing out there in the rough." He released her hand, folded his arms on the table, and leveled his steely eyes upon her.

"I know you and Whit sometimes have your squabbles. For a couple of preachers' kids, you fight like two polecats."

Polecats?

"He will show you exactly how things are done. Do what he tells you, watch for flying hooves, and you'll be fine."

Pop's eyes glistened and his mustache quirked. "Your grandmother would be proud."

"Did she ever work the roundup with you?"

A deep sigh threatened to cleave the dear man's chest. "Oh, yes. Our first year here, it was just the two of us roping and branding calves. Your mama helped too, the little sprite. Had her on the stamp iron. We didn't have that many cows back then, but it was a sight to behold, this old cowboy and his two female hands."

He chuckled and slapped both hands on the table as he pushed back. "Think I'll turn in. We've got a long day ahead with an early start."

Livvy stood and planted a kiss on his cheek. "If Buck doesn't hurry back, I'll save these potatoes for tomorrow morning."

The back door banged open and Livvy flinched.

Pop shook his head.

"Got the canteens here for you, Miss Livvy."

She gathered the dishes and joined Buck in the kitchen. "Thank you. Leave them on the counter there and find your fork. You can clean up the leftovers."

Buck grinned like she'd given him an entire pie and nearly had the remains of their meal cleaned off the platter before his backside hit the chair.

Livvy set the dishes in the pan, shaved in a soap curl, and added hot kettle water. Three canteens lay on the counter.

"You brought only three canteens, Buck. Didn't you want to fill yours?"

He swallowed his last mouthful. "Them's all there was. That one with the red stripe is mine. The other two must be your grandfather's and Whit's, unless Whit has one in his tack that I don't know about."

A tingling burn raced down Livvy's throat. How could she ask her grandfather to share his water? And she'd rather die of thirst than beg from Whit.

Tomorrow might be more difficult than she anticipated.

CHAPTER TEN

A faint glow edged the distant rimrock. Whit itched to scale its face and find the cougar he knew prowled there, but other work needed tending to.

The scent of pinion, juniper, and damp earth hung in the air, fallout from a brief rain that had settled the dust. Hidden birds twittered their pre-dawn songs.

Oro stamped a foot and tongued his bit, impatient to leave. Whit checked his cinch and stirrups, the oilcloth slicker he kept rolled behind the cantle, two ropes coiled and strapped on the right side of the saddle, a full canteen on the other.

He repeated the routine for a sleek bay mare and Baker's stout little gray gelding, Ranger. The man insisted that Livvy ride the gray. Whit shortened both stirrup straps a notch. Instead of a rope, the leather thong on her saddle snugged an old flour sack—Livvy's provisions for their midday meal. Her efforts dulled the irritation that chafed like a splinter under his chaps. But only slightly.

Buck should be checking his own mount, but he was probably still filling himself full of Livvy's bacon and biscuits.

The kitchen door opened, and pale yellow light spilled across the yard. Baker walked out followed by a slight-built boy. Had Jody Perkins wised up and returned in the night? His bunk was empty this morning. Maybe he'd sneaked in before breakfast.

Anger churned in Whit's belly as the pair moved toward the hitching rail. Baker loosed the reins holding the bay and pulled himself into the saddle, stiff leg and all. The boy walked around to Ranger's left side, gathered the reins, and swung himself up with surprising grace. The move drew Whit's closer scrutiny. *Livvy.*

He should have recognized the hat.

Stifling a comment, he watched her set her booted feet in the stirrups. From his position on the ground, he could clearly see her eager eyes, her lips slightly parted as she settled in the seat, tested the stirrups. Her hair must be piled inside that toadstool she wore or else she'd whacked it off since last night.

She caught him with a shadowed look. "Just right. Thank you."

He jerked a nod and turned away.

"And for the gloves."

He stopped and spoke to his shoulder. "You're welcome."

He stepped up on Oro, waited for Buck to join them with the irons, and then turned his back on the sunrise and headed toward the mountain. They'd ride to the top and work their way down. If everything went as he hoped, they'd be done in three days.

Dawn lit the top of Eight Mile and melted down the sides and into the grassland like warm butter. Whit led the small party halfway up the rough side of the mountain toward a park where he expected to find a good number of cow-calf pairs. He looked back to find Baker and Livvy holding their own. Buck brought up the rear.

An hour later, at the edge of a long low saddle, Whit rode through a thick timber stand and broke into a wide clearing. A flat park spread before them, eighty or ninety acres. More than fifty cows grazed with their calves beside them.

If he had enough men, he'd set up a bunch ground, build a fire, and brand the calves up here. But it would take at least one other hand to hold the herd together while he roped and the others held them down and branded. He could hog tie them, but those little critters'd kick the bottom out of daylight, and if one of the mamas got on the hook, somebody would get hurt.

Baker had insisted that Livvy brand, but Whit insisted she do it in a corral. He pulled up and whirled Oro to face his scraggly crew.

"Buck, you take the left. Mr. Baker, you go with him, and Livvy and I will take the right. We'll ease 'em out into the middle and drive 'em nice and slow through this break in the timber. Don't let them get off in the trees. Any runaways on your side, Buck, you take 'em. I'll take any on mine. We'll push them all down into the upper corrals."

He looked at each person, waiting for agreement. Baker nodded and tugged his hat brim. Buck grinned and spun his horse around. Livvy swallowed and set her jaw.

Whit screwed his hat down and nudged Oro into an easy lope.

He skirted the park, drawing uplifted looks from a dozen cows that switched their tails and called their calves. Three maverick two-year-olds tossed their heads and broke from the herd. Buck better let 'em be. They didn't need a rodeo out here on the back of the mountain. He and Buck could always find those big fellas come fall, and if they didn't carry a brand, they'd build a fire and use the rings on 'em.

Oro's strong rhythmic gait and the sense of being part of something bigger welled inside him. How could any other job replace this? He'd die if he had to work in a store or bank or anywhere but in this open country on the back of a good horse.

A quick check ensured that Livvy was a length behind, the gray keeping pace with Oro but no lust in its eye to race. Guess ol' Baker knew what he was doing putting his granddaughter on a horse that wasn't out to take the leader. He prayed she had as much sense as her mount. Otherwise, they'd all be in for a Wyoming rodeo whether he wanted one or not.

He reined in until she came alongside, then they slowed to a walk. "When we get behind them, we'll push 'em easy toward that gap we just came through. I'll ride a little ahead of you in case any try to break out through the trees."

Livvy met his gaze and nodded, her mouth clamped tight. No smile, no words, all business. But her eyes betrayed her excitement and burned like blue embers.

How could he get her to look at him like that when riding wasn't involved?

He motioned her on. Heels to the gray, she loped ahead. A horsewoman for certain in her grandmother's denims. No daylight showed beneath—well, no daylight showed where it shouldn't.

~

It just kept getting better.

Livvy tried not to lean into the wind of the ride, tried not to encourage Pop's cowpony to pick up speed, but she couldn't help it. Life surged through her veins on the beat of the gray's hooves and the scent of grass and pine and cattle. Had she died and gone to heaven?

Longing to pull off her hat and let her hair whip free, she laughed aloud and the sound fell away with visions of Whit Hutton set back on his heels. She laughed again.

He resented her presence and she resented him for resenting her. How was that for a tune? She'd show him how much horsewoman she was. She'd show him that Pop's faith was not ill put.

The cattle began to bunch and move as a herd, away from her and toward the opening in the timber.

She pulled up when she reached the end of the park, turned to face them, and leaned down to rub the gray's neck.

"You're a good one, Ranger. Good and even tempered and truehearted. Unlike a certain cowboy I could mention."

Scanning the park for Whit, she found him where he said he'd be—riding flank, slowly pushing the herd toward the break. To her right, Pop and Buck were doing the same. If they kept out of the trees, they might make the corrals by mid-day.

The sun was not yet straight overhead, but it threw heat like a hot skillet. She was grateful for the hat, regardless of Whit's mockery. The gloves he'd given her snugged against her back, tucked in her waistband, and she admitted he wasn't all bad. Just bad enough to keep her guessing.

She'd never been so hot and cold over anyone in all her life. Well, not really hot and cold, more like hot and cool. Cold had never applied where Whit Hutton was concerned, and life would no doubt be easier if it had. He could set her blood to boiling with his arrogance and her heart to purring with his tenderness. What a maddening man.

Her eyes wandered to Pop riding easy on the bay mare, his gray hat pulled low. He looked like any cowboy trailing a herd, not a man well up in years with a bad leg. What had he been like when he first met Mama Ruth? A striking cattleman who filled the young Englishwoman with spit and fire the way Whit did Livvy?

More laughter bubbled up. Her gentle mother would cringe at such an unladylike phrase as spit and fire, in spite of her ranching heritage. She rode as well as any man and had been doing so long before Robert Hartman turned her head one Sunday morning in Cañon City. At sixteen, she'd recognized the man of her heart behind that pulpit. Why, Whit's father had married the two of them in an odd ceremony with three brides and three grooms, a feat not since repeated.

With the deep pull of a strong current, Livvy realized that her connection to Whit—if she dared call it that—went back to before she was born.

A holler drew her attention to the right. Buck leaned forward and kicked his horse into the trees, slapping his coiled rope against his chaps as he followed a cow into the timber. No wonder Whit had warned them all. In a moment Buck had vanished, swallowed by the thick woods.

Lord, don't let him hit a tree or a low-hanging branch.

Pop loped toward the leaders. Whit held his side, and Livvy tightened her hands on the reins. A little bit farther and they'd be through to the other side and headed downslope toward the corrals.

The opening narrowed at the end, not far from where Buck and the cow came crashing through the underbrush. Several cows turned their heads toward the noise, and suddenly the stray and her calf broke through the timber ahead of the herd with Buck hard on her tail. With a smooth, even motion, he built a loop, swung it above his head, and dropped it around the cow's horns. He turned his horse and dallied the rope around his saddle horn, jerking the cow around. The calf followed, its tongue hanging out from the hard run.

At an easy trot, Buck led the runaway toward the open corral gate, and in no time the others followed her through in a lowing stream of mottled brown and white and black. Pop and Whit rode in with them, and Livvy shut the gate behind the milling herd.

Buck ran his cow up against the fence, threw slack into his rope, and popped the loop off her head. Then he opened another gate as Whit cut several calves from the herd. Buck and Pop steered them into the next pen. Livvy rode around the outside. After twenty calves funneled into the second pen, Whit shut the middle gate.

Buck started a fire and laid in the irons. Livvy looped Ranger's reins around a corral pole and waved her arms.

Whit rode over.

"We can eat while the fire's building."

He looked at Buck and back to Livvy, nodded curtly and dismounted, draping his reins on the top pole. Pop did the same, and all three men squeezed between the poles to the outside.

Livvy took down her bag and set it on a rock a little ways from the corral. Using the sack as a tablecloth, she laid out the sliced bread and beef, a smaller bag of ginger cookies, and what biscuits were left from breakfast. Pop leaned against the rock, and Buck and Whit squatted nearby.

Pop removed his hat, sleeved his brow, and bowed his head.

"Thank you, Lord, for Your good help and this food. Amen."

Livvy smiled to herself. Pop had always been short on words, but he was long on heart. Certain that everyone had enough to eat, she stacked bread and beef and made quick work of it. Amazed at how hungry she was, she ate two cookies before remembering she had no water.

"Thank you, Livvy." Pop laid a hand on her shoulder. "That hit the spot."

Buck lifted his hat and grinned. "Thank you, ma'am. 'Specially for them cookies."

Whit straightened. "You ready to get started?"

Ungrateful beast. "As soon as I clean up here." She stashed what little was left over, tied it on her saddle, and glanced around, not finding what she wanted.

The men had returned to the corral, and Whit was already mounted, swinging his rope at a mottled calf.

She squeezed through the poles into the corral, then pulled on the leather gloves. They fit perfectly.

Of course they did. She held her hands out, inspecting the back and palm, the way the gloves were worn in places and already curved perfectly to each finger. As if made for her. Where would Whit get something like this if they hadn't been his when he was younger and smaller?

Grimacing at the irony, she reset her hat. In order to follow her heart and be herself, she had to don the trappings of others—her grandmother's britches, Pop's hat, and Whit's gloves.

The calf bawled when Whit's loop snagged its back legs and he dragged it to the fire. Her grandfather hop-skipped to the calf and pinned it to the ground with one knee, his stiff leg sticking out to the side.

Whit dallied and stepped off Oro, who stood stock still, keeping the rope taut. He grabbed an iron, returned to the squalling calf, and pressed the hot brand to its right hip. Hair sizzled and white smoke billowed around Whit, obscuring him in its cloud.

He stepped back and looked at Livvy. "That's how it's done. You up to it?"

She took the iron, walked to the fire, and shoved it in the glowing coals. Whit swung to the saddle and signaled Oro forward, loosening the rope so Pop could let the calf up. It bawled and raced to a corner with the others.

Whit built another loop, and dropped it beneath a second calf that stepped right in. The process repeated, and Livvy prepared for the next victim.

No—not victim. This was their livelihood, their very food for the table and the tables of miners in mountain camps and people in Cañon City and elsewhere. This was life, and she chose to partake.

Buck handed her the hot iron. He should be holding the calves, not Pop, but she suspected her grandfather's pride had played into the arrangement. Whit watched her, eyes squinted, expression grim. Taking a deep breath, she stepped to the calf, turned the iron so the Bar-HB was upright, and pressed it into the calf's right hip.

Instantly the hair singed and curled away to cinders. White smoke swirled, heavy with the smell of scorched hide. She coughed but held the iron firmly.

"Good," Whit shouted.

She lifted the iron and stepped back.

"You don't need to cook 'em." A crooked grin flashed briefly as he loosened his dally. Pop let the calf up.

Whit coiled his rope and built a loop for the next one. "Well, don't just stand there. Get the iron hot."

She gritted her teeth. What had she expected? A pat on the back?

Her throat screamed for water, and she looked at the remaining calves huddled in the corner, wondering if they were as parched as she.

CHAPTER ELEVEN

Whit had to concede that Olivia Hartman could brand with the best of 'em. Had to be the Baker blood in her.

A part of him was proud. The other part snarled, but he was careful not to let her hear, or she'd be after his hide with that hot iron.

The next calf was a bull, and Buck stepped in to hold a leg. Pop straddled the calf, pulled out his stock knife, and with a quick grab and slice turned the little fella's mind toward grass rather than heifers. Whit glanced at Livvy who stood gaping, horrified. Obviously, she hadn't seen the cuttin' side of branding.

"Run and grab that cookie sack and bring it over. We'll have calf fries tonight," Whit said.

She stood motionless, staring as if she were deaf.

"Go on, Livvy." Baker motioned toward her horse. "We can't hold him all day."

At her grandfather's word, she squeezed through the pole corral and returned with the small sack. Baker took it, dropped the tenders inside, and snugged the mouth of the sack in his waist. By then Buck had the iron hot, and Livvy laid the Bar-HB against the bawling animal's hip.

She had grit, he'd give her that.

By day's end, they'd branded sixty calves and had enough fries for a feast tonight. Whit chose to let Baker explain to his granddaughter how to cook them.

While Buck kicked out the fire, Whit opened the inside gate and let the calves return to their mothers. Pop was back on his horse and rode through the herd to open the outside gate. With little encouragement, the lead cow saw her opportunity and dashed through. The others followed.

The taint of singed hair and hide hung in the air, and deep satisfaction coursed through Whit's veins. A good day. With what he and the Perkins' brothers had accomplished earlier, they were more than a third of the way through the stock. If the cattle hadn't scattered too far, they might have this done in three days after all.

Whit brought up the rear on the ride home. From the way Baker and Livvy sat their horses, it looked like they'd nearly worn themselves out. Baker worried him more with his bum leg than Livvy did. She'd held her own. But Baker's leg might not last. He should take the fire and let Buck work the calves.

Livvy rode a few yards ahead and a sudden coughing fit drew her up.

Whit leaned forward, setting Oro to a trot. He reined in beside her and looked for her canteen. She didn't have one.

He unlashed his own and held it out.

She scowled over the hand across her mouth.

Had she gone loco? "Here, take a drink." He pushed the canteen toward her chest. With a final stabbing glare, she took it, removed the top, and drank like a drunkard.

"Did you really think you could go all day and breathe all that smoke and not need water?"

She coughed again and wiped her mouth on her sleeve, avoiding his eyes. "I don't have a canteen."

Confounded woman. "Why didn't you say something?"

She stared straight ahead.

"You can have that one."

She held it out to him. "Thank you, but no thank you."

He kicked his horse too hard and Oro lunged ahead in a hard trot, then settled to an easy lope. As he passed Baker, a few choice words from his boss's colorful vocabulary jumped to mind.

Rather than voice his frustration at female wrangling, he pulled up next to Buck, whose horse marched against a tight rein. "I'm glad you didn't try to chase down those mavericks up there today. We can get 'em later."

Buck's mount had the home pastures in his nose and was in a hurry to get there. "I figured as much." He checked the reins and the horse slowed. They rode a ways in silence before Buck shared his thoughts.

"She did all right, didn't she?"

Whit slid a sideways glance at the boy. "Yeah, she did all right. But she nearly choked to death on the smoke."

Buck scrubbed his hand over his face.

"What?" Whit knew that nervous gesture.

"We didn't have enough canteens. When Baker had me bring 'em in last night, I could only find three. Why didn't she say something to the boss?"

"Why does a woman do anything she does?"

Buck guffawed and Whit threw him a warning glare. "She can have mine. I've got one in the bunkhouse."

"I figured Baker'd have a couple extra."

"Did you ask him?"

Buck rubbed his face again. "No, sir. Didn't see him after supper and I didn't think about it this morning."

"She's got one now."

Whit heeled Oro ahead and they loped down the final slope onto the bottom pasture. The sun slanted low across the valley and washed the house and barns in a long yellow light. Gray clouds bunched above the rimrock beyond, and a distant rumble echoed off the mountains to the north. There'd come a rain tonight.

Crossing Wilson Creek, he noted it ran wider than two days ago, swollen with summer storms. More than a light rain tonight could spell trouble. They didn't need a flood spreading out and running in close to the buildings. He looked again at the bunching clouds as another roll of thunder grumbled louder. Closer.

A fickle woman, the weather.

Whit felt the sneer on his lips as he trotted into the yard and pulled up by the barn. Fickle didn't begin to describe Livvy. She was up to her old tricks again—fire and ice.

He unsaddled and brushed Oro, then turned him loose in the near pasture to roll and shake and feed on creek-watered grass. Buck rode in next, followed by Baker and Livvy. Whit headed for the bunkhouse. If he wasn't half starved, he'd skip supper. But the bulge in the bottom of the cookie bag made his mouth water. Hopefully, Livvy'd get it right.

To his great relief, she did.

She must have left beans in the oven all day because the pork-laced aroma wrapped around him when he stepped through the back door. Above it lay the crispy lure of calf fries sizzling on the stovetop. Livvy wore an apron over her denims and her loose hair fell down her back like a wild horse mane.

He'd marry that woman if she'd give him half a chance.

Disgusted, he stomped back out. Must be as barn-soured as Buck's horse, having such thoughts. He scrubbed his hands and arms for the second time and splashed cold water on his face and head, then combed his fingers through his hair and met Buck at the door.

"You'd better wash up if you don't want a tongue lashin'."

Buck grinned.

Whit swore it was the only reaction the boy had, regardless of the situation.

Livvy laid the work table in the kitchen for supper, too tired for the dining room's formality. She doubted Pop would mind. After he'd told her how to cook the calf fries, he'd retired to his room, where his boots had thumped to the floor and the bed squeaked.

Poor man. If he were half as sore and worn as she, he'd be needing his liniment tonight. She checked the corner cabinet to make sure they had enough, intending to borrow a little herself.

Grudgingly, she admitted that what she was frying in the big skillet smelled enticingly good, if only she could banish the knowledge of their origin. When Buck and Whit finally showed up, Buck wore his usual mindless grin and Whit looked about ready to drool.

Men. It didn't take much to please them when they were tired and hungry.

Her heart turned at the thought, and sadness knifed beneath it. How pleasant it would have been to ride beside Whit today if he hadn't been so certain she couldn't pull her own weight. Well, she had shown him.

And what had he shown her?

Kindness. The knife twisted. He'd noticed her coughing fit and offered to share his water. Insisted, in fact. She scooped more beans onto his plate and topped them with several fries.

As she set the plate before him, and one each for Buck and Pop, Buck's eyes darted between his helping and Whit's, and a rare frown wrinkled his boyish brow. Heat rushed up Livvy's neck at the obvious favoritism she'd shown, and leaving her own plate on the table, she quickly turned away.

"You men go ahead. I'll get Pop."

"I think she likes you better." Buck's hoarse whisper followed Livvy as she hurried through the dining room, and the flush climbed all the way into her cheeks. At least Whit couldn't see her.

Pop's muffled snore met her at the doorway to his room, and she regretted having to wake him. But if he rode again tomorrow, he'd need every morsel of food for strength. She'd make sure he had several eggs for breakfast.

"Pop?"

He groaned.

Fear took a lick at her heart, and she touched his shoulder. "Are you all right?"

"I'll be fine. Give me a minute to get my bearings." He sat up and swung his legs over the edge of the bed, flinching with the effort.

"Would you rather eat in here?"

An impatient hand waved her off. "No, girl, I'm not dyin'. I'm just stove-up." He pushed to his feet and softened his tone with a wink. "After supper you can find that liniment your grandmother always kept on hand. It'll do me some good tonight."

Livvy slipped an arm around his waist on pretense of affection, but as she'd hoped, he laid an arm across her shoulder and they walked together. As they reached the kitchen, he straightened and entered under his own power.

Did men ever grow old enough to not strut and preen?

Pop slid a chair out and dropped into it with a grunt. "Whit, you say the blessing tonight."

Buck's spoon stopped halfway to his mouth, and Whit coughed on a biscuit. Livvy swallowed her surprise and seated herself next to her grandfather.

Whit cleared his throat and glanced up as he bowed his head, catching Livvy's eyes before closing his.

"Thank You, Lord, for your help today, for keeping us all safe. And thank You for this bounty and the company we have in one another. Amen."

Did Whit count her as one of the company for which he was thankful?

Pop bit into a fry and followed it with a spoonful of beans. "Fine job, Livvy. Fine job. Aren't you going to try your own cooking?"

She stirred her beans, watching them swirl around the dish. "Maybe later." Looking these men in the eye was beyond her, knowing what they ate and relished as they did so.

Whit chuckled. Buck shoveled. Livvy prayed for someone to change the subject.

Pop obliged. "Buck, my leg is stiff as a stamp iron. Why don't you let me take over the fire tomorrow and you flank calves?"

Livvy bit the inside of her mouth to keep from thanking God out loud. She dared not insult the man's pride—or good judgment. Sighing, she relaxed her shoulders, and unrealized tension drained away. Thank God, indeed.

Whit nodded as he chewed, not at all inhibited by his full mouth. "Good call, sir." He traded his spoon for his coffee cup and took a swallow. "I'm thinkin' most of the cattle are up the northeast draw, over in the far park. That pole corral up there might hold forty, fifty head at a time, but we could drive 'em all down, let 'em graze and rotate 'em in."

No one commented. Too tired, Livvy supposed, and she wasn't about to say anything. Instead she savored the beans and biscuits and lamented the fact that she could not fall immediately into bed. Not with preparations for tomorrow's meal awaiting her after the men left.

"I agree." Pop wiped his mouth, downed his coffee, and pushed back from the table. "Get me that liniment, Livvy. I'm gonna turn in."

Bottle in hand and with a small piece of toweling, she fell in step behind him. "I'll help you."

"No." The curt hand wave stopped her. "You have enough to do tonight. We'll be leavin' tomorrow at the same time and needin' the same food as you brought today." He took the cloth and bottle. "See you all then."

At the dining room door, he paused and turned his head to the side. "Good job today. That includes you, Livvy."

Full of glory at her grandfather's remark, she watched him hobble through the dining room. At the fireplace he stopped, opened the gaudy French clock on the mantle and wound it, turning the key four times. The same as every other night, he tended Mama Ruth's favored timepiece.

Returning to the table, Livvy caught Whit's dark eyes above the cup he held to his lips. They took in her every move, from picking up her spoon to swallowing the rest of her beans whole. Why did he have to stare?

"I agree," he said.

She met his look head on, steeled by her grandfather's confidence. "About what?"

"Today." Both elbows rested on the table, the cup held aloft in his rough hands. "You did a good job."

The compliment shot holes in her defensiveness. She lowered her gaze, lifted a napkin to her mouth. "Thank you."

"Got any more beans?"

God bless Buck Perkins. In his typically awkward manner, he delivered her from what could have been an awkward moment.

"Of course." She ladled in an extra-large helping with no doubt in the boy's ability to finish it off.

Suddenly fatigued, she wilted beneath the ache in her back and legs and moaned inwardly at the thought of rising an hour earlier than they planned to leave so she could make biscuits and eggs and bacon.

Whit set his bowl in the dish pan, his gaze traveling the swath of hair that had fallen over her shoulder. He held her eyes for a long moment, then gave a quick nod of thanks.

Grabbing his hat on his way out, he jerked his chin at Buck. "Hurry up. We leave at daybreak."

Buck shoveled, scooted his chair, and sleeved his mouth nearly all at once.

Livvy shook her head at the boy's ability to be so effortlessly mannerless.

"Thank you, Miss Livvy." He handed her his dishes. "Mighty good."

A weary smile was all she could offer. Mighty good, indeed. And mighty tired, and mighty frustrated. She just didn't know which was mightiest.

CHAPTER TWELVE

On the third morning, the clock in Whit's head woke him to the tuneless racket of Buck snoring. Snorting was more like it. The kid gagged like a choking bull.

Their second day of branding had gone much like the first, and Whit hoped today was their last. In fact, he did more than hope—he prayed. The rain held off yesterday, but he'd smelled it on the breeze last night, and didn't want to get caught in a late storm today.

He pulled on his pants and boots, knotted his bandana and tucked in his shirt. A hard kick to Perkins's bunk shut off the noise. "Get up. Daylight's burnin'."

Wasn't burning, wasn't even smoldering, but it would be before the kid made it to the kitchen. They had farther to ride today and needed a fast start.

He gathered their horses, saddled them, and checked hooves, then led them to the hitching rail behind the house. Through the kitchen window he watched Livvy at the stove doing what she did best. One of many things, he grudgingly admitted. She was definitely full of skill and surprises. Maybe he'd get a few moments alone with her before Baker and Buck showed up.

But he'd not be apologizing for his earlier behavior. He was justified in his concern for his men, for the cattle. For her. They were all his responsibility. Hauling a woman in to do a man's job was not. Lucky for her it had turned out all right.

Lucky for him.

He pulled his hat off, stepped through the back door and into the warm yellow light.

She looked up from the stove, a pleased expression tilting her mouth in a pink curve. "Good morning."

"Mornin'." So far so good. He straddled a chair.

"Coffee?" She brought the pot and two mugs to the table, set one before him, and filled it near to the brim.

He nodded his thanks and took the cup in both hands, then pulled the steamy brew through his lips. Not many things better in a man's life than strong coffee from a beautiful woman first thing in the morning. He could get used to this.

She filled the other cup and sat down, catching his glance at the stove.

"Don't worry. Breakfast is ready. I'm waiting for everyone to show up so we can all eat at once rather than in shifts."

She had pulled her long hair back into a single plait, oddly disappointing him. "Your grandfather not up?"

She sipped. "He's up, but moving slow."

A faint trace of liniment mingled with the coffee's strong aroma. He leaned toward her and sniffed. "Did you rub him down?"

She blushed like the sky at dawn and hid behind her mug. Two laughing eyes peered over the top. "I was a little sore myself after two days, so when he fell asleep last night, I stole in and borrowed the bottle."

Another surprise. He chuckled at her admission. "I guess you might be. How long has it been since you rode?"

"It's been a while. There was no riding on our last visit for Mama Ruth's funeral."

The memory stripped the smile from her eyes, and he longed to bring the light back, tip her mouth in that pink curve again.

Baker walked in with a more pronounced limp as Buck came through the back door. Whit looked at his crew gathering around the table and prayed again. This time for a miracle. They'd need it if they were going to get the rest of the calves branded today and not get someone busted up.

Pop gave thanks and Livvy served bacon, biscuits with white gravy and eggs, and kept everyone's coffee hot and full. She ate standing at the counter as she packed her larder bag and filled the canteen Whit had given her. Good thing he saw her—he'd forgotten to fill his own.

"I'll be right back and then we'll leave." He took his dishes to the sink, gave Livvy what he hoped she'd consider a friendly smile, and beat it out the back door.

When he returned to the house, everyone was mounted. He filled the canteen at the outside pump and draped it over his saddle horn.

Oro rumbled deep in his chest and pawed the ground. "Enough." Whit slapped him good-naturedly on the chest, slipped the reins from the rail, and swung into the saddle. Buck carried the irons, Livvy had her bag, and everyone had a canteen. He turned Oro toward the east.

Dawn peeked above the rimrock, flattened by a dark blanket seeping orange and pink along the edges. Not a good sign. He drew in a deep breath and with it the promise of a storm.

They rode toward the jagged rock wall, and he scanned its shadowed lip. Near the base they turned north to follow the draw around a low hill. From the rimrock, a scream split the air.

Another scream behind him, and he whirled to see Livvy with Ranger's reins pulled to her chest. The horse danced backward, bouncing its front feet off the ground.

"Let up!" He charged toward her and pulled up next to the rearing gray. "Let up on the reins!" Leaning out, he jerked her hands down toward the saddle horn.

As soon as the reins went slack, Ranger stopped dancing. Trembling, his eyes rolled white at the fear he'd picked up from his rider.

Breathless and pale, Livvy held Whit with frightened eyes, her fingers clutching the horn with an iron grip. Whit's doubts returned and dug in their spurs.

"Easy, now." He spoke low, reassuringly, as much to Livvy as to the horse.

Pop rode over and checked the gray's headstall. "He'll flip over backward if you yank on him like that."

"I—I know. It just startled me." Livvy's chest heaved on every word and her hands shook.

She released one hand and leaned down to pat Ranger's neck, then looked to Whit. "What was that?"

He laid his hand atop hers on the horn and gave it a light squeeze. "A lion. Up on the rimrock. But it's all right. She won't come down here."

"Why does she scream like that? Did she kill something?"

Whit withdrew his hand and looked at Pop, who rode off.

A lot of help he was. "She's lonely."

A bit more than lonely, more like calling a mate, but Whit wasn't about to get into that.

Livvy ducked her head. She'd figured it out.

Buck had ridden back at the commotion. "It's enough to curdle your blood for sure."

Livvy raised her chin and nudged Ranger ahead. "She caught me off guard, that's all."

And that was exactly how Whit felt—caught off guard by a woman out in the breaks where she didn't belong, nearly yanking her horse over backward. He had never believed in omens, not with his God-fearing folks. But the stormy dawn and cougar's cry didn't bode well for the day ahead. He tugged his hat down and loped to the front of their small string. If any other surprises awaited them, he wanted to take the brunt.

Livvy's insides quaked and she concentrated on appearing calm and in control of her emotions. She might be able to fool the men but not Ranger. His neck arched, his ears pricked, and his walk was more of a nervous trot. Truth be told, she wanted to wheel him and run as fast as she could back to the ranch house and hide beneath the quilts on her bed.

Lord, help her! The fright in Whit's eyes tore into her nearly as deep as the mountain lion's scream. Was he afraid *for* her or *because* of her?

The red horizon faded to pink and into a blinding white as the sun climbed above the low cloudbank. Daylight spread over the hills and dripped into the ravines and creek beds. Black birds and meadowlarks called to one another, and hawks screed above them. How could such beauty hide such chilling terror?

By midday they had driven the cattle down to a new pole corral and had half the cow-calf pairs inside. Whit refused to eat until they finished branding every single calf. Argument danced on the tip of Livvy's tongue, begging to spring to life, but she bit it back and followed his orders. It helped to believe his sharp words were aimed at the entire crew and not at her personally.

Only twice did she stop for water, and she noticed with satisfaction that the men took a break at the same time. Against Whit's wishes, she passed out two cookies to each man and quickly downed one herself. She worried more about Pop's strength than her own, and if Whit gave her any grief, that was exactly what she'd tell him.

The sun balanced on the western peaks as they loosed the last calf. Livvy pulled her gloves and hat off and sleeved her brow as she watched the youngsters run to their mamas seeking comfort for their burned backsides. She almost felt guilty. But cattle from several different spreads roamed the mountains and parks together, and ranchers had to keep them straight.

Before each calf was branded, Whit read the markings on the cow. If it didn't carry the Bar-HB, he'd holler out the brand and Buck would heat the rings. Livvy didn't know how to handle those things without singeing her gloves, so Buck burned in any neighbor's brand that matched the one on the calf's mama.

But most of what they'd gathered belonged to her grandfather, and at the moment, they all huddled at the east end of the corral. Something about their lowing gave her pause, the way they pressed hard against the far poles.

While Buck stomped out the fire, she considered the cattle outside the corral, also bunched and facing east with their rumps to the west. Over her shoulder black-bellied clouds spilled off a range in the north, and a deep rumble rolled across the park. A fat rain drop hit her arm.

The cattle knew.

Her grandfather opened the far gate and let the penned pairs out. They ran to join the others pressing toward the end of the park, away from the storm that seemed to be circling from north to west. Livvy shoved her hat on, tucked her gloves in her waist, and ran to the gray. Buck and Whit were already mounted and she joined them.

"Should we ride into the trees?"

Whit and Pop both shook their heads.

"No," Pop said.

"But we'd be out of the rain, a little more protected." It seemed the only logical thing to do.

"And asking to be fried." Whit pulled his hat down and turned toward the draw they'd ridden through earlier. "It's comin' a storm, and we don't want to be in the trees when the lightning hits. We'll find a bunch of low rocks and hunker down opposite the storm."

With that, he kicked Oro into a lope and the others followed. Livvy had no choice but to do the same.

A sharp rifle-like crack tossed Ranger's head nearly into Livvy's face, and a fiery bolt shot from the clouds. Thunder bounced off the mountain's shoulder and rolled across the park. Whit leaned low over Oro's neck and raced toward a granite outcropping.

As soon as their boots hit the ground, the sky ripped open. Livvy clutched the gray's reins and pressed up against the rocks.

"Let him go." Pop jerked his head toward Ranger. "If he spooks, he'll run home."

None of the men were holding their horses. Reluctantly, she tossed the leather straps over Ranger's neck and he trotted off, ears flat in the downpour.

Another crack and Livvy flinched. She slid down, pulled her knees to her chest, and tried to squeeze her entire body beneath her hat brim. Rain pounded her hat and arms and bounced off the ground.

Bounced?

Kernel-sized hail popped out of the grass and off the rocks like buckshot. It stung right through her clothing, but there was nothing she could do. For all her childhood experience in the saddle, she'd never ridden out a storm in the open.

Whit unlashed the yellow roll behind his saddle and ran to her. He shook the slicker and spread it out like wings, then squatted next to her, covering them both with the yellow shield.

His body warmth drew her, and she pressed close against him as hail pelted the oil cloth over their heads. Glancing up, even in their near-dark confines, she could make out his grin—that boy-like smirk with the ability to fan an angry fire or stir unquestionable longing.

Oh, Lord, help her.

As the storm raged, Whit's arm lowered until it rested on her shoulders, and even through her wet shirt his heat seeped into her. Rivulets formed around their feet and cut paths through the grass. Lightning hit close enough to strike with the thunder, leaving no gap between. Surely the horses would bolt and run, leaving them to slog home on foot in the dark.

The lion's earlier cry shivered through her, adding to the chill of her wet clothes. Whit pulled her closer and she didn't resist. She tugged off her soaked hat and his breath warmed her ear.

He didn't have far to lean. In fact, he didn't have to lean at all for his lips to brush her hair with a raspy moan.

Pounding hail drummed in her ears, or maybe it was her heartbeat. If she dared raise her face to him, she'd kiss him back. Right there beneath his slicker with Buck and her grandfather taking shelter Lord knew how close.

Oh, Lord—again—help!

As if in immediate answer to her plea, the rain stopped. Suddenly and completely. Livvy stilled and listened. Whit raised his right arm and looked out. It was over. He stood and shook out the slicker.

Livvy's legs screamed as she straightened, but she clamped her mouth tight. No complaining, especially not when her grandfather must have suffered terribly, hunkered down in the rain. She spun in a circle. Where was he?

He hobbled out from between two rocks, his hat a floppy mess. Buck looked as bad but without the limp, and he trotted off to gather the horses that had wandered into a shimmering aspen grove. So much for being struck by lightning in the trees.

No birds sang, no cattle lowed, only the drip, drip, dripping of rain-drenched trees. The storm thinned away from the western ridge, riding an unseen current toward the lower hills and eventually the plains. All that remained of the sun was its fading trail.

They had little time to ride home before full dark.

Buck brought Ranger around, and Livvy hauled herself up. She may have never heard a mountain lion scream when she was a little girl, but the memory of what she'd been taught sent shivers up her back and into her hairline. Cougars were nocturnal beasts that preferred to do their hunting at a specific time of day.

The time of day-turned-night that was falling around them at that very moment.

CHAPTER THIRTEEN

Whit's chest thundered, and it had not one thing to do with hail or lightning.

She hadn't pulled away. Nor had she slapped him. But how would he look her in the eye now that she knew she'd tangled his spurs?

Livvy Hartman smelled sweeter than new grass on a spring morning. Even under that oil cloth after a full day's work.

He was in deep trouble.

Buck brought the horses round. Whit checked his cinch and retied his slicker. The sun had tucked tail and run, and there'd be no early moon. If they didn't want to let their horses lead them, they'd best be going.

Baker looked like he'd been rode hard. In fact, he had. They all had, and on empty stomachs, not that Livvy hadn't tried to wrangle Whit into lettin' everybody eat. Keep their strength up, she'd said. Good thing he hadn't given in. They could have been caught in the corral with a bunch of spooked cattle busting out, and had to come back tomorrow and chase 'em all down again.

As it was, his tally showed they'd branded most all the new calves. 'Course there'd always be more through the year, what with the bulls ranging wherever they pleased. But he'd keep everyone close tomorrow, stay to home. The few head they might have missed could wait until Jody got back.

If Jody got back.

But Baker, at least, needed the rest. If the old man took sick and died, Whit would blame himself the rest of his days.

Buck rode up, wet as a duck.

"You still have both irons and the rings?" Whit said.

The boy nodded and slapped his saddle. "Right here where I tied 'em."

Baker walked his bay in closer, and his hat flopped over his eyes. He lifted it with a finger and revealed a dripping mustache. "What are we waitin' on?"

Whit choked down a chuckle and reined Oro around.

Thanks to his slicker, Livvy had fared better than her grandfather and Buck. His mouth lifted with pleasure at the memory of her tucked beneath his arm—and her soft yellow hair against his lips. He pulled his hat down, hoping to block her scrutiny. No sense having her think he was laughing at her.

But it wasn't laughter that hitched his hopes for Olivia Hartman. It was anything but. He squeezed Oro into a lope and headed through the draw on the last thread of light.

By the time they reached the ranch house, the clouds had scattered and stars washed the sky to near daylight. Whit reined in, prompting Baker and Livvy to do the same. "Buck and I will take the horses."

Baker angled a resentful glare his way, but stepped down and handed Whit the reins.

"I can unsaddle my own horse." Livvy bowed up like she always did when her independence was threatened.

"I know you can." Whit scowled, put gravel in his voice. "But I don't cook so good, and I figure everyone is hungry."

"Well, if you had let us stop and—"

The scowl must have done the trick, for she caught her words in her teeth and clamped her mouth shut. She stepped off, untied the soaked larder sack, and went to the house.

About time she did something his way without an argument.

Wet leather. Wet saddle blankets. Wet clothes, and none too warm. Whit nursed memories of the Saturday night baths he'd grumbled over as a kid. What he wouldn't give to soak in a tub of hot water tonight.

He and Buck laid out the tack, turned the horses into the near pasture, and slopped through mud to the bunkhouse, where they changed into dry clothes for supper. After that downpour, at least their bodies were clean.

When they stepped into the kitchen, the aroma of fried potatoes, bacon, and beans hit Whit in the gut. Livvy wore her blue dress and apron but stood at the stove in her stocking feet. She caught the question on his face and grinned like Buck.

"Pop built a fire and we put our boots on the hearth. Why don't you two do the same? Socks too, if you don't mind eating barefoot."

Whit wasn't so sure he wanted to smell Buck's wool socks heating up while he ate. But dry boots sounded too good to turn down.

Baker sat in an overstuffed chair by the dining room fireplace, his stockinged feet crossed before him on the fancy carpet. Buck dropped to the floor and started yanking on his boots. Whit returned to the back door, where he knew a bootjack waited. Two smooth pulls, and he carried his sodden boots to the hearth. He'd grease them tomorrow, help keep them drier the next time he got caught in the rain.

"Supper's on." Livvy set the beans on the dining table, and Whit noted the fancy china plates and cups, spoons and knives already set in place. He shook his head. Didn't take her long to get them all feeling at home.

She returned with the coffee. "Well, are you going to eat or sit by the fire?" She filled each cup and set the pot on a thick cloth.

Pop grunted as he shoved out of his chair and moved to the head of the table like an old bull favoring a new injury.

Buck was a two-year-old coming into his own, rangy and full of himself. Livvy shone like a yellow filly with her hair hanging down her back, still damp from the rain. Whit—he just wanted to wrap his hands in that mane and hold on tight.

He coughed to clear his throat and head and took his place to Baker's right, catching the man's quick nod indicating an order for Whit to say grace. Guess it naturally fell to him as a preacher's son. Baker had been calling on him to do so more often.

"Lord, You are mighty good to us. Thank You again for keeping us all safe in the storm. Give us strength from this good meal. Amen."

"Amen" echoed round the table, and Livvy served heaping helpings of beans and bacon and biscuits. Happiness hovered over her like a plum tree in full bloom, and she had a smile for each man as she set his plate before him. She served Whit last and her cheeks pinked as she glanced at him.

"Thank you." Whit shoved his longing down to his damp socks and turned his attention to the full plate.

"We goin' back tomorrow?" Buck tossed the question out between two bites.

"No." Whit took control before Baker could intervene. "My tally book says we're near done with only a handful left to check. We can finish when Jody gets back. I figure we all need to rest tomorrow, but there's plenty to do if you're lookin' to stay busy. Fence to mend and hay... Well, the hay has to dry out before we can cut it."

He slid a look at Baker, who worked on his food and kept his eyes down but not his voice.

"Buck, you mend the garden fence with that roll of wire I brought back from town. Whit can soap tack, fix what needs fixin' in the near pasture, and check on the widow Overton." He lifted his gaze to Livvy. "You need anything in town?"

She laid her spoon aside and dabbed her perfectly clean mouth with a napkin, but Baker spoke before she had a chance.

"Take the wagon in tomorrow and get what you need."

"We are nearly out of coffee and a few other things. And I'll get another bottle of liniment from Doc Mason."

"You know I have an account at Whitaker's."

She gave her grandfather a loving look that almost made Whit jealous.

"I can get the mail too." She picked up her coffee and held it before her as if debating a proposition. "If I leave enough food prepared, do you think you could get by without me for a day?"

A sound protest jumped into Whit's throat, ready to bust out of his mouth in a loud, "No!"

Baker leaned back against his chair and considered Livvy's request a moment. "And what takes a whole day in town?"

She set her cup easy in its saucer and dropped her hands to her lap. "I want to stop and see Martha Hutton." Her face flushed a bit but she pressed on, keeping her eyes fixed on her grandfather.

"When Whit and I were in town last, Mrs. Hutton said I could stop by any time. I'd like to take her up on that. For a visit."

Whit would go with her.

Baker smiled for the first time in several days. "I think that is a fine idea, Livvy. You need other women's company. Stay the night. I'd rather you not drive back alone near dark, and the three of us can hold this place together in the meantime."

But if Whit went with her ... *the three of us?*

Her smile ravished the fire's light and kindled anxiety in Whit's middle. Livvy gone? For an entire day and night?

~

Gratitude flooded Livvy's heart for her grandfather's generous understanding, but her thoughts raced at the sudden shock plastered across Whit's face. He'd blanched white as her apron and looked like he'd swallowed a boiled egg whole.

Surely it was his eyes she felt following her as she refilled coffee cups and cleared her dishes to the kitchen. She had to get away from his scrutiny. She had to *breathe*. The tension between them had somehow shifted, and it was—well—stifling. She prayed that her grandfather and Buck didn't pick up on it.

Of course Buck didn't pick up anything that didn't go into his mouth, so she was safe there.

But Pop was not easily duped. Not that she was sneaking around or doing anything she shouldn't. Her neck warmed at the memory of riding out the storm beneath Whit's slicker.

Too much heat, that's what it was. She opened the back window and let the night air rush in, cool and fresh after the storm. A hesitant moon edged above the rimrock, and she shuddered remembering the lion lurking there. Lonely, Whit had called it. That meant only one thing in the animal world. Her neck flamed again. Goodness—could she not think of anything without flaring like a wind-driven wildfire?

As much as she longed to fall across her bed, she needed work to keep her mind on more suitable thoughts. And she had plenty of it to do before leaving tomorrow. Another roast in the oven, fresh bread. She'd sweeten the deal by leaving Annie Hutton's apple butter on the kitchen table for the men to enjoy in her absence. A small price to pay for a day in town and a chance to visit with other women. *Hutton* women.

Oh dear.

She busied herself as the men filed out and off to bed, and she finally settled into the mundane chores that required little if any conscious thought—washing dishes and preparing food. An entire day with Annie and Marti Hutton held as much anticipation for her now as Christmas morning had as a child.

With the Dutch oven banked in coals, and bread dough rising on the counter, Livvy dragged herself to bed, too tired to pack but mentally going over what to gather in the morning. Her back and legs ached from the less than customary movements required in branding. She longed to soak in Mama Ruth's fancy copper tub, but Livvy was too tired to drag it out and wait for enough water to boil for even a tepid bath, much less a hot one. Her pitcher and basin would have to meet her needs.

In the morning she startled awake, only mildly surprised that she'd fallen asleep across her bed still wearing her house dress and apron. The mantle clock struck five. Daylight teased at her window and birds warbled out a welcome. She hurried to the kitchen, where she checked the roast, set water to boiling, and put three loaves of bread in the oven.

After her morning bathing ritual, she chose a fresh dress and buttoned on her Sunday shoes. Spending longer that usual on her hair, she coiled it tightly at the base of her neck and laid out her best bonnet.

The aroma of baking bread drew her back to the kitchen to thump the brown loaves with a finger. Perfect. She smiled, pleased with her culinary skills and aching only slightly from her recently acquired wrangling talents.

In her excitement she'd forgotten to gather eggs. She hurried to her room, where she changed shoes, then rushed outside with the basket on her arm. Thanks goodness Buck would be mending the garden fence. Deer had ravaged her radishes and kale—even nibbled the rhubarb. At least they'd left the herbs and lavender alone.

Did they eat columbines, those lovely purple flowers she'd first seen during the picnic lunch she'd packed for the crew? Her pulse quickened at the memory, and she ushered her wandering thoughts along to the henhouse.

A dozen eggs would feed the men this morning, and she left three beneath a brooding hen. She must mention the cross old thing at breakfast so whoever gathered eggs tomorrow would leave her be.

Ha! As if the men cared to gather eggs in Livvy's absence.

At the kitchen pump, she rinsed the eggs, then arranged them on a towel. The coffee began to boil and she moved the pot a bit and spooned bacon grease into the big skillet. Fresh bread and eggs and coffee should fill everyone. With a sudden change of heart, she whisked the apple butter off the table and hid it behind the egg basket. Let them find it after she left rather than finish it off first thing this morning.

When her grandfather shuffled through the dining room, she cracked the first eggs into the skillet.

"Smells mighty good in here." His mustache hitched as he came to the stove and reached for the coffee. "Like it did when your grandmother started the day with her fine cooking."

Again, Livvy's heart swelled at his compliment. She had come all this way to help, and she took pride in knowing that she had succeeded. Surely that kind of pride was not a sin. Even the woman in Proverbs 31 knew that her work was good.

He dropped a couple of coins in her apron pocket. "Give those to Doc Mason for Tad's care. And if the boy's up to it, bring him back with you and we'll get him home."

"That's very generous of you, Pop, but are you sure you will be all right today and this evening without me?"

His gray eyes twinkled as he sipped from a stoneware mug. "I will do just fine. But I won't hazard a guess where Whit is concerned. I dare say he might pine away while you're gone."

Livvy's sudden gasp brought a chuckle, and Pop made his way to the kitchen table, where he sat and extended his leg.

She turned to the eggs popping in the too-hot grease and pulled the skillet away.

"Don't be so surprised, Livvy, girl. That boy is already roped and snubbed. No other reason explains him spreading his slicker over you in a storm fit to drown a goose when he could have kept it for himself."

He knew. That meant Buck did too. Oh, Lord, help her. Heat leaped from the stove to her face, she was certain. If only she were not so fair skinned, she could ward off the annoying blush. Maybe if she didn't wear her bonnet today, let the sun burn her face on the way to town, she'd have an excuse for her constantly flaming cheeks.

"You could do worse, Livvy."

She stole a peek at her grandfather, who was watching her with a keen eye, as if measuring her reaction to his words. "He reminds me of myself when I was young and wanting my own spread. He's a good man—with the upbringing he's had, better than I was. You would do well to give him a chance."

Livvy flipped three eggs and broke the yoke in every one. There was no discussing such things with her grandfather even though she knew he loved her dearly. The ruined eggs went onto a plate for herself, and she broke three more into the skillet. She must get them right or she'd not have enough to feed the men.

Dare she tell Pop that his foreman had already turned her heart as well as her head?

Buck blustered through the backdoor, his perpetual grin beating him into the room. "Bess is all hitched and ready to go, Miss Livvy. The buckboard is out back here ready whenever you are."

Whit followed, apparently not nearly as pleased with Buck's news. He tossed his hat on a chair back and took a seat with as surly an attitude as Livvy had yet seen.

Biting the inside of her mouth, she squelched a laugh. He looked the same way he had as a boy when his mother made him sit out of a game. Well, she'd cut him more slack this morning, not laugh in his face. She wanted him to treat her with grown-up grace, so the least she could do was return the favor.

As Livvy expected, the men hate heartily and quietly, apparently enjoying the fruit of her labors. Deeply satisfied, she almost regretted leaving them to their own devises. Almost. A day and night with two bright, intelligent women outshone even the lilacs that bloomed round the ranch house.

Besides, they'd all be here when she returned—the lilacs.

And Whit.

CHAPTER FOURTEEN

If Buck didn't swallow that stupid grin, Whit would feed it to him fist first and tamp it down with a stamp iron.

Fine thoughts for a preacher's son.

He swigged the hot coffee, hoping to burn away the fact that Livvy was riding into town alone and was as happy about it as a sparrow at a wormhole.

Baker was in a chipper mood as well, which made it all worse somehow. Soaping tack was not the work Whit needed today. He needed bronc busting, maverick chasing, hard riding—something to wear him out and down to nothing.

He needed to drive Livvy to town himself.

And he'd have better luck skinning a live skunk than getting that idea past Baker. Whit ground his teeth and swallowed a growl.

She ate quicker than a coyote, swept everyone's plate away and into the sink, and left Buck with his mouth full and a fork in his hand. When she came back and snatched the fork, Baker laughed outright and shoved away from the table.

Livvy faced them all with her hands on her hips ready to shame each and every one of them. "Who will be gathering eggs tomorrow morning?"

Whit jerked a thumb at Buck, who couldn't speak for himself. "He will."

Baker hooted again.

"Buck, use this basket." She pushed it to the end of the counter. "And let that old red hen alone. She's setting, and we need some hatchlings this summer. Besides, she'll peck a hole in your hand if you try to rob her."

By the glint in her eye, Whit knew Livvy was toying with the boy, but Buck didn't. He nearly choked on the half of a biscuit in his mouth and quickly downed the last of his coffee.

"Yes, ma'am."

Livvy peeled soap into the dish pan and informed everyone and no one in particular that deer had gotten into the garden again last night. "If you all want any more greens—or rhubarb pie, for that matter—you'll be needing to fix the fence."

"Deer don't eat rhubarb." Whit's ma had told him that years ago. Said the leaves made them sick.

"Tell that to the deer." Livvy cast a blue light over her shoulder, and he nearly squinted in the brilliance.

He grabbed his hat and stormed out the door before he shamed himself by begging her not to go.

Infuriating woman.

Bess dozed in the traces, and Whit checked her riggings just to have something to do. He'd already greased the axils and made sure the wheels were sound. Livvy didn't need to break down between the ranch and town. She didn't need to ride off alone at all. Somehow, he had to get Baker to listen to reason.

And then the woman herself flew out the back door with her bonnet and satchel and a look in her eye that warned him not to get in her way. Like a green-broke colt.

"I'll be back by noon tomorrow." Livvy set her satchel in the back, hiked her skirt with one hand, and held out the other hand to Whit.

He took it and grasped her elbow as she climbed the wheel. She settled onto the seat, spread her skirt about her feet, and gathered the reins.

"Be careful." He swallowed the kiss he wanted to give her. "Don't let her run with you."

Livvy rewarded him with a true smile. She leaned over and laid her hand against his cheek. Quickly he covered it with his own, curling his fingers around it.

"I will be fine, Whitaker Hutton. You take care of my grandfather while I'm gone."

He turned his head and kissed her palm, heard the catch in her breath, and reluctantly released her hand. The bonnet hid her face, but when she flicked the reins she glanced his way, washing him in a blue gaze that set his insides afire.

"Giddyap, Bess."

Like a lost pup, he stood in the yard and watched her drive away. *Lord, keep her safe.*

The back door shut, and Whit turned as Baker lumbered over, hat in hand. He slapped it on his head, stopped a few paces off, and leveled a hard eye on Whit. "You thinkin' about puttin' your brand on her?"

Surprised by the bold question, Whit hesitated to tell the man he was in love with his granddaughter. But he was. That was the truth of the matter, and he might as well face the old bull head on.

He straightened his shoulders, stood square on both feet. "Yes, sir, I am."

Baker's silver mustache twitched at one end and he jerked his head in a sideways nod. "'Bout time." Then he hobbled off toward the barn.

If Whit's horse had talked to him, he could not have been more surprised. Those words constituted a blessing.

Joy split his insides and he could feel his face cracking in a Buck-grin. He wanted to whoop. He wanted to jump on Oro and catch up to Livvy and ask her to marry him and kiss her good and long right there on the wagon seat.

A sudden, sober thought punctured his dream, and he screwed his hat down and headed for the barn. A woman wanted her father's blessing as well. Whit couldn't take the time to ride to Denver and ask Reverend Hartman for his daughter's hand. Besides, what did he have to show for himself—a foreman's salary, a good horse, and a saddle. Not much for a young bride who deserved a whole lot more.

Suddenly the morning light glared harsh and unforgiving.

How would he ever get Olivia Hartman to be his bride?

~

Livvy's left hand burned as surely as those calves' hides. She turned it over, surprised to see no seared brand smoking in her white palm. Whit Hutton had kissed her hand. *Her hand!* Not like an English gentleman dips his head to a lady's gloved fingers. But ... intimately.

Shivers ran up her back, and she slapped Bess into a trot. If she had to take an easy walk the entire ten miles to town, she'd jump out of her skin.

What she wouldn't give for a moment with Mama Ruth. Her grandmother would know what it felt like to be swept away by a cowboy's charms.

A bouncing laugh escaped her throat as Bess clopped merrily along the ranch road. Her grade-school teacher would qualify "cowboy's charms" as an oxymoron. But Livvy knew better. The two words fit together like bacon and beans, and they came in the shape of one Whitaker Hutton.

The kiss wasn't his first tender overture. What of that day in the columbines? Or the huddled moments beneath the slicker in the hail storm. Even his roughly insistent offer of the gloves and canteen showed his protective nature. Somehow those small tokens had swept away every barb he'd ever thrown at her. She clucked her tongue and flicked the reins.

What might it feel like to really kiss him? Pushing her bonnet back, she let the sun do the kissing.

The sky spread strikingly blue above Fremont Peak and the lesser hills guarding the gorge where men fought over the right-of-way. She sobered at the thought of Tad and Jody getting mixed up in the so-called war. Whit would never do such a thing.

Doubt wiggled beneath her breastbone and she pressed a hand against it, forbidding it to spread. Whit was too level-headed, too smart to be caught in a foolish fight over a railway.

As she neared the bend that turned sharply along the river and into town, cottonwood trees waved a shimmering welcome. The Arkansas rushed along at their feet, shouting to be heard above Bess's hoof beats. Children played outside the hotel across the river, and couples strolled hand-in-hand across the foot bridge that dangled mere inches above the swollen river.

She drove by the massive stone wall of the territorial prison and passed carriages and lone horseback riders headed to the hot springs. Mules pulled by with freighters' heavy wagons bound for the mining camps. What would happen to those supply wagons and the men who drove them once the railroad won passage through the mountains to Leadville?

The number of people increased as she drove farther into town, but this time she sat proudly in her fine bonnet and Sunday shoes. Hers might not be the latest, most fashionable dress, and she had no parasol, but contentment spread through her clear to her fingertips and she sat a little straighter. What she *did* have was a pair of denim britches and the ability to hold her own with a branding iron. She doubted that any fine women she saw on the boardwalks could say as much.

At the church, she turned Bess into the lane and the mare quickened her pace for the secondary home and hay crib ahead. Livvy pulled into the yard behind the parsonage, where Whit's mother knelt weeding the columbines that edged the porch.

Annie stood and pressed her hands against her lower back, then shook out her skirt and greeted Livvy with a bright smile.

"Welcome!" She extended a hand as Livvy climbed down and then enfolded her in a gracious hug. "It's so good to see you again, and so soon."

Annie's brow knit together, and she stepped quickly aside to peek in the wagon. "Oh," she breathed. "I was afraid you had another wounded young man with you. This train war has gotten completely out of hand."

Livvy's shoulders relaxed at Annie's welcome. "No wounded men, only my satchel in case…" She hesitated and glanced at her shoes not knowing exactly how to phrase her request without begging or sounding presumptuous.

"Oh, by all means, you must stay the night." The woman's coppery eyes twinkled with comprehension, and the arm she linked through Livvy's confirmed her sincerity. "I can't tell you how much Marti and I will enjoy a good woman-to-woman visit."

"Thank you so much. I need a few supplies from the mercantile, and I'd hoped I wouldn't be an imposition."

"You must always think of us as an open home. Come in, come in."

Arm in arm they headed for the shady back porch, where Annie halted suddenly on the lowest step. "Did you come alone?"

Livvy hated to disappoint the woman, aware that Annie would love to see her only son. "Yes, I'm sorry. Whit is busy at the ranch."

Annie snorted—a most shocking reaction that Livvy surprisingly adored in this lovely woman.

"He is a man now and can't be chasing off to visit his mother."

Livvy's palm tingled with Whit's send-off. "I believe he wanted to come, but Pop won out. I think giving me a day to do as I please was his way of thanking me for my help with the branding."

Annie opened the door to the kitchen, a question rising. "You helped with the branding. You mean you cooked?"

Livvy untied her bonnet strings, laid the light cotton cover on the table, and settled into a chair. "Yes, I cooked, but I did that at the house. On the roundup I branded. I ran the iron, as they say."

Annie's head wagged as she pumped water into a tea kettle and set it on the stove. "My, but you do have pluck, young lady. It sounds like those men are working you to the bone."

"I loved it. Really. It was so exciting to ride again and help gather the cattle." She squelched the memory of her near wreck on Ranger.

"Surely you didn't do all that in a skirt?" The way Annie said it made Livvy want to snort herself.

"I wore my grandmother's denims."

Annie joined her at the table while the water heated. "That sounds absolutely wonderful. I am nearly jealous of your adventure."

The front door opened and someone entered through the parlor with a cheery "I'm home." Ruddy cheeked and exuding unbridled energy, Martha Hutton rushed into the kitchen with a stack of papers and books. She dropped them on the table and fell into a chair.

"Oh—Livvy. Did my beastly brother chase you off?"

"Marti!" Annie reddened at her spirited daughter's outburst.

"Oh, Mama, you know I'm only joking."

"Ladies do not joke, Martha Mae."

Livvy stifled a laugh and gave Marti a teasing frown. "You know, we will have to discuss that. Sometimes I could absolutely whack him with a carpet beater."

Marti leaned back in her chair and laughed remarkably like her brother.

Shaking her head, Annie rose to attend to the water and bring cups to the table.

After a lively visit, Annie went to the hen house with a young fryer in her sights. Livvy made herself useful by scrubbing and peeling potatoes for a salad, only too happy to be busy. Marti set half a dozen eggs in a small pot on the stove.

"You're going to think I'm terrible, but I hope Mother doesn't call me out to help her ring that chicken's neck. I can't stand to do that." The girl shuddered and her fiery red curls shook in agreement.

How would she ever survive on a ranch? Livvy glanced at the books on the table. "Are those papers last year's school studies?"

Marti brightened. "Oh, no." Swiping her hands down her white apron, she dried them front and back from the egg water that had splashed them. "These are library books and the papers are notes I took at Mr. Winton's museum this morning." She sat down at the table and spread out the papers.

"Really, it's just a curio shop next door to the saloon, but some people have recently been referring to Winton's collection as a museum. Two years ago he had an absolutely marvelous display there of fossils uncovered at the Finch ranch dig."

Livvy frowned. "A dig?"

"Yes, a paleontological dig." Marti's voice assumed a dignified tone as she enunciated the foreign-sounding word. "Our school superintendent has been excavating near Garden Park for quite some time and has uncovered the most amazing dinosaur bones."

Livvy's newspaper hat lining came to mind.

"Two years ago they hauled off five wagon loads of fossils all believed to have come from the same animal. Can you imagine anything so large?"

Marti's face fairly glowed as she shuffled through her notes.

"Where did the wagons go?"

The girl paused in her rearranging and looked at Livvy in scholarly surprise. "Why, to the Academy of Natural Sciences in Philadelphia, of course."

Of course.

A most unladylike huff followed. "Papa wants me to go to school to be a teacher, but I want to be a paleontologist. It sounds ever so much more exciting."

"Well, at least those animals would have no blood or feathers to contend with."

Marti burst out in that hearty Hutton laughter. "Oh, Livvy, you are so right!"

The back door opened and Annie stuck her head inside. "I need your help with the feathers, Marti. Bring a bowl we can drop them in for washing later."

If Marti had been a balloon, she could not have deflated any quicker or more completely. Casting a remorseful eye at Livvy, she rose and took a bowl from the sideboard with all the excitement of a funeral procession. "Coming, Mother."

Livvy adjusted the damper and set the potatoes on to cook. Martha's parents wanted her to be a school teacher. Livvy's wanted her to be a nurse. Did the Huttons want Whit to be a preacher like his father, or a storekeeper like his grandfather?

She let out a heavy sigh. No one asked *them* what they wanted to do with their lives.

With the eggs and potatoes cooking, Livvy dried her hands on a towel and poured herself more tea. At the table she added a heaping spoon of sugar from the double-handled bowl. Tarnished by daily use, the old silver relic boasted a dull patina rather than a shiny polished exterior. A well-used dinosaur.

Livvy assuaged her guilt at not volunteering to pluck feathers by setting the table for four and hunting down a jar of pickled cucumbers for the potato salad.

When Marti returned from her most dreaded chore, she washed her hands and arms at the sink and splashed water on her face.

"Would you like to go with me to the mercantile for supplies? We could even stop by the curio shop and you could show me Mr. Winton's bones."

The girl perked up immediately and yanked off her apron. "They're not Mr. Winton's bones. He's not even dead yet."

Livvy laughed. "Oh, where did you get your delightful sense of humor?" She set her half-finished tea on the counter and picked up her bonnet.

Marti ran upstairs and back down before Livvy made it out to the porch.

"I'm running errands with Livvy, Mama. Any messages for Grandma and Grandpa?"

Livvy watched Annie's face for disapproval of her daughter's quick escape but instead found the usual sparkle in her eyes. "Tell them I love them and to come for supper tomorrow."

Marti bounded into the wagon seat.

Annie's head wagged again. She dangled a quite naked and headless bird in one hand and pushed graying strays from her temple with the other. "I don't know what I'm going to do with that child." Sending an encouraging look Livvy's way, she continued. "Maybe your housekeeping and cooking sense will rub off on her. I dare say mine hasn't made much of an impact."

Livvy climbed up next to the girl and, with a parting wave, turned Bess down the short lane to Main Street.

Immediately, they were in the thick of things. Even her parents' home wasn't this close to the markets. But Denver was so much larger than Cañon City, a person couldn't live so near to downtown without taking a room above a store front or in a rooming house. Livvy shuddered. Living that close to so many people and so much noise? How could she ever?

Visions of purple columbines bobbed into her thoughts, whispering their secrets in the cool aspen shade. The palm of her left hand warmed around Bess's reins, and Livvy tried to measure which was softer—the mountain flower's delicate petals or a certain cowboy's kiss.

"You passed the mercantile."

Marti's voice jerked Livvy from her high-meadow musing and back to Cañon City.

"Yes." Daydreaming could land them at the opposite end of town. "We will come back after the museum."

"Oh, good." The girl straightened and pointed ahead on the right. "Just ahead in the next block, this side of the saloon."

Wonderful. Livvy was escorting the preacher's daughter into the neighborhood of the saloon. Lord help them.

CHAPTER FIFTEEN

Whit's imposed day of rest for everyone nearly drove him crazy. Without something to do, he'd be loco by noon and cutting wet hay wasn't his idea of a good distraction.

Two colts waited in the near pasture. He could run them into the corral at the barn and start working on them. His gut told him that wasn't a good idea either, not with the way his mind kept wandering off after Livvy and the buckboard.

But he'd lose it for sure soaping saddles, mending tack, or helping Buck repair the garden fence. He watched the boy wrestle with the new-fangled barbed wire that Baker wanted strung in a double row above the top rail. It clearly lived up to its name—the devil's rope—with those spiny points laced through it.

Whit hunted for Baker and found him in the barn resetting a shoe on Ranger. His boss let the horse's back left hoof slide off his leather apron and stood straight. Stooping over didn't seem to bother the man as long as he didn't have to bend his right leg.

"I'm riding up to Overtons'. See if she needs help with her chores."

Baker dropped his hammer in a small wooden box, unbuckled the apron, and hung it on a nail. "Tell her we'll come brand her calves in the next few days. See if she has irons. If not, I'm sure Buck can work out her brand with the rings."

Whit nodded and turned on his heel, not interested in conversation or in explaining his jittery condition to his steely-eyed boss. He saddled Oro, swung up, and struck out for the widow's, six miles west as the creek ran.

And the creek was more than runnin'. The usually clear stream gushed across the meadow. Muddy with mountain storm water, it swamped its banks like syrup on hotcakes. Oro pranced across, tucking his chin and twitching his ears at the chattering late-spring runoff. Yesterday's storm had hurried the high-country snowmelt and most likely set the Arkansas to churning.

Not any more than Whit's gut. That little catch in Livvy's breath when he'd kissed her hand had spurred his heartbeat as sure as any rowel could set a bronc to twisting. And she'd not jerked away. From the look on her face, she'd liked it. But that didn't solve his problem of getting her father's blessing and having something to show for his own worth.

He should have bought those cows when he was thinking about it instead of chewing on the matter. Three, four head even. Anything was better than nothing.

Whit rode over a draw in the near hills and paused to look down on the Overton place. The woman still lived in the tent her husband had put up, for an unfinished cabin slouched next to it. Another winter like that and she and her no-account son might freeze to death.

Whit took the trail down in plain view of the camp and waved his hat over his head hoping the widow would see the movement if she didn't hear him coming. He didn't need a startled woman peppering him and his horse with buckshot or bullets.

She stooped over a campfire tripod stirring something in an iron kettle. Supper, he supposed. Beans and a little pork wafted toward him. She set the spoon aside, returned the lid, and straightened. As he reined up next to the half-built cabin, Whit could easily see the worry lines creasing a face too young to look that old.

Would that happen to Livvy if she married him?

The thought cut him like a barb on Buck's new garden wire.

The widow pushed hair out of her face with the back of her hand. "Good morning, Whit. What brings you over?"

He stepped off Oro and dropped the reins, then removed his hat and walked to the fire. "Mornin', ma'am."

She handed him a tin cup of strong-smelling coffee. He nodded his thanks and sat on an upturned stump. She took one opposite, with the tripod between them, and cradled a similar cup. Even from a distance her hands revealed the rough, cracked skin of hard work.

"I've come to see if you need any help with your chores." He glanced around for some sign of what needed to be done.

The woman looked over her shoulder at the tent, then returned her attention to Whit. "We're doing all right. Tad's been getting stronger every day, but he's resting now. Takes it out of him in the mornings."

The tent flap pulled back and the boy stepped out, his arm in a sling and his hair dirty and wild like a mountain man's. Gaunt and weary, he lowered himself onto a stump, and his ma handed him her coffee.

Surprised to see Tad, a knot yanked into Whit's gut. The odds were against these two. Sure, he and Buck could finish the Overtons' cabin before winter, but would the widow and her boy get enough food stored up? Did they have warm clothes and enough ammunition to keep varmints away?

Did they have any money for supplies?

An old buckboard sat behind the tent, and two horses grazed a ways off.

"We're makin' out." The boy's defiant tone made Whit think otherwise.

"How many head do you have?" Whit swirled the thick coffee, watching it lap around the inside of the cup rather than catch the boy's eye and get his back up.

"Twenty cows," the widow said. "At least that's how many my husband bought." She looked down at her hands, and her hair fell across her tired eyes.

"You be interested in selling them?" Whit spooked himself with the question, wondering how it had fallen out of his mouth without so much as a serious consideration.

Mother and son exchanged a look, and she sat a little straighter, pushed her hair back again.

"You offering?" the boy asked.

Was he? Baker had tried to buy her out in early spring, but she'd refused. Had loneliness, back-breaking work, and her son's stupidity changed her mind? Whit made an offer—every last dollar he had in his bedroll.

The boy looked at his ma, and she jerked a nod.

"Done." Tad walked to Whit, sticking his left hand out in an offside handshake. "They're yours."

Whit stood and took the boy's hand but kept his eyes on Mrs. Overton. The cattle were more hers than her son's. The transaction was hers to make.

She looked at Whit. "You can have the land too, for a hundred more."

Whit didn't have a hundred more and wasn't sure he wanted the place. Things were gettin' outta hand. Helping with the Overtons' chores was a lot different than buying the whole kit and caboodle.

"I'll see what I can do." Again his gut knotted. He'd already done too much.

She sighed and a few worry lines slipped off her face. Whit looked again to make certain, and sure enough, she seemed ten years younger already. She almost smiled.

"We can be out tomorrow. Can you get the money by then?"

She didn't beat around the bush any more than Livvy.

"There's no hurry, ma'am. You can take your time. I might not be able to get back over here tomorrow."

Her shoulders slumped and she shrank before his eyes. Tad coughed and wiped his mouth on his dirty sleeve. "Doc Mason told me he needed a nurse, or someone who could help him with his patients. I told him Ma here was right good at fixin' people, and he said he'd think on it. We could sure use that job 'fore somebody beats us to it."

We? Us? Whit wanted to thrash the boy. "What will you be doing while your ma's working for the doctor? Taking pot shots at the railroad crew?"

Whit's conscience barely nipped him as a scowl curled Tad's brow into a dark snake. With a bold stare, Whit dared the boy to make something of the remark. He'd gladly give him the lickin' he needed.

"We'll be ready when you come with the money." Mrs. Overton stood, and Whit heard goodbye in the movement. He handed her his coffee cup and put on his hat.

But Tad wasn't finished.

"I ain't the only one worked on the rail lines." He smirked as if his information was valuable.

Whit took the bait. "Is that right? Someone from around here?" Suddenly Jody galloped through his thoughts.

"You missin' a hand over at Baker's spread?"

Whit stepped toward the boy. "You know something you should be tellin' me?"

The smirk held but Tad moved behind a stump. "Jody Perkins rode through here three days ago, first day I was back. Said he was gonna lay rail."

"Hush, Tad. You don't know if he really went to work for the railroad. He could have been full of bluster."

131

Tad snorted and hung the thumb of his good hand in his waist. "He's there. Makin' three dollars a day at it. A whole lot better'n punchin' cows."

Whit wanted to wipe the sneer off the boy's face, but he figured he'd have a she-bear on his back if he tried it. He shoved his hat down hard and gave Mrs. Overton a nod. "I'll be back tomorrow."

Curious, indeed. Livvy looked at the sign above the store as they left: *Winton's Curiosity Shop*. She had read about prehistoric creatures that once roamed the earth, had even seen drawings of their massive bones the size of a man. But to see an actual fossil right before her eyes was an experience she'd never dreamed of. In a small way, she understood Marti's fascination with the unusual and her rejection of the mundane.

Not that teaching children was mundane. It was honorable work for any woman. But studying fossils and discovering secrets of the past offered the mystique of the unknown.

Livvy drove Bess around the corner, two blocks east, and back to Main Street, where they stopped at the rail before Whitaker's Mercantile. Marti jumped down with a young boy's enthusiasm rather than a lady's grace and restraint. No wonder Annie Hutton had fits over her daughter.

The girl dashed through the door, setting the bell to singing as she raised her own melodic "Hel-lo-oh."

Livvy set the brake, looped the reins, and followed through the open door. The smells swept her back to childhood days of visiting her grandparents and stopping here for a sweet. And Mr. Whitaker looked the same, with his snowy hair and mustache and rosy Father Christmas cheeks. Marti greeted him with a kiss and a hug, then hurried to the back where her grandmother Martha ground fresh coffee beans. Arbuckle's,

Livvy guessed from the rich aroma. Mentally she added several pounds to her list.

Livvy held her hand out to Mr. Whitaker. "Good day, sir. How nice to see you again after so long."

He smothered her hand in both of his and cocked one white brow. "It's Daniel to you, young lady. Why, you're nearly kin, you know."

Feeling as much, she appreciated his welcome. "I feel the same, Daniel. Thank you." Withdrawing her hand, she turned to survey the goods and stopped at the sight of a bright flag hung on the store's back wall—new since her last visit. Thirty-eight white stars gleamed against a deep blue field, flanked on the right and below by white and red stripes.

"Is this the first time you've been down since Colorado earned statehood?"

Livvy tallied the years. "The first time I've been in the mercantile. The last time we came was for Mama Ruth's services, and we didn't stop in then."

A sudden sadness flickered in the man's eyes. "So sorry to lose her, dear. So sorry."

He came around the counter. "Well now, you must be here for supplies. I understand you are helping your grandfather Baker at the ranch."

"Yes." She felt in her skirt pocket for the list.

"Did Whit ride in with you?"

Against Livvy's deepest wishes, warmth raced up her neck and she turned away, suddenly interested in the nesting salt boxes against the opposite wall. "Not this time. He had too much work." She bit her lip at the near lie, assuring herself it was partially true.

A deep chuckle rumbled in the man's throat, and she suspected Daniel Whitaker saw through most of his customers' defenses. "I was hoping the boy would take over the store for

Martha and me, but he's set on cowboying. Gets that from his father, you know. He wasn't always a preacher."

Livvy did not know. That story had failed to make it to the dinner table. "No, I've not heard about Pastor Hutton's younger days." She faced the storekeeper hoping to hear more.

Instead, he held out his hand for her list.

She complied. "I will also have five pounds of that wonderful Arbuckle's I smell cooking."

"I married a mighty smart woman." He glanced at Martha and her namesake, their heads bent together over some intriguing topic. "We've sold more coffee since she keeps it going all day instead of only in the morning. People can't resist the smell."

Within an hour, Livvy had her flour and sugar, coffee and toweling, and a few other things not on her list that she knew her grandfather wouldn't mind. Daniel had the wagon loaded, and she stood at the counter as he wrote out her ticket.

"In a way, I'm glad Whit did not come to town with you."

Livvy caught his quick glance.

He pulled letters from her grandfather's mail slot, handed them to her, and lowered his voice. "There's going to be trouble over that railroad." Leaning over the counter, he dropped his voice to a whisper. "Santa Fe hired a Kansas sheriff to come head the fight and got the U.S. Marshall's office to pin a star on him."

Livvy blinked and held her breath.

"W. B. Masterson. Bat, they call him. A fast gun, I hear. He brought in his pal J. H. Holliday to gather a posse of sorts, and they're holed up at the roundhouse in Pueblo."

The hushed urgency in the man's voice chilled Livvy's blood no less than the mountain lion's scream. "Why are you telling me this?" The mail trembled in her hand, and Daniel enfolded it in his.

"I'm sorry, Livvy. I didn't mean to frighten you, but I know you are a praying gal. Both you and Whit were raised by godly parents, and you could not do any better than to pray that this so-called war comes to a halt."

His bushy brows locked together. "If it comes to a fight, it's not the wealthy train barons that will be catching lead. It's the young men from this community."

CHAPTER SIXTEEN

Whit opened the kitchen door and sucked back a hoot that nearly knocked him over. Baker stood at the stove flipping hotcakes, Livvy's apron tied high around his chest.

"Mornin'." A hearty cough mangled his greeting as he hung his hat on a chair.

Baker scowled over his shoulder. "Least you didn't say *good* mornin'." He poured a saucer-sized round of batter, then picked up the coffee pot, a bandana bunched on the handle.

Whit snagged a cup from the counter. "Thanks."

"Buck's pickin' eggs." Baker grunted as he flipped the hotcake over. "Livvy's got him plumb scared of that red hen."

Whit marveled at Livvy's ability to keep them all doing her bidding. And missing her like a pup missed its ma.

"What'd you learn at Overtons'?"

Whit swallowed a mouthful of coffee and flinched. A shade or two stouter than what Livvy cooked up. "The widow wants to sell."

Baker flopped the cake onto a stack next to the stove, shoved the griddle back, and took the plate to the table. "Grab the syrup."

Whit found a tin on the side board and, tucked into the corner, a jar of his ma's apple butter. He brought it too. Served Livvy right if they ate it all while she was gone, leaving them the way she had.

Feeling all of twelve years old, he set the jar and tin on the table and took a seat.

Baker forked three cakes onto his plate and reached for the apple butter. "How many head does she have?"

Confession was good for the soul, Whit's pa had always said. "None."

His boss looked up.

"I bought every blasted one, sight unseen." Whit slumped beneath the weight of what he'd done. He'd have to work for Baker another four years just to earn back what he'd spent in less than four minutes.

Baker grunted, cut into his hotcakes. "How big a herd?"

"Says there's twenty cows but could be forty head by now countin' yearlings. Don't even know if they've been branded."

Baker sopped up a mouthful and chewed for a moment. "That will get you started. You gonna run 'em with mine?"

"I'd like to. Been thinking on a brand, but I haven't registered one yet."

Baker watched him with that gunmetal glare. Whit wasn't about to tell him of his idea—a double H for Hutton and Hartman beneath a mountain peak. He had to tell Livvy first, that was if her father allowed the union. The thought soured even his ma's sweet apple butter dripping off his hotcakes.

"You takin' the land too?"

"Can't." Whit cut another bite and chased it with coffee. "She wants a hundred dollars for it."

Baker pushed his plate aside. "They prove it up yet?"

"Started a cabin, but it's not half finished. She's still living in a tent."

"I'll stake you."

Whit sucked air and coughed until he thought he'd lose his hotcakes.

"Don't choke up on me, son." Baker's mustache quivered on one side, a sure sign of pleasure in his joke. "You can pay me back in calves. Take you a year or so, but it'll work out."

"Thank you, sir." Whit's thoughts swam around like panicky cows fording a swollen river.

"Overtons' land borders mine, doesn't it?"

"Yes, sir."

"Good. That'll make it easier." Baker swirled his coffee. "When will you take her the money?"

Whit sat straighter, tried to stretch out his lungs, open his burning throat. "Today. She was in a hurry to leave. Has an offer from Doc Mason, Tad said—he's back home already. Said Doc needs help and she's handy at fixin' folks. Other than bullet wounds, I suppose. Anyway, she said they'd be packed and ready to leave when I showed up."

Baker shoved his chair back. "If her cattle are close, drive 'em back over the draw and run 'em in with our bunch. That might keep rustlers from pickin' 'em off."

"There's one other thing."

Baker stilled.

"Tad said Jody rode through their place three days ago. Said he was gonna sign on to lay rail for the Santa Fe."

Baker rolled a couple of words around under his breath and snatched his plate off the table.

"I want to go get him." Whit waited for his boss to break in half over that piece of news, but the man held his tongue and set his dishes in the pan. He jerked off Livvy's apron and faced Whit. "Don't get yourself shot."

Whit added his plate and cup to the pile. "There isn't anybody else to bring him home. No family other than Buck and us, and with Buck's luck, he'd get his head blown off if he showed up in the gorge."

Baker turned for the dining room. "Come by my study before you leave, and I'll give you the money for the widow."

"Thank you, sir."

The back door flew open and Buck lurched in with a basket full of eggs and a bloody hand. "That fool chicken attacked me!"

Baker shook his head and lumbered into the dining room.

Whit grabbed the basket. "Give me those before you drop them." The eggs were still warm. "Boil some water and wash the dishes. It'll clean out your hand."

"But I'm starving."

Whit jerked his chin toward the table. "You can have what's left."

He set the eggs on a towel like he'd seen Livvy do, and on his way past the table, snatched a hotcake and rolled it up for the ride.

"Hey!" Buck's offended tone rankled.

"That's what you get for messing with that hen when Livvy told you not to."

Four cold cakes should hold the boy, and what was left of the apple butter. If Whit remembered right, Ma had given Livvy *two* jars. The other one had to be around there somewhere, but he'd look for it later.

At the bunk house, he stuffed his savings in his waistcoat, strapped on a gun belt, and picked up the rifle and scabbard. No intention to join the fight, but no sense being foolhardy and unprotected, either. Sometimes looking well-heeled kept the roughs off your back. He hoped for as much today.

He led Oro around to the hitching rail in front of the house and out of habit, peered at the lace window curtains. No white square today, tipping him off to Livvy's attempted secrecy. Pressure built up behind his ribs and he pulled a deep draught of clean, morning air. Columbines might do the trick. He'd help her plant 'em by the back door. Like his pa had for his mother.

He jerked his hat off and scrubbed his head, digging deep for his brain. What was he thinking? This wasn't his place. And what kind of cowhand went around digging posies?

After stomping his boots on the landing, he stepped inside. Baker sat at his desk in the small study off the dining room, opposite the front door.

"Come on back."

As Whit approached the big walnut desk, he noted an intricate floral pattern carved into the lid of a wooden box on the desktop. Must have been Ruth's. What was it with women and flowers?

Baker withdrew the money and returned the box to its drawer. Then he folded the bill in half and handed it to Whit. "You going to Texas Creek after Overtons'?"

"Should take me half a day to get up there and haul him back. Then we can push the widow's cows over the draw on our return." He tucked the bill in with the rest of his money.

"Buck and I can handle things while you're gone." Baker studied him. "You tell him what you're doing?"

"No, sir."

His boss nodded in agreement.

Whit hesitated.

"What?"

"If Jody's not where I think he is, at that rock fort, I'm gonna hunt for him. He could be someplace else along the river."

"Face down."

A muscle in Whit's cheek flinched. He truly hoped the boy hadn't gotten himself killed.

Baker waved his hand in dismissal. "Don't get shot." He leaned back in his leather chair, both hands grasping the worn arm rests. "I don't think Olivia could take it."

Whit's collar tightened, and he suddenly knew why Baker was staking him on the Overton place.

Livvy thought sure a good night's rest would smooth her ragged nerves, but that required sleep and there had been precious little of it.

As soon as dawn pinked the sky, she bathed at the wash basin and stepped into her petticoat and dress. She scrubbed her teeth with a small brush and baking soda from a tin in her satchel, then rebraided her hair and twisted it low at her neck. Buttoning her good shoes with a hook, she regretted not wearing her boots instead. Less trouble.

She repacked her satchel and smoothed the star quilt, wanting to smooth away her worry over Whit as easily. Easing the bedroom door open, she glanced at Marti's closed door. Annie's stood slightly ajar. A light glowed at the bottom of the stairway, and Livvy suspected the lady of the house was making biscuits or gathering eggs.

She crept down the stairs and stopped near the bottom. Annie Hutton sat at the kitchen table with a lamp drawn near and a Bible opened before her. Her forehead rested against her two opened hands and her lips moved. Feeling intrusive, Livvy grasped the railing and stepped up to the previous stair, catching her skirt in the process. Her petticoat ripped.

Annie looked up.

"Good morning." She rose and came toward the stairs. "I see you are an early riser too."

"I'm so sorry I disturbed you."

Annie reached for the satchel and returned to the kitchen. "You are not bothering me in the least. I was merely starting the day the way I always do." She set the satchel by the back door and went to the stove where coffee simmered. "Want a cup?"

"Yes, thank you." Livvy took a chair, glancing at the open Bible. Proverbs 3.

"'Trust in the Lord with all thine heart; and lean not unto thine own understanding.'" Annie poured two cups as she recited the verse and brought them to the table with two spoons.

"You know it by memory." Livvy deflated with a stab of guilt for not being more familiar with the Scriptures. And she, a preacher's daughter.

Annie seated herself and pulled the tarnished sugar bowl closer. "That is exactly the reason. Those words go straight to my heart every time I read them. And when I need the Lord's comfort and strength, reciting them is the quickest and shortest route I know."

Livvy waited until Annie had sugared her coffee before dipping her spoon into the bowl. "I don't read as much as I should, at least I haven't since coming to help Pop at the ranch. It seems like every waking moment is spent cooking or cleaning or gathering or washing. Some household chore always needs tending to."

"Or branding?" Annie's eyes sparkled with mirth.

Livvy muted a laugh behind her palm. "Oh yes, branding. And dare I admit that I liked it better than most any other chore?" Because it put her close to Whit.

"I can't say I blame you, though I'm sure my hands would suffer from such a task."

Livvy felt a certain affinity with this kind woman, one she believed she could trust. "Whit gave me a pair of sturdy leather gloves to use. I think they were once his." She dared not meet Annie's gaze, affinity or not.

"It's no surprise to me that he looks after you like that. His affection for you was clear when you were here last."

Livvy stole a quick glance to see if Annie meant those revealing words. Who knew a man better than his mother?

A knowing smile followed. "He cares for you, I am certain. May I be so bold to ask if you feel the same?"

Livvy should have let the sun scorch her face yesterday on the way to town. Better that than its current competition with the brightening dawn burning through the windows.

"Yes, I do." So faint was her answer she doubted if Annie heard it.

The woman reached out to grasp her hand. "That does me good to hear, Livvy. I have been praying for you both." With a quick squeeze, she rose and set about starting breakfast.

Livvy felt as obvious as a thistle in a columbine patch, certain her cheeks were just as brilliant. But hearing that Whit's mother prayed for her—for them—touched something deep in her soul.

The hot coffee was warming her more than necessary, so she went for the egg basket. "I'll gather for you this morning. Is the coop behind the barn?"

"Attached on the left side. Two hens are setting. A red and a black-and-white speckled."

Livvy thought immediately of her grandfather's surly russet hen and wondered if Buck had survived the chore.

Later at breakfast, all the Huttons were in a better mood than the previous night at supper when Livvy had asked her unfortunate questions about the railroad war. Which side was in the right? Was the whole thing really worth dying over? Marti had fled from the meal and remained in her room the rest of the evening.

Undoubtedly, the display had something to do with young Tad Overton, for Pastor Hutton had raked his brows together and made guttural noises just like Whit. Livvy's insides had quaked.

But in the light of morning, Marti came to the table with swollen eyes that quickly brightened as she shared about Livvy's visit to the curio shop. The girl's obvious delight in fossil remains pulled her toward a scholarly pursuit, though not the scholarly pursuit her parents imagined. However, if it drew her affections away from the Overton boy, Livvy guessed her family might accept it.

Eager to be on her way, Livvy folded her napkin and gathered her plate and cup. "Thank you for breakfast, Annie.

And for supper last night and your wonderful company, all of you." She looked to each one to emphasize her sincerity.

"Maybe you can persuade our son to come with you next time." The pastor held his coffee mug in both hands, elbows resting on the table like Whit.

Livvy's chest tightened. "I will try." She smiled, hoping it masked her worry over Whit's uncommon sense of duty where the Perkins boys were concerned.

"And remind him that Papa Whitaker wants him to take over the mercantile." Marti tacked on the afterthought with a dash of sibling impishness.

Livvy looked away to hide a grin. And a jealous tug. She did not want to marry a store clerk. She wanted to marry a cowboy. A *particular* cowboy.

Oh, Lord, how self-centered she was.

"Do you have any idea how early Doc Mason is up and around?"

Pastor Hutton leaned back in his chair. "Depends on how late his last call was the day before. But don't mind knocking good and loud."

Annie brought two jars from her pantry, wrapped them in toweling, and tucked them into Livvy's satchel. "If he doesn't answer, you will simply have to come back to town."

Livvy pushed the jars deeper into the bag. "Thank you for the—apple butter?"

Annie nodded. "Of course."

"I left one jar out for the men while I was gone, hoping to appease them in my absence."

Annie kissed her lightly on the cheek. "You are a good woman, Livvy Hartman."

Marti rose and took Livvy's hand. "Come back soon and we can go to the library. They have books on paleontology. And if you stay long enough, we could take the buggy up to the quarry to see the dig."

"Perhaps, Marti. Don't make rash promises." Her father's remark dampened the girl's spirit only briefly, and she shot Livvy a sly wink and quick nod.

Outside by the columbines, Livvy paused for one last look. "Thank you all again. I will be sure to give Whit your best wishes."

"You could give him a big kiss too."

Annie's quick swat nearly knocked her daughter off the porch.

Livvy was grateful she had turned toward the wagon, already hitched and waiting. She climbed aboard with the pastor's hand at her elbow, and his laughing eyes reaffirmed the Hutton family's playful spirit.

"Annie and I are riding up the river today, something we do quite often, as a matter of fact. Hopefully, she'll take her daughter's advice to heart."

Blushing at the comment, Livvy hardly knew what to say, though she certainly knew where Whit came by his outrageous remarks. Yet how could the pastor take his wife up river with all the shooting?

She gave him a worried look, considering how best to warn someone older and wiser against such an unwise outing.

His mouth quirked up like Whit's "We don't go past the hot springs. Not until things are settled with the railroad."

Relieved, she situated the satchel at her feet, waved at the close-knit family, then clucked Bess ahead. With a quick slap of the reins she was on her way down the lane and on to Main Street. One stop at Doc Mason's, and then home. She should be at the ranch well before noon, within three hours at the most if she hurried.

And for some unknown and uncomfortable reason, her heart said to hurry.

CHAPTER SEVENTEEN

Whit rode in at a slow walk.

True to her word, the widow had all her worldly possessions—which wasn't much—loaded in the old buckboard and a sorry-looking horse hitched to it. The other horse was tied to the back. She and Tad waited on stumps around what used to be the fire, cold and scattered now. The spider and tripod were gone, but the tent remained.

Mrs. Overton stood, tension sluicing off her thin shoulders. "The tent is yours and whatever else you find. I have no need of anything to remind me of this place and what I've lost here."

Whit stepped off Oro, dropped the reins, and reached into his waistcoat. "This is for your livestock." He waited as she counted through the money, disregarding the insult since she was more than likely unaccustomed to such things.

"And this is for the land." He held out the folded bill.

Tad reached for it.

Whit snatched it away and drilled the boy with a hard look, melting him into the background.

"As agreed."

She added the bill to the others.

"Do you have papers?"

She pulled a folded piece from her skirt pocket and handed it to Whit. Without another word, she and her son climbed into their wagon and drove away.

They did not look back.

Suddenly alone, Whit exhaled what he recognized as relief. He had not asked the lay of the property, but the paper in his hand would say. He slipped it inside his waistcoat to read later.

The camp huddled in a small meadow fifty yards from the full-running stream he had crossed. Grass-covered hills swelled around it, and behind them rose the timbered ridges and rock-strewn mountains common to the area.

A nice spot. A place that could be home if a man had the right woman. Livvy's scent whispered by and he turned, expecting to see her standing there. Just the breeze playing tricks with his heart.

He walked around the cabin. No floor. He'd lay Livvy a wood floor, someday add a fine carpet like her grandmother's. And build her a real house.

A huff rose up in his throat. He hadn't even found the Overtons' cows yet and here he was dreaming away the morning.

A muffled sound jerked his head toward the tent. His right hand went straight to his gun, and he eased closer to the shabby shelter. Was a coyote poking around?

There—again. His fingers curled around the butt of his pistol and he pulled it from the leather, cocked the hammer. With the barrel he pushed the tent flap aside and squinted as his eyes adjusted to the shadowy interior. And then he saw it.

A black-and-white head poked out from beneath a cot. Two white paws inched forward and a whimper followed. A small dust cloud rose at the swish of a tail.

Whit eased back the hammer and slipped his gun in the holster before squatting. The animal looked away, its paws scooted forward, and the whimper repeated.

Kind eyes. Not spooked or wild. Whit held out his left hand. "Come on, fella."

The whimper strengthened to a plea that tugged at Whit's insides. How could they leave a dog behind?

And whatever else you find.

He edged forward, hand outstretched. A cowering dog wasn't worth its keep—just what he didn't need.

The animal bellied its way out, hope and distrust mingled in its black eyes.

Whit lowered his voice. "It's all right. Come on."

At the sound of promise, the dog crawled to Whit's hand and tucked its head beneath his fingers. He rubbed the smooth head, the ears. The dog wiggled closer, and soon Whit had both hands on it, running them over the bony back, feeling every rib, and itching to get his hands on Tad Overton.

"What's your name, fella?"

The dog stood to its full height, a youngster, not more than a yearling, maybe less. Its feathery tail wagged like a parade flag, and hungry eyes drank in Whit as if he were God himself.

"Lord, what am I gonna do with a dog?" He remembered the rolled hotcake in his saddle bag. "Guess that's an answer, isn't it."

Whit rose slowly and backed through the tent opening, then walked to Oro lipping grass a few feet away. He pulled out his stash and turned to see the pup sitting behind him, head cocked, ears up. One ear flopped at the tip, the sign of a not-grown dog.

"A sharp one, you are." He held out the rolled cake, and the dog sniffed once before inhaling the offering in a single swift gulp.

"Don't choke on it." He laughed out loud, recollecting Baker's similar warning not an hour earlier. Gathering Oro's reins, he swung into the saddle.

"You comin' or stayin'?" Fool question for sure, but he'd soon learn if the dog was the fool or not.

A small yip answered and the pup wagged its tail.

Whit rode toward an open draw that cut around Eight Mile and pointed to the river gorge. The dog still trotted behind him, far enough back not to get kicked.

No fool there.

A wide park opened on the other side of the mountain, and Whit followed its western reach into higher country. An hour later it narrowed between rocky ridges and sidled up alongside the Arkansas River as it churned down the mountain, white-topped and roaring through rocky stretches, placid and smooth in others. Like a certain woman he knew.

Just as the valley opened out at Texas Creek, he turned Oro down toward the river, through the brush and juniper. A hunch told him where he thought men might build a rock fortress. He was right, but no one was there.

The stonework stood mute and unmanned. The new rail lay not far from the abutment, but without ceremony or defender. The dog trotted closer, sniffed around the rock work, and looked at Whit as if to ask the purpose.

"You're right. Pointless. Absolutely good for nothing."

Whit reined his horse through the trees and headed upstream. Martin Thatcher's spread lay along Texas Creek. He'd turn in there, see if they had any word on where the railroad crews were.

Obliged for the Thatchers' hospitality and information, but eager to get down the mountain, Whit thanked them for dinner and urged Oro back down to the river and onto a wagon road that led into Cañon City. The dog ran beside him, its tongue hanging out and a near grin pulling at its jowls.

"You're a real maverick, aren't you?"

Black ears lifted and the dog looked up as if agreeing.

"You like that name?"

A slobbery grin.

"I'm talking to a dog."

Whit slowed to a walk, pulled off his hat, and ran his sleeve across his forehead. Would Baker allow a dog called Maverick on the place? He huffed. Maverick pricked his ears. They'd soon find out.

It was early evening before they made it to town.

This was not how he had planned to spend his time—dragging into Cañon City with a half-dead dog, looking for a foolhardy boy who joined a gang of roughs fighting somebody else's war.

Martin Thatcher had told him both railroad crews had beat it into town and on to Pueblo and the roundhouse there. What were they going to do—fight over the train station? They'd just end up fillin' each other with holes.

But according to Thatcher, the Denver and Rio Grande boys and the Pueblo County sheriff intended to *borrow* the cannon from the armory and blow one Bat Masterson and his gun-slingin' friends back to Kansas.

Whit turned Oro down the lane beside his father's church and rode back to the parsonage barn, where he watered Oro and Maverick and scooped cool trough water over his own head. Tired from riding and keeping a tight rein on his swirling emotions, he left Oro at the hitching rail and told Maverick to stay.

The dog dropped and laid its head on its paws with a heavy sigh. If Jody Perkins had as much sense, Whit could have been at home courting Livvy. Or at least trying to.

He slapped his hat against his thigh and stopped at the back porch steps by the columbines. They looked corralled, bunched together. Not free and spreading at the meadows edge in aspen shade. But he knew his ma's love for the purple flower. Just like Livvy's.

The back door opened and the woman herself stepped out.

"What are you doing here?" A knife in one hand and a carrot in the other. If one didn't get him, the other would.

"Nice to see you too, Ma."

Her tense shoulders relaxed and she let go a sigh. "I'm sorry, but Livvy told us you couldn't come with her because of your work."

He combed his wet hair back with one hand, watching his ma's eyes narrow at the gesture and then drop to his sidearm.

"She was right," he said.

"And how is that, since here you are?"

Women sure had a way of complicating a man's life.

He moved up the steps, planted a kiss on her cheek, and stepped past her into the kitchen. "Do you have any coffee left? I could use a cup."

Sweeping in with her usual grace, she soon had a full mug before him on the table and one for herself with a spoonful of sugar. Rather than her typical silent stirring, the spoon clanked against the cup indicating her concern.

"One of our hands, a boy about fourteen, lit out after the Denver railroad crew. Since we finished branding, I figured I could ride over to the river and haul him back by the ear. But they're gone. Every last one, and a rancher told me they all headed to the roundhouse in Pueblo itching for a fight."

His ma seamed her lips and laid her hand on the family Bible. "I have been praying about this war." She slid a glance his way. "Among other things."

Whit was undoubtedly one of the other things.

"Appreciate that." He took a swig and held in a grimace. The pot had cooked down some. Fit to float a horseshoe.

"Before sunup we heard them ride through town. Some in wagons, the rest on horseback. Your father is over at the mercantile now, trying to learn what he can." She raised worried eyes. "Do you think Tad Overton rode with them?"

Whit snorted. "Not unless he lit out after I saw him this morning."

"So he is at home, with his mother?" A two-sided question if Whit ever heard one, and the weightier side concerned his sister, Marti.

He glanced toward the stairs.

His ma read the look. "At the library, or so she said."

"Reading about dusty professors digging up dustier bones."

"Don't change the subject." A coppery gaze held him, the same one that had peeled the veneer off many a tall tale. He might as well cough up the whole sorry story.

"Overtons don't have a home any more. I bought it."

She froze in her chair, her coffee cup halfway to her mouth. The copper turned to brass. "You *what*?"

"The widow wanted off the land. Too many bad memories. I bought her cattle, and Baker staked me on the land. It butts up next to the Bar-HB and we'll run the cows together."

She set the cup in its saucer and drew her hands into her lap, mulling over the news. "Did the Overtons leave the area?"

"I wish I could say they had. But Doc Mason evidently needs a nurse, and the widow is fit for the job, according to Tad." He held the mug to his mouth, considered another swallow. "She didn't do much for the boy the day he was shot, but I guess I shouldn't fault a mother's fear."

"No, you should not." She raised a hand to her throat, fingered the top opened button of her dress. "So they will be living in town."

"If Doc takes her on."

She took her cup to the sink and it clattered against the saucer. "Will you be staying to supper?"

The quiver in her voice decided him. "Yes." He loved his parents, but an unfamiliar urgency was starting to gnaw at his gut. He drenched it with a final swallow. "If you'll have me."

She turned with a tight smile. "Of course we will have you. You are always welcome." She tipped her head. "As is Livvy."

He was wrong. It wasn't a smile she wore standing there with her arms folded across her waist. It was the leer of a professional inquisitor.

CHAPTER EIGHTEEN

The ranch house, barn, and outbuildings spread across the verdant meadow like welcoming arms, and Livvy ached with longing. Not for home in her parents' fine Denver parsonage, but home here, on the ranch. With Whit.

She was ruined for city life. For buggy rides through the park, for the stately brick church house, and for girls her age paying more attention to their latest fashions than to her father's sermons.

Her father. The joyful bubble burst with a painful prick. The dear man had swept a rancher's daughter off to the city to be his bride and here he was losing his only child to that same rancher's foreman.

If he allowed it.

If Whit wanted it.

Panic tightened her chest and inched up along her throat. Pop may have made his opinion known where Whit was concerned, but Whit had never come right out and declared his feelings. And her father did not even know she and Whit had been working so closely. Of course he knew Whit worked for her grandfather, but he knew little else.

At least her trip back to the ranch had been faster than she'd planned to take with an injured passenger. Tad Overton was already gone when she'd stopped at Doc Mason's. His ma had come for him days ago, Doc said as he took Pop's money. And as Whit had assumed, she'd had nothing to pay the doctor's bill.

Livvy slapped Bess into a jolting lope and every board in the wagon squawked in protest until she pulled up in a dust cloud at the barn. She looped the reins on the brake and leaped, very unladylike, from the board. Skirts were such a nuisance. Satchel in hand, she marched into the barn.

The shady interior hung like night, and she blinked several times, adjusting to the dim alleyway. The stalls stood empty and no one worked on anvil or tack. She strode to the side that opened into the corrals and the near pasture and counted the horses.

One was missing. A tall black-stockinged buckskin.

She hurried to the house and stopped at the kitchen door with her pulse pounding in her ears. Gripping the satchel's handle, she pulled clean mountain air in through her nose and concentrated on slowing her heartbeat. With one hand she shook out her skirt, then checked her braid to find it still coiled in place. Another deep breath and she reached for the door knob.

Pop's voice boomed from his study, rolled around the dining room, and shot into the kitchen. "That you, Livvy?"

She closed the door quietly behind her, determined not to match his uproarious greeting though she wanted nothing more than to run through the house like Marti would, jump into his lap, and confess her affection for his foreman.

Glancing at the untidy sideboard and dishes piled high in the wash pan, she continued into the dining room, past the wilted lilacs on the dusty table, and stopped at the door to her grandfather's study. "Hello, Pop."

Poise. Grace. Restraint. She drew them all together like ribbons on a package and pinned on a smile. "Did you miss me?"

The man looked up and his gray eyes sparkled. "You are a bright flower among dull sage brush. Come here, child."

Delighted by his tender greeting, she pulled the mail from her satchel and dropped the bag before stepping into his still-powerful arms that encircled her in a great bear hug.

"We missed you, Livvy."

We?

"I was gone for only a day and night. Surely you could get by without my cooking for that long."

"Not just your cooking." He held her at arm's length and gave her a squinted appraisal. "I do believe you are more beautiful than when you left. Just like your mother and Mama Ruth."

She giggled and worked free of his hands. "You are trying to get on my good side so I'll give you fresh biscuits and Annie Hutton's apple butter."

He leaned back against his leather chair and twisted one side of his mustache. "That was mighty good what you left behind. We finished it off."

"So soon?" She laid the mail on his desk. "I should have known. And my guess is that Buck ate the most."

He grunted. "Not a chance with Whit keeping the jar at his plate, a knife in one hand, and a sour eye on anyone daring to reach for it."

Laughter bubbled up and she walked back to the door. "I have your liniment here, and two more jars of apple butter. But I'll need Whit and Buck to unload the supplies."

Pop's mustache fell and jerked her hopes down with it.

"Where are they? Out chasing mavericks?"

"I imagine Buck has his boots off at the bunkhouse." Pop stood. "I'll go get him."

"Can't Whit do that?" *Why* can't Whit do that?

Her grandfather stopped directly in front of her and held her with a loving gaze. "He's gone after Jody."

A gasp slipped away before she could forbid it, and her right hand tightened on the satchel handle.

"Now don't you worry. That Whit's got a fine head on his shoulders, don't doubt that for a minute."

It wasn't his shoulders she was worried about. "Where did he go?" *Not the railroad war. Please, not the war.*

"Overtons told him Jody joined up with the Santa Fe boys layin' track."

If she did not sit, she would faint and show her grandfather she was no better than the wilting lilacs. She leaned against the door frame, afraid to attempt the great distance to the nearest chair.

Pop took her by the arm and led her to the dining table, where he pulled out a ladder-back. Grateful, she fell into it and clutched the satchel to her breast as if it held all her strength and fortitude rather than tooth powder, a hairbrush, and Annie's apple butter.

Pop took the next chair and turned it to face her. "Whit left the same morning you did with a couple things on his mind." At that, the man's eyes clouded with a private notion and his mustache jerked to one side. "He has some news I am sure he wants to tell you himself rather than have me spill the beans."

Curiosity gained a foothold over worry, and Livvy relaxed as she leaned forward.

"No, I am not going into that,"—he raised a calloused hand—"so don't ask me. But you should know that he is determined to bring Jody back from the rail war."

She tightened her arms around the satchel again and considered pulling out Pop's liniment to use as a smelling salt.

"He might be gone for a few days. But I'm sure he will be safe." Pop fingered his mustache and nodded with a far-off look over her shoulder. "I've seen him use that Winchester a time or two."

Maybe her grandfather *wanted* her to swoon, fall out right there across Mama Ruth's beautiful dining room carpet.

Oh, Lord, please don't let Whit get involved in the railroad war.

Whit's ma's chicken pot pie was bested only by his grandmother's, and Whit raised a hearty "amen" after grace as he set about proving it. It was a wonder his pa wasn't as big as a horse from his ma's great cooking and a preacher's sedate lifestyle. But the Reverend Caleb Hutton had never been one to simply sit by and let other men do the hard labor. Townsfolk still called on him when their foaling mares were having a hard time.

The man had a reputation.

Whit chuckled around a mouthful at memory of the oft-told tale of how his pa had delivered a foal during his first Christmas Eve service in Cañon City. Dolly, his ma had named the filly, and they had her still.

Soon he and Livvy would be creating their own family stories.

He hoped.

Suddenly sobered by the reminder that he needed to talk to Livvy's father, he cut a glance at his own. "You going to Denver anytime soon?"

Marti, always two steps ahead of everybody else's thought processes, held him in a calculating gaze. "What's got you wanting to go to Denver?"

Whit straightened his back, hoping to bully her with his bigger bulk. She intimidated as easily as Livvy—not at all.

His pa took a healthy bite and closed his eyes as he chewed, clearly relishing his wife's handiwork before he replied. "I want to stay close until this train war is cleared up."

Whit's ma made a clutching sound in her throat, and Marti's attention suddenly fell to her half-empty plate.

"I understand that is the reason for your visit," his pa said.

Guilt poked Whit like a pitchfork. He could take time to follow a fool boy into town but not for a legitimate visit with his folks. He coughed hard and ran the napkin across his mouth.

"Yes, sir, it is."

His ma pushed pie crust around on her plate.

"Ma said you heard men ride through here early this morning, before daylight. Did you happen to look out and see anything? Specifically a stout little black horse with a white blaze?"

"Didn't look out, but I saw that horse at the livery this afternoon. One of yours?"

His father's characteristic calm set Whit on edge—like it always had. Rarely did his pa get excited about anything. A fine quality in a preacher, Whit supposed, but there were times when it drove him crazy with impatience.

He forced himself to stay seated, not dash out the door and run across the street to the livery. "More than likely." But what was it doing here if Jody rode with the railroad men?

A sudden pounding at the front door jerked Marti from her chair before their ma could tell her to keep her seat. Whit followed, grateful for an excuse to use his legs.

Marti had the door opened wide to a breathless boy standing on the threshold.

"Mr. Sutton told me to run this to the pastor." The youngster gulped air. "He in?"

"I'll take it for him." Whit held out his hand.

The little chest heaved, but the telegram remained tightly gripped in grubby fingers.

Whit scowled.

His pa came from the kitchen. "Thank you, William. Tell Mr. Sutton I appreciate it." He slipped a coin into the boy's hand and the youngster repaid him with a grin and dashed across the porch, down the path, and into the lane toward Main Street.

No wonder he'd waited for Pa.

Whit closed the door and followed his sister to the kitchen where they all resumed their seats. His pa laid the telegram beside his plate and picked up his coffee. A bronc-y gleam danced in his eyes as he ignored his baited family.

"Pa-ah!" Marti spoke for everyone, and for once Whit appreciated her impudence.

"Caleb, really," his ma chided. "Tell us what it says."

"Oh, you mean this?" He lifted the thin folded paper.

Marti stamped her foot underneath the table.

"Martha Mae, hold your foot." Their ma fought her own battles against foot stomping, and Whit grabbed his coffee cup to hide that bit of knowledge.

Slowly and deliberately, his pa unfolded the paper and silently read the message, moving his lips as he did so. Marti made growling noises, and Whit's ma scraped her shoes back and forth on the braided rug beneath the table.

"DRG to armory with Sheriff Price to commandeer cannon. Masterson and ATSF in possession. Stormed telegraph office. Shots fired. On to roundhouse. Masterson surrendered. Most well."

"Most well?" Whit's ma held trembling fingers to her lips. "Does that mean someone was shot?"

Pa refolded the paper and slipped it into his waistcoat. "Most likely we will know more tomorrow. But it sounds like it didn't turn into the blood bath I feared, thank the Lord."

"But who stormed the telegraph office?" Marti's eyes flashed with a mix of excitement and fear.

"I heard talk at the mercantile that the Denver crew rode to Pueblo to seize the cannon. But this telegram says that Masterson and the Santa Fe men already had it."

"Then why did Masterson surrender?" Whit could make no more sense of the telegram than his sister and ma.

"We'll have to wait until our so-called posse returns to get the whole story. And I am certain that it will be the talk of the town for weeks. The trick will be getting the story straight once we start hearing those men boast and gloat."

Whit's ma went to the sideboard and returned with a vinegar pie.

His mouth watered for the "in-between" desert they always ate before the peaches came on. She must have been saving her strawberries for jam.

"But who won?" She sliced a generous piece for each member of the family. "If you can call it winning."

Whit's pa laid a gentle hand on his wife's arm and looked into her worried eyes. "I'd say the town won."

As good an answer as any, at least until they had more details.

Whit cut into his pie and let the sweet custard and flakey crust melt in his mouth. The railroad would run through the mountains' heart to Leadville—one way or another. He'd prefer men not die over it. Especially young men.

If some hadn't already.

The next morning, Whit left before sunup and stopped at the livery. The whoosh of Pete's billows seeped through the crack in the massive barn doors. The smithy was getting a head start before the day's heat vied with his furnace, and the twang of hot metal nipped Whit's nose as he tied Oro at the rail.

He walked the alleyway, checking each stall for a stout black gelding with a white blaze, and found it in the fourth one, feeding on grass hay.

"Mornin', Whit." The ping of hammer on iron punctuated the man's greeting. "What brings you into to town so early?"

Whit stopped near the anvil, watched Pete's massive arm flex as he gripped an L-shaped piece and shoved it into the fire.

"Stayed at my folks last night, and I wanted to see you about a job before I left today."

The blacksmith withdrew the glowing iron from the coals, laid it over the anvil's horn and hammered it around. "What kind of job?"

"I need a brand."

Pete glanced up, repositioned the piece. "The Bar-HB got so many cows they need another iron?"

Whit thumbed his hat up. "I'm starting my own herd."

The blacksmith set his hammer down, laid the piece across the anvil, and mopped his sweaty face with a rag. "Show me."

Whit squatted and smoothed the finely-ground dust with his hand. Then he drew the double H with a wide inverted V across the top.

"Like a rafter," Pete said, looking over Whit's shoulder.

"Wider. It's a mountain. Spreads over both letters here." Whit retraced the angled bars that, to him, resembled a mountain peak, then straightened and wiped his hand on his pants. "Any way I can get it today?"

"After dinner is the best I can do."

Whit was hoping to be home before that. "No sooner?"

A thick arm swept toward the anvil. "Got shoes to make."

"All right. Afternoon it is."

He repositioned his hat and, remembering his other task, jerked his chin toward the alleyway. "Who brought in the black gelding?"

Pete picked up his hammer and chuckled. "I saw the Bar-HB when the sheriff brought it in. Wondered how it got all the way down the mountain with a saddle and no rider."

Whit's throat tightened. "Sheriff? No rider?" Not one thing funny about that.

"Then he told me he locked the boy in the jailhouse. Said to keep the horse until the Denver railroad crew got back from Pueblo. Even paid me."

"He being the sheriff?"

Pete nodded, grabbed the tongs, and shoved the bent iron back into the fire. "You gonna take the black with you?"

Whit dragged his hand over his face. "Yeah, I'll take him when I leave. Put the brand on Baker's tab, if you don't mind. I'll square up with him."

The smithy returned to his work, and Whit headed for the door and fresh air.

Dawn flushed the horizon, and he thought of the cougar. Hoped she hadn't taken another calf while he was gone. Hoped even more that Baker hadn't heard her scream again and gone out looking for her.

Urgency slinked in and started gnawing at his gut. There'd be a hole clean through him by dinnertime, and he wouldn't be able to eat even if he wanted to.

He swung into the saddle and struck out for the mercantile. His grandfather would have the coffee on, few customers this early, and plenty of time to hear how his grandson was going into the cattle business.

CHAPTER NINETEEN

A cow bellowed, and Livvy's eyelids fluttered open. Sparrows chittered from the lilac bush near her window, and she burrowed beneath her quilt, listening, delighted to be back on the ranch.

And just that quickly, worry nibbled a hole in her comfort. Was Whit back? Or was he still riding the countryside looking for Jody Perkins and meeting up with God knew who?

Throwing off the quilt, she sat up and stretched her arms above her head. Her Bible lay open on the bedside table, and a ribbon marked the passage she'd read the night before. "'Trust in the Lord with all thine heart and lean not unto thine own understanding.'"

Trusting God with her eternal soul had been easy. Raised to take Him at His word, she believed what He said about salvation. It all made sense to her—God's gift of love and forgiveness in Jesus.

But trusting Him with her heart where Whit was concerned? For some reason, that was harder.

"Oh, Lord, please protect him from gunmen and his own brash ways." Tears pricked her eyes and she knuckled them away. What choice did she have other than to trust God? She looked again at the passage. *Lean not on thine own understanding.*

That was her only option, and she knew full well that her own understanding fell far short on so many things. She could not see Whit at the moment. She could not perceive his thoughts, nor did she know his next move. She didn't even know where he was.

"Oh, God, help me trust You."

Fear pressed in and took a bite. If she truly placed Whit in the Lord's hand and removed her own clutching fingers, she could lose him.

What if God chose not to bring him home safely?

What if a future with Whit was not in God's plan for her life?

She closed the Bible, determined to commit that particular verse to memory as Annie Hutton had. Maybe that would calm her quaking heart.

After washing and dressing for the day, she tied her hair back with a blue ribbon, and plucked the egg basket from the kitchen counter on her way to the hen house.

Sweet mountain air filled her lungs and soul with fledgling hope, and even weeds sprouting in the garden failed to discourage it. Though she'd pay dearly for a week's neglect—three days spent branding and two in town—at least Buck's prickly new fence looked to be holding out the deer.

She lined the basket with pink rhubarb stalks, then went to the coop where she found the red hen napping atop her clutch.

He shall cover thee with his feathers, and under his wings shalt thou trust.

The old childhood verse flew across the years. "Again, it's trust," she whispered to the old hen. Blinking away a rising sting, she stepped back, watching the docile creature that could become a vicious defender if necessary.

How much more so the Lord?

Forcing herself from thought into action, Livvy quickly cleaned out the remaining nests and left the coop. Daylight was burnin', as Whit would say. The memory of his voice tugged at her insides.

And Buck Perkins tugged at the back door, stomping his feet on the step. Behind him, Livvy cleared her throat loud enough to be heard. He looked over his shoulder and opened the door wider, stepping aside for her to enter.

"Thank you, Buck. And thank you for washing before you come inside."

His mumbled "Yes, Miss Livvy" faded behind the closing door, and she smiled at his reticence. She'd make a civilized man out of that boy if it was the last thing she did.

The morning flew by with rhubarb and egg-custard pies, cinnamon cookies, and the scrubbing of what had not been scrubbed in a week. By then it was time to feed Pop and Buck again. As soon as she finished cleaning up after dinner, she hung her apron over a chair back, went to her room, and traded her blue calico dress for a blouse and Mama Ruth's denims. She'd forego the hat since the sun was edging away toward the western peaks.

Pop snoozed in his desk chair, his stockinged feet crossed on the desk blotter and his mustache ruffling as he snored. Easing past the door, she chose not to wake him. She'd be back in an hour or two, in plenty of time to serve leftovers for supper, with bread and apple butter. And more pie.

Maybe it was habit that prompted her to saddle Ranger rather than another horse. He had proved such a stalwart fellow during the branding. His surefootedness comforted her, and he wisely avoided badger holes long before she even saw them. She could ride Ranger and relax, enjoy the mountain beauty without being overly alert. And that was exactly what she wanted to do.

She set the sturdy gray to a leisurely walk and angled him across the meadow toward the rimrock. Cottonwoods clustered at the base of the red wall and she expected to find columbines hiding in their shade. The sky hung like a blue curtain, a sharp contrast to the cliffs and quivering green trees.

Ranger's ears pricked forward and he raised his head higher as they approached the towering wall. Livvy tried to follow his gaze, but saw only the multi-hued strata of rock and sediment laid down over the centuries. Perhaps a deer or mountain sheep had sent a loose stone tumbling, catching the horse's keen hearing.

In a moment, he relaxed his neck and plodded onward, matching Livvy's peaceful demeanor. She marveled at such color so far from town, more varied and brilliant than any dressmaker's work or gaily painted house. And with the afternoon sun behind her, shining directly on the scene, the rocks and trees and grass shimmered with near incandescence.

Tranquility embraced her. No shouting freighters and rattling wagons. No rowdy miners. No bickering women haggling over a merchant's prices. No people sounds at all. Simply peace.

A sigh escaped her lips and she settled even deeper into the saddle.

The cottonwoods were farther than she anticipated—a phenomenon she'd noticed during the branding. Pristine air made the mountains and ridges appear closer than they really were. But the ride was pleasurable, and as she approached the trees, her expectations were rewarded. Fragile purple heads clustered in gossipy groups.

When she stopped at the clearing's edge, Ranger immediately began lipping the tender grass. She untied the old flour bag she'd brought for holding columbines on the return trip. A heavy cooking spoon, perfect for digging, weighted it down.

Slipping to the ground, she dropped Ranger's reins, confident that the well-trained horse would stay nearby.

She stepped carefully through the patch, intent on her hunt, and stopped at the most prolific clusters to dig up a clump for transplanting. Without her notice, the afternoon waned.

A distant cloud's pass across the sun alerted her to the fading day.

One more clump, and then home.

An unexpected pile of leaves and brush caught her eye, and she turned aside to inspect it. Persistent buzzing hung about, and a septic odor wafted her way. Odd that she would smell an open wound here in the meadow so far from people.

Whit's words at a long-ago breakfast hit her memory like a rifle shot: *I found her latest kill in the cottonwoods, half covered with leaves and brush.*

Livvy's breath locked in her lungs as she stopped dead still. The fine hair on her arms rose, and a spidery shiver crawled up her back. Someone—or something—was watching her.

~

Whit made Jody Perkins ride next to him on the way to the ranch. Maverick trotted drag, unaware of the insulting position and grinning as if happy to be included at all.

The pride-busted boy sat his horse like a seed-corn sack, slump-shouldered and sullen. Three times before they cleared town, Whit convinced himself not to whip the stuffing out of him. Buck would more than likely see to that.

Jody had to keep reining in the black, determined as it was to lead. He'd check the horse with quick jerks on the reins, and Whit would check him out. Was he mad at being found in the hoosegow or was he mad that Sheriff Price had locked him up so he couldn't follow the Denver bunch to Pueblo?

Jody Perkins didn't know how lucky he was.

A heavy sun hung in the late-afternoon sky by the time they made the ranch road. The boy hadn't said two words and that suited Whit just fine. He had other things on his mind.

If he didn't care so much for his horse and the black, he'd over-and-under it all the way home. His scalp itched and it wasn't due to his pa's trough water from the day before. It went deeper.

His blood simmered with warning, yet their surroundings offered no clue. Oro gave no sign that predators lurked. Even Maverick was unaffected, though his carefree countenance could simply mean he had as much sense as Jody Perkins and wouldn't know a mad bear if one slapped him on the rump.

Whit slid his Winchester partway from the scabbard and slid it back in. He did the same with the Colt on his hip, made sure the pull was smooth and unhindered. He flexed his right hand, and the gesture drew a worried glance from Jody.

Served him right.

Whit's nerves bunched in his legs and his back, and he urged Oro into an easy lope. Another half hour and they should see the barn roof and the rimrock across the valley.

Rimrock. The word rippled through his arms and down his back. He was more nervous than a prairie dog at a badger picnic.

Watch her, Lord. Please, watch out for Livvy till I get there.

Until he got there? What an arrogant prayer—as if he had more say-so than the Almighty. Maybe there was a bite of truth in Livvy's stinging reprimand of him for not praying. He needed to trust the Lord more and stop thinking everything depended on his doings. But that'd be a whole lot easier if he could see Livvy from where he sat atop his good horse.

When they loped into the yard, the place was deserted. No Buck, no Baker, no Livvy. No lights in the house, and the sun had pulled itself behind the first ridge. Before long it would tuck tail and run for cover of night.

"Check the house for Buck and Livvy," he told Jody. "I'll check the corral and pasture."

The boy hit the ground running.

Whit loped to the barn and around to the back pasture. Baker's gray was gone. Either Whit's boss or the woman he loved was out riding.

Jody ran out the kitchen door and halfway to the barn before he yelled. "Neither one's here. Just the boss."

Buck's horse was in the barn. That left Livvy out alone. Hurt? Trapped? Lost?

The yelling drew Buck from the bunk house, barefoot and shirtless. Whit slid Oro to a stop before him and tossed him the Colt. "Fire this three times if Livvy rides in." Buck held the gun as if it were hot iron and nodded so fast Whit thought his head would fly off.

He whirled Oro around and squeezed his heels. The buckskin lunged forward and landed on the gallop, straight for the fading red rimrock.

Baker's gray caught the last of daylight as Whit neared the meadow's edge. He slowed to a trot, saw the horse's reins dragging as it grazed. At Whit's approach, it jerked its head up and rumbled a greeting.

Livvy was nowhere.

Had she fallen? Had Ranger thrown her into some spot Whit couldn't see in the waning light? Or was she off climbing the outcroppings, getting herself in a fix.

And then he saw her yellow hair. She stood a hundred feet beyond the gray, against a bank of cottonwood trees, as still as stone, looking down. Every fiber in Whit's body wanted to run to her and sweep her into his arms, but his instincts told him to look closer.

Only the cottonwood leaves moved, fluttering in the early evening breeze. And a long golden rope that whipped soundlessly from side to side atop a small pile of boulders.

Whit's blood froze. A shout formed in his throat but he checked it.

He drew out the rifle, cocked the hammer, and took aim. The gray's ear swiveled at the metallic click. Livvy didn't move. Daylight faded by degrees. He hadn't warned Livvy about riding out alone. How could he have been so careless? Why hadn't he hunted that cat down when he had the chance?

Regret dug its rowels deep. *Oh, God, please...*

His finger snugged the trigger as he sighted just to the left of the boulder that hid the cougar's body. Only the movement of its tail betrayed its position. If he shot too soon he'd miss. If he shot too late...

Slowly, calmly, Livvy raised her head and looked at him. She knew.

Don't run, Livvy. Don't run.

How he loved her! Helplessness burned a hole clean through him as she turned around. Her gasp reached his ears as her hands reached her face.

The cat leaped. Whit fired.

CHAPTER TWENTY

The rifle's report bounced off the rimrock and set Ranger to prancing. Whit kicked Oro into a run and jumped off before the horse came to a complete stop.

His eye and his rifle never left the cat stretched the length of Livvy, its tongue lolled across her hair. Blood soaked her blouse.

Neither of them moved.

He kicked at a plate-sized back paw. No response.

"Livvy." The word scraped from his throat, dragging his soul with it.

Finger on the trigger, he knelt beside her, laid a hand on the lion, feeling for a pulse. Satisfied the animal was dead, he knelt and rolled the cat off Livvy. His heart stopped.

Her chest barely rose with each shallow breath, and her hands covered her face—bloody hands, striped with seeping gashes that widened and spilled down her arms.

He choked out her name and lifted her to him.

She curled into his arms. "I thought—I thought—"

"It's all right now, darlin'. You're safe. I've got you." He kissed the top of her head, felt her heart pounding against his. *Oh, God, thank You. With all my life, I thank You.*

Easing her onto his leg, he gently lifted the fingers of one of her hands, afraid of what he'd find. But her fair face bore only the wash of her tears.

"We need to get you back to the house. Take care of these scratches on your hands."

A great soundless sob racked her body and she lowered the other hand. "What scratches?"

More like gouges. They dripped onto the denims she was so proud of, and when she finally saw them she cried out.

Whit pulled off his neckerchief and wrapped it around her right hand, the more deeply cut of the two. Then he stood, easily lifting her in his arms. "Can you ride?"

She nodded. Of course she'd say yes. He was proud of her stubbornness, but he couldn't have her passing out. "I'm putting you on Oro. I'll sit behind you and lead Ranger."

He looked deep into her shining eyes, so round and terror-filled. "Are you sure you can sit the saddle?"

Livvy hadn't been waited on since she was twelve and sick with a fever. But she had no say in the matter. The laudanum Pop administered at annoyingly regular intervals left her head fuzzy.

Whit was worse, seeing to the bandages that swathed both hands, tenderly changing them each morning and even more tenderly, applying a healing salve.

But more healing than Doc Mason's cure-all ointment was the love in Whit's eyes. If he never spoke the words in her lifetime, she knew he loved her. The admission spilled over with every touch and every smoky glance that sent shivers coursing through her body.

She yearned for him.

And he knew it.

For that she could kick him and would if she could stand without feeling light-headed and woozy. Yet for all her fussing and grousing, she thanked God for Whit's attention and Pop's medication.

Only twice since the attack had she wakened in the night with a cold, incalculable fear clutching her heart. She must have cried out, for both times her grandfather had come immediately, murmuring soothing words, assuring her she was safe, tucking the quilt around her as if she were a child again.

But in the daylight she had been remarkably calm.

Again, she was resting—as Pop insisted—with her legs extended on the dining room settee. She adjusted her skirt and gingerly flexed her fingers, forcing the stiffness from them.

Her hands would always be scarred. When she'd held them unbandaged before the mirror, side by side as they'd been that day against her face, the red swath of three razor-like claws declared how close she'd come to disfigurement. To death. The cuts were smooth, deep, precise.

She'd never understand why she had raised her hands. But she didn't have to understand. God's timing had been even more precise than the lion's attack.

Restless rather than restful, she swung her legs down and stretched her back, considering a trek to the kitchen pantry.

Every morning for a week, Buck had faithfully delivered a basketful of eggs. But the morning he discovered hatchlings peeking beneath the old red hen, he'd strutted more than the rooster.

"You should see them babies," he cackled at breakfast.

"*Those* babies," Livvy murmured.

Buck shot her a shy glance. "Yes, ma'am. Those babies."

"You act like you had something to do with 'em." Pop's mustache twitched.

Buck blushed and ducked his head. "I did. I left her alone."

Whit snorted. "After she nearly peeled the skin off your hand the first time you reached in there."

Jody hooted, fitting in more comfortably than he had for a few days. Buck had worn him out, and he'd no doubt think twice before he lit out after any more hired guns.

Livvy had awkwardly spread apple butter across one of Pop's famous hotcakes, getting more on the plate than the cake. Whit reached to help her, and she stopped him with a deadly glare. He smirked and withdrew his hand before it suffered the same as hers, but from a well-aimed fork.

Chuckling at the memory, she prepared to stand when Pop came out of his study and straight at her with a bottle and spoon.

She shooed him off. "I am done with that, thank you very much. I must get my mind clear, and you've got me all cloudy and befuddled with that whiskey you're giving me."

He stopped short, stared at the bottle, then held the label side toward her. "It is *not* whiskey. See here? It's laudanum."

"Oh, Pop, I'm teasing you. But I cannot take any more. I need to start thinking straight. Why, I could barely make sense of the newspaper article about the train war."

He grunted and stuffed the cork back in the bottle. "Makes no difference if you ask me. Far as I can tell, Masterson went back to Kansas. Some folks think he was paid off. But I think he got smart and figured he'd let the train barons fight it out." A bushy brow raised. "Denver did have a court order, you know. Proved they had the right-of-way through the gorge."

She vaguely remembered reading something about that on a page of her hatband stuffing, but regardless, the whole affair sounded like a bunch of roughs on both sides working themselves up for a fight that was already won.

"Won't be long until we hear the whistle all the way up here when the train runs through to Leadville." Pop lumbered back to his study and returned with an envelope.

"This was in the mail you brought the other day. Didn't you see it?"

Livvy took the envelope and read the return address. "Mother and Daddy. No, I didn't." She looked at her dear grandfather. "Thank you. I must have been too distracted over the rail-war news to notice."

She held out the envelope. "Open it for me, please?"

After a quick swipe of his stock knife, Pop handed back the letter. "I'll be in the study if you need me."

Livvy unfolded the thin paper, smelled her mother's light rosy scent, and read news of her parents and home. Their lives were the same—the daily duties of a pastor and his wife. She missed them, but she did not miss Denver. A frown drew her brows as she read of their plans to visit in the fall. Did they expect her to return home with them?

She could not. Even if Whit never declared himself, she could not go back to Denver. Not after living here. Surely her grandfather would let her stay and care for him, cook for his crew …

The kitchen door opened and a familiar boot step crossed the floor and stopped at the dining room. Livvy looked up at the handsome cowboy, hat cocked to the side, a confident gleam in his eye.

Her pulse quickened. "Have you come to take me beyond the bounds of these crushing walls, Mr. Hutton?"

A slow smile spread. "'Bout time you got off your pretty pastime, don't you think, Miss Hartman?"

She fanned the letter in front of her face, feigning embarrassment at his forward remark. "Really. Such language."

Whit strode to the settee and bent to scoop her up.

She resisted. "My legs work just fine."

His face close to hers, one side of his mouth lifted in an unspoken comment and her flush rose with it. No doubt her complexion matched the burgundy cushion beneath her.

Laying the letter aside, she slipped a bandaged hand in the crook of his arm as he straightened. "A walk would be lovely."

They left through the front door and strolled toward the barn, Maverick frolicking beside them. The fresh air invigorated her, reminding her of the life that flourished beyond the confines of the ranch house, and the beautiful countryside surrounding it.

Whit led her to a rough bench against the barn, shaded now in the afternoon light. He sat beside her, looped his left arm through her right one, and cradled her bandaged hand in both of his. Then he raised her hand to his lips and kissed the palm side of her fingers.

A storm stirred in his eyes as fierce and powerful as the squall that had pinned them at the rocks, and his pulse pounding against her wrist hammered a heavy counterpoint to her own running heartbeat.

"I love you, Olivia Hartman."

His husky voice rippled through her, and she took a moment for the current to subside. "Well, I'd say it's about time you figured that out."

His eyes darkened, narrowed as he searched her face.

She raised her left hand to his rough chin and glazed the stubble with her fingertips. "I love you, too, Whitaker Hutton. Whiskers and all."

He swallowed. "Would you marry a cowboy?"

Unable to resist the temptation, she rounded her eyes and struck an innocent pose. "Do you have one in mind?"

The growl came from deep in his chest, and she shivered in delight, holding his dangerous gaze.

"Will you marry *me*?"

"With pleasure, Mr. Hutton."

Leaning toward him, she closed her eyes in expectation of a kiss—that never came. Chagrined, she straightened, scolding herself for being so brash and bold.

He released her hand, left her briefly, and returned with a canvas roll. Standing before her, he withdrew a long, wooden-handled stamp iron she didn't recognize. Then he smoothed the dirt with his boot and stamped the brand. When he stepped back, a wide inverted V hung above twin Hs.

Puzzled, she looked up.

"That's you and me—Hutton and Hartman—beneath the mountain. That's our brand."

"Our brand?" She leaned over and traced the imprinted dirt with her finger, a spark of joy flaring in her breast. "But we—you—have no cattle. Why do you need a brand?"

Gently he raised her to stand, and with his hands grasping her arms, leaned down and brushed his lips against hers. "I bought out the widow Overton, and your grandfather staked us on the land. We have our own herd now, our own place."

"You—you had this made before you even asked me?" She stiffened at the realization, stinging from the emotional hail pelting her reasoning. "You arrogant—"

Lightning struck and he pulled her against him, pressing his mouth to hers with a hunger that both startled and thrilled her. When he broke away, he buried his face in her hair with a hoarse whisper. "You had to say yes, Livvy. What would I do with all those cows without you?"

Laughing, she wrapped her swathed hands around his neck. "Confident, aren't you, Mr. Hutton." She kissed him back, more heatedly than she'd thought possible, then took her fill of the love pouring from his eyes. "I'm sure you'll be needing my help come branding time."

He lifted her off the ground and swung her around with a cowboy's whoop that shot straight to her heart.

And that was exactly where she intended to keep him.

~~~

The Cañon City Chronicles

Romancing the Widow

Davalynn Spencer

For all who hope in God's unfailing love.

"Now faith is the substance of things hoped for, the evidence of things not seen."

—Hebrews 11:1

CHAPTER ONE

Cañon City, Colorado
September, 1888

Martha Mae Stanton yanked the satin ribbon beneath her chin and jerked off the ridiculous black hat. Digging her nails into the fine netting, she ripped the veil away and tossed it on the seat beside her.

A long, hot train ride was one thing. Making that ride while behind a socially dictated curtain was quite another.

Across the aisle, a matron gasped and clutched her reticule to her bulging bosom.

Martha picked up the veil, leaned into the narrow walkway, and dropped the netting on the woman's shelf-like lap. "Here. You wear it. I've had enough."

The matron sputtered and huffed and swatted the black tulle from her knees as if it were a stinging hornet.

A smile almost made it to Martha's dry lips but died for lack of sustenance.

She leaned back against the plush green seat and squeezed her eyes shut. The late afternoon sun broiled through her window. Grit dusted her teeth, and perspiration gathered beneath her arms and slid down her back. Late summer had never been so sticky—not in the Rocky Mountains.

Mimicking the matron a half hour later, the Denver & Rio Grande wheezed to a coughing stop at Cañon City's depot. Steam hissed along the wheels, and a knot tightened in Martha's neck. She retied the hat as impatient travelers rushed the aisle. Weary mothers herded their petulant young ahead of them, reminding Martha of her former students—and the children she would never bear.

The porter stopped at her seat with a shining smile and tip of his cap. "This be your stop, ma'am. Last one today."

"Yes—yes, I know." Through the open door at the end of the car came happy shouts and endearments of reuniting families. She gripped the seatback ahead of her and stood, giving her legs a moment to remember how to proceed.

"May I carry that for you, ma'am?" He reached for her bag.

"No. Thank you." She curled her fingers into the handle, desperate for something to ground her, something to keep her from running back down the rails.

She made her way to the exit and paused, searching the crowd for her parents.

Caleb and Annie Hutton stood apart, the only two people not huddled with arriving passengers. Upon catching sight of her, a smiling mask formed hard across her mother's gentle face, one Martha recognized from the countless times her father had dealt with the more unpleasant duties of his clerical calling.

Regret slid from the back of her damp collar and pooled at her waist. Returning had been a mistake. She did not want her family to see her as an unpleasant obligation.

The porter cleared his throat. "You all right, ma'am?"

She plucked at her high collar. "Quite. Thank you."

Breathing in a dusty draught, she descended to the step and then the ground.

Her father approached and drew her into his arms. Silent. Strong. He held her close, knowing as always exactly what to do.

Her mother wrapped an arm around each of them and bent her lilac-scented hair toward Martha. The fragrance embraced her as closely as her parents and drew her back through the years.

"I am so sorry." Mama's whisper fell as gently as her scent.

Martha pulled from their arms and met troubled eyes—her father's black as her mourning dress but shining with love. Her mother's burnished and beautiful as ever, though age had etched their corners.

"Thank you," Martha said. "Both of you. Let's go home."

It was a short walk to the buggy, and she and her mother climbed in while the porter helped her father strap her trunk to the back. Settling her carpet bag at her feet, Martha glanced toward the depot's long covered platform. In a shadowed corner, an abutment jutted from the building and a man leaned against it. Had the sunlight not cut from a sharp angle, she would have missed him in his dark clothing, hat pulled just below the level of his eyes. One knee bent with a booted foot resting on the wall. His thumbs hooked his trousers, draping back a black coat.

It was too hot for a coat of any kind.

She didn't realize she was staring until he raised his head a hairbreadth and met her eye to eye.

Steeled, perhaps by months of grief, she held his study without reaction, measuring him as he measured her. Lean and alone, like a wolf. So unlike her beloved Joseph.

Dressed in black, as was she in her widow's weeds.

Her jaw clenched at the phrase, and the tightness coupled like a freight car to her cramping neck. It was bad enough to be shrouded in spirit, bereft and singular after sharing life with a fine and caring man. Her eyes pinched at the corners, dry and tearless. Depleted.

She looked down at her pale hands clutched tightly against the gloomy skirt, as white as Joseph's still face. The memory seared through her chest, scorching what little vibrancy remained. All her hopes and promises of a future lay buried in a pine coffin.

Her father climbed to the seat, gathered the reins, and tapped old Dolly's rump.

A shudder rippled through Martha. Cramped as they were, her mother leaned even closer with concern. "Are you ill, Marti?"

The old name rang foreign in Martha's ears. No one had called her Marti since she graduated and married Joseph three years ago. She glanced over her shoulder as if searching for the name's rightful owner. The stranger's eyes caught hers.

Foolishness flooded her cheeks, perhaps a convincing enough sign for her mother to think she was feverish.

"No, Mama, I'm fine. Just—just noticing all the changes in Cañon City." A flimsy excuse, one sure to wither beneath years of perfected detection.

But the woman had pity on her only daughter and simply patted Martha's folded hands.

"Yes, a lot has changed since last you were here."

~

Everyone looked the same to Haskell Tillman Jacobs—road-weary, dusty, and glad to be off the train. Everyone but the red-haired beauty in black.

Anonymity suited him, and he preferred to blend in with whatever background presented itself. But she had stared straight at him as if she knew the man he sought and could tell him the varmint's whereabouts.

Obscurity returned when the parson drove away from the depot and turned east onto Main Street toward his home at the opposite end. Knowing what people did and where they lived was one of the better aspects of Haskell's job.

He just hadn't known about *her.*

He pushed from the wall, stepped off the wooden platform, and stopped at the second car. When the porter leaned down for the step, Haskell pulled back one side of his coat, revealing the star on his vest.

The man straightened. "Yes, sir?"

"Anyone else on the train?"

"No, sir. This our last stop."

"I'd like to see for myself."

The porter stepped aside. "Yes, sir."

The interior smelled of sweaty clothing, coal smoke, and sour lunches. Haskell walked the narrow aisle, checking the seats for any telltale sign or forgotten belonging.

The porter followed.

"There ain't nothin' left behind, sir. I done looked."

The man obviously took his job as seriously as Haskell took his, but he continued on, pausing at each bench.

Something lay on the floor halfway back. He bent and snatched up the dark netting, wadding it into his coat pocket. Continuing to the next car, he repeated his inspection, then turned to his dogged follower.

"And a fine job you've done."

"You huntin' somethin' special?"

The man's voice carried more than the cursory question. He saw more than most.

"Where did the woman in black board the train?"

"You mean the widow Stanton? Kansas City, sir."

Haskell fingered the netting. "You pick up anyone in Pueblo today?"

"Just a mother and her two youngin's. If'n somebody else jumped on the back, I couldn't say." Coal-black eyes lifted to the low ceiling. "We carried a body or two without knowin' it at the time." He regarded Haskell coldly. "But not in a *long* time." His thick brown fingers flexed open and closed.

Haskell nodded and stepped outside. "I'll have a look."

When the train arrived, he'd seen no movement on top of the cars, saw no one jump. At least not on the depot side.

5

He climbed up to view the length of the train and found what he expected—nothing. Squinting back along the rail bed, he noted the few houses huddled near the track with small fenced yards hedging the narrow road between the gravel and their gates.

Working his way down, he jumped clear and walked downtown.

Word had it that the man he sought was last seen in La Junta and headed this way by train. Obviously, the speed and comfort of such travel balanced out the risk, especially for one so gifted at slipping into a crowd unseen.

But Haskell could have missed his prey once the widow stepped down. She'd drawn his eye like a prospector's nose to a nugget. The hazards of a solitary life, he figured, though he had no intention of being turned from his purpose.

The black netting snagged his calloused fingers as he pulled it from his pocket. Intricate needlework hung from one side, torn thread from the other. Crumpling the ripped piece, he dropped it in a wire basket just inside the front doors of the McClure House.

Across the lobby, the dining room beckoned, and he took his usual table in the farthest corner. A seat against the wall offered a clear view of the guests who dotted the room. He set his hat on an empty chair.

The Yale University professor with more hair on his face than his head dined with his entourage, each member intent upon impressing the Easterner with some tidbit of knowledge.

A serving girl interrupted Haskell's observation with her coffee and inviting smile.

"Good evening, Mr. Tillman." She righted the cup on his saucer and filled it to just beneath the brim.

"Evening."

"Did you enjoy your day?"

She waited expectantly for him to answer, but he didn't chit-chat with girls young enough to be his daughter and obviously angling for a beau.

"What's on the board tonight?"

Her good humor slid away and she pulled the coffee pot to her waist. "Roast beef, mashed potatoes with gravy, green beans, and peach pie. Will you be dining alone again?"

She didn't give up easily, he'd give her that.

"Yes." He reached for the coffee, dismissing her.

She huffed away in a swirl of skirts and stopped at the Bentons' table, her smile back in place, her coffee at the ready.

If the food wasn't so good, he'd fill himself in his room on canned peaches and jerked beef. But it wasn't often he found fare like the hotel offered. Cañon City had more to recommend it than its bath house and hanging train bridge in the canyon.

Which were a couple of the reasons he'd given thought to staying a while. Maybe even settling down.

The young widow's bold gaze rose before him, framed by her black hat and coppery hair.

Her image nettled him. Irritated him. He had business to tend to and could not be distracted by a beautiful, aloof woman.

"I tell you, the second quarry will be as forthcoming as the first."

Drawn by the professor's insistent tone, Haskell raised his cup and tuned his ear to the conversation at the far wall. An animated man, the Easterner waved his fork like a band leader's baton.

"Finch has made further discovery across the gully and has been digging there for several weeks now with great success."

The listeners murmured over their plates, and from the gleam of fortune in the speaker's eye, Haskell guessed the man and his absentee companion—Finch—had uncovered an oil bed or a rich ore vein.

"I am confident that these bones will rival the Allosaurus and Diplodocus unearthed here a decade ago. Perhaps another Stegosaurus will be discovered, even more complete that the first."

Haskell coughed as the hot coffee slid down his wind pipe. He set the china cup in its saucer and wiped his mouth with a linen napkin.

If he recalled his school days accurately, the bald professor in the fine jacket was talking about dinosaurs.

CHAPTER TWO

Martha stood in the doorway, taking in her old room—that of a girl on her way to college. She set her bag on the trunk her father had placed at the foot of the iron bed and flopped onto the bright fan-patterned quilt. Running her fingers along the fine stitches, she recalled the piercing needle that bit repeatedly until she got the feel of the thimble.

She removed her hat and tossed the dreary thing aside. With a heavy sigh, she hugged a pink pillow to her chest and fell back across the bed.

Life had not turned out as she'd hoped.

Familiar footsteps sounded on the stairs, but Martha had no energy to sit up and invite her mother in. Nor had she the right. This was no longer her home, though she had called it such at the station.

"Supper's in a half hour. Will you be down?"

She turned her head toward the door. "Perhaps."

Her mother came in and sat on the bed. "There is a new seamstress in town. We can visit her in the next few days and pick out some lighter fabric for a new dress or two."

Martha sniffed. "You don't like my widow's weeds?"

"No, I do not."

Such characteristic honesty did not surprise Martha, but it bolstered her enough to sit up.

"It's been more than a year, Marti. You are young and smart and beautiful, and it breaks my heart to see you grieving away to nothing." She pulled one of Martha's hands from the pillow and pressed her fingers. "Life goes on—like the river. Ever the same but with new water every day, fresh from the mountains."

Martha turned her hand over and closed her fingers around her mother's. "It's hard, Mama. It's not only that I miss Joseph so much, I just don't know how to go on living."

Her mother nodded but said nothing.

"It's as if I buried myself with him." The whisper fell so lightly that Martha doubted it had been heard.

An aching smile pulled her mother's lips. "I know, dear. Not exactly how you feel at losing your husband, but I know how it feels to lose someone you love. That person leaves an irreplaceable hole in your heart—like your grandfather did in mine." She tightened her fingers. "But we go on in Christ's strength. He shares our sorrow, just as He did when He grieved for His friend Lazarus."

Martha pulled her hand free, resenting the comparison. "But Jesus brought Lazarus back. He hasn't brought back Grandpa or Joseph, and Joseph was a minister. A preacher, like Daddy, who loved his wife and his congregation. A man who should not have been struck down by a stray bullet in a street brawl."

Anger stiffened Martha's already aching neck and her fists clenched involuntarily.

Her mother stood and faced her. "I could not agree more. Life is not fair. But it is life. And while you are home with us, I pray you will take it up again." She leaned forward and lightly kissed Martha's forehead. "Come down when you're ready. We'll be waiting."

Martha let out a deep sigh and, seeking distraction, studied the book shelf her father had built when she was in grammar school. A china-faced doll sat on top in her beautiful blue taffeta dress. Below, an assortment of rocks and fossil fragments remained where Martha had left them beside a stack of books on paleontology.

At one time she fancied herself a pioneer in the male-dominated field. Her enthusiastic pursuit had earned her a seat at Michigan's Albion College where Joseph studied. How quickly his kind nature had turned her interest from things long dead to the handsome seminary student so full of life. She had gladly laid aside her earlier passion to be his wife.

And now he lay beneath the same earth that had hidden her once-cherished fossils.

The irony bit into her with a carnivorous crunch.

She replaced the pillow against the head board and slapped her hands on her lap. Dust blossomed from her skirt and powdered her palms. She removed her short jacket and hung it over the footboard to beat outside tomorrow along with her skirt. For this evening, her shirtwaist would do.

Time allowed a quick scrub of her hands and face before joining her parents at the table, and the lavender-scented water in the pitcher refreshed her from her doldrums.

Food held no appeal, but a cup of tea might sooth her stomach and her spirit.

She unpacked her satchel, loosed her hair, and let it fall unhindered. With the porcelain-backed brush and comb set Joseph had given her on their wedding night, she smoothed the knots and tangles until her fingers pulled smoothly through the length. Then she plaited it into a long rope and secured the end with a ribbon. Joseph had liked her hair down rather than up in the style of the day, and it had been her delight to please him.

Placing the matching set on her dressing table, she caught a younger version of her mother in the glass. At least Martha knew how she would look someday. But aging as gracefully as Annie Hutton in manner as well as appearance was far beyond Martha's capabilities. That required faith, and at the moment, hers was shaky at best.

Downstairs, she paused at the kitchen doorway, not surprised that her parents still ate there rather than the formal dining room. Some things never changed, and when she entered the kitchen, her father stood and offered his hand. Martha took it and allowed him to draw her into a brief embrace. She kissed his cheek and took the chair she hadn't claimed in seven years.

Such a short time. Yet it felt like a lifetime.

The plates already held cornbread and sliced ham, and her mother brought coffee to the table as well as a pot of tea.

"I thought you might prefer tea this evening," she said as she placed each vessel on a hot pad.

"Thank you, Mama. You were right." Martha pulled the old silver sugar bowl from the table's center and spooned in a helping, then poured the aromatic brew. She set the pot on its thick cloth, then laid one hand in her father's upturned palm and the other in her mother's as she bowed her head.

"Thank You, Lord, for bringing Marti safely to us," her father said. "Comfort her, Lord. Heal her with Your love, in Your timing. Amen."

Papa never had been one to preach a sermon in his prayers, and for that she'd always been grateful. But he also used her informal name—the moniker that had stuck until she enrolled at Albion.

Indeed, some things never changed, but she had. She may have come home, but she could never be who she once was.

The warm corn muffin broke apart in her hands and she buttered half. "So who's minding the mercantile now?"

A current shot between her parents like sheet lightning across the sky. She took a bite and waited for what must be bad news. Had they sold it since Grandpa Whitaker's passing two years before?

Mama held a napkin to her lips then picked up her coffee. "We wanted to talk to you about that."

Martha laid the muffin on her plate. Talk to her? About the mercantile? "Did you sell it?"

"I couldn't. Can't." Her mother's brows pulled together over pained eyes. "Foolish, I know, but I can't let it go. It's outdated and old-fashioned and other modern stores out-shine it. But the mercantile is what brought Daddy and me here, what introduced me to your father—that and Bess and Dolly." She reached for his hand, and he caught hers with a loving smile that tightened Martha's chest.

"We wondered if you might be interested in running the store." His thumb idly stroked the back of her mother's hand. "Just for a while, until we find someone to run it full time."

The suggestion made Martha's head hurt. She hadn't been required to make a decision since the deacons told her they would take care of all the funeral arrangements and asked her to choose a headstone. The reasoning part of her brain didn't work, and she rubbed her temples hoping to prod the lax organ into action.

"I—I don't know."

"You don't have to answer now." Apology tainted her mother's voice. "We had not intended to spring it on you so suddenly. Take your time and think it over. Your grandmother still works every morning, and a young man is helping in the afternoon until we find someone more permanent. We just thought—"

"You just thought it would be good for me." Martha regretted the steel in her voice, but they were doing it again. And she a grown woman now. They had sent her away to school to protect her—they said—from Tad Overton. They had suggested she become a teacher—they said—because she had such a way with the children at church. And now they had planned the rest of her life here in Cañon City, tucked safely behind the counter of Whitaker's Mercantile.

"If you'll excuse me, I'm rather tired from my trip." She took her plate to the sink and scraped her meal into the chicken scrap tin. When she turned around, her parents still held each other's hands. Mama's head dipped forward, hiding her expression.

"We'll see you in the morning, Marti." Her father's words offered acceptance. "Sleep well."

Aching with regret and frustration, she dashed up the staircase and slammed her door with the unreasonable anger of a twelve-year-old.

More shame.

Leaning against the door, she slid to the floor. At last the tears came, burning and purging, like great stinging drops of acid.

~

Haskell stood at the east window of his third-floor room, watching dawn crest the Main Street buildings. Within a month the sun would slide south along the horizon and rise a half hour later.

But his internal clock woke him at the same time every morning, summer and winter. Something he had learned from his father.

Paying extra for the corner room was well worth the view of the depot a few blocks to the south. Steam and smoke rose from the train's stack as it coughed and cleared its throat, preparing to pull through the narrow gorge and up the grade to Leadville.

He rubbed his face and ran both hands through his hair. One more day and he'd visit the barber. But today he'd walk the road that hugged the south side of the tracks. Keep an eye out for any last-minute passengers hopping a car.

He grabbed his hat and locked the door behind him.

Few people were on the streets at this hour, but enough to garner his scrutiny. Merchants, bankers—those he'd seen before. No new faces. He cut down a side street and crossed the tracks east of the depot. Lights shown from the row houses fronting the narrow road, and ribbons of frying bacon laced the morning. His stomach growled and an old yearning stirred.

Food wasn't all he longed for, but a warm smile and a loving woman to come home to. A family, maybe a few acres of his own outside of town. The law was a mean-spirited mistress and had kept him on the move far too long. It was time.

The widow's face flashed before him, sober, pale, bold. Not exactly what he had in mind for a wife. But her image dogged him and he couldn't shake free of her. Even in his dreams she stared, peeling away his veneer as easily as skinning a spud.

Who was she—other than the parson's widowed daughter come home to mourn? That much he'd overheard in the hotel parlor last night after supper. But *who* was she? *What* was she that she stuck in his mind like a bur to a saddle blanket?

He shook his head and cleared it enough to focus on the empty street that stretched before him. A cottonwood stood sentry halfway between the houses and depot, and he took up his post on its west side with a clear view of both. If anyone crossed over, he'd see him. And if someone jumped the cars without benefit of a ticket, Haskell would be obliged to help him detrain.

He pulled his watch from his vest pocket, ran his thumb over the engraved *TJ*, and flipped open the cover. The watch face read a quarter to seven.

The train whistle blew, right on time.

He slid the timepiece in its shallow pocket and reset his hat. If his quarry were here, he'd be showing himself any second now.

The tree's rough bark bit through his coat sleeve by the time the train built up a full head of steam and eased out of the station. No one stole from the houses across the tracks. No one dodged out at the last minute to swing onto the back of a car. Haskell rubbed his arm. Maybe his information was wrong. Crossing the tracks, he headed for the telegraph office.

The sleepy-eyed operator opened the door, clearly displeased at being asked to send a telegram so early. Haskell penned a coded message, signed the agreed-upon alias, and pushed the paper across the counter. "Send it to Captain Teller Blain, Colorado Rangers, Denver."

Two bits followed the paper and he answered the operator's curious regard with a cold stare. "You can reach me at the McClure House."

He reset his hat and walked toward the hotel. He'd eaten there twice a day for the last five and though it was good, he needed a change. Smoke curled from a mercantile chimney in the next block. He crossed the street and stopped before the door, held open by a flatiron. The front windows were filled with the usual wares—stoves, dishes, barrels and sacks of provisions. Toward the back, two men sat in front of a pot-bellied stove, though it wasn't the season for that sort of thing.

An older woman poured coffee from a blue-speckled pot and saw him as she lifted her head. Her hand beckoned, and out of respect he removed his hat and stepped inside.

The aroma of fresh biscuits lured him to join the other hapless prey at the stove. If the pan-fry lived up to its smell, it'd be worth sitting so close to a fire on a late-summer morning.

Shadowed at the back of the store, another woman worked at a long counter. A thick braid hung to apron strings tied at her waist, and the hair's color registered a warning, but she turned before he took notice. Her dark eyes locked on him, nailing his boots to the worn wooden floor. Expressionless, her porcelain skin did not pink as did that of the young waitress at the hotel.

In a breath, she collected herself and continued forward, bearing two plates of biscuits floating in syrup. She gave one to each man without so much as a word.

"And you must be hungry yourself, young man."

He turned to the diminutive white-haired woman who wore rosy sunshine on her face and offered him a tin cup filled with coffee. Few people called him young anymore, but she had the right, judging by her snowy crown.

"Thank you, ma'am." He took the remaining empty chair and acknowledged the other two men as briefly as possible.

Without her black suit and hat, and with her auburn hair hanging down her back, the widow appeared younger than she had at the train station. Softer. But not in her countenance. It remained stony and unresponsive as she handed him a tin plate with two syrup-covered biscuits.

He'd never eaten syrup on biscuits, and it didn't necessarily appeal to him. "Thank you."

Her eyes skimmed past his before focusing beyond his shoulder.

"You are welcome."

Did he imagine it or did he actually hear it?

Her voice was a wind whisper in tall pines, a sigh of evening breeze across prairie grass. It chilled him and warmed him at the same time.

He stared at his plate, telling himself to use the fork that lay across it.

The others ate as if they were about to be hanged. He set his cup on the floor and balanced the deep-lipped plate on one leg.

The first bite threw the hotel's heavy bread into disgrace. The second pulled his heart up through his gullet, and the third finished a biscuit. The word fell short of describing the fare, as far short as red told the color of the widow's braid.

Without watching her, he followed her movements, felt the shifting air as she passed, smelled the faintest lavender when she reached for his empty plate.

Again the voice, stronger this time. Purer. "Do you care for more?"

He studied her hands, avoided her eyes, for they would make a beggar of him, ranger or no.

Shaking his head, he gave up his plate. "But thank you." The hot tin cup offered distraction, and he gripped it, drawing the coffee's burn through his fingers.

The other men left, the older woman filled his cup again, and time stood still. The fire died, his brow cooled, and he remembered what he was about.

He raised his head to find the widow gone and a doorway at the back of the store closed. It'd been open earlier. Clapping his hat on, he stood and set the cup on the cold stove. At the counter he laid his money down and thanked the older woman.

"She makes the best, wouldn't you agree?" Her pleasant voice broke through his clouded state.

Ignoring his silence, she continued. "Marti makes the best biscuits in these Rocky Mountains. Just like her mother, Annie, did years ago." His coins clinked into the till drawer. "Drew me in, I tell you. That and Marti's handsome grandfather, God rest his soul. But she's got her mother's touch, that's for sure."

The matron sent him off with a cherubic smile. "You come back, now."

He touched the brim of his hat and made for the open door and fresh air. Had he dreamed it all or had he just spent the morning in an old mercantile, mesmerized by a beautiful young woman?

The sun's position agreed with his pocket watch.

He turned toward the livery at the end of town. A hard ride would do him good. He'd scour the river, search for cold campfires, maybe find what he was looking for. Get his wits about him.

And decide if Marti was a shortened form of Martha.

CHAPTER THREE

Martha ran down the alley behind the Main Street stores until she came to the livery. Leaning against the old gray barn, she gathered her breath and her composure. The dark stranger unsettled her, and it had cost every ounce of her shaky strength to conceal the fact. Her legs trembled from the brief sprint and her pulse hammered in her temples. She'd never felt so poorly. A year of inactivity, other than teaching, had weakened her, left her vulnerable. No horseback riding, no long walks, no working in a garden since Joseph had died, and now she felt she might follow him at any moment.

She pressed her back against the rough boards and drew in long, deep breaths. She surely *would* die if she didn't find something to do with herself. But working in the mercantile was not the answer. Not with men like…like…disarming strangers who could be outlaws or gunslingers or ne'er-do-wells of any sort.

Twice she had seen him in as many days, and both times he'd affected her the same way, making her shamefully curious about a man other than her beloved Joseph.

She rubbed her hands down her skirt front, annoyed to see the apron. It must be returned, but not now. Not today. She loosed the strings, folded the white cloth and rolled it into a bundle. If Mama hadn't insisted she go to the mercantile…

She stomped her foot. Oh—it was happening again. People telling her what to do and how to do it. She'd not be a storekeeper, not even temporarily.

The recent reminder of her grandmother's cheerful countenance flooded Martha with remorse. How could she, the woman's name-sake, *not* help?

Deflated by an inbred sense of duty, Martha twisted the apron as if wringing water from laundry, and walked up the alley between the livery corral and the boot maker's. She'd return the apron tomorrow.

At Main Street, she watched a passing buckboard with laughing children jostling in the back. A man and woman sat on the bench. They pulled up in front of the mercantile, and the woman turned to the youngsters. Even from a distance, her ultimatum was clear. The squirming bunch quieted and stilled and nodded their blond heads.

Joseph was blond. His children might have looked such, if she had been able to bear them. Her mind's eye filled with the doctor's shaking head and death-like pronouncement.

Clutching the rolled apron, Martha stepped into the street. The sudden scramble of iron-shod hooves, a man's shout, and a horse's breathy snort were the last she heard before slamming the hard-packed road with her head.

The ground pushed hard against her, gritty and gouged with wheel ruts. Her dress must be ruined. She turned her head to the side, tried to inhale but her chest refused the air. Panic licked her spine.

Where was the apron? She tried to sit up, but pain shot through her ribs and shoulder.

"Can you hear me?" Deep, the voice came. Urgent, like the dark visage above her, frowning over piercing blue eyes.

"Blink once if you can hear me."

She blinked. Slowly, heavily. When she looked again, the face was still there, but closer. So close she could see a lavender rim circling blue irises and smell coffee on the lips beneath them.

"Can you move?"

She made to sit up, but fell back at the sharp stab in her right shoulder.

Another man came into view, the blacksmith, judging by his stained leather apron.

"She's the parson's daughter," he said. "They live behind the church across the way."

Impatience rolled through the blue gaze, and their owner straightened. "I know." He spoke to the smithy. "Tie my horse to the rail. I'll be back."

Again, he leaned close, his features softening. "I'm Haskell Jacobs. I'm going to pick you up, get you off the street. Blink once if you understand."

She complied.

He slid one arm beneath her shoulders, cringing when she flinched. The other arm slipped beneath her knees, and he lifted her as he stood.

Nausea roiled in her stomach.

O Lord, the very man I feared has me in his arms and I am defenseless! Forcing her eyes to stay open, she tried to guess his intended destination. He crossed the street and took the lane beside her father's church. At least he was headed in the right direction.

Against her will, her eyes closed and her churning stomach threatened to expose everything she had eaten that morning. She gritted her teeth and the pressure increased. Her left arm was pinned against a hard chest and her right lay across her lap. She wiggled her fingers and raised her hand to her face, wincing at the effort.

"Don't try to move."

The deep voice rumbled against her ear. Gruff yet gentle, as much a paradox as flashing eyes beneath a black scowl.

She fingered her temple and found gravel and dampness.

"You hit hard. You're bleeding, but you need not be frightened. I've got you now."

She looked up as he spoke and caught the comfort he offered in spite of his dark air.

"Marti!"

Her mother's cry startled her, and pain shot through her shoulder again. Closing her eyes, she turned her face against the stranger's chest. A man's smell filled her senses—warmth, sweat, an equine earthiness. His heart pounded as hard and fast as the horse's hooves had danced around her. His horse's hooves? He had nearly run her down and now he was carrying her up the porch steps.

"Is she all right?" Anxiety rippled her Mama's voice as footsteps led them to the parlor. The stranger—Jacob?—set her gently on the settee and tucked a cushion behind her neck before pulling his arm away.

"Do you have a doctor in Cañon City?" he asked her mother.

"Yes. Doc Mason's place is at the other end of town."

"I'll ride down and get him. It's the least I can do."

Martha fought her heavy eyelids to catch her mother's expression.

"What do you mean? What happened?"

"She stepped in front of my horse at the livery. When he reared, a front leg knocked her to the ground. She may have broken her shoulder." He touched his hat brim and backed toward the door. "I best be getting the doctor, ma'am. My apologies. I'll cover any expenses."

The front door closed with Martha's eyes. Skirts whispered near, and Martha forced her eyes open again.

Worry pinched her mother's brow.

Martha's eyes refused to focus and she surrendered.

A gentle hand pressed her forehead. "I'll be right back. I'm going to get a cool cloth and clean you up a bit."

She tried to nod but the effort increased her nausea. She heaved a sigh and sank into the cushion.

23

Haskell heeled Cache into a lope and kept a careful eye on the boardwalk and cross streets for anyone who might be fool enough to rush out in front of him. He didn't need to run down another careless pedestrian.

What was she thinking, charging out that way? Did the widow have a death wish?

She'd caught him off his guard at every turn, and as she'd lain ashen and unmoving in the street, death was exactly what he'd feared. The gash on her head had stopped his heart. Stopped the very blood in his veins. Thank God, she lived.

He hadn't thanked God for anything in a long time.

He reined in at a yellow two-story house with green shutters. A sign hung from the porch: *Marion Mason, M.D. ~ Surgeon, Dentist.* Dismounting, he tossed the reins over a fence picket. At the covered porch, he knocked on a door marked *Surgery* and stepped inside.

"Hello?" He took off his hat.

A harried woman came from an adjoining room, wiping her hands on a white blood-stained towel. "You need something?"

He'd never met a woman doctor. "You Doc Mason?"

Her thin brows wrenched together. "No. He's washing up. Give him a minute and he'll see you." She gestured to a row of mismatched chairs against the front wall. "Have a seat."

He remained standing.

"Suit yourself."

Her manner, not her gender, made him glad she wasn't the doctor.

She returned to the surgery, and muffled voices blended above a groan. Haskell made out the word *laudanum* and watched the doorway. Feet scuffed on the hardwood, a chair scraped across the floor.

He turned to the window. Cache danced wide-eyed and nervous after the collision, ears swiveling at every street noise. The dark gray sidled up along the fence to keep one eye on the road.

Haskell huffed. Even his horse knew better than to have its back to the door.

At a clearing throat, Haskell spun, caught less prepared than his gelding.

"May I help you?" A balding man with wire-rim glasses halfway down his nose and shirtsleeves rolled halfway up his arms walked to the center of the room and waited. His hands were ruddy from a recent scrubbing, and the scent of alcohol wrapped his short stature.

"A woman's been hurt. She's the parson's daughter. Can you come and look at her?"

The doctor rolled down his cuffs as he returned Haskell's query with one of his own. "Which parson? There is more than one, you know."

Haskell clenched his jaw. He couldn't keep his thoughts clear when the widow had them in an uproar. "At the other end of town, behind the white clapboard church. She's a widow. The daughter, I mean."

The doctor perked up. "Marti Hutton—er, Stanton? Pastor and Annie Hutton's daughter? What happened?"

Haskell's jaw cramped tighter. He didn't need questions, he needed action. "She was knocked to the ground by a horse. Stepped into the street without looking."

"I'll get my bag and meet you there. My buggy's out back." With that, the doctor left Haskell standing in the parlor like a dismissed child. A back door closed hard, and he took that as his cue to leave. Shoving his hat on, he went back outside, lifted Cache's reins from the picket, and swung up.

So much for a ride along the river.

At the livery, he pulled off Cache's rig and carried it inside, where hammer pings rang from the back of the barn.

Pete Schultz wasted no daylight. Every door and window was fastened open, and a draft pulled through the alleyway, sweeping the furnace heat from the stable.

Haskell stowed his tack and returned to the parsonage behind the church. A buggy waited in front of the house with a sleepy-eyed nag in the harness. Doc Mason's.

Covering the three steps in one leap, he paused at the screen door.

"Yes, he brought her in just moments ago, then rode to fetch you," Mrs. Hutton said.

Being the subject of a woman's conversation wasn't the most comfortable thing he'd endured, especially since the accident was his fault.

Check that. It was *not* his fault.

He knocked on the door frame.

Mrs. Hutton pushed open the screen. "Come in. The doctor's just arrived."

He snatched his hat. It'd been in his hands more that day than on his head.

Mason sat on a low stool pulled close to Marti—or Mrs. Stanton or Miss Hutton. What did a man call a widow, especially one as young and striking as this one? The blue velvet settee backed her copper hair as if designed to do just that.

Mason leaned close to the widow's ear and gentled his voice. "Can you tell me exactly what happened?"

Haskell cleared his throat. "I can."

The doctor turned and glowered over his wire frames. "Well, speak up."

"She stepped in front of my horse."

Expressionless, the doctor continued to stare. "And?"

"He reared and when he came down, his knee knocked her to the ground."

"Didn't you see her coming?"

I was distracted. Haskell stiffened. He didn't have to answer to this man, or anyone. "She hit hard."

His eyes flicked to the purple swelling beneath the now-clean gash. "May have broken her shoulder."

Mason turned back to his patient and held his hand against her brow. An odd resentment prodded Haskell.

"Come over here and help Mrs. Hutton. I'm going to palpate Marti's shoulder and you'll both need to hold her still."

Annie Hutton's eyes locked on Haskell's as if daring him to harm her daughter again. A she-bear ready to charge. He laid his hat beneath a chair and took his place at the widow's feet.

He'd set his share of bones, but out on the trail, not in a parson's parlor. And they'd been men's bones, not those of a fragile young woman with a worried mother at hand. Just to be safe, he pulled the widow's skirt hem over her buttoned shoe tops, then wrapped both hands around ankles he could snap with a flick of his wrist.

Mrs. Hutton placed a hand on her daughter's left shoulder and slipped her other arm over her chest and around her ribs.

This was awkward at best.

Doc touched the right shoulder, pressing with seasoned fingers. The widow lurched, but her mother held firm. She kicked against Haskell, hard enough to break her own ankles, but she did not cry out.

He'd seen men fare far worse.

"It's not broken." Sweat beaded on the doctor's forehead. "Dislocated. Hold her now. I'm going to pop it back in place."

Haskell squeezed. Mrs. Hutton leaned into her daughter. Doc Mason yanked.

The widow jerked as if she'd been shot, then she fell slack and her head lolled to the side, her mouth open. Out cold.

Haskell let go and shoved his shaking hands in his pockets. What was wrong with him?

CHAPTER FOUR

Martha sat at her dressing table, basking in Joseph's attention. He stood behind her, pulling the hand-painted brush through her hair with long, smooth strokes. Smiling, she lifted her eyes to meet his in the glass and gasped at the dark visage there. Ice-blue eyes bore into her with unsettling possessiveness.

Martha's eyes flew opened and locked on the parlor ceiling above her. Her parents' parlor. A sling bound her right arm against her chest, and her feet flounced awkwardly over the short settee's armrest. She struggled to sit upright and movement behind her warned of an approaching presence.

"Allow me."

A deeply tanned hand took hold of her left arm and steadied her as she pulled herself up and swung her feet to the floor. The effort spun her head like a top, and she raised her left hand to her temple.

"Are you all right?"

Again, that voice. She leaned against the settee's back, gripping an armrest.

"I'll get you some water."

"I don't want any water." Her abruptness scratched her own ears, and she glanced at the tall stranger standing in her parents' home, so committed to her well-being.

Training at a pastor's knee forced a quieter remark. "But thank you."

The man's face bore the lines of one who squinted long and tirelessly into the sun. A deep indentation ringed his head, evidence of a hat normally worn over black collar-length hair. His shadowed jaw could have buffed her nails if she dared raise them to it.

Curling the fingers of her left hand, she slid it beneath her skirt and softened her tone. "Who are you and why are you here?"

He pulled a footrest closer. Martha fully expected it to collapse beneath his weight, but it held him, though his knees pitched high and he looked up at her as if he perched on a milk stool.

In spite of his awkward seating, he relaxed and the tension in his jaw loosened. "Haskell Jacobs, ma'am. I carried—brought you in from the street where you fell."

That explained the sling.

"Why are you here?"

He swallowed. "I brought you in—"

"I know that."

Blue lightning flashed.

She would not be intimidated. Not in her parents' home by a man squatting on a footstool. "Why are you *here*, in Cañon City, Mr. Jacobs?"

The light dimmed as a shade drew down, shutting her out from what lay in those icy depths. "Business."

The next logical question jumped to her lips, but she bit it back. Instead, she raised her chin. "I see."

Footsteps approached from the kitchen, and Mr. Jacobs shot up from the stool.

Mama appeared with a tray. "A cup of tea is just what you need, Marti. I'm glad to see you've wakened."

Evidently she thought Mr. Jacobs needed one too, for the tray held three cups as well as the silver sugar bowl and three spoons. She stopped at Martha's knee, searching for signs of fever, illness, nerves, rash, pox—all the things a mother feared would overtake her offspring, regardless of their age.

"Thank you, Mama."

A weak smile. Her mother turned to Mr. Jacobs, whose hand dwarfed the tea cup. Surprisingly skillful with the china, he declined the sugar and held the cup and saucer unwaveringly as he seated himself in a nearby chair.

Those hands would swallow her hair brush.

Betrayed by the uninvited image, Martha smarted at the heat in her face and bent her head to hide her humiliation.

Mama took the chair on the left, facing Mr. Jacobs. Silence encased them in a delicate web that Martha cared not to break herself. She sipped the hot chamomile, her favorite.

Sunlight slanted through lace curtains at the west window and cut ornate designs on the carpet. Clearly, she'd spend most of the day flat on her back in the parlor, hopefully not under the continued observance of Mr. Jacobs. Shouldn't he be leaving?

Head down, she peeked at his boots, dusty and black like the rest of his attire, other than a gray shirt beneath his shadowed chin. A coat brush would do the man a world of good. Had he no wife to care for him?

Oh, Lord, I am surely losing my mind.

Her head ached with the search for clear thought, and one bobbed to the surface.

"The apron." She looked at Mr. Jacobs. "Did you see an apron?"

He stared as if she were a halfwit.

She stared back.

"Were you wearing an apron from the store?" Her mother's cup landed hard on the saucer.

Martha flinched. "No. I had rolled it up. It was in my hands, I think."

Mr. Jacobs retrieved his hat from beneath the chair and stood. "Thank you, Mrs. Hutton." He set his cup and saucer on the tray atop a side table and turned to Martha. "I'm glad to see you are feeling better. Next time, check both ways before you step into the street."

Fire rushed into her temples. How dare he speak down to her. She was not a child. *He* ran into *her*. As she opened her mouth to set him straight, her mother rose.

"Thank you, Mr. Jacobs, for bringing Marti home safely. I do appreciate your concern." She followed him to the door and clasped both hands at her waist.

He held out a silver piece.

"No, but thank you. We can cover the doctor's expenses. Really, it is not necessary."

He laid the coin next to the lamp by the front window, jerked his hat on, and nodded to them both.

"Ma'am. Miss." Then he left.

Mama ignored the silver and joined Martha on the settee, reaching for her left hand. "I'm sure he meant well."

"I am sure he meant nothing of the sort."

The set of her mother's mouth forewarned a lecture. Martha withdrew her hand. She was not a child. Did everyone see her as such?

"Marti—"

"Why do you insist on calling me that? I am not a school girl. I am a grown woman, an *educated* woman."

That had not come out as she intended.

Her mother's face paled and her jaw line tightened. She peered directly into Martha's eyes.

"Educated enough not to step in front of a man on horseback?"

Martha's anger evaporated.

"What if he had run you over? What if he had trampled you and left you in the street?"

The suggestion certainly described Martha's feelings at the moment. Tears clogged her throat and stung her eyes. She fingered the neck of her bodice.

Her mother's tone softened. "What were you thinking?"

At such gentleness the barricade broke, and words gushed out on a wrenching sob. "I was thinking of children—the children I will never have."

Martha leaned into her mother's embrace, much more a school girl than a woman. "Oh, Mama, I don't know what I'm going to do. I believed I could go on without Joseph, but I can't. I've tried, and everywhere I turn I think of him, of what might have been."

Straightening, she pulled a hanky from her sleeve and held it to her eyes. "I'm sorry."

"You've been sorry quite long enough for something you've no need to apologize for. Is this what Joseph would want you to do—grieve your life away? Or would he want you to remember him for the good days you shared? Be the vibrant young woman he fell in love with?"

"At twenty-four I am no longer young or vibrant."

Her mother's brow knotted and she clutched her skirt in both fists as if fighting for Martha's life. "Start over, Marti—Martha."

"But how could I ever love anyone other than Joseph?"

Again her mother reached out. "You make the fresh start, dear, and let the Lord take care of your heart. Get involved at the mercantile or someplace else. The Women's Reading Club. Perhaps you could lead a children's group at church, or teach at the school this winter. Or spend some time at the ranch. The twins are a handful for Livvy, you know."

Children. Always someone else's children. Or the mercantile.

Martha spread the damp hanky on her lap. "I don't want to be a store keeper, but I know Grandma could use my help."

"And you could use hers." Her mother's voice thickened. "She knows what it means to lose your life's companion."

"I'm sorry, Mama. You must miss Grandpa terribly."

"I do. But I concentrate on what he gave me, not on what I lost when he passed on. My prayer is that you will do the same. Joseph is with the Lord, whom you both love. Trust that God will lead you as you face the rest of your life."

Martha wrapped her arm about her mother's shoulders and kissed her graying temple. "I love you, Mama."

"I love you too, dear. But not nearly as much as our Lord does."

~

Haskell strode down the short lane to Main Street, paused for a mule-drawn wagon, and crossed to the other side. He snatched up a crumpled roll of white fabric and swiped at brown hoof marks imprinted on the sturdy cloth. It would take more than the brush of his hand to make it right.

His gut twisted like the cloth. Making things right involved more than the widow's apron. He wanted to make things right with her.

He was a fool.

Folding the roll in half, he turned up the street toward the laundry. If they couldn't get it clean and like new, he'd have another one made to replace it.

Decision made. The knot in his belly eased.

Life had been predictable and simple when he came to Cañon City. He had a man to find, a duty to do, and a plan to carry it out.

And then that woman stepped off the train.

In the time it took to cock his pistol or cuff a wrist, his life had jumped the track.

He stomped into the laundry and slapped the apron on the counter. A sweaty little man rolled it out to its full length and gave Haskell the once-over.

"Can you make it look brand new?"

The man's eyebrows dipped and he turned the cloth around. "Can do. Five cent."

"Today?"

"Tomorrow."

Haskell slammed a coin on the counter and turned to leave.

"Name!"

"Tillman."

His stomach pushed him toward the café.

Few patrons remained this late in the afternoon, and he took the table against the back wall, chair facing the door.

A thick man with thicker hair brought coffee and a heavy mug, then poured without asking. Haskell nodded his thanks.

"Beef stew's all we got left. And biscuits."

Haskell's mouth watered at the memory of the widow's biscuits. "That'll be fine."

The coffee was charred, but it jolted him back to reality.

He was old. Too old and too hard for a woman like the widow. At thirty-three he'd taken part in more than his share of brawls and killings, and he didn't know the first thing about settling down.

But that was what he'd been aiming at the last few years. The exact reason he'd convinced the captain to let him take this job. He intended to scope out more than horse thieves and train jumpers. He wanted to drop his reins on a piece of cow country with a steady flowing creek and sweet grass. Grow a few fruit trees, raise a family. Stay in one place.

But men like him didn't get to live that kind of life.

The waiter returned with a steaming bowl and set it before him. "There's a little more where that come from if you're still hungry." He held out his hand. "Four bits. Coffee's on the house."

Haskell dropped a half-dollar in the open palm. The man glared at Haskell, and left.

If the stew was palatable, he'd leave a short bit on the table. The biscuit was cold and hard, but the well-seasoned beef and vegetables made up for it. He broke the bread into chunks and stirred them into the stew. Martha Hutton Stanton must be the only one around who could make a decent biscuit.

He jabbed at a chunk of meat and splashed gravy on the tablecloth. That woman wouldn't let him be. She drew him off course at every turn. He needed to find his man and leave town.

A half hour later, he headed Cache toward the Arkansas and turned upstream. Cottonwoods grew thick and green along the banks, and Canada geese poked their way through pastures that sloped down to the water's edge. Few fences blocked his path, but where they did, Cache easily took the lazy current at a slow walk. The water ran smooth and low this close to town, unlike the rapids farther up the canyon.

Again he turned Cache onto the bank, then reined in. A canvas tent snugged against the trees, and a dying fire sent wavering heat circling round a spider and tripod. A blackened coffee pot sat on the stones.

He called out.

An old man bent beneath the tent flap. From the looks of his hat and beard, a miner gone bust. He squinted at Haskell, stepped out, and stood as straight as his old bones allowed.

"What kin I do fer ya?"

"You alone here?"

A bony hand slipped into the pocket of his dungarees. "Who wants to know?"

Haskell pulled his coat flap back. "I'm not huntin' trouble. Just a horse thief."

A grin cracked above the unshorn beard. "'Tain't me." The other hand swept around the camp site. "As you kin see, I ain't got no horse flesh here." A laugh bounced out. "I hardly got any flesh o' my own."

The man hobbled to the fire, poked a stick under the coffee pot lid, and peeked in. "I can give ya coffee and that's about it."

Haskell looked upstream. He should move on. Cache tossed his head in unspoken agreement. "I'll take you up on that offer." Stepping down, he dropped the reins.

The grin widened and with a lighter step, the old timer disappeared into the tent and returned with a tin cup. "Don't get many callers down here like in the old days." He pulled a rag from his pocket and lifted the pot.

Haskell straddled a log and took the offered cup. "Much obliged."

The man retrieved another tin from behind the fire circle and filled it halfway.

"Here's to good huntin', son." He raised the cup in a mock toast.

Haskell tested the brew with a cautious swallow. Second time today he'd been referred to as young. He shook his head.

"Not to your likin'?" The old man's eyes narrowed.

"No, sir. It's fine. Just fine. I was thinking about something else."

A cackling laugh. "Outlaws or women?"

Haskell shot a glance at his host. He didn't need a prophet in the mix, but with different clothes, the old timer would fit the bill.

"Both are trouble, but one's more fun 'n the other."

Haskell took a swig of tepid coffee. "I can't argue with you there."

The man wiped his coat sleeve across his bushy-bearded mouth. "Seen a fella walkin' the river last night, leadin' a string o' mighty fine ponies. Didn't know I was watchin' him."

Haskell lowered his cup, listened for what wasn't being said.

"I figured he didn't own any of 'em. Otherwise, why sneak 'em by here after dark and not ride 'em through town in the daylight?"

"Was he headed upstream?"

"He was. Had a full moon last night, and after he passed, I follered him. He walked near the length o' town before cuttin' off into the trees. I figured we was at the other end of Main Street by that time."

Haskell swirled the dregs. "Why'd you follow him?"

"Why not?" A gap-toothed grin pushed through the whiskers. "Like I said, don't get many visitors out here nowadays, and I figured he was up to no good. Wanted to make sure he didn't come back and cut my juggler."

Haskell tongued coffee grounds out of his cheek and set the cup on a smooth river rock. He pulled a silver dollar out of a vest pocket and laid it one rock over. "Thank you for the Arbuckle's."

The miner's eyes narrowed and he angled his head away, watching his guest out the side of his face. "What's that fer?"

"The coffee." Haskell stepped easy to his horse, aware of the old timer's hand back in his pocket. He swung up and tugged his hat brim. "And the information."

The man picked up the coin and turned it over a couple of times before tucking it away.

Haskell rode upstream a half mile, picking out a jumble of hoof prints along the way. At least five horses. At a clearing in the trees, the tracks turned north, and he followed an overgrown trail to a barn just this side of Main Street.

Right behind Doc Mason's place.

CHAPTER FIVE

Martha winced as she rolled to her left side and swung her feet over the edge of the bed. Any movement—large or small—managed to find its way to her right shoulder. Whether it started with her foot or her head, it landed in a dull ache that throbbed into her neck and down her arm.

A restless night had left her weary and irritable. If Mr. Haskell Jacobs crossed her path today, she'd tell him exactly what she thought of his horsemanship and his unseemly manners in the parlor yesterday.

And then she would stop thinking of him altogether.

Last night Mama had filled the copper tub with hot water and let her soak in luxury until the water cooled. It eased the pain and soothed her simmering temper, and she'd give almost anything to repeat the process this morning. But that was unlikely. One did not bathe in broad daylight in the kitchen.

At the washstand in her room, she squeezed out a cloth with one hand and scrubbed her face and neck and shoulders—as much as possible. She needed her mother's assistance with her hair, her dress, and her shoes. Grateful that she hadn't fallen on her left shoulder, she dipped a small brush in tooth powder and cleaned her teeth, then unfastened her braid and pulled it free. It hung over her shoulder and past her waist, and she pulled the brush through it, scrapping the bristles against her body.

Joseph was gentler.

Would she ever complete the morning ritual without thinking of him?

You make the fresh start and let the Lord take care of your heart.

The words pushed against her memories, making room for themselves among other unpleasant reminders.

She'd believed the Lord *was* taking care of her heart. Yet all along He had known it would break when the bullet crashed into Joseph's skull.

Her chest tightened, and in the mirror she stared at the fossilized bones edging the bookcase across the room behind her. If God were to open her rib cage and lift out what remained of her heart, He'd find it as cold and hardened as her stony collection. Lifeless.

A tap on her door. "Mar—*tha?*"

"Come in, I'm up."

Mama walked straight across the room, pushed the curtains aside and opened the window as far as it would go. "It's stuffy up here. And dark."

Like me.

"May I help with your hair?"

Her mother waited, hands pressed flat against her apron as if holding herself back with an obvious effort.

Would Martha act any differently if she were watching her daughter flounder?

She'd never know. But that didn't mean she had to be unappreciative and difficult. "Would you, please?"

The relieved light on her mother's face nearly outshone the early sun. "How do you want it? Up or down?"

"Down. In a braid."

Martha closed her eyes against the pain. Each tug of nimble fingers pulled a stinging thread through her very core. As determined as she was to be independent, here she sat having her hair braided by the one who had done so before she could do it herself.

A cruel twist to come home bereft of husband and end up nearly helpless. She sighed heavily.

"Impatient?" Mama addressed the mirror. "I'm almost finished."

"No, that's not it at all. I'm frustrated. I feel absolutely useless."

"I can imagine. You've always been so active." Her mother finished with a brown ribbon at the end, and then helped her into a dark shirtwaist and skirt. "Let's turn this into an opportunity to get you some new dresses."

"My trunk holds several other skirts and blouses. I've just not shaken them out yet."

"And I'm sure they are lovely." Her mother went to the door and paused as if waiting for Martha to follow. "But you are as much a woman as I, and I know how it makes me feel when I get something new to wear."

The sparkle in her mother's eye won her over, and Martha stooped to pick up her shoes. "Only if you'll help me with these in the kitchen."

"Of course."

She handed over the shoes.

At the stairs, Martha reached under the sling to hold the handrail with her left hand as she descended—a completely awkward maneuver, but less painful than tripping down the stairs and dislocating something else.

"Good morning, beautiful." From the kitchen table, her father acknowledged her over the top of the *Cañon City Times*.

"Thank you, Papa." She kissed his cheek and pulled out a chair.

"I do believe he was addressing his lovely wife." Mama planted a smug kiss on his lips and tossed Martha a wink. "Hold up your foot."

She slipped one shoe over Martha's dark stocking and buttoned it, then repeated the process, ending with a gentle pat against her ankle. "I have tea, Martha, if you prefer it this morning."

Sensing her father's curiosity over the name change, she avoided his eyes and adjusted the sling to a more comfortable angle. "I'll take coffee. I think I'm going to need it."

Her mother set three cups and saucers on the table, each bearing a delicate pink rose pattern trimming the edges.

"These are new. They're beautiful." She didn't miss the shy smile before her father hid once more behind the newspaper.

"To commemorate our anniversary." Her mother filled each cup and set the pot on the table before taking her seat.

Martha reached for the sugar bowl. "How thoughtful of you, Papa."

The paper rattled. "I know."

Her laugh erupted on its own, startling her with its spontaneity. Laughter and humor had nearly rusted away from neglect in the past year, and she'd had no hope for their return. A thin fissure ran up the hard spot in her chest.

Hotcakes, eggs, and bacon were more than she could stomach, but she nibbled the bacon and managed a few syrupy bites. "Will you be making apple butter this fall, Mama?"

"Oh, yes. Our trees are quite full. But the Blanchards—you remember them—invited us out to pick as much as we could haul home. They insist this year's crop is the best they've had in twenty."

Her father finished his breakfast, gathered his dishes, and took them to the sink. "I have an appointment this morning at the church, so I need to be off. What do you ladies have planned for today?"

He came up behind his wife and wrapped his arms around her, chair and all, and kissed the top of her head.

Martha lowered her eyes. The affection her parents had consistently shown one another over the years was something she had longed for in her marriage. Joseph had been loving in his own way during their few years together. But he'd not met her expectations where affection was concerned. Now that he was gone, guilt chewed on her raw edges. Was she simply greedy and ungrateful by nature?

"We are going to visit the dressmaker." Mama leaned her head back against his chest and linked his arm with her fingers. "Who are you meeting so early?"

"Haskell Jacobs. Said he had something confidential he wanted to discuss with me about one of our citizens."

Martha stilled like an unwound watch, waiting for her breath to catch up and flow freely.

Her father noticed.

"Don't be alarmed, Marti. It's just a meeting. But I do think there is more to Mr. Jacobs than meets the eye."

Her mother sobered instantly and stood to face him. "Why do you say that? Do you think he's an outlaw?"

He chuckled in the way men did when thinking they knew better than a woman.

Guilt took another bite from Martha's soul for categorizing her own father as such.

He gripped his wife's waist and kissed her soundly. "I think he's a good man, and I will give him the benefit of the doubt until he proves otherwise."

Martha snorted.

"I won't turn my back on him, Marti, but I'm not often wrong about reading people. They are a lot like horses, you know."

Immediately a long-eared equine relative came to mind, but she knew better than to voice her uncomplimentary vision of Haskell Jacobs.

Her father gave her a light peck and headed through the house for the front door.

Doc Mason had been as forthcoming yesterday as Haskell expected: not at all. His assistant was worse. He'd never seen such a sour visage on a woman's face, as if his questions insulted her own kin.

Which implied the need for a different perspective. He passed up the sheriff and other ministers in town, and caught Reverent Hutton exiting the mercantile. His gut told him Caleb Hutton was the man to see.

The preacher agreed to meet at the white clapboard church house this morning at eight sharp. Haskell flipped open his watch. Five minutes till.

He planted an elbow on the church hitching rail and leaned back, critiquing the horses corralled across the street. Cache held his own in the livery pecking order, and a lightning-quick kick sent a surly mare on her way. Haskell grunted his approval.

At a metallic click, he turned. The front door opened outward and Hutton stopped on the threshold. "Right on time. Come in."

Haskell mounted the steps and pulled off his hat. "Thank you for meeting me this morning, Pastor."

"Caleb." The parson extended his hand in greeting. "I'm more comfortable on a first-name basis." A genuine smile accompanied his welcome. No snake oil here.

Haskell felt oddly at ease, considering how long it'd been since he'd been in a church.

Sunlight filtered through the eastside windows, buttering the pews with a yellow glow. Hutton walked to the front of the room and sat in the first pew, turning slightly to the side.

Haskell joined him—again, hat in hand. It was getting to be a bad habit.

"I'd like to begin by telling you I know what happened yesterday with my daughter."

Haskell slid on his lawman's mask and gave no response one way or the other. He had yet to categorize the parson, and a father's reaction to his daughter's injury was not to be underestimated.

"Thank you for bringing Marti home and fetching the doctor."

At that, Haskell's jaw eased a notch and he studied his hat. "I'm sorry about the accident. I should have—"

"That is exactly what it was, I believe. An accident." The preacher's dark eyes probed Haskell's very brain, if that were even possible, but didn't give away his own thoughts. The man had the makings of a ranger. He crossed a boot on his leg and stretched one arm along the pew back. "You wanted to ask me something."

Haskell dangled his hat on his fingers. "How is she doing today?" The question shocked him, but apparently not the preacher.

"She's her old sharp self. A little stiff, that's all. I expect she'll be slowing more at the street corners now." His expression sobered. "But that can't be all you have on your mind."

No, it wasn't, but he wished it were.

A casual tug on his coat revealed the star pinned to his vest. Hutton caught the movement without surprise. He'd probably heard and seen just about everything in his line of work.

"I'm with the Colorado Rangers out of Denver, and I'm looking for a horse thief that's said to hole up in these parts."

"There are a lot of places for a man to hide around here. Plenty of abandoned mines and narrow canyons in this country."

"Yes, sir. But you might know him."

The preacher's right eye twitched.

"Without knowing he's a thief."

Hutton uncrossed his leg. "How do you figure? Think he's one of my congregants?"

"I think he's connected to Doc Mason."

The eye twitched again, and the preacher rubbed the back of his neck.

"I rode along the river yesterday afternoon and came upon an old man camped back in the cottonwoods. He told me a fella traipsed through the night before with a string of four good horses. Said he followed him and the man turned toward town at the other end of Main Street."

Hutton nodded. "That would be Goldpan Pete you met. Went bust years ago, but seems content to live down there on the river." He considered Haskell. "But if there were strange horses in town, I'd know it. And I haven't seen any."

"I'm not surprised. They're stabled in Doc Mason's barn. Haltered and filling themselves on mountain hay."

Hutton held his eye.

"I followed the old timer's lead, ended up at Mason's barn, and checked inside." The partial truth jabbed Haskell in the preacher's presence. "I made a brief visit. That's when I saw the fresh brand on their shoulders, recently burned with a running iron."

"You think Mason's a horse thief?" Hutton's deadpan gave nothing away.

"No, I don't. But I think he's housing one. When I rode down there yesterday to bring him back for Marti—I mean your daughter—Doc and his nurse were working on a fella in the surgery. I didn't see him, but I could hear him. He was hurting. When the nurse came out, she was curt and hostile. Had a bloody towel in her hands. She and the Doc had been talking about laudanum, and I heard them shuffling someone to another room before she came out to see me.

Hutton frowned and rubbed his neck again. "Have you spoken to the doctor?"

"Yesterday before I found you. He wouldn't tell me anything about his patients. Said he couldn't talk about them, even if they were outlaws or horse thieves. Especially to people who weren't kin."

"Does he know you're a ranger?"

"Yes, sir."

Hutton blew out a breath. "I'm bound by a similar standard. I can't discuss other people's problems and troubles. But I can tell you this much—the nurse is Delores Overton. Several years ago, her son Tad got himself shot during the Railroad War here between the Denver & Rio Grande and the Santa Fe. A lot of good men got caught up in that, but there was always something about her boy Tad that didn't set right with me."

"Can you put your finger on it now?"

A shadow crossed the parson's face and he turned his gaze toward the windows.

Haskell clenched his jaw. He didn't need vague impressions, he needed information.

"We sent Marti away to school about that time. She was sweet on him."

But not that kind of information.

CHAPTER SIX

Martha cleared the table, scrubbed the counter, and returned each piece of china to the dining room hutch—work that required only one hand. She placed the delicate dishes just so, arranging them as her mother had, who was obviously proud of such finery.

"Let's walk to the dress maker's, Mama. It's been so long since I've done anything physical—other than stepping in front of a horse."

Her mother hung her apron on a hook and tucked a smile between her lips. "We shall stay to the boardwalks this morning. How does that sound?"

"Wonderful. And let's stop in at Mr. Winton's curio shop. I want to ask if he is still taking people up to the dig." She caught her mother's frown. "Is his shop still open?"

"Oh, yes. And he is still exhibiting remarkable fossils from Garden Park before they're crated and shipped out on the train to the university. But going to the dig in your condition could be dangerous, and not just because of the footing. Vandals are smashing some of the bones, and poor Mr. Finch—the farmer who's leading the dig—is beside himself. On top of that, he lost another son since you've been gone."

Martha wilted at the news. Not uncommon to lose a child, but grieving over one's beloved children must be worse than grieving over children never born.

"Mr. Finch reopened the second quarry across from the first one, and Yale University sent another paleontologist to help him with his work. But from what I've heard, the site may be exhausted."

Old dreams stirred in Martha's breast as they left through the front door. She had to make it out to the dig at least once before it was shut down, sore shoulder or not.

Her mother swept her with a worried look. "Are you sure you're up to walking today? We can just as easily take the buggy."

"Nonsense. I need the exercise."

From the corner of Main Street, the open church door was obvious. Haskell Jacobs sat inside with her father talking about—what? Dig-site vandals?

That wasn't exactly confidential information. And the man didn't strike her as the type who would be interested in a bunch of old bones anyway. She wasn't quite sure how he struck her, other than with his horse.

She snorted—a childish habit that had resurrected since her return.

Her mother glanced over. "A penny for your thoughts."

"Nothing important. Just thinking about recent events."

The least of which was her absolute lack of concern over what Haskell Jacobs did or did not do. Or talk about with her father. It didn't matter.

Twisting her reticule drawstring around the fingers of her right hand, she stepped up her pace. "My arm is not broken, you know. Doc Mason said as much. Maybe this sling is too confining and I should be working out the stiffness." She tugged at the knot behind her neck.

"Leave that be." Her mother swatted her hand away. "You don't want to make matters worse. Give it a week and we'll have the doctor assess it again."

A week. In a week she'd lose what little of her mind remained if she did not find some outlet for her restlessness.

They kept to the south side of the street, and Martha marveled at the smart storefronts replacing what she'd remembered. Several new establishments boasted brightly painted signs. In the next block they turned in at the dressmaker's, which resembled a shop straight from St. Louis.

Evidence of scented soap and sachet hit Martha square in the face as they entered, but it did not overwhelm her any more than the countless hats, parasols, gloves, reticules, and petticoats that covered every inch of counter, wall, and shelf space. Women clustered in every nook and cranny, chattering over the latest fashions and patterns.

"It is surprising, isn't it," he mother said. "I reacted just the same the first time I came here with your grandmother."

Martha didn't know what to consider first—material for a dress, or a new hat. With feathers, ribbons, or lace? Nothing in the store said *schoolmarm*, that was for sure. They headed for the back, where fabric lay stacked on the counter.

Her mother picked up a length of light-weight wool and held it next to Martha's face. "This would be lovely with your hair."

The exact color of Haskell Jacobs' eyes.

And what if it was? He was not the only fair-eyed man in the world. Just the only one to run her down with his horse.

Martha tugged at a dull gray. "What about this?"

Her mother propped a hand on her hip and pegged Martha with a warning. "Must I spell it out? I'm trying to cheer you. Look at this place." She twirled around like a girl in a candy store. "Have you ever seen anything like this?"

For her mother's sake, Martha picked up the cornflower blue and held it to her chin. "Five lengths?"

While they waited for Martha's turn to be measured and sized, they fondled delicate thread for tatting, several soft yarns, and the most beautiful hair combs Martha had ever seen. Her mother pushed thoughtfully at the combs she had worn since time immemorial, and Martha made a mental note for Christmas.

By the time the seamstress finished, Martha's stomach was growling like a cur. "I'm starving, Mama. Let's save the curio shop for another day and go home for dinner."

Outside, her mother linked arms with her and turned toward the center of town. "Let's not." She marched up the boardwalk, and Martha was obliged to follow. "I've heard about the wonderful food at the café. I think we should give it a try. What do you say?"

Apparently, it mattered not what Martha might say, for they were already at the corner, stepping into the street. She quickly looked to her left and flexed her right arm, which shot a pointed reminder to her shoulder.

"But what about Papa?"

Her mother chuckled. "Did I ever tell you how he lived before we were married?"

"Yes, you've told me." The matter had been discussed countless times during Martha's younger years. "I could recite it by heart."

"Well, then, no need to ask. I dare say your father will fend for himself. It's not every day I get to step out on the town with my daughter."

A departing couple exited the café as Martha and her mother approached, and a most delicious aroma followed them out the door. Her empty stomach noticed, and she pushed against her waist to stop the rumbling.

A waiter seated them at a window table in clear view of the busy street and boardwalk. Fewer freight wagons rumbled by than she remembered, no doubt replaced by the train that cut through the mountains to Leadville and points beyond.

"We shall have whatever it is that smells so delightful," her mother said.

The waiter poured coffee into two mugs. "It's pork chops, ma'am, with gravy and beans and potatoes."

"Wonderful." She waited for Martha's confirmation.

At the moment, Martha could eat almost anything. "May I have extra gravy, please?"

The mustached waiter bowed briefly before turning on his heel for the kitchen. Amused by the man's formal attitude, Martha relaxed and reached for her coffee. She lifted it to her lips and looked up. A sharp intake jerked her hand, and coffee splashed to the checkered cloth.

Her mother leaned toward her, worry darkening her eyes. "What is it? Are you all right?"

Martha set down the mug and dabbed at the stain with her napkin. "Quite." She peeked again, relieved that Haskell Jacobs was too busy dismembering his pork chops to notice her. At least she hoped so.

Scooting her chair to the left, she allowed motherly concern to block her view of the arrogant Mr. Jacobs. "I just recognized someone I did not expect to see, that's all."

Her mother turned.

"Mama!"

She stopped at Martha's frantic whisper and cocked a thin brow. "And why not?"

"It's Mr. Jacobs. I don't want him to see me." She'd said too much.

Her mother leaned back in her chair and tilted her head. "Is your father with him?"

"No."

Martha squirmed again, feeling all the school girl beneath her mother's scrutiny. The woman expected some sort of confession, admission of, of … what? Martha would gladly bare her soul if only she understood what was hiding there.

Haskell saw them enter the café. He saw *everyone* who entered the café. It was his job to be aware, take note. But his bucking pulse at Marti Hutton's arrival was not.

He busied himself with the meat, forked a bite in the gravy, and kept his head low as he chewed. Haskell Jacobs backed down to no man. So why did he react to the presence of the young widow wearing a sling?

Maybe it was the sling. He'd been thinking of her and not paying attention when she stepped in front of Cache yesterday morning. Distraction could get him killed. It nearly got her killed.

He cut off another bite and, from under his brows, saw her flinch and spill her coffee. The mere sight of him distressed her.

He looked again. She had moved to her left, positioned her mother between them.

The meat turned to wood in his mouth and he laid down his fork. He was not a man to run from trouble, and this situation with Marti Hutton or Martha Stanton or whatever her name was, was trouble. It was taking its toll on him, costing him precious time, and dulling his observational skills.

Decision made.

He'd take the apron to her this afternoon and confront her head on.

About what, he had no idea.

He caught the waiter's eye, paid for his meal, and tugged his hat down as he left.

Outside on the boardwalk, he blew out a hard breath, feeling he'd escaped a fate worse than being shot. A strange sensation.

He freed Cache's reins from the hitching rail and swung up, then rode toward the west end of town, hunting a topic other than the widow and her one-time affection for a possible horse thief.

Tad Overton. The pastor said his son, Whit, knew the man. Whit ran cattle about ten miles out of town, and a visit appealed to Haskell. Might give him a chance to see the country, maybe locate a few acres that needed a new owner.

But did he want to settle in Cañon City near a woman who drove every reasonable thought from his head?

He slowed Cache to a walk at Doc Mason's. A buggy waited in front and the surgery door was open. Busy man.

The prison walls rose ahead, and a ways beyond them across the river, the Hot Springs Hotel. Fifty cents bought a bath in the thermal waters, according to the newspaper. The steamy image appealed to him—a good hot soaking after dark, followed by a slow walk behind Mason's barn on the way back to McClure's.

He turned north up First Street and rode in the shadow of the penitentiary walls. Seemed like a waste of time to drag a horse thief back to Denver when Haskell could just as easily chuck him over the high stone battlement. He grunted at the idea. That'd be quite a sight for the town's residents.

But due process was due process. Even a thief deserved a trial.

Grand homes faced the shady streets running north of and parallel to Main, and Haskell passed fanciful structures of rose quartz and granite. Two- and three-story houses boasted yellow or green gingerbread reminiscent of Denver's grandeur. Much gaudier than the Hutton's parsonage with its simple white clapboard and broad porch.

His house would have a porch. And a swing for summer evenings when the sun washed coppery gold over the Rockies. And a wife with hair the same color.

He squeezed Cache into a lope, disgusted with his slack discipline, and rode back toward town. The sooner he got the apron chore over with, the better. At the laundry, he yanked his horse to a stop, dismounted, and stomped inside.

Voices chattered from behind a wide curtain, but no one manned the darkened store front. His hand slapped the counter and the voices stilled. The curtain moved, and dark eyes peeked through a slit, followed by the fellow who told him the apron would be ready today.

The little man pulled a bundle from below the counter and handed it to Haskell.

"Thank you." He strode to the door, then stopped and turned. "Was it ruined?"

"Just dirty." The washer man grinned. "Now clean."

Haskell nodded and shut the door, then pulled the reins from the post and swung up.

At the livery, he tied Cache out front and gave a boy there a nickel to keep an eye on him, then tucked the apron under his arm and walked to the parsonage. The widow sat on the porch swing and stopped its motion when she saw him.

He also stopped, expecting her to flee indoors to her mother. Instead, she pushed against the porch floor and resumed the swing's movement. His heart resumed beating.

"Evening," he said as he took the steps and stood before her.

She glanced at the bundle. "Good evening, Mr. Jacobs."

No wind whisper or prairie sigh tonight. Her tone raised a wall as cold and stony as the prison's. He held out the paper-wrapped parcel. "Here's your apron."

Surprise raised her brows. She stopped the swing again and reached out with her left hand. A question lit her face.

Rather than wait for her to ask, he answered.

"I had it laundered."

She regarded him with something near gratitude before tucking the expression safely inside. "I see that."

What had he expected? A sweet "thank you" for running her down in the street?

He turned on his heel. He wasn't going to apologize.

"Please, won't you have a seat?"

Like a well-aimed bullet, her offer stopped him cold and he looked over his shoulder. She held out a delicate white hand, indicating a chair at the end of the porch. For reasons beyond his comprehension, he accepted her offer.

His boot steps resonated on the old wood, the naked sound drawing him out into the open. Away from the comfort of shadows. He sat.

She laid the bundle on the swing and raised her eyes to his hat.

He removed it and hung it on one knee.

She almost smiled.

"Thank you for finding the apron and having it cleaned."

He could nearly hear the top stone layer crumbling from her wall. He gritted his teeth to keep his jaw from gaping. "My pleasure, ma'am."

"You may call me Martha."

Another layer toppled, and he risked a question. "Is it Stanton or Hutton?" Hearing the query aloud convinced him it was none of his business.

She rolled her lips as if holding back a verbal thrashing. He was a fool.

"That is a very good question, Mr. Jacobs." Her attention shifted to the back of the church house a few yards beyond the front gate, and she absently fingered the bundled apron. "I began as Hutton, spent a short while as Stanton, and now I am Hutton again, I suppose." She turned her focus to him, bold and unembarrassed, just as she had at the train station. Had it been only two days and not his entire life that she'd muddled his judgement and clouded his mind?

Wicked and deadly men had dared look him in the eye, and none had the effect of this injured woman. The sling mocked him.

"How is your shoulder?"

She tilted her head to the right, and the guileless gesture shot an unwelcomed dart of sympathy through him.

"Stiff, but that is to be expected. The sling is bothersome, and it seems I can do nothing but sit and think." She raised her left hand to her injured shoulder and touched it lightly.

"I apologize."

Her gaze flicked sideways. "Thank you, sir." She lowered her voice. "I should not have plunged into the street unaware."

Now it was his turn to be surprised.

The steel in his jaw melted like an icehouse afire, swamping his good sense. "It's Haskell."

CHAPTER SEVEN

Martha stilled before the sapphire scrutiny, cool and clear as a mountain lake. So much for her resolve to rebuke the mysterious Mr. Jacobs. He'd been headed off the porch and out of her life. Why had she stopped him?

"The name's Haskell," he repeated.

Quite aware of her tendency to stare, she forced her eyes down. "Haskell it is, then."

The screen door creaked and her father stepped outside. "I did not realize we had a caller, Marti." He crossed in front of her and offered his hand in greeting.

Haskell stood. "Sir."

"Good to see you again, Mr. Jacobs. What brings you by?"

"Haskell, sir, if you don't mind."

Her father nodded and threw her a quizzical look. "Have you invited our visitor for supper? I'm sure your mother has plenty, and I happen to know she has a peach pie set aside."

Martha's stomach clinched and clear thought fled. Invite the man to supper?

He put his hat on and moved toward the porch steps.

"By all means, Mr.—Haskell—please, stay to supper."

He looked at her father as if testing the water, then nodded once. "Thank you."

Her father offered his right arm as she rose from the swing. "Let's not keep your mother waiting, Marti." His mouth quirked at one end, a sign she recognized all too well. A joke was at play and she was more than likely the brunt of it. She had half a mind to tell Haskell Jacobs to go eat with his horse. But when he stepped forward and held the screen door open, she swallowed the words.

Papa was right about the peach pie. Its flaky aroma threaded around her empty belly. She hadn't eaten much at dinner after noticing a certain man at the opposite end of the café. Now she had to face that man at her parents' table. Lord help her.

"Annie, you remember Haskell Jacobs," her father said. "He's agreed to share our supper this evening."

Her mother turned a startled expression on the three of them but quickly softened it with her usual grace. "It's my pleasure, Mr. Jacobs. Caleb, please bring another chair from the dining room."

Martha moved to her place at the table, but their guest anticipated her. He pulled the chair back, waited for her to seat herself, and then gently assisted her in scooting forward.

Her mind swirled like a river eddy. What kind of man met privately with her father, paid good money to launder an old apron, held her chair—and looked for all the world like a dark and handsome villain from a dime novel? Not that she read such things.

She pulled the napkin onto her lap and her mental ledger to the forefront. He'd even apologized for something she was at least partially responsible for.

That final admission tugged her chin down in chagrin. Four marks for Haskell in the positive column and one in the negative for running her down with his horse. Two, maybe. His dark demeanor could be noted as secretive. But *handsome* might slip into the number five slot on the other side.

Unfaithfulness jabbed an accusing finger as Joseph's fair image dimmed.

Her father returned. Haskell waited until Martha's mother was seated before taking his own chair.

Circumstances were against her. Or was it God? She pleaded silently that her parents break with their custom of holding hands in prayer, but her plea was denied. Mama sat across from her, to her father's right. This forced their guest to the end, placing Martha between the men.

Her father laid a hand on her right arm. She hesitated. At an arched warning from her mother, she lifted her left hand to Haskell, who took it in his as if it were the most natural thing in the world.

Well, he had held her in his arms like a sack of flour, so he might as well hold her hand.

Her neck warmed. If her pulse flashed through her fingers as it did her throat, he'd know and she would die of humiliation right there at the table.

"Amen."

With blood pounding in her ears, she'd not heard her father's prayer and sat momentarily frozen. Haskell raised his brows in question, and she jerked her hand from his. Laughter sparked in his eyes. Would it be completely inhospitable to stab him with her fork?

After the tasty remains of a beef stew, her mother dished up large servings of warm pie and passed around a pitcher of cream. With a childhood favorite before her, Martha almost forgot her current predicament—until she lifted her fork and realized that Haskell Jacobs was observing her.

She cut through a golden slice of peach, pretending he wasn't there.

"I'm going to take you up on your advice, sir, and visit your son, Whit."

"Good." Her father poured cream over his pie and set the small white pitcher in the center of the table. "I'm sure he can give you solid information."

Martha and her mother exchanged an unspoken question and waited for the men to reveal what lay behind their cryptic conversation.

They said nothing.

She had never been good at keeping her thoughts to herself, especially where her brother was concerned. "About?"

Haskell set down his coffee with what seemed to be deliberate restraint. "I'm looking for someone, and your father believes Whit may be able to give me some insight into the person's behavior."

That was about as unspecific an explanation as she had ever heard. Her left hand paused against the table's edge, peach juice dripping from the fork tines onto her rose-edged plate. She regarded her father with expectation, years of practice ensuring that he sensed her curiosity.

He ignored her, continued eating his pie, and addressed her mother.

"Weren't you thinking of driving out to visit Whit and Livvy and the boys, dear?" Avoidance pooled around his eyes as thick as the cream around his peaches. She had never judged her father as one to hedge. And she had learned long ago that leaving in a huff was most undignified, as was stomping one's foot beneath the table. It took everything in her to do neither.

Her mother shot Martha a peculiar look. "Yes, I was, but I'd not had opportunity to discuss it with Martha, see if she felt up to riding out to visit her nephews." She paused, teacup in hand, watching Martha over the rim.

Felt up to? Mama had thrown down a gauntlet and had done so deliberately. Martha despised prissy women who feigned frailty as the weaker sex and her mother knew it. The woman had imbued her with the opinion, for heaven's sake.

She adjusted the sling and smoothed her lips into a sickeningly sweet smile. "I'd love to. We could go tomorrow."

"Perfect."

She stared at her enthusiastic father.

"Perhaps you wouldn't mind Haskell riding along with the both of you. You could show him the way, and he could serve as a sort of escort."

Martha's jaw must have banged against the table but she couldn't help it. Never had she or Mama been *escorted* to Whit and Livvy's. She stole a glance at Haskell, who wore a mask as impenetrable as hammered steel.

By the meal's end, conversation had swayed from picking apples and the price of hay to the start of school and a basket social planned at the church, with Haskell invited, of course.

Martha rose to clear the table.

Haskell stood as she did but did not retake his seat. Instead, he lifted his hat from the back of his chair.

"Thank you, ma'am, Pastor, for sharing your supper." He nodded to her. "Miss Martha."

Her father accompanied him to the front door.

Martha stole to the parlor entry and waited on the kitchen side, out of view.

"I hope you find what you're looking for here in Cañon City." Her father paused. "I know I did."

Haskell mumbled something low that Martha could not decipher and then left.

She hurried back to the table and grabbed the empty pie tin before her father reappeared. Combing through her family history, she searched for what he had found in Cañon City. She came up with two items: his renewed calling and his wife.

~

The Hutton women's cooking could pull a man's heart out through his gullet and plop it in his plate. Haskell crossed the street to where Cache stood dozing at the livery rail with a back leg cocked. He stripped the reins and swung up, hoping the Hot Springs Bath House hadn't closed for the evening.

The prospect of accompanying the widow and her mother to Whit Hutton's ranch held all the promise and curse of a double eagle: a valuable commodity a man could lose his life over.

Riding out of town, he followed the railroad tracks to the mouth of the gorge where a path veered toward a footbridge suspended across the Arkansas River. He tethered Cache at a railing with two other horses and took to the plank bridge. Halfway across, he stopped and peered over the side at the dark water. The steady wash raised a voice unheard unless one stood close enough. Persistent, unchanging. Rising in volume only as the seasons changed their colors, he surmised. He imagined the river raging with spring floods, whispering beneath an icy mantel. Constant, none the less. Always there.

Lights flickered through the hotel's windows, and he continued toward them.

Not much was constant in his life, other than the hunt for those who broke the law. Again an unnamed longing surged through his soul, a swollen stream of discontent. But its churning did not sooth him. It merely emphasized his isolation.

The Royal Gorge Hot Springs Hotel offered a bath for fifty cents and he bought two. The newspaper and pamphlets had been right. Thermal waters eased the tension in his neck and shoulders and back. If Cache were not waiting across the bridge, Haskell would rent a room and spend the night.

As it was, his relaxed legs barely carried him back across the footbridge.

Accustomed to the cool evenings of the Rocky Mountains in late summer, Haskell wakened enough to mount his horse and ride for town with a clear plan. At First Street, he turned south and then paralleled the river to the overgrown path he'd followed the day before.

He ground-tied Cache and moved soundlessly on foot through the trees toward Doc Mason's barn. A dim light glowed between the siding slats, and tense voices rose within.

"You won't be bringing any more horses to this barn. Do you hear me?" Doc Mason's high-pitched tones quivered with anger.

Haskell picked his way through the leaves and fallen branches behind the barn and stopped near the back door, closed but leaking light at its edges. A lantern on the far wall backlit the doctor's face and that of a taller, slightly built man. A cloth bound the taller man's right thigh, and he held his hand fisted against it.

"They aren't here, are they?" The thin man gestured wildly toward the empty stalls and flinched at the effort.

"I don't care. I won't have stolen horses in my barn. And you should be in bed with that gunshot wound." Doc swore and took the lantern from the wall. Shadows fell across their faces, but in the lowered light Haskell saw the shine of blood oozing through the thin man's bandage.

"That ranger was asking about you yesterday. I should have let him haul you off. Would have, it if weren't for your ma."

Haskell ground his teeth. The doctor just incriminated himself in harboring a fugitive. And Haskell's instincts about the nurse had also been right. But he needed evidence, and without the horses, witnesses, or a direct confession, he had nothing.

Pastor Hutton's hunch had panned out. Tad Overton was his man, and as far as Haskell could tell, the lanky fella favoring his right leg was none other.

Doc left the barn and Overton followed.

A horse nickered out front—Doc's buggy nag, more than likely. Haskell stole around the far end of the barn and up to the corral, where the horse flicked an ear his way. Doc and

Overton went up the back porch steps and inside, and the light dimmed as they made their way to the front of the house.

Those four stolen horses could be anywhere by now. Overton could have sold them to the Utes or the hack owners who carted people back and forth to the hot springs. A careless rancher could have run them in with his own band of horses, turning a blind eye to the new shoulder burns.

He retraced his steps to Cache and led the horse downstream to a clearing where he mounted and continued to the livery.

Would Whit Hutton buy stolen horses?

Haskell doubted it. Something about that family felt strong and true, like a deep-running current that held them all together. But he'd find out for himself in less than twelve hours, for tomorrow morning he was accompanying the Hutton women to the ranch.

Crickets raised a chorus. A dog yelped and a gate hinge squeaked. Ahead of him a yellow orb inched above the horizon like an out-of-place sun. He pulled up to watch.

The full moon hefted itself against the night, appearing bigger at the horizon than it would later as it mounted the sky. Haskell chuckled to himself at the phenomenon that had puzzled him as a child.

"It's all in your eye," his father had said. "It's no different when it starts than when it reaches its zenith."

His father had him hold a penny at arm's length, right next to the rising moon, and note its size. Together they'd spent the night on bedrolls by a campfire—Haskell and the man he admired most in the world, Tillman Jacobs, a Jefferson Territory Ranger.

Hours later, his father woke him. The moon dangled from the night like an empty saucer.

"Hold out your penny," his father had said.

Haskell would never forget the sense of discovery that washed over him when he lifted the copper coin and saw the moon was the same size as it had been when it first peeked through the pines.

"That's called perspective, son. Things are not always as they appear. Judge wisely—with evidence—and you will do well."

Those words still guided him. Haskell had spent most of his life pursuing that first taste of discovery. That thrill of uncovering the hidden or solving an enigma. It was the drive that pushed him to be a ranger, like his father, and it fueled his determination to find those who spurned the law and to see justice done.

Anticipation gripped his insides. Tomorrow would bring him closer to the horse thief he sought. And closer to the complex Martha Hutton Stanton, now Hutton again, as she had put it. A day in her company might wreak havoc with his powers of observation, for if he admitted the truth to himself, he was drawn to pursue her as surely as he pursued the snake that stole another man's horse and profited from it.

The copper-haired beauty pulled him like night pulled the moon across the sky.

He had to get Whit Hutton alone, away from the women, and talk to him in private. Hutton might have a tip on the horses, information connecting Overton to them, or word of their whereabouts.

Without a sound lead, Haskell had no grounds to bring Tad Overton in.

And if he did make a viable connection, what would Martha think of him then—when he rode away with her former beau in handcuffs?

CHAPTER EIGHT

Sitting in the parlor as her father read by lamp light and her mother darned socks was absolutely out of the question. What was Martha supposed to do? Stare out the windows into the night and fume?

Betrayed. Bested. Beaten. A vocabulary list formed in her mind, filling with words disloyal to the parents who had raised her and loved her. But they still tried to control her. She stood and walked to the door, where she paused at the screen and breathed in the night air.

"I'm going to sit outside for a while." Without waiting for a reply, she escaped to the porch swing and fell into its restful arms. Haskell's tall presence seemed to linger on the porch where he had sat earlier in the day.

If she had not allowed herself to be baited into inviting him to supper, the man would not be "escorting" them to Whit and Livvy's tomorrow. How could her father do such a thing? What had he and Haskell discussed that morning that so influenced his opinion of the man?

She hissed at the memory of Haskell's vague explanation. If one of her former students had given such a non-answer to a direct question, she'd have kept him after class to beat erasers.

She toed the swing and focused on her nephews. Her first and only glimpse of the twins was a cabinet card her brother had sent one Christmas, and they were babes in their mother's arms. They were nearly seven years old now, a handful, Mama had said. But as boys they must be Whit's delight. Surely he had them riding and roping already.

A child-shaped emptiness throbbed in her breast.

Bitterness was taking hold there. She recognized it as clearly as she'd identified the horseradish that grew behind the small parsonage she shared with Joseph. If even a mite of that ugly tuber remained in the soil, it sprouted. Oh, how she had worked to rid her garden of it.

A familiar Scripture ran through her mind, warning her to weed out the vicious root of bitterness. Was it defiling her and her family as well, as the passage suggested?

"Oh, Lord, help me." These seemed the only words she prayed since Joseph's death. Did God hear? She'd been raised to believe so.

"Help me dig out the bitterness," she whispered into the darkness. "Help me accept barrenness as readily as Whit has accepted the blessing of children."

Bitter. Barren. Blessing. More words for the new list.

Mama's soft laughter floated through the screen door, and Martha stopped the swing to listen. Now she could add eavesdropping to her catalogue of sins.

"He is a good man, Annie. I am sure of it."

Who? Martha scooted to the end of the swing closest to the door.

"But he is so secretive," her mother said. "Did you notice how he avoided Martha's question at the table?"

Haskell Jacobs. Martha held her breath.

"He has good reason."

"And that is?"

Not a word. Only the whisper of evening through the giant elm in the front yard.

Mama huffed.

"Why are you calling her Martha now?" Her father's tone had changed, softened.

"Because it is her wish. She does not want us thinking of her as a child, and the name we used in her youth makes her think we still see her that way."

"I will always see her as my child—my lively, fiery beauty."

Martha covered her mouth, squelching a sob.

Her father's voice lowered into rich tones meant only for his wife.

Again, Mama's soft laughter. "Oh, Caleb."

All too well Martha knew the intimate moments between a woman and her husband, and her mother's voice betrayed such tenderness. She rose from the swing and slipped through the door and onto the stairs. Once behind the safety of her closed door, she fell onto the bed and cried until she slept.

The morning sun slid beneath a cloud bank, as reluctant to rise as Martha was to leave her quilts. Her shoulder ached again from lying on it in the night, and she pushed herself up, rubbing at the soreness.

The washstand pitcher held warm water—her mother's doing. Martha had been no help since her arrival, thwarted first by sorrow and now by injury. And she still hadn't found anything to do. The schools had a full roster of teachers this late in the year, but she could ask at the library. Someone there might be interested in her scientific studies or her sketching. She could teach basic drawing if nothing else, or return to the Garden Park dig.

Or mind the store.

Never.

As if stirring banked coals, the idea fanned her irritation over a pre-determined future. She would find her own way. Even if she couldn't fasten her dress, button her shoes, or fix her hair by herself.

She tucked her hairbrush into the sling, and clasping her shoes in one hand, descended the stairs in her stocking feet, more confident than the first time she'd tried it. Of all days to ride out to Whit's, it had to be cool and cloudy. Sunshine would have felt so good on her face. Yet the possibility remained that the clouds might burn off and not bank against the mountains into a late rain storm.

There was hope.

The word fluttered soft against her soul like a falling aspen leaf.

"Good morning." Her father took her shoes and offered his arm as he led her to the kitchen table. "Would you like me to nail these on for you?" His brow furrowed in his best mock frown.

Martha snatched them back. "Very funny. I am not a horse." She kissed his cheek before taking her seat. "Mama, have you already fed the chickens and gathered eggs?"

"Yes, dear. How many do you want for breakfast?"

Martha grumbled, drawing her mother's puzzlement.

"One, please. But you must let me make myself useful. I think I can manage tossing scraps to the hens and gathering eggs until my shoulder is ready for heavier tasks."

Her mother set tea before her with one hand and poured coffee for her father with the other.

"So you're off to Whit and Livvy's today." He lifted his cup.

How could a man be so totally guilty and innocent-looking at the same time?

"I do believe Mama and I could have made it out there without an escort." Martha watched closely to determine her father's mood.

His expression remained placid, unaffected.

She gathered her nerve. "Why do we need Mr. Jacobs to accompany us when we safely made the trip dozens of times before I went away to school?"

"You don't."

She stared.

One brow flicked up and his eyes took on a calculating glint. "It is he who needs *your* escort."

At the remark, her mother turned to face him, a question clearly about to crest her lips.

"But enough of that." He stood, took his cup to the sink, and left a lingering kiss on his wife's neck.

Martha ached at the familiar gesture, something she had always wanted Joseph to do. But he simply had not had her father's spontaneity when it came to affection.

"Off with you," her mother fussed, pushing at the thick knot of hair at her neck, her cheeks tinted with a becoming rose. "If you are not going to stay and eat a good breakfast, then don't be distracting us in our preparations to leave."

"A distraction now, am I?" Martha's father aimed the question at her as he lifted his hat from the peg and his mouth in a smile. With a wink and a chuckle, he was out the back door and off to the barn.

"That man," her mother said. "You'd think after twenty-eight years he wouldn't be such a flirt."

"You don't know how blessed you are, Mama." Not accustomed to chiding her own parent, Martha stared into her teacup and tried desperately to blend in with the embroidered table cloth.

"Wise words, I must say, dear."

The hint of pity soured Martha's tea. She did not need pity. She needed something to do.

Her mother brought two plates with eggs and biscuits, took her seat at the table, and grasped Martha's hand atop the table.

"Thank you, Lord, for this family and our home and this food. Bless Caleb today and keep him in Your care. And please watch over us as we ride out to Whit's. Amen."

Expectation rushed the meal in spite of Martha's best efforts at nonchalance. The prospect of an entire morning with

Haskell Jacobs had her more jittery than she cared to admit. Her mother made quick work of the breakfast dishes, and Martha wiped down the counter and brushed the table for crumbs. Bending to scoop them into the palm of her cradled right hand, she caught a movement through the back door's glass. Haskell stood next to the buckboard while her father adjusted Dolly's harness.

As dark and tall as her father, he seemed a match in body if not in spirit. He pulled his coat aside and reached into his vest pocket, revealing a long-barreled side arm and holster. In the breaking sunlight, something metallic flashed on his vest.

Her breath caught.

"What is it?" Her mother's gaze shot to the wagon and she lifted a determined chin as if irritated with her husband's wishes. "Let me brush out your hair and we'll be on our way. The sooner we leave, the better."

Martha sat sideways on the chair so the ladder back didn't interfere—and she could watch for Haskell Jacobs to repeat his move. Had that glint been a badge? Was that why he was so evasive?

Catching sight of the gun tore open a poorly healed wound. Not that guns were evil. Goodness, her father had several, and he'd seen to it that she and Whit knew how to properly care for and handle them.

But a gun had stolen her precious Joseph. What if gunplay erupted on their way to the ranch? What if another stray bullet took someone else's life—her mother's or her own? Her blood chilled.

"Let's not go, Mama." She felt the tug at the bottom of her long braid and turned her head. "We don't have to go. There is no law that says we must ride out of town today. Let's wait until…until…I'm feeling better."

Her mother laid the brush on the table and picked up her satchel. "We can do this, Martha." She peered into the satchel's depths. "I have preserves for Whit, new linen for Livvy, and peppermint sticks for the boys."

"But Mama, what if—"

"Martha, you can what-if your life away if you're not careful. Come on." She gathered her wrap and straw hat, then fairly ran out the back door.

Martha had no sun hat, and that silly thing she'd worn on the train was upstairs. Besides, it did nothing to shield her face.

She lifted an old garden hat from the pegs by the door. Better to hide beneath the wide brim than freckle her nose on the way, for the sun had indeed pushed through the clouds and promised to shine on them today.

~

Haskell watched Mrs. Hutton march to the buckboard and accept her husband's hand to the seat. Martha followed like a flitting bird, less dignified and trying desperately to hide beneath a wide-brim straw hat. He sucked in the side of his mouth to keep from laughing.

The parson handed up his daughter also, waiting as the women situated themselves.

Haskell returned to Cache at the fence and swung up. He tipped his hat to Hutton and pulled up beside the man's wife.

"I'll follow you out of town, then come alongside once we make the turn at Soda Point."

Mrs. Hutton gathered the reins. "That will be quite acceptable." She snapped the leather on the mare's rump, and the wagon jerked ahead. He got the distinct impression that he was not welcome on the outing.

So be it. The less obliged he'd be to make small talk with two women.

He glanced back. Hutton leaned against the corral, arms folded at his chest, a pleased expression on his face.

Haskell's hands started to sweat. The same way they always did just before he rousted an outlaw.

They rode past the paint shop, a book store, a druggist. The city bakery, a meat market, millinery, hardware store, and several clothing and dry goods establishments. Cañon City had everything a larger city offered, except the crowds and smell of too many people in one place. Every morning since he'd arrived, he'd noticed the clear air, clearer even than Denver.

At Soda Point, they followed the road around the end of the hogbacks, as locals called the jagged ridge. He nudged Cache into a quick trot and pulled up beside the women.

Not that he expected—or wanted—conversation, but he was a man of his word.

Neither looked his way. He might as well not be there.

A few miles on at the next bend, Mrs. Hutton turned off on a road to the northeast that Haskell assumed led to the ranch. Immediately, Cache stiffened beneath him and shot his ears forward to the water-gouged roadbed.

The mare jerked to the side, reared in the harness, and screamed before shying off the road. Haskell kicked Cache ahead and reached for the mare's bridle. The wheels rolled over a deep crevice and the wagon pitched to the right, threatening to toss its passengers and flip the crazed horse.

Homing in on the hissing rattle, he pulled his .45 and separated the coiled body from its fang-bared head.

The women screamed. Cache danced backward, and the harnessed mare rolled her eyes white with fear as she strained against the unyielding buckboard.

"Jump to the road!"

Mrs. Hutton stared at him with her mouth open.

He holstered his gun. "Jump or break your neck when the wagon rolls."

She reached back for Martha who was clinging to the tipped seat with one hand.

"Alone!" He heeled Cache clear of the spot Mrs. Hutton should land. "Jump alone. I'll get Martha."

With a last desperate prayer of a look, she jumped and pitched forward onto her hands and face with a groan.

Haskell swung his leg over and leaped from the off-side of his horse. He helped her to her feet and turned back to the groaning wagon. Both left wheels cleared the ground. "Jump, Martha. I'll catch you."

He gripped the front wheel with one hand and held the other out to the white-faced woman with one arm in a sling.

She didn't move.

CHAPTER NINE

Time slowed as Haskell's expression pleaded with Martha to let him save her. Again. His voice she could not hear, for her hammering heart sounded over and over in her ears, "We should not have come."

His lips moved again, forming the words "I'll catch you." What choice did she have?

Dignity was of less value than one's life, and she gathered her skirt as high as possible. The wagon shimmied and groaned, urging her haste. Pulling in a sharp breath, she sent a frantic prayer flying, and pushed off into Haskell Jacobs' waiting arms.

He crushed her against his chest as if desperate to keep her feet off the ground, her slinged arm pressed between them. Her other arm looped instinctively around his neck.

"I've got you," he whispered against her hair. "You're safe now."

The urgency in his voice and the pounding of his heart made her question which of them had been the more frightened.

"Marti!"

Her mother's voice brought Martha's head up, and she looked into sea-deep eyes darker than the last time she'd been so close to them. She squirmed, and when he failed to take notice, she pushed with her free hand.

"Let go. Mama's hurt."

As if startled by her comment, he set her down and stepped back.

Martha spun around and the motion unbalanced her.

A steely grip fastened onto her left elbow and rich tones brushed her ear. "Maybe you should sit down and let me tend to her."

She jerked her arm away, instantly shamed by the ungrateful response. But Mama was hurt. They should not have come. When would people listen to her and take her seriously?

The shade dropped over Haskell's arresting eyes, and she softened her reply. "Thank you, but I'll be fine." Trying her legs and finding them sound, she hurried to where her mother sat in the road.

She knelt and pushed back the straw hat for a better view of a swelling, graveled rash.

"Ow!" A quick hand swatted hers away.

"Can you stand, Mama?" Frustration and relief twisted a tight rope around Martha's insides. She didn't know whether to laugh or cry, but she pulled her dusty mother to her feet.

Haskell stood beside the wagon as if afraid to approach.

So much for chivalry.

"I hurt my ankle." Her mother's voice was tight and breathy.

Together they hobbled to the road side where her mother leaned against a large boulder and plopped her hat on, but tipping it farther back off her forehead. "I don't think I can walk the rest of the way."

Martha looked to Haskell as if he had the answer to all their problems and then chided herself for doing so. She helped her mother into a sitting position and elevated her right foot on the rock. "We'll figure something out," she said, patting her hand as if Martha were the parent.

She wiped her face against her sleeve and flipped her braid behind her shoulder, then walked back to the wagon that leaned precariously on two wheels.

"We can pull it upright," she told Haskell, who had begun unharnessing the mare.

"No, we can't."

Martha planted her free hand on her hip. Men were absolutely mulish at times. "And why not? We can leverage enough weight between the two of us to right it."

He stopped his fiddling and looked her up and down in a most forward way and then scoffed. "Right."

If he had been closer, she would have slapped him.

"Why do you want to exert all that energy for nothing?"

Did she have to sketch it out for him? "So we can ride on to the ranch, of course."

He went back to fighting the twisted leather and didn't look at her at all. She wasn't sure which was worse, his ogling or his disregard.

"See the front axle?" He pulled a knife from his boot and deftly sliced through the trace.

The wood had splintered just inside the right wheel. Clearly, they'd not be taking the buckboard anywhere.

She turned away and stared up at the cedar-speckled hills. Patches of red rock pocked the landscape, and a hawk screed above them. The sky was terrifyingly clear, burned free of every cloud by a bold, late-summer sun. She reached for her hat. It was gone.

"You and your mother will ride the horses."

The voice was so near that she whirled into it and nearly into its owner. He'd approached her without a sound, like a bandit. Like the snake that was suddenly there.

But a snake didn't wear such longing on its face that she wanted to clutch it to her breast. She stilled as he stepped closer, smelling of sweat and dust and horse. His coat had been tossed aside and the star on his vest lay flat and dull with his back to the sun.

"Can you ride?" The look in his eyes tore away any possibility of pretense on her part. There was no place to hide, no words to shield her from his scrutiny.

"Yes. It's been a while, but yes. So can Mama."

"Good. I'll put you on Cache. You can trust him. And your mother will be more comfortable on her own horse. She'll be bareback, but she has two good arms to hold on with."

Again Martha's foolishness came home to roost, and she flexed her right hand against the stiffness, earning a heated dart to her shoulder. "What about you?"

"I have two good legs." A scant smile flickered before he strode away.

Martha followed.

"Do you think you can ride the mare, Mrs. Hutton?" He knelt on one knee before her, like a knight before a lady. The image shocked Martha, but she pushed it aside and listened for her mother's reply.

"Dolly? Oh, yes, I believe I can. I raised her. If I can't ride her, I'm a poor excuse for a horseman's wife." She stood, favoring her right ankle and swatting dirt from her torn skirt and sleeves. "If you'll help me get on her." Raising her chin with a characteristic air of determination, she limped toward the horse now loosed from the dead wagon but still quivering from the accident.

Haskell had cut the reins shorter and knotted them for easier handling. Her mother stood close to the mare, stroking its neck and calming the animal with her soft murmurs. Haskell handed her the reins, she nodded her acceptance, and with his hands around her waist he hefted her up. She threw her right leg over and perched atop the old yellow horse as if she did it every day.

Martha nearly cheered.

Then he led Cache to where she waited, looped the reins over the horse's head and linked his fingers together like a stirrup.

"Grab the horn, step into my hands with your left foot, and I'll lift you high enough to throw your leg over."

His mention of her limbs brought a blush to her face, but this was no time for proprieties. If it were not for Haskell Jacobs, she and Mama would be walking.

A sudden truth adjusted her perspective. Were it not for Haskell Jacobs, they could be dead beneath an overturned wagon.

"Well?" He looked up from his stooped position, and his expression betrayed impatience with her dawdling.

"Certainly." She hiked her skirt, stepped into his joined hands, and had barely a moment to grab the saddle horn before she shot into the air above the horse. She swung her leg over and landed unceremoniously in the seat. Taking a deep breath, she felt for the stirrups with her toes.

"If you will allow me," he said with that near smile, "I'll set the stirrups for you."

Burning with embarrassment, she hiked her skirt again—a regular occurrence in the last half hour—and bent her leg at the knee. Haskell quickly shortened the leather straps and then repeated the process on the other side.

"You are a might shorter than I am," he said as if he appreciated it.

"Mr. Jacobs." Martha's mother reined the mare around. "I had a satchel with me on the seat. Is there any way ..."

Haskell's jaw flexed. It was too much to ask, but Martha kept her opinion to herself. Let the knight prove just how gallant he might be.

Adjusting his hat with quick, sharp movements, he walked around the back of the forlorn wagon. It teetered at the top of a steep draw, and Martha suspected the slightest movement might send it rolling down the embankment. It wasn't worth a few jars of preserves—or Haskell's life. Anyone's life, she corrected, as if her feelings were on display.

For several moments, Martha and her mother sat silently waiting for Haskell's return. Martha strained her ears for any indication of his success or hazard, but only the wheeling hawk pierced the hot silence, with an occasional chirp from a ground squirrel and the trickle of loose rocks tumbling down the ravine. She wiped her face and neck with the hem of her skirt.

Finally he came up at the wagon's front end, balancing his climb with one hand and holding the satchel in the other. The sight of his dusty clothes, sweat-soaked shirt, and that satchel must have weakened her mother's reserve, for she nearly fawned over the man as he lifted the battered bag.

"Oh, Mr. Jacobs, you are so kind." She reached for the satchel. "Thank you so much. I appreciate—"

"You can't ride and carry this, too." Standing close to Martha's knee, he tied the bag to the front of the saddle. His armor may not be shining—not even his star shone—but he was definitely winning the joust with her mother.

~

Small talk had been Haskell's chief concern as they started out that morning. He grunted. It should be that simple.

As should getting to the ranch. Martha could have ridden behind her mother, but she had only one good arm to hold on with. The same reason he had for not pulling her up behind himself on Cache. She needed stirrups for her balance, and he did not ride behind a woman. Which meant he walked.

From what the parson had told him this morning, Haskell figured they were about four miles from the ranch. He'd hoofed it farther and in worse conditions.

At least he had a hat.

He checked his back trail, Martha bringing up the rear, her face burning redder by the minute. She rode well enough. Her mother was in obvious discomfort with her swollen ankle dangling low, but it bore no weight.

His presence had turned out to be rather providential after all. What else could account for him being nearby with a gun when the women needed one most?

Providence. Now there was a word that didn't often trail him. He kicked a stone from the path and rehearsed what the Good Book said about man being alone. The phrase had rubbed him raw in recent years, but particularly so since Martha had stepped off the train. If he ever prayed again, he'd be askin' about the parson's daughter and how she might figure into his future.

Their shadows were short and the sun high as they trudged into the ranch yard, and it had to be noon or thereabouts. Two youngsters and a black-and-white dog came running to greet them, the dog more cautious than the boys.

Its bark must have called an alarm, for a fair-haired woman appeared from round back of the long, low ranch house, a basket on her arm and a hand shading her eyes.

When she recognized the lead in their procession, she dropped the basket and came running.

"Annie! Whatever happened? Are you all right?"

The mare tossed her head as Mrs. Hutton reined her in. The younger woman grabbed the headstall and pegged Haskell with a blistering glare.

"Oh, Livvy." Mrs. Hutton reached over the mare's neck. "It's so good to see you, but we hadn't intended to come dragging in like this." She turned to Haskell with an expectant look. "Would you be so kind as to help me down?"

If Martha aged as well as her mother, she'd still be a handsome woman in twenty years. Haskell shelved the thought and slid Mrs. Hutton from the mare's back. Livvy came round to catch her mother-in-law's arm across her shoulder.

"Let's get you inside with a glass of lemonade and you can tell me what happened. Did you fall? Oh, your skirt—it's torn. And your head!"

She fussed and bustled, and Haskell left her to it. He turned in time to see Martha's attempted dismount and made it to her just as she lost her balance. She landed in his arms rather than in the dirt, and he suspected her dignity took more of a beating than her backside would have.

"Oh!" she blurted. "Thank you." Righting herself and brushing at her dusty clothes, she met his eyes again with that bold, unabashed regard that loosened his knees.

"What would we have done without you today?"

What would he do the rest of his life without her?

The words nearly fell out of his mouth.

"You must be parched. Please, come inside for some lemonade." She touched his arm.

"I will after I see to the horses."

The two youngsters bounded up, offering their assistance, and the dog joined the melee and sniffed about Haskell's boots and trousers.

"We'll help, mister. We can each take a horse."

"You must be Whit and Livvy's boys," Martha said as if she'd never met them.

Two grins popped out beneath their blue eyes, a reflection of their mother's. The dark hair must have come from Whit.

"You kinda look like Grandma," said one.

"But younger," said the other, more diplomatic of the two.

Unoffended, Martha spread her good arm. "Come give your aunt Martha a hug, boys. And tell me who is who."

A knot in Haskell's gut tightened.

The boys obliged.

"I'm Cale."

"And I'm Hugh. I'm oldest."

"Just by a minute."

Martha embraced each in turn and then tousled their hair. His children might look like that if he ever had any. But that required a wife, and right now the likeliest prospect he'd met stood before him, spitfire and all.

Squirming beneath their aunt's affection, they politely ended the encounter and turned to Haskell.

"Our pa taught us everything there is to know 'bout horses," said one.

"That's right," said the other. "Ask us anything."

Rubbing his jaw, he feigned consideration and then posed his query. "Which eat more, black horses or white horses?"

Puzzled, the youngsters discussed it between themselves.

"Seems as we don't rightly know," the first one said.

"Well, now. I was under the impression that you knew everything."

One kicked the dirt and the other stuck his chest out at the challenge.

Chuckling, Haskell made them an offer. "If you'll rub down our mounts, give them water, and turn them out in that pasture over there, I'll tell you how to find the answer."

They each grabbed a horse's reins and were on their way before one yelled back, "Thanks, mister."

Maybe if he had a lick o' luck, they'd someday call him "uncle."

"Now you have no excuse." Fatigue edged Martha's voice, but she tugged at his arm and her touch seared through his sleeve and into his skin. "Come in the house, have something to drink, and rest. You must be weary from that long, dusty walk."

Was this the same woman who had scorned him three short days ago from the velvet settee in the parsonage?

Or was this the woman he longed to take in his arms and into his soul and never let go?

CHAPTER TEN

The old ranch house boasted a new front porch, but when Haskell opened the heavy front door for Martha, it still led directly into the dining room. The last time she'd been there was for Whit and Livvy's wedding.

A new carpet covered the floor, setting off the same elegant furniture Livvy's grandmother had brought from England. A crystal vase on the dining table held a fistful of bright sunflowers, and their upright, happy faces momentarily eased Martha's weariness.

Haskell removed his hat and waited, observing her without watching. He did that a lot, a trait she now realized had to do with his work.

Voices drew her to the kitchen, where Livvy tended her mother, bare foot resting in a basin of water. Mama's face colored at Haskell's approach until she lowered her skirt around the basin.

If Martha were not so worn out, she'd mention her mother's undying sense of propriety. But the woman had borne enough today, and it was all Martha could do to drop into the nearest chair.

Livvy squeezed out a cloth and pressed it to Mama's brow, chattering like an old maid on Sunday morning. She glanced up as Martha joined them and reached for her hand.

"Oh, Marti, I didn't mean to ignore you." She drew back, eyeing first one woman and then the other. "You two look like you had a time of it getting here." She glared at Haskell, who stood apart and aloof.

Defensiveness fired in Martha's breast, a need to inform Livvy that Haskell was not the cause for their unkempt condition but rather, their rescuer. She gestured toward him, avoiding his eyes. They had power to open the door of her affections.

"Livvy, this is Mr. Haskell Jacobs, a friend of my father."

In spite of the gun he carried—thank God he carried it today—he seemed less intimidating than before, less daunting. His stony expression remained in place, but he doffed his hat and gave a slow nod.

Martha flipped her braid behind her shoulder. "Haskell, this is my brother's wife, Livvy."

"Nice to make your acquaintance, ma'am."

A bowl of lemons sat on the counter next to a wooden press—not yet the refreshing drink she'd expected. Martha went to the sink, where she filled a cup with cool water and handed it to Haskell. He'd parch to death if he had to wait for the lemonade.

She sensed his scrutiny as he took the cup, careful not to touch her fingers in the process. A quick glance confirmed her instincts.

"Thank the Lord, Mr. Jacobs was with us today." Mama appraised him from a more relaxed and dignified position, but true appreciation shone in her eyes.

"What happened?" Livvy handed the damp rag to Martha. "Can you do this while I get the sugar water off the stove?"

Her mother snatched the cloth. "I am perfectly capable of washing my own face."

Livvy set the syrupy mixture aside and brought the bowl of lemons to the table with a pitcher, knife, and press. "Did you meet with outlaws on the road to the ranch?"

"Excuse me, Mrs. Hutton?"

All three women looked at Haskell.

He cleared his throat. "That is, Miss Livvy. Is Whit about?"

She sliced a lemon in two, clamped half into the wooden press, and held it over the pitcher. "He must be out with the cattle or he would have come up at all the commotion." She shrugged. "If you don't mind riding out, you might find him down at the lower corrals. Just head for the rimrock east of here and watch for the windmill. You can't miss it."

He slapped his hat on. "Thank you, ma'am."

He slid a look to Martha, and all her insides backed up against her spine. She swallowed hard and accepted his empty cup. Another nod and that near smile tipped one side of his mouth.

Now she was noticing his mouth.

"Let me help you with that lemonade, Livvy." She set down the cup and dragged the bowl and knife toward her as the front door clicked shut.

The knife blade slammed against the wooden table and lemon juice squirted her mother.

"Martha! Use the board or you'll slice right through Livvy's kitchen table." She wiped her face with the damp rag and sloshed her foot in the pan. Hiking her skirt above her knee, she leaned over to assess the damages.

"Swelling's gone down some."

"But it should be raised," Livvy put in. "Since the men are all gone, let's get your foot higher." She lifted the basin to a low stool beneath the table. "Pop used this stool to rest his bad leg. Good thing I kept it."

Martha managed to slice three more lemons and picked up the press but couldn't work it with just one hand. "What have you done with the old Overton place Whit bought before you were married? Did he ever finish the cabin?"

Livvy fetched the sugar water and dumped it in the pitcher. "Oh, yes. But since we moved back here, he just uses it as a branding camp. We didn't live there long, not after Pop got so crippled up and needed us closer."

"Give me a spoon," Mama said. "I can at least stir while I'm sitting here like an invalid."

"It's so good to have you both here." Livvy handed her a long wooden spoon. "I'm just so surprised, that's all. I didn't know you were coming back to Cañon City, Marti, though it seems like the natural thing to do." Her blue eyes rested on Martha with compassion, and she lowered her voice from its cheerful pitch. "I was so shocked to hear about Joseph."

Martha inhaled deeply, hoping to head off the old pain. "Thank you. I wanted to finish the school term and then I lingered in St. Louis for the summer. Uncertain, I suppose." She sighed, disgusted with her limitations. Tentatively, she lifted the knotted sling over her head and pulled the cloth from her right arm. With less pain than before, she hunched her shoulder and straightened her elbow.

Her mother watched with concern. "How does it feel?"

"Tight," Martha said. "Like I haven't used it in a few days."

"Well, you haven't. And you probably want to keep it in that sling until we get home this evening."

Martha tensed at the mother-hen response, but she had no chance to reply.

"How long have you known Haskell Jacobs?" Livvy squeezed another lemon into the pitcher.

Mama watched her with a stoic expression and continued stirring.

Another deep breath hid the little flame that flickered in Martha's belly at mention of his name. "Just a few days." Since she stepped off the train and into his notice.

"Well, I think he's taken with you."

Martha stared. "What makes you say that?"

"He looks at you as if the sun and moon and all the stars rose in your face."

The heat rose, that was for certain, as did Martha before walking to the kitchen door and opening it to the clear mountain air. She pushed at her mussed hair with both hands. How could she ache for Joseph with one breath and have her heart race for another man in the next?

"I don't mean to say he's besotted with you. More like watchful, I suppose. Protective, as if trying to anticipate your moves. But adoration is definitely lurking."

Mama laughed nervously. "It's a bit early for that. We've known Mr. Jacobs such a short while. Though I must say, he is quite gentlemanly, in spite of his attire. Which reminds me…" She scooted her chair around. "Martha, did you bring in my satchel?"

"No, I left it on the saddle. I'll get it for you." Anything to escape Livvy's speculation on Haskell Jacobs' unsettling observation.

From the way the approaching rider sat the saddle, Haskell pegged him as the son of Caleb Hutton.

The rancher pulled up near the house and dismounted, eyeing him with caution. "You lookin' for someone?"

"Haskell Jacobs, Colorado Ranger." He extended his hand. "Pastor Hutton suggested I see his son, Whit, about a matter. I accompanied the pastor's wife and daughter here today. I take it you are Whit?"

The man's sun-squinting gaze took in the empty yard, then the pasture, where the boys were hand-feeding grass to two strange horses.

Haskell read the question. "A rattler spooked the mare. The wagon's tipped at a deep gully just after the turn-off. Broke the front axle. Mrs. Hutton and her daughter rode my horse and the wagon mare the rest of the way here."

At that, the rancher swept Haskell's dust-covered clothing with a quick appraisal. "Let's see what I've got in the barn in the way of an axle and you can tell me why my father sent you."

One way to answer a direct question.

From the corner of his eye, Haskell caught Martha in the shade of the ranch house. Was she planning to eavesdrop on what her brother had to say? She didn't know Overton was a suspect, but disappointment wedged itself between Haskell's hopes and better judgment. He followed Whit to the barn.

"Was the snake coiled or sunnin' itself?" Whit dropped his horse's reins at the corral, unsaddled it, and draped his rig over the top pole.

"Coiled."

Whit stepped into a tack room just inside the barn door, came back with a brush, and looked pointedly at Haskell's side arm. "I take it you solved the problem."

"Changed its mind."

Whit snorted. "Best solution I know of."

The twins were pulling grass and feeding it to the horses. Whit brushed his mount and turned it out. "Nice gray."

"Thanks." Haskell couldn't agree more. Cache was the closest thing he had to a friend, besides the captain. The realization made him feel old and lonely. "He's sound and true."

Whit took his rig to the tack room, and they walked the brief alleyway to an open area where a buckboard sat between two wide doors on either side of the barn. Haskell paused at the last stall for a view of the ranch house. Martha was nearly to the barn.

"So what am I supposed to know?" Whit set a bucket of axle grease in the buckboard and pulled a spare axle away from a pile of timber against the wall. Haskell hurried around to get the opposite end, and they hefted it into the wagon.

"I'm trailing a horse thief rumored to be holed up in the area. Your father thinks there's a possibility that he could be the son of Doc Mason's nurse."

The remark hitched the rancher's otherwise smooth and easy movements, and his expression hardened. Evidently, he didn't think kindly of Tad Overton.

Whit lifted his hat and wiped the sweat from his forehead. "More than a possibility. He was through a couple of days ago with a string of four horses. Tried to sell 'em to me, but the freshly run brands told me they weren't his to sell." He muttered something under his breath. "Like he thought I wouldn't notice."

"How well do you know him?" Haskell said.

Whit made a sound in his throat. "Better than I care to."

"Do you know which way he headed?"

"West, toward Texas Creek."

"How far is that?"

"Half a day's ride." Whit eyed him. "From town, not here. You could make it quicker from the ranch."

"Sounds like you wouldn't mind seeing him caught."

Whit snorted. "I couldn't just take off and ride into town to tell the sheriff about the horses. Overton's been a no-account all his life. Left his ma in the lurch and got himself shot during the train wars, abandoned a good dog when it was a defenseless pup, and now he's stealin' horses. Yeah, I'd like to see him get his due."

"I understand he fancied your sister at one time." What that had to do with Haskell's manhunt he was unwilling to admit.

Like a hot poker, Whit's look burned right through him. "Fuel for the fire." He grabbed a heavy hammer and tossed it in the wagon. "Let me know if you want a hand hauling him in, and I'll ride with you."

Haskell appreciated the man's willingness, but he didn't need a gut-driven vigilante shooting his suspect. "I'll keep that in mind."

A clearing throat turned both their heads to the alleyway. Martha stood with hands clasped before her—minus the sling—and her chin reaching for the rafters. "Excuse me, but have either of you seen my mother's satchel? You remember, Mr. Jacobs. You tied it to your saddle as we were leaving the wagon."

Mr. Jacobs. She'd heard enough to learn his intentions but not enough to know the intention of his heart.

"Your nephews may know its whereabouts. I asked them to care for the horses."

She turned with a sharp jerk of her head and the braid snapped like the tail of a bull whip. Before he could reach her, the twins came running through the alleyway and nearly knocked her down in their hurry.

"Whoa, whoa, whoa!" She snagged each one and flinched when one boy hit the end of her right arm's reach.

He stepped forward. "What'd you boys do with the satchel that was tied to the saddle?"

The pair stopped wiggling and looked as if they didn't know what he was talking about.

He nailed each one with a hard glare. "Where's the saddle?" If it was lying in the pasture, it would take more than the presence of their father to prevent him from whipping them both.

One pointed sharply to the tack room and the other's mouth opened as if attached to the finger. "It's hanging on a rack in there. With all the other rigs."

His jaw relaxed. "Good work, men." He clapped one on the shoulder as he squeezed past the boy and Martha.

In the dim interior, he finally spotted his saddle on the bottom rack, the satchel still attached and looking like it'd been dragged up the ravine again. He untied the leather thongs and slapped off the dirt. When he turned for the door, she stood at the threshold, her face a study in sculptured control.

And beauty.

She held out her hand. The chin remained aloft. "Thank you."

He wanted to explain but doubted she'd listen. Offering her the bag, his grip on the handle forced her eyes to his. Cold water could not have doused him more than her silent, icy reproach. He let go, and she strode from the barn.

Whit joined him in the alleyway, frowning. "She heard us. Didn't she know what you rode out here for?"

"She didn't know I was a Ranger before the wagon incident."

"That matters?"

Haskell tamped down the personal side of things. "It might."

"I take it you're not aware of how her husband died."

Haskell wasn't sure he wanted to be.

"A stray bullet caught him in the head. Died right there in a St. Louis street. He was a preacher too."

The news hit Haskell like the lead that dropped Martha's husband. Not only had she been the wife of a decent, God-fearing man, she was the widow of one brought down by a gun.

No wonder the site of his Colt made her tense up.

He didn't have a chance.

CHAPTER ELEVEN

Hot tears swelled behind Martha's eyes. So much for the gallant Mr. Jacobs. He was convinced Tad Overton was a horse thief and no doubt planned to shoot him down in the street the first chance he got.

How dare she give a gunman a second glance—lawman or not. She should have known better.

She burst through the kitchen door, dropped the satchel on the table, and hurried through to the dining room, away from curious eyes. With no other place to hide in her humiliation, she stepped inside the adjacent study, closed the door, and leaned against it.

A man's study. The smell of leather and oiled wood filled the room, shooting fine pin pricks against her already aching sensibilities. She locked the door and turned the large desk chair to face the window overlooking distant bluffs and green pastures. Dropping onto the worn leather seat with a hiccup, she let the tears slip down her face unchecked.

Betrayal crawled in and curled up next to her heart.

She didn't cry for Tad. Her childish infatuation with him had dissolved years ago when she fell in love with Joseph. She didn't even cry for Joseph. He was with the God he loved, as her mother had said. The God *she* loved. But sometimes the Lord seemed so distant, so in cahoots with every other man in her life, like her father who turned Haskell Jacobs onto Tad's trail.

A few tears, she admitted, were for the tall ranger. What a fool she'd been to think something might grow between them.

She sniffed and wrapped her arms around her middle, crying for herself, fully aware of pity's suffocating grip. Fishing in her skirt pocket for a hanky and finding none, she wiped her eyes with her sleeve, pulled up her petticoat hem, and blew her nose. Mama would be appalled.

All she wanted was a loving marriage like her parents had. And children. Fresh tears burned, and she coughed against the tightening in her chest.

At a knock on the door she flinched and her shoulder tightened with a sharp stab.

"Marti?"

Livvy. "Yes?" She cringed at her soggy tone.

"Are you all right?"

No, she was not all right. "Yes. I'm fine." The break in the last word ruined her prospects for taking up lying as a profession.

The door knob rattled, then lay still in its place. "May I come in?"

Martha pulled her petticoat up again and pressed it to her face. Livvy was asking to come into a room in her own house. Humiliation flared. "Just a moment."

Drawing a shaky breath, she stood and smoothed her skirts, then at the door, turned the key and stepped back. She stiffened at Livvy's worried expression. They were so close in age, yet so far apart in wisdom and experience.

"Of course you may come in. This is your home. I apologize for locking the door."

Livvy stepped inside, quietly closed the door behind her, and pulled Martha into her arms. The gesture drained every drop of resolve in Martha's body.

Groping inwardly for composure, she pulled away and held her arm against her eyes. Livvy took her other hand and pressed a hanky into it.

"Thank you." So many tears clogged Martha's nose and head that she didn't recognize her own voice.

Livvy pulled a side chair to the end of the desk. "Come and sit," she said, leaving her grandfather's desk chair empty. "What is it that has you tied in such a knot?"

Martha walked to the window and stood for a long moment drinking in the expansive sky, verdant meadow, and rocky bluffs. Such contrasting elements that balanced the scene rather than warring within it. So unlike her inner landscape.

Discouraged, she sank into the leather chair and faced her sister-in-law. Not long after Livvy and Whit married, Martha had left for school. She'd not had much chance to get to know her brother's wife, and she steeled herself for an inquisition.

Instead, a kind smile settled in Livvy's eyes and she said nothing, but simply waited, unhurried and unflustered.

Martha sucked in a broken breath. "I have no life."

The declaration informed Martha herself as well as Livvy. She'd not faced it head-on, but as she sought to explain, she realized the depth of her problem.

"I have no husband, no children, no substance."

Livvy folded her hands on her apron and looked out the window over Martha's shoulder. Her yellow hair reminded Martha of Joseph. They could have been siblings.

"I am not surprised you feel that way." Livvy took in the same ranch land that Martha had regarded. "When I first moved here, I was running away from the mundane life of a preacher's daughter entombed in a city. I longed for something else, I just didn't know what."

Her gaze shifted to Martha. "Until I saw the ranch and your brother."

A reactionary huff. "You knew Whit when we were all children."

"Not the Whit he became as a grown man."

Martha still considered him an overbearing big brother, though she'd tried to cut him free of that image.

"But it was more than that." Livvy continued. "I took care of Pop, fed the crew here, tended to the garden and chickens and canning and cooking. I had a sense of purpose and felt needed. Like I belonged." Her focus returned to the window. "And I had your mother's encouragement to trust the Lord with my heart and stop trying to figure things out on my own."

Shame bent over Martha and breathed heavily down her neck. She'd not listened enough to her mother's counsel. Usually she bristled against it.

"I know you see her differently than I." Kindness softened Livvy's laugh. "I certainly don't view my own mother with the same regard, and for that I confess my sin. It's often difficult to see a parent's wisdom when you know their weaknesses so well."

Martha's back eased, the tension in her shoulder lessened. Whit had made a good choice for a wife.

"But it is worse for you."

Perhaps she had judged too soon. Her eyes locked on Livvy, waiting for the ax of accusation to fall.

"You have had a purpose and a life, as you put it, and lost it. No wonder you feel bereft."

Livvy's tender words threatened to open the floodgates anew, and Martha blinked hard. She had no more use for tears. They swelled her face, blurred her vision, and did her no good.

"But never doubt that you have substance. I know what your mother would say: 'Faith is the substance of things hoped for.' You have faith and you have hope. Therefore, you have substance."

Martha sat numbed by the simplicity with which her sister-in-law spoke. The verse Livvy referenced had been one of Joseph's favorites. Why had it not come to mind since his death?

~

Haskell's head turned at the brilliant clang coming from the ranch house. He'd nearly forgotten the sound of a stirring call to dinner and envisioned the woman rounding the bar against the triangle. Little hope was left to paint in the face of Martha Hutton.

He and Whit had worked amicably for an hour, switching out a broken pole in the corral, laughing at the boys as they scattered hay in a mock brawl and then grumbled their way through raking it into a neat pile.

"If you ever change your mind about the Rangers, you'd do all right on a ranch." Whit leaned his shovel and the boys' rakes against the wall. "Might even hire you on myself. If you can rope from horseback, that is."

The younger man pushed up his hat up with his arm. A wide grin broke through a week-old beard. Haskell suspected Livvy would soon be after her husband with a straight razor.

Whit turned to his sons. "Go wash up. Don't keep your ma waiting."

"But Mr. Jacobs owes us for takin' care of his horses." One dark-haired youngster stood his ground and held a narrowed eye on Haskell.

"You're right." Haskell snagged his gun belt from a high nail, strapped it on, then rolled down his sleeves.

"And what might that be?" Whit said to the boys. "You're not takin' money for being hospitable."

"'Tain't money, Pa."

"It *isn't*." Whit hammered the words with a frown. "Your mother'll have my hide if she hears you talking like that."

Haskell sucked his cheek between his teeth and grabbed his hat.

"He said he'd tell us how to figure what kind of horse eats more—a black one or a white one."

Whit scrubbed his face and made a rough noise behind his hand.

Haskell squatted before the boys and looked one in the eye and then the other. "Count 'em."

Two pairs of dark brows tucked down in puzzlement and they turned to each other as if pulled by the same string.

"Count what?" said the narrow-eyed challenger.

"The horses. How many white ones, how many black ones?"

Light cracked in the blue eyes of the other boy and he let out a whoop. "Ha! You got us good." He hopped around on one foot and slapped his brother on the back. "Don't you see? If you got more white horses than black ones, the white ones eat more. And the other way 'round if you got more black horses."

Whit laughed, grabbed each boy by a shoulder, and turned them toward the house. "Off with you. Dinner's waitin', and don't forget to wash."

The pair ran off, shoving each other like two unruly race horses on the final stretch.

"Cale! Hugh!" Like a whip crack, they stopped their antics and walked the rest of the way until they rounded the corner of the house and out of sight. A high-pitched "Hey!" rolled across the yard to the barn, and Whit shook his head.

"They're good boys," Haskell said, heading for the house.

"But they're a bucket full o' bobcat, I tell you what." The disclaimer did nothing to dim the pride in the young father's eyes.

Haskell tasted envy on his tongue. A bitter and unpleasant flavor.

Nearly as unpleasant as dinner with Martha sitting feet away and miles apart. She refused to acknowledge him, yet was a lively conversationalist with everyone else. It was as if he didn't exist, and she made it clear that she wished it so.

He scooted back from the dining room table. "Thank you, ma'am." He nodded to Livvy, who responded with a kind smile.

"You are quite welcome, Mr. Jacobs."

To Mrs. Hutton he added, "Whit's offered us the use of his buckboard. I'll be saddling up so we can get on the road and have your wagon repaired before dark."

"I quite understand, Mr. Jacobs. Martha and I will help clear things away and be right out."

If he had his way, he'd be taking Martha Hutton out to the porch and clearing things away between the two of them. He was too old for games, and he wasn't about to chase her like a spring calf. Either she'd have him or she wouldn't. And the sooner he found out what was wrong, the better.

The axle was an easy fix between the men, and within a couple of hours, Haskell was driving to Cañon City, seated on the bench next to Mrs. Hutton. Martha rode Cache, who had decided to show his gentle side, and Whit was driving his wagon home with two youngsters in the back, as full of boyish pranks as Haskell had ever seen. He chuckled to himself and the sound drew Mrs. Hutton's attention.

"Do you find humor in this situation, Mr. Jacobs?"

The woman's voice so resembled her daughter's that he cut a sideways glance to banish his doubts. Martha still rode next to the wagon with a stiff back and stiffer jaw. She'd regret it come morning.

"Only in the boys, ma'am. They are quite a pair."

At mention of her grandsons, the woman's formal attitude eased and she sent him a beaming smile. "Aren't they? Oh, but they are so like their father when he was that age. Full of vinegar yet with little hearts of gold."

Martha snorted.

Annie took to studying her hands, and Haskell couldn't see beneath the brim of her straw hat. Something intangible shot between the two women. An unspoken regret. He skirted that badger hole and gave the reins a light slap as the yellow mare turned onto the main road.

By the time they pulled up at the parsonage, he wished he'd eaten more at dinner. Lights had still shone from the hotel dining room as they passed the McClure House, and he hoped they'd have something left after he unhitched the wagon and bid the Huttons' good evening.

A saddled horse stood tied to the corral. He reined in the mare, and the preacher bounded down the back porch steps.

"Ten minutes more and I was coming to find you." He took in first his wife and then his daughter seated atop Cache.

"What a day," Annie said as she reached for her husband's shoulders and allowed him to lift her from the wagon. "We have quite a story to tell you, but let's get supper on the table first. Give me your arm, dear. I've sprained my ankle and am not quite my quick-footed self."

Haskell caught the parson's suspicion. He'd talk to the man later, after the womenfolk gave him their rendition of the day.

Looping the reins around the break handle, he jumped down and offered his hand to Martha.

"Thank you, but I can dismount a horse, Mr. Jacobs." If her chin jutted any higher she'd drown come the next rain storm.

Considering himself an all-or-nothing sort, he linked one arm around her waist and dragged her from the saddle. She'd stomp into the house without a word if he set her down, so he caught her under the legs with his other arm and made no move to take her inside.

She had instinctively circled his neck with both arms and he liked it. Her heart fluttered against him like a bird in a hunter's hand.

"Set me down this instant."

If she screamed, he was done for, but her demands contradicted her actions. Both arms remained round his neck. Which signal did he act on—her words or her gestures?

"We need to talk."

She blinked but held his eyes. "About what, Mr. Jacobs?"

"About you calling me Haskell, among other things."

She relaxed a hair.

"Very well, *Haskell*. Kindly set me down."

The edge she added to his name confirmed that she'd bolt the minute her feet hit the ground. Her body warmth seeped into him, melding them together, and he intended to keep it that way for as long as possible.

"Do you promise not to run off?"

She looked away. "Yes."

"You're lying."

She went rigid again and knifed him with a cold glare. He wanted to laugh aloud, swing her around in his arms, and feel her lips against his. Instead, he bounced her up as if to drop her, and she tightened her grip and tucked her head against his shoulder.

Much more and he *would* taste those lips. Instead, he dragged reason to the surface and laid out the facts.

"Number one: I am not going to drop you."

She raised her head and looked straight into his eyes.

"Number two: I am not your enemy."

Her tight jaw relaxed a fraction.

"Number three: When we arrived at the ranch you were sweet as molasses, and when we left you were cold as stone."

She swallowed hard, an act that drew his eyes to her slender throat.

"Why?"

Her arms loosened, but she didn't let go and addressed her comment to her father's horse tied to the corral. "Why what?"

He bounced her and her head jerked back to face him.

"Look at me and ask me that."

Twins as close as her nephews shouted from her dark eyes—one anger and the other fear. The first he expected, the second set him back.

He lowered his voice. "You have nothing to fear from me, Martha."

"Really? You are holding me against my will and yet you say I have nothing to fear? Were I to scream, my father and all our neighbors would be out here in an instant ready to lynch you from the nearest tree. Ranger or not."

"Then scream if you're truly afraid."

She hesitated and his chest seized.

At last she let out a defeated sigh. "Fine. I won't scream."

His arms ached, more from wrestling earlier with the overturned wagon than from holding her small warm body. "Promise me you won't run away and I'll let you down."

She nodded.

He couldn't hold her all night, as much as he wanted to, so he lowered her feet, keeping one arm around her waist. She stood against him, her hands resting on his chest. Had she forgotten or did she want them there?

She looked up. "Why what?" Her tone had softened.

"Why did you distance yourself when we left the ranch—no—before that. At dinner. You had a word for everyone but me."

Eyes as dark as the deepening night searched his own with more than the question on her lips. "Why do you care if I spoke to you or not?"

He let go of her waist. "You answer my question first and then I will answer yours."

Her hands slipped away, and the sensation left him feeling abandoned. She clasped her fingers and dropped her gaze. "I overheard you speaking to Whit in the barn about Tad Overton."

Though he already knew their past, her admission twisted a jealous knot inside him. "Are you still fond of him?"

A small sigh escaped and she shook her head. "That was many years ago and I was a child. I haven't even seen him since my return. But I don't want to see him—shot."

Her hand flew to her mouth and the two dark pools welled.

He reached for her other hand and held it between both of his. "Do you suspect he's a horse thief? Is that why you think I'd shoot him?"

She did not pull away, but lowered her free hand to her waist.

He leaned nearer.

"I've seen a man die from a gunshot wound. I don't care to see another." Her small hand stiffened in his. "Now you must answer my question."

CHAPTER TWELVE

Haskell linked his fingers with hers, and Martha found herself responding. It was too easy to yield to his strength, to be captured by his attentions. Three times he had held her, but this time not from necessity. Though she'd insisted he set her down, she had felt safe in his arms, protected. More so than she had in months.

It was as if he knew.

Perhaps Whit had told him about Joseph or mentioned her one-time fondness for Tad.

How *much* did he know?

As doubt and mistrust hefted themselves into a formidable wall, Haskell raised her fingers to his lips and held them there. His intensity invaded her, the day-old scruff on his jawline tempted her to cup her hand against his cheek.

Instead, he pressed it to his chest. His heartbeat pounded into her hand and down her arm until it mingled with her own.

"I care about you, Martha Hutton. I care that you talk to me, smile across the table at me like you do for others. I want to hear your voice and your dreams and…" He stopped, startled by his own words, it seemed.

Her temples throbbed, and she struggled for clarity of mind. Was Haskell Jacobs declaring himself to her?

Releasing her hand, he stepped back. "I apologize. I had no right to force myself upon you in such a manner."

She wrapped her arms about her middle, suddenly chilled without his touch.

The back door opened and her father stepped out. "Supper's on, you two. Best hurry before it's gone."

Haskell reset his hat. "I'll unhitch the wagon, settle your horse for the night, and be on my way."

Dare she ask him to stay? She'd done so once before and regretted it. But this time she was afraid she'd regret *not* asking him. Make a fresh start, Mama had said. Oh, if she could just sort out her emotions.

The jangling harness broke through her confusion.

"Stay."

He turned his head toward her, his face shadowed. Martha held her breath. The slow dip of his chin served as reply, and he finished unhitching the mare.

As if waking from a dream, she became suddenly aware of her surroundings. The sun had long since set and night was creeping up against the house and barn. She gathered her skirts and mounted the back steps with care, her pulse suddenly racing as if she'd run all the way from the ranch. At the door she turned. Haskell looped his horse's reins on the corral rail, then unsaddled her father's horse and led it into the barn.

I care about you, Martha Hutton. So did her mother and father and grandmother. Did he mean what she hoped he meant?

She curved her fingers at her lips, the way he had held them against his own. Something tore free in her breast, dropped and floated away like a wearisome black veil.

Livvy had stated the obvious. Yes, Martha had faith. Old faith, trained into her as a child though sorely tested as an adult. She also harbored hope, but she hadn't expected it to materialize in the form of a Colorado Ranger hunting the boy she'd once fancied.

With a twist of the door knob, she stepped into the welcoming atmosphere of the parsonage. Though separated by several feet and different tasks, her parents' affection for each other laced the room. Like a tangible thread, it had held her and her brother firmly within the family fabric of their childhood.

Tad had grown up with the opposite—a gaping hole. His father's death embittered his mother, and he had no one to teach him how to be a loving, helpful son. In spite of—or because of—the hard places of loss, he had chosen the wrong path.

Papa read by the gas light hanging from the ceiling above the kitchen table and glanced up as she walked past. At the sink, she washed her hands and dried them on a dish towel, considering the things in her life over which she'd had no control—primarily her husband's death and her barrenness. Like Tad, she too had the power to choose her response to those inequities.

She peeked at her father. How often she'd chosen to resent his involvement—his *interference,* she had called it.

At the stove, Mama leaned heavily to her left, favoring her right ankle. Even if Martha did not take her advice about fresh starts, that was still a choice.

She pressed her mother's arms from behind, brushed her cheek with a quick kiss, and shooed her away. "Go sit and put that foot up. You know what Livvy said."

Her mother groused but retreated to her chair at the table, where Papa lifted her foot into his lap, much to her distress. Martha shook her head. What if Haskell walked in on such an affectionate display?

When he opened the door, Mama nearly turned her chair over. To no avail, she tried to free her foot from a husband who took too much delight in teasing her. His eyes danced in the lamp light, but he finally conceded by scooting closer to the table, hiding her foot beneath the cloth.

Haskell's hand suspended above his hat on the way to remove it.

"Please, come in," Martha said, failing to keep the laughter from her voice. Her parents were as lively as her nephews and always had been.

So close to the man who had recently held her and then threatened to drop her, she shivered at the memory. Had he been playing? Teasing her as her father teased her mother? The possibility sent a tremor up the back of her neck.

From the pie safe she removed two vinegar pies. In-between pies, they'd always been called, made prior to the apple harvest.

Their Black Arkansas trees were heavy with fruit, but there wouldn't be enough for the winter, not with her father's sweet tooth and her mother's fame for apple butter. Hence, the Blanchards' invitation to come out and pick as many apples as possible. A sweet, sappy scent played in Martha's nose at the thought of a day in the orchard.

Four place settings already topped the table, and Martha added the pies and a tureen of left-over soup that might stretch among them. Another parental trait—making do with what they had and sharing even that with outsiders.

Somehow, there was always enough.

Haskell filled the room with his hesitation, no longer the decisive ranger or gallant knight come to rescue the ladies. He waited at the door, hat in hand, and combed his fingers through his dark hair.

"You can wash up right here." Martha pulled a clean towel from a drawer, laid it on the counter, and then moved out of the way. Far away. As far as she could go to the other side of the table to fill each cup with coffee and catch her breath. She set the pot on the table and took her seat as Haskell joined them with an inscrutable expression.

Had he misspoken outside by the wagon? Did he regret his hastily confessed affection?

Keenly aware of him and feeling still the strength of his arms, his lips on her fingers, and his breath on her face, she steadied herself as she raised her hand to his. Her father's strong grip encased her other hand, and his deep voice carried them all before the Lord.

"Thank you, Father, for bringing these three home safely. Thank you for Haskell's protection and help with the wagon, and for Whit's generosity. And thank you for Your grace and this food. Amen."

Mama must have told him about the snake. Martha prayed she hadn't mentioned Livvy's bold observations.

Her mother ladled soup into the men's bowls, and Martha sliced the first pie and set a piece on each person's plate. The informality of their family meal relaxed her, and an old Sunday school lesson came to mind of Jesus knocking at a door, asking to come in. As Livvy had that very day in her own home.

Martha regretted her immaturity and noted gratefully that everyone was intent on their meal and not her emotional fluctuations.

"So I hear you're a dead shot." Her father lifted his spoon to his mouth and his eyes to Haskell who, in turn, gave Martha a quick look.

Gripping her coffee cup, she raised it to her lips and hid behind it.

"On occasion." Haskell spooned a mouthful.

"This one for sure, thank the Lord," Mama put in. "He fired once and that was that. I can't imagine what Martha and I would have done had we been alone."

Martha focused on the coffee pot. One shot had killed Joseph.

Coffee splashed onto her plate. She eased the cup to the table and prepared to excuse herself when her father's touch stopped her.

He leaned close, his voice a near whisper. "It's all right, Marti. You can do this. You can face it."

His dark eyes as well as his gentle hand held her in place. He was right. She could not keep running every time a gun was mentioned. She'd be running her entire life. She clasped her hands in her lap. Lord help her.

"Did I mention that Mr. Jacobs also rescued my apple butter jars unscathed from their trip over the gulley's edge?"

Thank you, Mama. Martha puffed out a tight breath and picked up her fork.

"That is a rescue, indeed." Her father raised a brow at Haskell. "If you didn't get a chance to sample it, then you'll want to attend our fall basket social next Sunday after church. Annie always donates her last jars of the season to the fundraiser. We'd love to have you."

~

It was bad enough that this family welcomed Haskell into their home on such equal standing. It was bad enough that Martha had not rebuffed him for his earlier empty-headed ramblings and sat within arm's reach. But now they had invited him to a social event. He, a gunman, a blatant reminder of what a bullet could do, and a man set on bringing in the one-time object of their daughter's affection.

That must be it.

Cold confirmation soured the sweet vinegar pie on the first bite. The custard melted in his mouth and slid down with a plop onto the Huttons' ulterior motives.

With Tad Overton out of the picture, they could stop worrying about Martha and see that she was married off to a more respectable man. A younger, more stable man like a banker or a merchant. Maybe that telegraph operator at the depot or a young farmer from their church.

As far as they were concerned, Haskell was just a hired gun with a badge, and they were paying him off with kindness. He choked on the flaky crust.

All three Huttons paused and stared.

"Did I add too much vinegar?" Concern tainted Mrs. Hutton's voice.

"No." He set his fork down and coughed into his napkin. "It's very good. It just went down the wrong pipe."

Martha's mouth tipped in an appealing way.

Reaching for his coffee, he stole a look at the pastor who, by all outward appearances, was a man at peace with God, himself, and the world.

The evidence at the table said these were honest people with open hearts. So why did he suddenly mistrust them?

Frustrated and unsatisfied with his conflicting observations, he excused himself a short time later, led Cache to the livery across the street, and walked a circuitous route back to the McClure House.

~

By the next Sunday, Haskell was no closer to finding Tad Overton and more agitated than he could ever remember being. Concentration fled like a startled rabbit, and he found himself retracing his steps and coming up empty.

Goldpan Pete had no news. No more horses had tromped through the old-timer's camp in the middle of the night. Nor had there been any more in Doc's barn as far as Haskell could tell from sneaking around in the dark. He had even dropped word at the livery that he was looking for anyone who had come into ownership of new horses. The truth hit a high, strained pitch when he kept his badge out of sight and insinuated he might be requiring a new mount.

But he could take no chances. The smithy knew everyone in town and then some. Which meant the man could tip off a friend and have him gone before Haskell saw his dust.

He looked in the glass that hung above his washstand. What happened to his cold objectivity? Rubbing the linen towel over his face and across his hair, he formulated a telegraph for the captain. Maybe Overton had moved on. He needed to do the same. The more distance he put between himself and Martha Hutton, the clearer his thinking would be.

Decision made.

Tossing the towel aside, he pulled on his clean shirt and tucked it in his trousers. If he hadn't given Pastor Hutton his word, he'd ride out now. Instead, he was headed to a Sunday morning service and something called a basket social.

That part wouldn't be in the telegram.

He set out for the church house at the other end of town, passing a much larger, elegant brick building on the way. Well-dressed people streamed inside the broad doors and a bell tower chimed out the fact that he was late. Another professional value gone by the wayside since landing in Cañon City—promptness. He was losing his grip.

Discipline. His father's admonition rang in the bells' after tones. *Discipline over hunger, temper, loneliness. Keep a tight rein on your desires. They'll lead you by the nose if you let them.*

Right now, number three was tugging so hard he could feel the steel ring.

Two blocks later, lively singing penetrated his dark mood as he mounted the steps to the church. The pews were filled, and several men stood at the back, hats in hand. Martha should be toward the front, if not in the very first pew.

Out of sight, out of mind.

Right.

She was as much out of his mind as she'd been out of his arms when he pulled her from Cache's saddle. Had he read more into her invitation to supper that night than she'd intended? Had his heart taken the bit in its teeth and run off with his common sense?

Song books closed like buckshot spitting across the sanctuary.

It didn't matter. He'd never pass the Hutton's muster for their daughter, even if she was of age.

"Please be seated." Pastor Hutton met his eye and tipped his head in acknowledgment. A small russet-haired woman delayed seating herself and looked toward the back. Her shy smile pinned him to the wall as certain as a sharp shooter's trigger finger.

The man to his right grunted and slapped his hat against his leg. Haskell hadn't met him, but something about him felt familiar. His slight frame, an impatient air bordering on disrespect. Haskell ran his hand through his hair and cut a side glance. A smirk curled the younger's man's lip. Had he thought Martha smiled at *him*?

Maybe she had. The idea sobered Haskell and he pushed his shoulders back, straightened his stance.

"What is faith?" Hutton's voice reached all the way to the back of the cramped room, louder than Haskell had heard him before.

"Some say it's trust. Others say it's hogwash."

Several parishioners *tsked* and others snickered at the remark. In the few sermons Haskell had heard, the preachers hadn't used such common language. Maybe he'd been missing out all these years.

"Doesn't matter what some folks say. It matters what God says. And he's told us in the letter to the Romans that faith is the essence of what we hope for and evidence of what we can't see."

Haskell's attention honed in on the preacher.

"Faith is knowing. It's banking on what God tells us. It's proof of the invisible—like Him. We don't see God Himself, but we can see His handiwork around us and His love in our families and neighbors. We *know* He's with us."

Evidence was a word Haskell handled every day. He knew it inside and out. But he also followed his gut at times, without any real proof. Usually, he was right.

The young man grunted again. Haskell looked straight at him and conceit looked back.

His hands began to sweat.

CHAPTER THIRTEEN

He came.

But so had Tad. Martha would recognize those roguish good looks anywhere, though he'd aged considerably. Yet hadn't everyone?

And Haskell stood right next to him. Hopefully he wouldn't cause a scene during the sermon, throw Tad down and drag him away in shackles.

Martha twisted a wad of skirt into a wrinkled knot and then smoothed it out. She toed her basket from under her seat for another peek at the wide satin ribbon encircling the wicker. A flamboyant bow blossomed on top, the same color as Haskell's eyes. She'd paid extra for that ribbon at the mercantile—against her grandmother's attempts to give it to her free of charge.

Her pulse kicked up. Would he notice? Did men see such things? Likely not. But he'd be sure to notice the fragrant fried chicken and fresh biscuits she could smell from where she sat.

A few years ago, she'd have stood on her head to get Tad's attention to buy her basket. Now he seemed like a mere boy standing at the back of the church next to Haskell Jacobs. A boy much too sure of himself, if she read his expression correctly. She'd seen that look in her pupils' eyes, particularly young ruffians who thought they had pulled a prank she didn't know about.

Tad had not called on her since her return, nor had Martha seen him in town when she walked to the library or the mercantile. What was he up to these days? Could he really be stealing horses?

Pushing the basket beneath the pew, she tried to concentrate on her father's sermon. Her childhood training to recite three points from the message had stayed with her all these years. Even with Joseph—whose image fled her best efforts to bring him into focus. She strained to capture his features in her mind's eye and recall one of his many sermon topics.

"Faith is the substance of what we hope for." She blinked back to the present and her father standing behind the pulpit, obviously invigorated by the words he spoke.

All right, Lord. I get it. First Livvy, now Papa. God was indeed pressing the point.

But she'd always had faith. She'd grown up believing, knowing. Wasn't that enough?

"Let us pray."

Ashamed that she had missed so much of her father's message, she bowed her head and absorbed his benediction.

Afterward, all the women gathered at the front of the church, as was the custom for the fall basket social, and placed their ornately decorated baskets along the platform's edge. Haskell remained oblivious to what was going on.

Martha wanted him to bid on her basket. Not Tad or any other man, and not some old codger out to get a good meal, Lord forgive her.

"All right, ladies, please be seated toward the back of the room," her father said. "Gentlemen, step forward and we'll get underway. My stomach's empty as a new post hole, Mr. Russell, so kindly start the bidding."

Howard Russell, a rotund man with a bushy red mustache stepped to the platform and shook her father's hand. An auctioneer who prided himself at the speed with which he could singsong people out of their money, he puffed out his already protruding chest and thumbed his suspenders. Her father lifted the first basket, and the bidding began.

Several baskets into the bidding, Martha's agitation drove her from her seat. Who cared if she was being unseemly? She forced her feet into a dignified pace and strolled toward the back until she caught Haskell's eye. He leaned against the wall with no apparent intention of participating. Tad had disappeared—to the front with the rest of the men, she assumed.

She stopped next to Haskell and cleared her throat. When he made no comment, she repeated the sound, louder. His jaw worked like a horse straining at the bit, his tension palpable. What had gotten into the man?

"Blue is my favorite color."

He looked down at her, arms folded across his chest, his black hat gripped in one hand.

Did she have to sketch it out for him? "I thought you might want to know."

"Oh." He pushed away from the wall and stood evenly on both feet. "All right."

He was obviously distracted. Maybe he figured out who had been standing right next to him. But wouldn't he have left with his quarry if he'd known?

Tad's voice suddenly cut through the room. "Four bits."

Her basket dangled in her father's fingers, a not-so-happy expression on his face.

"Four bits, I have four bits," Mr. Russell sang. "Do I hear six bits a dollar?"

"Haskell."

Realization dawned. "Six bits," he bellowed.

Several men turned to see who had bid, and before they could turn back around, Tad barked, "One dollar."

Oh my. Martha's throat tightened. She might be dining with Tad Overton at one of the picnic tables scattered across her parent's front lawn. *Please, no, Lord.*

"Two."

Haskell's booming bid made her jump. He threw a challenging glare toward the location of Tad's voice.

"Three!"

A murmur rippled through the congregants as they turned to gawk, and now everyone in the room saw her standing next to the tall stranger.

Why couldn't she have stayed in her seat with Mama?

Mama. She searched for her mother and realized she was probably in the yard spreading tablecloths and setting up a lemonade stand on the porch. Martha should go help, but she couldn't pull herself away from the bidding war.

"Four."

She flinched. Haskell was willing to pay four dollars for her basket? Surely that would bring an end to this public display, and they could enjoy her chicken in the quiet shade of her parents' giant elm tree.

Tad stood and held a shiny gold coin above his head. "I'll give the church a double eagle for that pretty little basket with the big blue ribbon."

The room went deathly quiet. Martha's heart all but stopped, and Haskell tensed beside her. His left hand curled into a fist.

"It's all right," she whispered, hoping he could hear her. She touched his arm and felt hardened steel beneath her fingers. Oh, Lord, help them all. The men mustn't come to blows right there in her father's church.

Haskell took a step forward, and she dug her nails into his arm, forcing his attention to her. "It's all right. I don't mind. I mean—thank you."

The tension in his arm eased but his eyes burned with a hot, blue flame.

Mr. Russell slapped the pulpit as if prompted by the Spirit. "Sold! For twenty dollars to the young man on my left. Come claim your prize, sir."

Martha shuddered at the insinuation. Her father's expression dared Tad to pry the basket from his hands. Tad's lips curled in what Martha had once considered a sly and secretive smile, but now it made her skin crawl. She released Haskell's arm and straightened her shoulders. How had Tad known which basket was hers?

"Mama's basket has a yellow ribbon and a yellow checkered cloth draped over the top." She couldn't be any clearer. If Haskell missed her cue, there was no helping him.

She waited by the door as Tad dropped the gold piece into Mr. Russell's hand and took the basket from her father—her kind and loving father, whom she'd never known to stare daggers at anyone until now.

If Tad didn't read the warning, he was a fool.

~

Haskell's jaw ached and his fingers were numb. He'd squeezed the blood clean out of them. The silhouetted figure from Doc Mason's barn had outbid him for Martha's basket. At great cost, he reined in his temper.

He watched the thin man through slitted eyes. No wonder the palms of his hands were sweating. He'd been standing right next to the sidewinder through the whole sermon.

Tad sauntered to the back of the room, stopped, and saluted Haskell with a finger to his forehead. Then he placed his hand intimately against Martha's lower back and directed her out the door.

Haskell nearly lunged for him over the possessive gesture. If Overton touched her in any other way…

Sudden laughter tore his attention from the door to Pastor Hutton holding a basket with a yellow ribbon. The impulse took him before he could reason it out.

"Ten dollars."

A collective gasp and the room stilled again.

The auctioneer twitched his mustache. "Well, the Hutton women have certainly drawn some serious bids today. Sold!" He slapped the pulpit and everyone applauded.

Haskell's hard stride bounced off the crowded pews as he went forward and solemnly claimed his dinner. Pastor Hutton gripped his right hand and transferred the basket with the other. "Thank you for trying. I appreciate it."

"Three more baskets are all we've got left," Russell warned. "A few of you are going hungry today unless you can bribe someone into sharing."

Mrs. Hutton wasn't there—probably outside since the pastor had mentioned the parsonage yard as the gathering place.

Haskell trotted down the front steps and around the side of the church. Several tables were scattered across the clover lawn and couples and families were already seated enjoying their meal. Martha's mother served lemonade from the near end of the porch, and another table stood empty at the opposite side. The perfect vantage point.

Overton and Martha sat beneath a large shade tree with Martha's back to the yard and Tad facing the group. He smirked as Haskell entered the front gate and walked toward the house.

Haskell ground his teeth, refusing to take the bait Overton dangled in his arrogant eyes. He could break the man like a match stick and wanted to. But that would not serve the purpose of his assignment. Nor would it endear Martha Hutton to him. He may be just a hired gun as far as her parents were concerned, but he still cared for their daughter.

More than he should.

As he took the porch steps, Mrs. Hutton looked up from her ladling. "Oh, Mr. Jacobs. How kind of you to bid on my basket. I hope you don't mind starting without me. Just have a seat at the table there, and I'll bring you a glass of lemonade."

He gave the cheerful woman a curt nod and attempted a pleasant expression.

Setting the basket on the table, Haskell seated himself at an angle to Overton. From the cover of his hat brim he watched the scoundrel flash a brazen smile and lean low across the table, mouthing something only Martha could hear.

She moved discreetly backward every time Overton leaned toward her. If Haskell weren't so drawn to her himself, the situation would be comical. Like a see-saw, the two of them leaned back and forth across the table. The signal was clear.

Mrs. Hutton brought the promised lemonade. "Please don't wait on my account, Mr. Jacobs. The chicken is cold already, but there is a jar of my apple butter tucked inside for the biscuits."

"Thank you, ma'am." He tipped his hat. "I'm sure everything will be as good as it smells."

She laid a hand on his shoulder as she turned away. Evidence of—what?

He pulled the bow, set aside the napkin, and investigated the contents. A small jar nested in one corner and he set it on the table with two knives and forks. Two small plates of fried chicken followed, with another cloth holding several biscuits like those he'd had at the mercantile. He picked up one.

The memory raised his eyes to the pair seated under the tree and his gut twisted. Overton had moved to Martha's side of the table, straddling her bench.

The see-sawing began again.

Martha scooted to her right. Overton followed. Haskell crushed the biscuit.

He glanced at Mrs. Hutton, hoping she hadn't seen him destroying her food without eating it, but she was chatting with another woman and two small children who held their cups out expectantly.

He dusted the crumbs from his hands and reached for another biscuit just as Overton reached for Martha.

Haskell's chair fell back and he was off the porch by the time she had pushed the polecat away.

A sudden hush draped the yard, and Haskell stopped inches from Overton, drilling him with a cold promise as he spoke to Martha. "Miss Hutton, is everything all right?"

Overton's jaw clenched and his face reddened. He threw Haskell a dismissive wave. "Yeah. Everything's right as rain."

Haskell fisted his left hand, raised the other waist-level and curled two fingers around his coat flap. "I was speaking to the lady."

Overton swung his inside leg over the bench and rose to the challenge. A full head shorter, he was forced to look up. Anger brimmed in his eyes and his hands opened and closed.

An easy read that could go one of two ways.

Instead of throwing a punch, Overton stepped back and stretched his lips in a cold sneer. "Good to see you again, Marti. Maybe next time we can dine without interruption." He picked up his hat and leaned close to her ear. "And by the way, you and your dinner were worth every dollar."

He strode across the lawn, out the front gate, and into the side street.

Picnickers resumed their pleasant conversations. Haskell breathed again.

Martha gathered her basket and took his offered hand as she stepped over the bench. "Thank you."

He placed his other hand atop hers. "Did he hurt you in any way?"

Her lips quivered in a slow, sad smile. "No, he did not hurt me. He simply opened my eyes to things I hadn't seen years ago. Perhaps I didn't want to then." She withdrew her hand and looked around at the others enjoying their Sunday afternoon.

"Would you join me on the porch? Your mother and I haven't eaten yet. She's been busy serving lemonade and I, well, I…"

"Of course." She held the basket with one hand and gathered her skirt with the other as they walked to the front steps.

Her father was making the rounds of the tables crowding his front yard, thanking people for donating to the church's support for the coming winter.

And keeping one eye on his daughter and Haskell.

CHAPTER FOURTEEN

Every inch of Martha's skin tingled, which made her look eastward for gathering storm clouds. But the only storm brewing did so in her jumbled thoughts. Haskell had rescued her again—this time from public humiliation, for she was about to shove Tad backward off the bench. Either that or stab him with a drumstick.

In a way, she pitied the boy who was stunted somehow, trapped in the same spot he was in when she'd left. He'd aged, yes, but he had not grown.

Martha took the stairs with Haskell close behind. Perspiration glimmered on her mother's forehead as she served a never-ending line of lemonade lovers. When Haskell joined her at the table, Martha handed him her basket.

"Please, insist that Mama eat something. I'm going to take her place serving. She should also put her foot up, but…"

Haskell looked like he'd been asked to attend a quilting bee.

"Never mind. Just make her eat something."

She stepped behind the serving table and took the ladle. "Thank you, Mama, it's my turn. Haskell is waiting for you. Make sure he has some of your fine chicken and potato salad *before* he finishes off your apple butter."

Her mother dabbed her forehead with her apron hem and gave Martha's shoulder a squeeze. "Perfect timing, dear. Perfect."

Martha's timing was not all that was perfect. She accepted a cup from a freckle-faced little boy and peeked at the tall, dark-haired man seating her mother at the table. A new definition of perfect was developing with increasing clarity.

She tipped the crock and ladled out enough to wet the little boy's whistle. "That's it. You got the very last drop of lemonade."

He grinned his thanks and bounded down the stairs. Martha's father dodged quickly enough to avoid a collision with the youngster and then joined his wife and Haskell on the porch. Martha wiped her hands on a towel by the crock and did the same.

Taking her seat with a sigh, she relaxed for the first time that day. Relief washed over her like the afternoon sunshine, clarifying and defining more than the tables and people scattered across the yard. Martha was beginning to see herself in a different light, one that illuminated possibilities there in Cañon City, possibilities that might include a certain Colorado Ranger.

Then again, what reason did he have to stick around once he found what he was looking for?

Staving off a flare of disappointment, she pulled her basket closer, revealing a pile of biscuit crumbs swept into a neat little pyramid. She cocked a brow at Haskell, who was busy working over a chicken leg, but her mother caught her question.

"That one didn't make it," she said with a laugh.

"Best social event of the year so far, Pastor." Foster Blanchard stood among Mama's peonies that fronted the porch, no doubt breaking off several stems. "I think your missus and daughter raised more for the coal-bin fund than the last two years put together."

Blanchard laughed at his cleverness, but as the church treasurer, he was probably right.

Martha bent her head toward her raised napkin, avoiding the need to comment.

"Don't forget," Blanchard continued. "We've got a bumper crop o' apples this year and I hate to see 'em go to waste. Come out and pick whatever you can haul off." He gave Martha's mother serious regard. "Best there is for that apple butter of yours, Mrs. Hutton. Right good."

"Thank you, Mr. Blanchard," her mother said. "We do appreciate it."

As the man blazed a path out of the peonies, she whispered, "He says that every year. I think he takes great pride in that apple butter."

"As do I," Martha's father said, squeezing his wife's hand.

"But I can't pick apples this year."

Martha felt the sudden shift, and a sense of foreboding crept up her shoulders and spread over the otherwise pleasant setting. Reluctantly she looked up from her napkin to see that she was right. Her mother spoke volumes in molasses-colored tones.

"You know I can't go hobbling around out in that man's orchard. Not with my ankle in the shape it's in." She blushed the slightest bit and lowered her eyes. "Pardon me, Mr. Jacobs, for speaking so personally."

Haskell coughed, caught unawares by the apology. "No pardon necessary, ma'am."

Martha scripted out the next comment before it hit the air.

"And your father can't go either, can you, dear?" Mama's ability to communicate the unspoken was matched only by her husband's ability to hear it.

"No. I'm sorry, but I can't." He reached for the last biscuit. "Too much to do around here in the next several days. And I need to get the church ready for winter." He spooned a large helping of apple butter on his biscuit. "I guess that leaves you, Marti. If you can find someone to go with you, that is. I'd

125

rather you didn't drive out to Blanchard's by yourself. Maybe one of the ladies from the library would like to pick apples. Or a student working the dig up at Finch's quarry."

Haskell seemed oblivious to their machinations. Not Martha. She'd come in on the train and she was about to be railroaded again with Haskell Jacobs, straight for Blanchard's apple orchard. Why must her parents interfere so blatantly?

She dropped her hands to her lap and opened her mouth to speak, but Haskell picked up the trail.

"Might I accompany your daughter to the orchard?" He looked her father in the eye as if she were not sitting at the table with them. As if she were twelve and he needed permission to go with her. Of all the—

"A wonderful idea, Mr. Jacobs." Mama smiled demurely, effectively masking the manipulative nature that lurked just below a glowing surface.

Haskell turned to Martha as she fumed. "What day would you like to go?"

His question demanded a clear answer and his laughing eyes banished her anger. A day with Haskell? She should be so fortunate. He was indeed stealing her heart, and yet...

Doubt slipped a cold hand around her neck and reminded her that she knew very little about the man. However, she knew quite a bit about Tad Overton and she'd take Haskell's company over Tad's any day.

"Wednesday." That day required their necessary return in time for the mid-week service, ensuring they'd be home before dark. And it left two days open for a trip to the fossil quarry.

"Wednesday it is."

"I shall pack a lunch for you," her mother said. "It's the least I can do."

Martha rolled her eyes and wondered if Haskell had any idea he'd been set up.

Monday morning's nine-mile ride to the fossil site in Mr. Winton's cab proved dustier and rougher than Martha remembered from her youth. Then again, at her age with a still-sensitive shoulder, she was not the young woman she'd been at seventeen.

Enthusiasm seemed to have waned over the dig, as her mother had suspected, for few people joined the excursion. Golden cottonwoods paraded along the creek bed that marked the road into the red, rocky canyon, and an azure sky reminded her that fall reigned in the wide Arkansas Valley.

At the wash that held the quarry, Mr. Winton was careful to hand her down from the cab and lead the way up the ravine to the site. With her sketchpad under her arm, she paused to tie on the straw hat her mother had insisted she take. The sun made a furnace of the hard-baked earth and yellow stone that formed the gully's walls. Not a green thing grew at the dig site other than stunted juniper trees that clung with gnarled fingerlike roots to barren rock.

From a distance, Mr. Finch appeared much the same as she remembered, hunched over his work with a small pick and brush, pitifully shaded by his soiled farmer's hat. Hesitant to lose her footing on the loose shale, she held back as others ventured across the site to join in the careful scraping and brushing. She situated herself on a large flat rock, a suitable spot for sketching the scene before her, one that allowed her to give special attention to details.

But those details had lost much of their appeal. The area looked the same, but the intriguing mystery of what lay beneath the ancient streambed had been replaced by wonder at what stirred in her heart for a certain, very much alive, Colorado Ranger.

Not much in Haskell's Monday morning telegram to Captain Blain resembled the one he'd planned Sunday before church. Nor was it the only thing that had changed since then.

He slid the paper across the counter, followed by a coin. Outside the train station he lingered, watching people buy tickets and leave trunks on the platform. He'd hoped to be leaving by this time as well, with a prisoner cuffed to his arm and Cache tied in a box car. His original purpose in Cañon City had faded next to his growing affection for Martha Hutton, and he needed to get back on track. Lack of discipline almost had him hobbled.

That accounted in part for nearly wading into Tad Overton in the parson's front yard. He'd let a beautiful woman distract him. The case might be wrapped up with the crook in custody if he hadn't been drawn off course by the widow's charm.

He checked the street, and then crossed toward the café. Nothing about Martha Hutton said widow any longer. In two weeks' time, she'd shed her dark dresses, and her pale features had warmed with life. Just that morning he'd trailed her and a group of bone hunters to the bluffs in what the locals called Garden Park. Who spent all day in the sun digging for dead animals, regardless of how large the bones were?

Martha Hutton, for one. He'd even overheard the starchy professor commenting one evening at the hotel about Miss Hutton's admirable sketches of the quarry site.

He stomped his boots outside the café door and entered to a full house. One small table sat empty in the far corner. The perfect spot to no one but him.

With his back to the wall and a clear view of the door, he ordered steak and eggs and coffee and was pleased to see that the meal also came with a pile of fried potatoes. He forked the eggs onto the steak and dug in.

He needed a plan.

If Overton had sold off the stolen horses—demonstrated by the double eagle he'd brandished in church Sunday—how could Haskell prove the man was the culprit? He needed evidence.

He shoved down a curse unspoken, a recent tendency inspired by intrusive thoughts of Martha, her family, and their God.

It wasn't that he didn't believe. Of course he believed. But God didn't get involved in his work and Haskell didn't invite Him to. He stabbed the steak with his fork and cut off a chunk.

Whit Hutton had mentioned Texas Creek. It was worth a half day's ride up the canyon to find out who bought the horses, and it'd have to be tomorrow. Wednesday he was picking apples.

Egg yolk bled across the meat, as yellow as Overton's twenty-dollar gold piece. The Huttons were good people, but he wondered if they'd try to pay him for his armed protection on the apple-picking outing. He chuckled remembering Martha's discomfort at the table as they herded her toward a hired-gun chaperone.

"Something funny?"

The aproned waiter stood with a steaming coffee pot and a puzzled frown.

"No." Haskell wiped his mouth and held his cup out. "Thanks."

The man considered him with suspicion, but Haskell did not explain anything to anybody he didn't work for. Which brought the captain to mind. He'd think Haskell had gone loco.

With a sniff and a shake of his head, the waiter moved off to another table.

It wouldn't hurt to stop and see the sheriff again. He was aware of Haskell's assignment, and if he wasn't in cahoots with the thief, he might have heard something he was willing to share.

He certainly wasn't out beating the bushes for the snake himself. Fact was, Haskell didn't know what the sheriff did other than gouge the top of his desk with his spurs. A man didn't need spurs if he didn't ride—unless he just liked the sound of his own jingle bobs and boot chains.

And that was how Haskell found him when he walked into the sheriff's office after breakfast. Feet up on the desk, hat slouched over his face, fingers laced across his belly. The door slammed shut, and the man scrambled to keep from tipping backward.

"Mornin', Sheriff." Making enemies wasn't Haskell's way, but this man wasn't smart enough to be his enemy.

"Jacobs." The sheriff coughed and righted his hat. "Ya find your horse thief yet?"

"No, that's why I stopped in. Wondered if you'd heard anything."

The man stood and hitched his britches, then walked to the board where he displayed wanted posters. He mumbled the names to himself and returned to his desk chair, spurs a janglin'. "Can't say that I have."

Or wouldn't say.

"Have you heard talk of any new horse flesh around? Anyone buy a few head lately with blistered brands? Like maybe up around Texas Creek?"

The sheriff cut his eyes sideways and pulled on the end of his mustache. "Nope. Not lately. 'Course, we don't hear much from up the canyon without ridin' up there, seein' as how they ain't got no telegraph till Salida."

Haskell reset his hat and turned for the door. "Thanks anyway."

The desk chair creaked. "Say, Jacobs. You thinkin' on stayin' in these parts? Settlin' down, maybe?"

Haskell faced him. "Why do you ask?"

"Well, election's in a couple months. They'll be needin' a sheriff seein' as how I'm goin' back to Kansas. Thought you might be interested in the position, you bein' a lawman yourself and all."

The man had more nervous twitches than an old woman on chewing tobacco.

"That right?" Haskell folded his arms. "No takers around here?"

The sheriff snorted. "Can't get nobody. Ain't enough goin' on around here to keep a man busy. Not worth the trouble."

That depended on the correct definition of trouble. Haskell reached for the door. "I'll think about it."

He thought about it the rest of the day.

And all the next. He thought about it while he brushed and saddled Cache and rode to Texas Creek. He thought about how he could find that place he wanted and raise a few cows, maybe a couple of youngsters like Whit and Livvy's boys.

And build a house with a porch that faced the sunset.

He pressed a fist against an ache in his chest.

As he rounded the bend to the junction, a small park spread out from the river and the mountains leaned back against a clear sky. A mighty hand had cut this land and forested these slopes. A hand Haskell could use help from right about now.

He cleared his throat, rubbed his jaw. "Lord."

Cache's ear twitched back at the sound.

"I know we haven't spoken much lately, but I'd be obliged if You'd turn me in the right direction where Overton is concerned."

The horse shook his head and tugged on the reins.

"And help me win Martha."

Cache nickered.

Fool horse was laughing at him. "Amen."

Yellow cottonwood trees flared along the river, their gold leaves quivering like paper coins against a blue sky. Autumn came early in the Rockies, and its sharp edge cut the fine air, invigorating Haskell as he stepped off his horse at the Texas Creek General Store.

A man had ridden through the week before with a string of ponies, the storekeep told him. "Wouldn't have minded havin' the little mare for myself," he said as he stacked canned peaches on a shelf behind the counter. "Green broke, fresh branded." He faced Haskell with the air of a busy proprietor. "But I don't got time to be breakin' no horses."

"What did this man look like?"

"Younger than you. Thin, dark hair. When he came back through, he didn't have the horses."

"Any idea who he sold them to?"

"Rancher, I expect. But wouldn't know which one. I'll ask around though. Send word if I hear."

Haskell drew a pencil and paper out of his coat, wrote his name, and handed it to the man.

The storekeep read it. "Tillman," he said and glanced up.

"I'm at the McClure House. They'll take a message."

On the way down the mountain, Haskell studied on how he'd explain two last names if he ran for sheriff.

If Martha Hutton would have him.

CHAPTER FIFTEEN

In the last two weeks, Martha had joined the Women's Reading Club, worked now and then at the mercantile, and ridden up to the new dig at the Finch quarry north of town. Her sketches there had resulted in an invitation to give drawing lessons at the library.

Between helping her mother and keeping up with her new activities, she'd found herself thinking less and less about Joseph.

She pulled the hairbrush through loose tangles, closed her eyes, and tried to picture him as he brushed her hair in the evenings. Though she loved him still, his features more and more often blurred and melted into a murky memory. She plaited the long strands and coiled the braid at the base of her neck to keep it from snagging on tree branches or falling across her face. A full day's work awaited her. A full day with Haskell Jacobs.

A shiver ran up her back, and her gaze fell on the matching set on her dressing table. Lavender forget-me-nots trailed around pink and yellow roses on the porcelain backing. Was she forgetting? Was she being unfaithful to consider another man?

"Martha?"

Her mother might push into Martha's affairs, but she never burst through her closed door uninvited.

"Come in. I'm up."

Aproned and wide awake from preparing breakfast, her mother sat on the edge of the bed and smoothed invisible wrinkles in the colorful quilt. "I remember when we made this and how often I had to soak out blood stains from your pricked fingers."

Martha chuckled and sat down to pull on her boots. "It took me awhile to get the feel for the thimble, didn't it?"

Mama had not come up before breakfast lately, so something itched to get out beyond Papa's hearing. Martha pushed a stockinged foot into one boot and began pulling the laces.

"I'm sorry I can't go with you today."

Martha paused, then continued tightening the laces. She'd never known her mother to be untruthful, but the woman was stretching the facts as tight as Martha stretched the black strings in her fingers.

"Please be careful."

Tempted to jump into a tirade about her parents manipulating the entire situation, Martha instead considered the worried crease between fading brows and unruly gray wisps flaring from her mother's hairline.

"If you are truly worried about me in Haskell Jacobs' company, why did you and Papa work so hard at getting him to take me to Blanchard's orchard today?"

Her mother spread reddened fingers on her lap and pressed them against her apron. "What I meant to say is, be careful with your heart." She looked at Martha's small fossil collection. "Don't keep it on a shelf as a monument to the past. Be open to what the Lord might have for you."

All the breath left Martha's chest. This was not the usual mother-daughter talk she had suffered through during her school-girl years, pining over Tad Overton.

Mama folded her hands and raised her chin. Martha tensed.

"God has given us a great capacity to love, but the choice is ours. I love both you and Whit more than I can explain. Differently, yet the same. One of you is not loved more than the other. And now Livvy and the boys have my love as well."

Martha tied off the first boot and reached for the second. "But you've had only one husband. Could there ever have been anyone else?"

"It's a hard question, I know. And I've not been faced with that loss as you have." Her voice softened. "You will always love Joseph, but you have enough love for Haskell as well. And loving him in Joseph's absence from this earth does not mean you are betraying Joseph."

Martha tugged on the laces as her heart strings tightened in her chest. Her doubts did not suddenly fly out the window, but they tested their wings.

She tied off the second boot, then stood and held out her hands. "Thank you, Mama. I think the Lord must have sent you up this morning."

A quick embrace and she stepped back to press one more question. "But why Haskell? You don't know him any better than I."

Her mother pushed at her hair combs, then turned to smooth the bed where they had been sitting before looking Martha in the eye. A mirrored look, that made Martha feel like she was peering into her future.

"I have never seen you more yourself than when you are in his presence." With that, she turned and left Martha standing by the bed, feeling less a daughter and more a woman than she ever had before.

By the time they finished washing the breakfast dishes, the clop of horse hooves echoed off the barn. Towel in hand, Martha watched through the door's glass. Haskell stopped at the corral and looped his horse's reins over the rail. Papa was readying the wagon, and Haskell led Dolly from the barn, already harnessed, and backed her between the shafts. The men worked in tandem, as if each read the other's mind. Like Martha and her mother.

She dried her hands and patted her hair.

"Take my new hat." Her mother lifted a broad-brimmed straw from the hooks by the door. "You don't want to look like a baked apple after spending all day in the sun."

"I really need to get one of my own, but I don't think of it when I'm at the mercantile." She plopped it on and hurried to the mirror in the front hall. With a nervous giggle, she tied the ribbons beneath her chin. All she needed was a daisy in the hatband.

The backdoor opened and Martha's heart flipped in her chest. Why did such a divided pathway seem to stretch before her? Only one road led to Blanchard's apple orchard east of town, but she sensed she'd be choosing between two that day.

Lord, help me choose well.

When she entered the kitchen, Haskell's face brightened with—what? Was he laughing at her foolish hat, spreading nearly as wide as her shoulders?

"You're ready." A pleased expression pulled at his mouth, and he curled the brim of his hat, held loosely in one hand.

Her mother handed her the picnic basket and gave her a peck on the cheek. "Don't be late for services."

"We won't."

Haskell offered his characteristic nod and stepped aside for Martha to exit.

A crisp fall morning greeted her. Stacked bushel baskets filled half the wagon bed, and she set the picnic lunch beneath the bench seat and shoved it to the center. A handy distance for reaching from the ground, plus a safe divider. A woman must be wise.

The memory of Tad's inappropriate advances at the social on Sunday shuddered through her.

"Martha." Mama stood on the back porch holding a quilt and light wrap.

"I'll take them," Haskell said, reaching for the bundle.

He laid the quilt and Martha's cloak in the nearest bushel, then offered his hand. Strong and gentle, it gripped hers as she climbed up, and he steadied her elbow with the other.

Safe. He made her feel safe. Protected. Quite unlike Tad Overton had.

The wagon creaked and swayed slightly when he pulled himself in and settled beside her, kicking the picnic basket with his foot. He looked down and a slight twitch tugged his mouth. Detecting a blush coloring her cheeks, she turned her head, grateful for the wide brim.

He gathered the reins and flicked the mare's rump, and they set off at a lazy pace down the lane, east onto Main Street, and into the open country that stretched between town and the Blanchard's farm. It would take at least an hour before they reached the sheltered valley where apple orchards quilted the landscape.

Clear sunshine warmed her hands and her body, and cloudless skies promised a fine day. As they jostled along, Martha turned halfway around and counted the bushels. They assured several hours of hard, hot work in the kitchen. Love's labor, Mama called apple harvest with its cooking and canning and drying and baking.

Facing forward again, she bemoaned the hat, for it prevented any side glances at her companion. On pretense of viewing the countryside, she turned her head enough to study his profile. Strong. Kind. No tension in his jaw. No coat, just his vest but without the star. He seemed genuinely relaxed, and a slow smile lifted his mouth. Quickly, she looked ahead.

A soft laugh rumbled deep beside her. She straightened her back and stared at Dolly's bobbing head.

"This road is smoother than the one to your brother's ranch, wouldn't you say?"

She felt his scrutiny and chanced a peek. The coil that was her stomach loosened. "Much. Even if we came across a sunning rattlesnake, we wouldn't risk turning over."

Surprised by her unwitting mention of the snake, she glaned at his hip. As always, his gun lay easy there. She hadn't noticed it earlier. It was such a part of him that she no longer noticed it at all.

Feeling bundled as tightly as a Christmas package, Martha untied the ribbon and set the hat aside.

"Much better." Haskell studied her hair and face with such appreciation that it rippled clear through her.

Her cheeks blazed again, but replacing the hat would send the wrong message. "I'll need the hat later, when the sun is higher and relentless. Right now it feels good on my face."

"It *looks* good on your face."

Leave it to Haskell to speak his mind so easily. This outing might be more than she expected. She needed to keep the conversation on safe ground. "Have you picked apples before?"

He laughed aloud. Free of mockery, the sound encased them, drawing them together in a shared and secret moment. Something feathery brushed against her heart.

~

Haskell slapped the reins on the lagging mare. At this point in his life, he figured he'd done most everything that qualified as new and adventurous. Apple picking wasn't one of them, but he fully counted on it to top the list.

"No, this is my first venture to an apple orchard, but I'm sure it will be worth the day's work for the pies and apple butter I've sampled at your table." And the uninterrupted time spent with a woman whose cheeks bore the same tender glow as the smooth, firm fruit.

They topped a rise, and orchards spread before them in blocky green patches, some edged with a tarnished warning that the season was changing. Farmhouses and barns peeked out of scattered clearings, and dogs barked in the distance.

Martha clapped her hands.

"I love this part—the surprise of seeing the valley so green and full and awaiting harvest." She took a deep breath. "Can you smell it? The rich, sweet nectar?"

He inhaled and drew in only dust from the mare's steady hoof beats. "Not exactly." He coughed.

Martha laughed and leaned toward him. That picnic basket would *not* be between them on the ride back to town.

"I'm sure it's my imagination. Or anticipation. But this is the only fun part of picking apples. Everything else is a lot of hard work."

He looked at her sideways. "But it has great rewards."

"As you said, you've never picked apples. Wait until you're up a tree with the fruit just out of reach and you're risking your neck if you take another step."

He groaned at the irony.

She turned to face him. "Is something wrong?"

"No." He shook his head and chuckled. "You just have a way with words."

"Well, I was a teacher, you know."

"No, I didn't." But he should have. "Why aren't you teaching now, here in Cañon City?"

She faced forward again and folded her hands. "I wanted to do something different, at least for a while. So I joined the Women's Reading Club, and I go on excursions to the fossil dig, and I may give drawing lessons to a few people interested in sketching landscapes."

At least he knew those things. "Sounds like you have plenty to do without adding school teaching to your list."

She smiled up at him, and his backbone turned to apple sauce. She had more power over his nerves than any gun slick he'd ever faced.

"Maybe after Christmas. Mama and I will be busy enough canning and preserving for the next few weeks. November and December are full of preparation for the holidays. In January it will be too cold to go up to the quarry. Maybe the schools can use an extra teacher when classes start after the new year."

"How did you become interested in dinosaur bones?"

She cupped her hands like a bowl on her lap and stared into them. "Years ago the curio shop in town had fossils displayed that area ranchers had dug up on their land. It was like a miniature museum. Professors from Eastern universities came to see the massive bones, and they eventually set up digs in a heated race over who could find the best specimens. Wagonload after wagonload of gigantic bones were shipped to museums around the country. I was fascinated by the evidence of creatures that lived so long ago but no longer roamed this country. Or any country, for that matter."

The wagon's wheel hit a washout, and at the sudden jolt, Martha gripped his leg. Catching herself, she quickly withdrew her hand. "Pardon me. I guess I'm jumpier than I thought."

If that infernal picnic basket wasn't wedged beneath the bench, he'd pull her closer.

"Don't worry. You won't hurt me."

She gasped at his presumption and shot him a wicked glare that quickly turned mischievous. "Wait until I've got you up an old apple tree, Mr. Jacobs."

Wait until I've got you in my arms. He rubbed a hand over his face, hoping to clear the fog. He hadn't even checked for anyone following. Where was his head?

Their back trail proved empty. A good sign, but it would have been better from the top of the hill. They were already down the far side and into the valley.

"Turn in at the next farm on the left. That will be the Blanchard's place. He has ladders in his barn that we always use, so stop there first."

"Yes, ma'am." He flicked the mare into a trot, and they turned down a tree-lined lane that rivaled groves he'd seen in the East. Driving into a different world, they were immediately swallowed by apple trees. A wine-like perfume tainted the air. "I smell it now."

"Told you."

Her child-like anticipation infected him. Surrounded as they were by a lush orchard, it was easy to forget his job as a ranger. And he planned to do exactly that. At least for a day.

He pulled up at a neat red barn with green wagons parked nearby, and Blanchard himself ambled through the broad double doors in his dungarees, a pitchfork in hand. He swiped his head with a forearm but failed to hide surprise at Haskell's presence.

"Mornin', Miss Hutton. I see you've come to get those apples." He took in the bushel baskets. "I expected your mama to be with you."

Haskell jumped to the ground and waited at the mare's head.

"She wanted to come, but her ankle still bothers her from a fall she took the other day." Martha gestured to Haskell. "Mr. Jacobs here kindly agreed to help. May we borrow one of your ladders?"

Apparently satisfied that Haskell hadn't kidnapped Martha and brought her out against her will, Blanchard grunted something and motioned for Haskell to follow him into the barn. A moment later, Haskell shouldered a ladder and a long pole and laid them in the wagon bed.

"Thank you, sir," he told the farmer. "We'll bring them back before we leave."

He climbed in and picked up the reins. "Which way?"

Martha twisted in the seat and looked around. "I want the Gano variety. They ripen first and are good for nearly everything, but if I remember correctly, they're out a ways." She pointed to a narrow lane that led away from the barn. "Take that path."

They drove deeper into the orchard to where most trees hung full with green apples just beginning to ripen. As they continued, the fruit darkened to a bright red. "Here, she said. Pull up here and we can pick a few and see how they taste."

Before Haskell had a chance to loop the reins on the brake handle, Martha hopped to the ground, hiked her skirt, and made a beeline for the nearest tree. The woman wasted no time once she saw what she wanted.

Would she ever want him?

~

By midday, he'd climbed enough trees to appreciate good footing. He'd poled branches, knocked apples to the ground, and helped Martha scoop them into an apron she'd brought and then dump them into the baskets.

As she took off toward the next tree, he raised both arms. "Enough!"

She whirled and rested her hands at her waist. "Are you surrendering? Is that it, Mr. *Ranger*?"

He'd soon be loco with that playful look and taunting voice. No child on a schoolyard had a chance with her, much less a man like him.

"Guilty as charged." He dropped his hands. "I'm starving."

Her eyes flashed and she stooped to pick up a fallen apple. One eyebrow cocked like a pistol, and she bounced the red orb playfully in her palm. "Why not have an apple?"

"I wouldn't do that if I were you."

The picture of innocence tilted her head. "Do what?"

He ducked and the apple hit him in the arm. "That."

Laughter bubbled into her eyes and out of her mouth, and she grabbed her skirt in both hands and bolted away.

He was supposed to be chasing an outlaw, not a red-haired beauty flying through an overgrown apple orchard with her lace-up boots peeking beneath her skirts. Her laughter rolled out behind her like the Sirens' song, and he was powerless to go elsewhere but after her.

Out of breath, she stopped behind a tree, then circled one way. He lunged the other, then switched back, catching her off guard. She screamed and turned, but too late. He caught her left arm and she jerked around, falling against him, laughing and gasping for breath.

Without thinking, he cupped her head in his hand and pressed his mouth against hers. Sweeter than any apple, the taste of her drowned all reason.

He lifted his head and pulled her closer, her hands pressed against him but not resisting. Then she looped her arms around him and sighed against his chest.

And all of heaven and earth stood still in the circle of his arms.

CHAPTER SIXTEEN

Martha melted into Haskell's embrace—the strength of him, the steady beat of his heart beneath her ear. He held her as if she might fly away, and at that moment, she did not doubt that her emotions had done just that.

For he played.

The man she would never have guessed had a playful bone in his body had frolicked spontaneously, like a child. Without hesitation, he'd chased her and laughed with her and kissed her senseless. Surely he wasn't merely toying with her.

If her parents' approval was any indication, Haskell Jacobs was an honorable man.

The day would tell.

She pushed gently. His arms fell away, but not his blue regard that held her imprisoned and unwilling to flee. Yet like a jealous child, doubt whispered in her ear, *He'll soon be leaving.*

The overwhelming possibility of those words weighed on her spirit, and she shook the dust from her skirts to shake the warning from her mind. "We'd best be getting back to the wagon and our lunch."

She turned to lead the way and stopped short. In the chase, she'd lost all sense of direction. Even the mountains were hidden from view, surrounded as she was by row after row of apple trees. Fear slithered in next to doubt.

"What is it?" Haskell's voice deepened with concern and he reached for her hand, soon discerning what taunted her. He curled her fingers into his elbow. "This way."

As they walked, he watched the ground.

Of course. He was tracking their steps. Martha studied the path he took between the trees but saw no signs of anything other than grass and bird-pecked apples fallen from their branches. The sun bore straight down upon them. So much for Mama's garden hat.

And then she heard the mare nicker.

"Oh." Relief spilled out on a nervous sigh, and she fingered her bodice. Haskell's hand tightened atop hers and she looked up.

He faced her and took both her hands in his. "I told you once before that I will never hurt you. I meant that. Nor will I let anyone or anything—like being lost—hurt you."

Never. That was a long time. A word she'd cautioned her students not to brandish about. Did Haskell use it lightly, or did he mean it?

Without taking his eyes from hers, he lifted one hand to his lips as he had before. Her breath fled at the gesture, raising the question of which was more thrilling—a run through the orchard or the touch of his lips?

His stomach growled and she giggled, freeing them both from the moment. She hurried to the wagon for the picnic basket, and he followed, retrieving the quilt.

Kneeling on the bright patchwork, Martha unpacked two small crocks of chicken potpie, molasses cookies, and a quart jar of lemonade. She gave him a fork, a napkin, and one of the pies, and set the cookies and lemonade between them. Two empty apple butter jars served as glasses.

She poked through her pie crust but Haskell waited, pie intact and fork in place. Surely he wasn't disappointed in what her mother had packed. He'd eaten her chicken without complaint at the social on Sunday. Four pieces.

Then the obvious hit Martha squarely in her conscience and she set her pie aside. "Would you like to offer thanks or shall I?"

He held out his hand and she took it, melting a little at the way he linked his fingers through hers and bowed his head. "Thank you, Lord, for this day and this food and this company. Amen."

She squeezed her eyes tightly shut but couldn't prevent a smile from escaping at Haskell's brief and to-the-point prayer so like her father's. "Amen."

Mama had outdone herself. If Martha ate all of her serving, she'd not be able to finish filling the few bushels that remained empty in the wagon. Already she longed to lie back on the old quilt and nap in the shade.

But a lady did not fall asleep in an orchard alone with a man other than her father or husband, regardless of how honorable that man might be. Heavens. As it was, Mr. Blanchard was sure to set the gossip fires burning over her traipsing into his orchards unescorted by a family member.

But she was no young, inexperienced girl.

Haskell had given in to the urge and stretched out with his eyes closed. He'd linked his hands beneath his head and dark lashes rested against his tanned skin. How tempted she was to lean down and return the kiss he'd given her. How easily she could lay her head on his broad chest again and rest against the rhythm of his heartbeat.

Flushed, she grabbed the lemonade and filled one of the small jars. Such thoughts should be reserved for one's husband. And what made her think he'd ever consider a match between them? He knew little of her background and she knew less of his, and nothing of his intentions, for that matter.

One kiss did not a proposal make.

He'd have to leave once he caught the horse thief, and if not that, he'd be leaving to continue his search.

As much as she had resisted believing Tad was the culprit, she could see he fit the pattern. His sudden appearance with a twenty-dollar gold piece laid suspicion at his feet. He could have been stealing horses for years and Martha wouldn't know any different. Maybe the Colorado Rangers had good reason to be on his heels.

She filled the second jar, and Haskell's eyes opened. He sat up and stretched his arms overhead, flexing his shoulders and hands.

"So, when will you arrest Tad?"

Her question stilled his movements and his eyes narrowed. A ranger's mask slipped across his face, just as it had the first day she'd asked him what he was doing in Cañon City.

"Does it matter?"

Blunt, if nothing else. At least he spoke his mind. In that way, they were much the same, except propriety kept her from speaking her mind where he was concerned.

"I suppose not," she lied, careful to look anywhere but at him. "I just assumed you'd take him back to Denver or wherever you take your prisoners and go home to...wherever home is."

He watched her for a long moment and she dreaded what he might say—leaving tomorrow, never returning, moving on to the next assignment. She sipped her lemonade.

"I'd like to settle down here."

Coughing like a sick cow, she sloshed the contents of her short jar onto her lap and the quilt. While covering her mouth with one hand, she sopped up the spill with her apron.

"Would it be that bad to have me around?"

No tease tugged his mouth. He was dead serious.

"No. You...you just surprised me. I expected..."

"What did you expect?"

She'd better close her mouth before she talked herself into a corner.

147

"I don't know what I expected."

"But you do know you're a terrible liar, don't you?"

She regretted not grabbing her hat. Very well. If he wanted to play this kind of chase, she'd join him. She untied her wet apron and stuffed it into the picnic basket, then began packing their dishes and leftovers. He snatched the cookies before she got to them and shoved one in his mouth whole.

"I expected you to leave. To go on to your next assignment. I dare say Cañon City does not often draw infamous hoodlums to the river's banks, though we have had some trouble with vandals up at the quarry lately."

He crossed his legs Ute-fashion and bit into another cookie while watching her. She closed the basket and made to stand, but he stopped her with a light touch.

His gaze brushed across her hair and cheek and neck, leaving as much heat in its wake as a kettle full of apples cooking on her mother's stove.

"The sheriff asked if I'd be interested in running for office. He's going back to Kansas after the election."

Haskell Jacobs had a knack for stealing her breath, either with his lips or with what those lips had to say. "What did you tell him?"

"I told him I'd think on it."

"Well." Profound for a school teacher. She could have said nearly anything, like "Please do," or "Would you?" or "You'd be a wonderful sheriff." The last phrase nearly slipped out but he stopped her short.

"What do *you* think?"

~

The verbal chopping block's rough surface scraped Haskell's neck and he swallowed hard. Never once had he asked someone other than his father what they thought he should do. But he wanted to know, needed to know this time. It meant the difference between riding out and coming back or just riding out.

He'd catch Tad Overton, that was certain. Either in the act or through a witness. But what he did after that was up to Pastor and Mrs. Hutton's widowed daughter. If she'd have him, he'd stay. If not, he'd never look back.

An uncommon malady took a choke hold on his belly: cold, tight dread.

Indecision and something like yearning warred across Martha's features. One word from her, just one would be enough either way.

She fumbled with her skirt and folded and unfolded her hands, each gesture tightening the grip on his gut.

Finally she took a breath and held it in, then met him eye to eye. "I'd like it very much if you decided to run for sheriff."

The grip broke with such force that air gushed out of him as if he'd been belly-kicked. Those were all the words he needed from her, but he had a few extra of his own.

"There's just one problem. I have a confession to make."

She wadded her skirt in her fists and straightened her back as if bracing for a blow. If he'd believed things would get this far, he would have told her and her parents long ago.

"Different people in town know me by two different names."

She stared, brows drawn. "What do you mean?"

"My name is Haskell Jacobs. But it is also Haskell Tillman Jacobs. Sometimes I go by Haskell Tillman—at the hotel, the café, the livery. With others, I use Haskell Jacobs."

A sigh escaped her perfect lips and her shoulders relaxed. "I see." One hand fingered her bodice. "You frightened me. I thought you had deceived us."

"In a way I have. I should have told you and your family the whole truth. Then I wouldn't have to explain it when I ask for your hand."

Her fingers stilled.

He reached across the picnic basket for those fingers. "If you will have me."

She blinked, rolled her lips together, and looked into the orchard behind him as if she were looking into the future. Interlocking her small hand in his, she drew her eyes back to him and favored him with a sweet smile. "Yes, Haskell Tillman Jacobs. I will."

He laughed aloud and pushed the basket aside. She came willingly into his arms, and he kissed her deeply, longingly, then pulled back and pressed his lips to the top of her head. He wanted more—so much more—but that would lead him into dangerous territory, and he had given his word.

Could it be this easy? Had God really answered his prayer?

She eased back and spread her skirt over her feet. "Did Whit tell you anything about my marriage?"

Uncertainty edged her voice. Guilt called for another confession, but he wanted to hear her version, get that glimpse into her soul.

Resisting the urge to pull the pins from her hair and let the braid fall over her shoulder, he let his words fall between them instead. "I'd like to hear it from you."

She tugged at a loose quilt thread. "I was Mrs. Joseph Stanton for two wonderful years. Joseph pastored a small church in St. Louis and I taught school. One summer afternoon a year ago, Joseph was in town on church business and left late to come home. Near dark."

She drew in a shaky breath and continued in a careful tone, as if unfolding an old and faded letter. "He stepped out to cross the street, and a bullet from a drunkard's gun hit him in the back of the head." Her voice dipped. "We had no children."

Haskell ached to hold her, to kiss away the pain that etched her face, to shield her from the world's evil. But he let her finish.

"Your gun put me off for quite some time, though I am grown-up enough to know that not all men who carry guns use them for ill purposes. It may take me a while to become accustomed to one so close, but I am willing to try."

A smile trembled on her lips and his heart twisted. He would die protecting her, if need be. But he preferred to live out his life as her husband.

"I'll not be able to set it aside if I am elected sheriff."

She closed her eyes. "I know. But it's who you are. I cannot ask you to be anyone other than who you are."

He pulled her to him then and simply held her until the mare whinnied them back to the moment. Time had kept its steady pace, and already the sun had slipped past its zenith. He helped her to her feet, and they packed the basket and quilt in the wagon bed. She leaned over the back, surveying what they'd accomplished.

Only two bushels remained empty. They could hurry to fill them or come back another day, but he might not get the chance this season. It was his fault they hadn't finished.

He lifted a bushel.

"It's all right, Haskell." She moved to the mare and stroked its shoulder. "We have plenty. We'll need to unload before dark anyway, and I'd rather enjoy the trip back than overwork poor old Dolly trying to get her home too quickly with a full load."

A metallic click lifted the hair on Haskell's neck. The basket dropped and he slapped his holster.

"Ah-ah-ah." The voice closed in, and a gun barrel pressed between his shoulder blades as a hand slipped his Colt from the leather. It landed among the trees with a dull thud. "Have a seat, Ranger Tillman."

Martha froze beside the mare, her face pale as death. "Tad."

"Why, Marti, I'm so glad you're happy to see me."

The man walked around in front of Haskell and pointed the gun at his chest. "I said, have a seat."

Haskell lowered himself to the ground, keeping his eye trained on Overton's trigger finger. Anger at his own stupidity nearly overrode his good sense.

Overton waved the gun. "Take off the vest."

Haskell's hand went automatically to the pocketed watch.

"Now."

He shrugged off the vest and held it on the tips of his fingers, ready to drop it when Overton reached for it.

The man smirked. "Toss it to me."

Haskell ground his teeth and tossed the vest. Overton bent to retrieve it, eyes and gun steady on his target.

Martha stepped away from the horse and snapped a twig.

"Stay right there, Marti, darlin', unless you want me blowin' a hole in Ranger Tillman here."

She stilled without a sound, her face cold, eyes hard. *Not again for her, Lord. Not another killing.*

Overton put on the vest, felt in the pockets, and pulled out the gold watch. "Nice time-piece ya got here, Tillman." A guttural huff. "Guess I should say *I* got here."

The smirk broadened as he dropped the watch in the pocket and tugged at the oversized vest.

"Marti, got any rope in that wagon?"

"No." She crossed her arms at her waist.

"Then tear off the bottom of that pretty little petticoat you're wearing and bring it over here nice and slow like."

Haskell fisted his hands and leaned forward.

"Don't even think about it, Tillman." The gun raised to Haskell's face. "I'm not above killin' ya right here amongst all the ripe fruit."

"You don't want a poster with your name on it for murder, Overton. Stop now and come back with me, and you'll just be tried for stealing horses."

Overton hacked out a sharp laugh and shook his head. "You're right funny, Tillman. What makes you think I'm stealin' horses?" He stepped back at an angle that put both of them in his line of vision. "Hurry up with that petticoat. We don't got all day."

Martha turned her back and lifted her skirt. The tearing sound ripped Haskell's insides open, and all his regret and anger spilled out in a bitter gall.

God, please…

CHAPTER SEVENTEEN

Fear screamed in Martha's head, but she'd not give Tad Overton the satisfaction of hearing it.

Grasping the seam in her petticoat, she ripped it open, tearing away the bottom three inches and shredding her nerves. Birdsong mocked from the trees, and overly ripe apples vexed her nose.

"Good girl." Tad waved the gun barrel toward Haskell. "Now tie his hands. Good and tight, mind you. You don't want me shootin' him 'cause he got loose and followed us, now do ya?"

She gripped the torn cloth with fisted fury. His voice repulsed her, and his arrogance stoked a fire fit to scorch the orchard were she able to loose it. How had she ever found anything appealing or attractive about Tad Overton?

And how could she help Haskell now, here?

He held his hands out, crossed at the wrists.

Overton cackled.

"Nice try, Tillman." The gun fanned the air. "Behind your back." He straightened his arm, aimed at Haskell's chest, and steeled his voice to a deathly quiet. "You think I'm stupid?"

Don't answer. Please, Haskell, don't speak your mind, just this once. Martha knelt behind him and bound his hands with the eyelet-edged strip. Never had she dreamed the delicate trim would find such purpose as this.

She laid a hand on his shoulder and squeezed as she pushed herself up.

"Get away from him!"

She stepped toward the mare, clawing through her mind for a way to stop Tad, free Haskell, and escape.

Overton pulled off his bandana and dropped it. Then he drew a small vial from his trousers' pocket, pulled out the cork with his teeth and quickly turned his head. Stooping, he emptied the contents onto the neckerchief. Even at a distance, the pungent odor wrinkled her nose. *Chloroform.*

Panic filled her throat. He'd stolen the drug from Doc Mason, and she doubted he knew its potency. Fully expecting him to use it on her, she gasped as Tad picked up the neckerchief and walked to Haskell.

With a sickening grin, he circled behind his victim and reached around, covering Haskell's mouth and nose with the soaked cloth.

Tears fell involuntarily as Martha watched Haskell's weakening struggle. Finally he slumped sideways. Tad knelt and held the rag against his face again.

"Stop it! You'll kill him!" She started forward, and the gun quickly pointed her way.

"Not to worry. He's a big boy. Look at him." Overton grinned down at his helpless target and laughed again—the harsh, cold bark of a feral dog. "If a little is good, more is better, right?"

Martha bit her hand to keep from screaming.

Overton stuffed the rag in his back pocket, picked up Haskell's hat, and shoved it on his own head with a smirk. "Not so tough are you now, Ranger Tillman." He landed a stiff boot against Haskell's back and walked to the wagon.

Martha shook with rage. God forgive her, but if she had a gun she'd gladly shoot Tad Overton where he stood. She gripped her hands to steady them.

"Push those baskets out o' the wagon." The gun raked the air.

"No."

Without taking his eyes from her, Overton pointed the gun at Haskell's head. "What was that?"

Her jaw clamped tight enough to burst a vessel, but she climbed to the seat and into the bed. One by one, she shoved the baskets off the opened end. They smashed onto the ground, bursting apart like Martha's memories of the day she'd spent with Haskell. Apples bounced and rolled, and all their hard work, all their laughter and joy, spilled across the grass and dirt until the wagon was empty and dry as her throat.

"That-a-girl. We don't need that extra weight holdin' us back."

She glared at him, her fingers balled into trembling fists. "I'll never be a part of your *we,* Tad Overton."

His raucous laugh stilled the birds and scratched Martha's ears like little-boy nails across a chalkboard. "Take a seat, darlin'."

He climbed in beside her and scooted close as he reached over her lap for the reins. "Now ain't this cozy. Just like old times."

Remorse flooded her veins as his unwashed odor flooded her nostrils. If she hadn't fallen for his charms years ago, Haskell would not be lying in a heap in the orchard, his wrists bound and God knew how close to death. Tears spilled over. *Lord, have mercy.*

"Yah!" Tad slapped the reins hard against Dolly and she lunged forward, startled by such abuse.

Martha jerked back and gripped the end of the seat with her right hand. "Where are you headed?"

"Why, the Pueblo train depot, of course." The wagon rumbled down the narrow lane between the trees, but Tad slowed as they neared the barn. He pulled the hat low, laid his gun across his lap, and shoved the barrel into her thigh. "You tell old man Blanchard thank you and smile real pretty when we go by, ya' hear? Don't make no signs if you plan on walkin' again anytime soon."

Martha's last hope of escape died at the end of Tad's revolver.

Blanchard must have heard the wagon coming, for he stood at his barn entrance leaning on a pitchfork.

Martha waved and raised her voice.

"Thank you, Papa Blanchard."

Tad cocked the hammer.

Silently, she prayed the man would pick up on her hint. "See you Sunday."

She hoped.

Tad took the turn too fast, and she rocked against his shoulder. When she looked back, Blanchard was trotting after them.

"What about my ladder?" Winded, he stopped and stood scratching his head as if he'd just seen a peculiar sight. She prayed he had and would do something about it.

At the main road, the wagon wheels skittered in a hard left turn. She had to leave a sign—anything for someone to follow. Something like the breadcrumbs from the storybook tale of two frightened children, but she couldn't reach the picnic basket. Wagon wheels left no footprints. They would merely blend in with every other horse and wheel that traveled the hard-packed dirt to Pueblo.

Frantic to drop something, she bent over and fumbled with her boot laces. Tad said nothing and continued to drive the mare hard. Her mother's hat had fallen beneath the seat and she eased it up and over the edge praying Tad wouldn't notice the flutter.

Another *yah!* and Dolly lunged again. Soap-like lather clung to her neck and sides where the harness rubbed. She'd never keep up the pace. Swallowing the guilt, Martha dared to pray the poor horse gave out before they reached the depot.

Otherwise, there might be no chance of escape once they boarded the train out of town.

Haskell winced as he rolled to his back, crushing his bound hands beneath his weight.

Squinting into leafy branches, he searched his memory for where he was and why.

Martha. Her fear-filled eyes.

He jerked up and the orchard spun, forcing him to his back. She was in danger. Of that he was certain, but nearly everything else was a blur. Everything except Tad Overton's mocking laughter.

He eased up the second time and pulled at the cloth binding his hands but it held fast. Heaving himself to his feet, he waited for the spinning to stop, then stumbled toward a rough-barked tree. The cloth quickly tore and he jerked free. Rubbing his wrists, he walked in widening circles until he found his gun. He spun the cylinder—six cartridges remained. Overton hadn't unloaded it.

Anger warred with objectivity, and he steeled himself against the rising rage. He'd promised Martha he'd protect her and then he let a sniveling thief get the jump on them. Fury was a formidable enemy if allowed to overtake him. He needed hard, cold detachment to get Martha back, and he trained all his thoughts on that one purpose.

Holstering the Colt, he gathered his bearings and walked toward the lane. His pulse pounded at the sight of their morning's labor strewn across the ground—bushel baskets smashed in their heavy fall from the wagon and fruit scattered and damaged.

Forcing himself to breathe through his nose, he walked steadily in the direction of the barn, and by the time he arrived he was in a full trot. He needed a horse and he'd take one at the business end of his gun if necessary.

His badge lay in a hidden pocket in his vest. Another blunder.

"Blanchard," he hollered, approaching the barn.

The man ran out leading a saddled horse with one hand, a shotgun in the other.

The long double barrels leveled out. "Who are you?"

"I'm Haskell Jacobs, Colorado Ranger."

Blanchard's eyes narrowed. "No, you're not. He just left with Marti Hutton."

Haskell raised his hands, palms out, and took a step closer. "Look again. I sat at the table on the Hutton's porch Sunday afternoon during the basket social. You stood in the flowers by the porch and invited Mrs. Hutton out to pick apples—the best, you said, for her apple butter."

The shotgun dipped but the challenge held steady. "Then who was that with Miss Marti?"

"That was the man I'm tracking, Tad Overton. Wearing my hat and vest."

Blanchard's ruddy face went white. "I knew something was wrong when they didn't stop and unload my ladder."

Another step. "I need your horse to go after them."

Blanchard gave him the once over. "How do I know you're really a ranger?"

"If my badge weren't in my vest, I could prove it. You're going to have to take my word."

Blanchard rubbed his chin, still holding the reins. Haskell's palms began to sweat. Seconds raced by, carrying Martha farther away. If Overton made it to a depot...

He lowered his hands and rested one on the butt of his gun. "I need your horse, Blanchard. They're getting away—and I don't know which way they went."

Blanchard's eyes flicked to Haskell's gun hand. "I should have tried harder to stop them when they came flying through the yard here." He offered the reins to Haskell, stepped back, and cradled the shotgun in his arm. "I was gonna ride into town and see if Miss Marti was all right." He shook his head and stared down the lane.

Haskell swung into the saddle, itching to dig his boots into the bay's side and run for the wind. "Why do you say that?"

"She called me Papa Blanchard when they drove by." His forehead wrinkled. "Why would she say that when we're no relation?"

Haskell's fingers tightened to iron on the reins. The bay pranced, picking up its rider's agitation. "If you have another horse, I advise you ride in like you planned and tell Pastor Hutton and the sheriff. I doubt Overton'll go in on the main road. And he may have headed for Pueblo."

Blanchard raised his hand. "You best be goin'. I'll let them know what's happening and send a telegram on to Pueblo just in case."

"I'm much obliged." The spirited bay reared under Haskell's tight hand. "I'll get your horse back to you."

"He's a good one. Dodger, I call him, 'cause he can dodge a prairie-dog hole before you know it's there."

Haskell leaned forward and rubbed the bay's neck, already slick beneath the reins. With a flick of his wrist, he whirled the horse around and it charged down the lane to the main road.

Show me which way.

Haskell had prayed more in the last few days than in the ten years since his father took sick. And he prayed he'd get a different answer this time than he did to those long-ago prayers that failed to keep his father alive.

At the crossroad, he reined in and looked both ways. His gut told him Overton would head for Pueblo, where he wasn't as recognizable. He could catch a train south to Raton, hide out in New Mexico, or go north to Denver. Or he could go east.

From the valley floor Haskell saw only orchards, fields, and distant mountains—a poor vantage point.

"Which way, Lord? I need your help like I've never needed it before."

The bay swiveled its ears at his voice and pranced in a full circle. Haskell heeled him left toward Pueblo.

With the sun at his back, he chased his shadow. Just as he'd chased Tad Overton—always pursing, never catching. But this time he pursued much more than a thief.

Something in the road ahead caught his attention and he pulled up.

The bay danced around it, ears and nostrils strained at the wheel-flattened straw hat. Had Martha thrown it out on purpose or was she hurt?

His gut cinched and he flexed his fingers against their steely grip. "Steady, boy, steady." He rubbed the horse's lathered neck but the words were for himself. His father's words.

The hat was evidence that they'd ridden this way—not evidence that Martha was hurt. *Don't give your anger free rein, son. Steady. Hold steady.*

Leaning over Dodger's neck, he dug in his heels and the horse stretched into a dead gallop. The wind whipped sweat from Haskell's face as soon as it formed and blew dust and grit in his eyes. He pushed on the reins, giving the horse its head, counting on Blanchard's confidence that the animal could dodge a chuck hole if need be.

The road crested a small rise, and below, across the flat before the next hill, dust churned from the wagon as the old mare kept a frantic pace.

Joy leaped to Haskell's throat on its way to a shout, but celebration was premature. He had to reach them first.

"Catch them, boy." The wind tore the words from his lips, but their urgency telegraphed into Dodger's straining muscles. As if the bay knew, it charged into the dip and up the other side. With the heavy pull, the mare had slowed on the upward climb. Haskell was gaining on them.

A loud pop and hot air grazed his cheek. He ducked. Another bullet whizzed by.

Two shots. Four left. Haskell reached for his Colt. A few more yards and he'd be close enough to fire.

And close enough to hit Martha if the wagon veered. He holstered the gun and squinted into the wind. She didn't look back. She wasn't sitting straight but was slumped against Tad.

He'd chloroformed her.

Haskell slapped leather. His spurs were at the hotel, not needed for a peaceful wagon ride to an apple orchard. Another mistake. He knew better than to not be prepared. Never again.

Another pop and heat grazed his ear. He flinched and jerked the reins left. Dodger swerved and Haskell quickly pulled him back to center. Another crest and the wagon disappeared over the top, picking up speed.

But the mare was fading. As Dodger chewed up the distance, curses shot past Haskell like bullets. When a wagon's length closed between the buckboard and the bay's head, he kicked free of the stirrups.

Just a few more strides. Keep it up, boy, a little closer…

Haskell dove for the wagon. Overton swung his gun hand back as a front wheel hit a rut and his bullet fell short, biting wood from the bed.

Two shots left.

Overton shoved the gun against Martha's chest and screamed. "Jump out or I'll kill her."

Haskell leaped, knocking the gun forward. The bullet shot past the mare's ear, frightening her into a death race.

Haskell twisted the weapon from Overton's hand and threw it over the side. A left hook sent the man over the bench seat and into the wagon bed. He didn't move.

Haskell snatched the reins with one hand and reached for Martha with the other. She had slumped forward onto her knees and bounced against the end of the bench. One misstep by the faltering mare, and she could be thrown out.

The horse's ears were pinned against her skull, and her head bobbed with straining effort. Globs of white sweat flew back off her lathered hide.

Haskell looped his right arm around Martha's waist and held her upright as he reined in the mare, slowing to a painful lope, then a trot, and finally a limping walk at the road's edge.

The horse's sides heaved, her head hung, and her forelegs buckled. She went down and the wagon slammed to a standstill.

Haskell turned Martha to face him and cradled her lolling head. Enfolding her in his arms, he rocked back and forth as he prayed, frantic that he'd reached her too late.

"God, please. Don't let me lose her."

His vision blurred as he drank in her pale features and smoothed her hair from her face.

"Don't leave me, Martha," he whispered. "I want you to be my wife and fill our home with your fiery spirit." His voice broke on the last word, and he crushed her limp body against him.

CHAPTER EIGHTEEN

Painful hoof beats throbbed through Martha's head. Her face rubbed against a sweat-drenched shirt, a strong heart pulsing behind it. Steady, masculine, comforting. Haskell?

She pushed against the hard chest and looked up. The sun backlit the man, and she squinted against the light. But the smell, the tenderness, the substance of him confirmed who he was.

She breathed his name and felt a moan at her ear. The arms that encircled her set her upright, and a rough hand cupped her face on each side. She blinked, trying to see, and raised a hand to shield the sun.

"Haskell?"

"Thank God." His voice choked off and he drew her to him again.

The throbbing in her head lessened, and she finally scooted back to sit on her own. Without the sun in her eyes, she clearly saw the tear trails on his grimy face and blood atop his right ear.

"You're hurt." Gently she ran her fingers through his wind-whipped hair.

"Just grazed. I'll heal."

"Oh, Haskell. I was so afraid he'd killed you."

He pulled her to him again and pressed his lips against hers. "I'm sorry I didn't protect you," he whispered.

"But you did."

He leaned back and his hot breath swept her face like a thirsty man searching for water.

"You showed me how to leave sign, a trail to follow."

Relief gushed out on a moan and he kissed her again.

"You saw it, didn't you? You saw my hat?"

A smile broke white in his dirty face. "I'll make a ranger of you yet."

She sniffed. "I should hope not. One rough ride like this is entirely enough for me."

A groan from the wagon bed jerked their heads in unison.

"Give me your boot laces," Haskell said as he climbed over the bench.

Martha untied her boots, stripped the long black laces, and handed them to Haskell, who straddled Tad face down on the wagon's floor boards. He pulled the vest from Tad's back and bound his hands. Then he pulled off both boots and bound his ankles.

Haskell grabbed his hat and returned to the bench seat, where he slipped on the vest and patted the pockets. He drew out a gold fob anchored by a beautiful watch with scrollwork engraving the case in a fine *TJ*.

Martha laid her hand on his arm. "Where is the *H*?"

"There is no *H*. This was my father's watch—Tillman Jacobs. A Jefferson Ranger. He gave it to me the day he died. Someday I'll give it to my son."

A cold and heavy stone dropped to the bottom of Martha's core. How could she stand in the way of what he really wanted? She wrapped her arms around her middle to keep from breaking in half. "I'm so glad you got it back."

He pocketed the watch, then searched the vest's lining. Halting with discovery, he withdrew the ranger's star and pinned it to the front of his vest. "Blanchard wants proof I'm who I say I am when I take his horse back."

At that, he looked to Dolly who lay awkwardly in front of the wagon. Martha had been so woozy she hadn't noticed that the poor thing had fallen in the harness.

Haskell lifted her from the wagon and together they stripped away the rigging.

She knelt at the mare's head and stroked her sweat-soaked neck. "You poor thing," she whispered. "You poor, dear, faithful thing."

The smooth slide of steel against leather turned her head as Haskell cocked his gun.

He reached for her. "Stand behind me. You don't need to see this."

"No. Please. Can't we help her in some way?" Fresh tears squeezed up from Martha's soul, bitter with regret for having prayed for the animal's demise.

Pained features and a stern jaw met her pleading. "What would you have me do? Leave her here to be eaten alive by coyotes and buzzards?"

"We can get her up, get her standing. Oh, Haskell, please. I know she may not make it, but not now. Not like this." She covered her mouth with both hands to hold back a sob.

He stared at his boots for a long moment, then eased the hammer back and holstered his gun. They pulled the winded mare to her feet, and Haskell set the brake and tied her off to the front wheel.

"Thank you." Martha rested her forehead against his chest and looped her arms around him. He stroked her hair and in a low voice thanked the Lord for the animal's faithful heart.

Martha palmed tears from her face and stepped back. "Amen."

A whinny floated to them on the cooling breeze, and Martha looked east. A beautiful bay stallion stood next to the road, head high, reins still around its neck.

Haskell whistled and the bay flicked its ears and tossed its head. As if making clear the decision was his, he turned toward them and trotted to the wagon.

"Dodger." Haskell held his hand out as the horse approached and greeted them with a deep-chested rumble.

"You're definitely a runner." He slipped the reins off and dropped them to the ground, then he tightened the cinch and started to shorten the stirrup strap.

Martha stopped him. "Not this time, Haskell Jacobs." She patted the stirrup leather against the horse's side. "You are not walking back to town. You're riding. We're *both* riding."

His slow smile swirled through her.

"Don't look down," she said.

Her order doused his heated look and his brows raised in question.

"Better yet, close your eyes."

She lifted her skirt and wiped the dirt from his face. He squinted.

"No peeking."

He gripped her wrist and his eyes flew open—two fiery blue gems in a sea of sweat and grit. "A bit forward don't you think, Miss Hutton?"

"Not at all, Mr. Jacobs. I can't have my apple-picking escort looking like we chased halfway across Colorado."

Curses erupted from the back of the wagon. Martha whirled away, yanked at her petticoat, and tore off a wide strip. "It's ruined anyway. We might as well do something constructive with what's left." She stuffed the fabric in Haskell's hands. "Do you mind?"

"With pleasure."

Haskell gagged their captive and left him flopping like a trout in the wagon bed.

"I recommend you stay face down or the buzzards'll gouge your eyes out before the sheriff gets here."

At that, the flopping ceased, but not the guttural noises Martha equated with ungentlemanly expressions of wrath.

Haskell gathered the bay's reins, swung into the saddle and held out his hand. "Grab my wrist and I'll pull you up."

She complied and landed behind him astride the saddle apron. Wrapping her arms around his waist, she laid her head against his broad back, and they turned toward the sunset and home.

As relieved and grateful as she was, grief puddled deep within her like bitter rain. She had come so close to finding what she'd lost.

~

The dust cloud at the top of the first rise had to be the sheriff or Hutton. With daylight slipping behind the far ridgeline, Haskell couldn't make out which.

They met at the bottom of the dip, and Hutton rode up close and reached for Martha's arm. "You're safe." His voice was thick with emotion. "Thank God you're safe."

"Yes, Papa. Haskell got to us in time."

Hutton wiped his eyes with the back of his hand and looked at Haskell. "Blanchard told us what happened. The sheriff telegraphed Pueblo and he should be along soon. He's got a few men riding with him."

"The wagon's behind us about two miles. Overton's tied in the bed."

"With my boot laces."

Haskell bit back a grin at the pride in Martha's voice. He wasn't sure how her father would take such talk, but she pressed on.

"And that strip of white you'll find in his mouth—that's my petticoat."

Hutton held his tongue.

"Overton's gun is somewhere out in the cholla," Haskell said. "I didn't see where I tossed it."

"And Papa." The pride drained from Martha's voice. "Dolly's nearly done in. Tad drove her like a fiend."

Haskell softened his tone. "She ran her heart out and buckled where we stopped. I don't know that she can make it back to town."

Hutton dragged a hand down his face. "Better her than the two of you." He reset his hat and gave Martha a sad smile. "She was a good horse. Brought your mother and me together."

"I know, Papa. She was the little yellow filly, wasn't she?"

"That she was." He reined away. "I'll ride on and hitch the wagon to my horse, see how Dolly's doing."

Haskell shifted in the saddle. "She's tied to the off-side wheel."

Hutton left, and they continued on. In another mile, the sheriff and his posse reined up in a galloping dust cloud.

"Overton's in the wagon bed, trussed and ready for shipment, maybe three miles on." Haskell thumbed over his shoulder. "I'll testify against him to charges of kidnapping, assault, and attempted murder. I'm also certain he's the horse thief I was trailing, but we'll need a confession unless we can find those horses."

The sheriff pulled his hat brim. "Said you were the man for the job, didn't I?"

The eager group rode off, and Haskell headed Dodger toward the orchard. At the turn the stallion tried to lope, but he kept a tight rein to make Martha's ride as easy as possible.

Light filled the farmhouse windows and two lanterns hung at the barn doors.

Haskell threw his right leg over the bay's head and jumped to the ground, then turned to help Martha. With her hands on his shoulders, he pulled her to him, holding her close in the stillness.

"I've got you now," he whispered against her hair. "You're safe."

She wriggled against him. "Put me down, please."

With a quick squeeze and a chuckle, he set her on her feet. "I'll put you down but I'm not letting you go."

A shadow swept her face and she averted her eyes and stepped back. He couldn't believe it. She'd done it again—switched leads without so much as a stumble. What happened?

Blanchard came out of the house, his wife on his heels and three youngsters trailing behind.

"Lord be praised," he said, slapping Haskell on the back like a long lost relative.

A little pig-tailed girl peeked around her mother's skirts. "You really a ranger, mister?"

Blanchard pointed at Haskell's vest. "See that, Priscilla? That's a ranger's star. He's the real thing."

"Would you stay to supper?" Blanchard's wife said.

Martha moved her way, lightly touching Priscilla's hair. "Thank you, Sarah. You are so kind, but I expect Mama is beside herself with worry since we missed the evening service, and I hate to keep her waiting any longer."

The woman gave Martha a brief hug. "You're right, you know. She's near frantic, according to what Foster told me when he got back from town. But you two take our wagon home. The one there in the barn. The children and I gathered all your apples—all that weren't ruined—and loaded them in fresh bushels for you."

Martha covered her mouth with her hand.

"Thank you, ma'am." Haskell tipped his hat. "That's mighty generous of you."

"Can't have all that good fruit go to waste," Blanchard said, putting an arm around his wife. "Not when Mrs. Hutton's apple butter is at stake."

Haskell envied the man his family, but pushed such thoughts aside. "You've got a fine horse here, Blanchard. As good as you said, if not better."

The man's chest swelled. "Got him for a song, I did. About two years ago, down in Raton. Off some fella who said he was fast as sheet lightning and sure-footed as a dance hall gal."

"Foster!" Mrs. Blanchard clapped her hands over Priscilla's ears.

Blanchard himself blushed and ducked his head. "Sorry, Miss Marti. His words, not mine."

Haskell swallowed a grin and headed for the barn. Blanchard hurried forward and took the reins. "I'll take care of him. You get Miss Marti and those apples home. I can get the other horse and the wagon when I come to town Sunday."

Haskell shook his head at the man's generosity. "Thank you, Blanchard. I'm much obliged."

The wagon held baskets filled to the brim. More than they started with, if Haskell's count was right, and a horse stood ready and harnessed. He extended his hand to Martha, who came to his side with eyes downcast. His gut twisted. Something had sapped her joy and left her fragile and weak.

He handed her up and settled beside her. With a flick of the reins, they drove out of the open barn, past the small family, and into the night. He ached to feel Martha's warm body against him but she sat apart, straight and stoic.

If it were a man who had stolen her tenderness, he could fight him, defend her. But his foe was beyond the reach of his gun or his fists.

His instincts told him words were the culprit, and words had never been his weapon of choice.

As helpless as a lost pup, he headed out of the valley and up the last rise toward Cañon City.

CHAPTER NINETEEN

The evening star hung singular and bright in the paling sky, a shining ornament strung above the mountain silhouette. Solitary, like Martha, though she sat inches from a man to whom she would gladly give her heart and her life. She breathed in the cooling air and her insides chilled. Brimming like the new bushel baskets behind them, she was bursting with love for this man who had risked his life for her. He was so much more than she could have ever hoped for.

And she was so much less than he needed or wanted.

Once he knew the truth, he'd not be so eager to marry her.

A shiver rippled up her back.

Haskell pulled her beneath his arm. "You cold?"

Frozen rigid. "A little."

Unable to resist his warmth, she tucked against his side.

"It won't be long. The lights of town are just ahead."

He squeezed her arm, pressing her closer. The gesture deepened the pain of what she was about to lose all over again—the love and acceptance of a caring man.

As they drove into the quiet town, the horse's plodding hoof beats echoed off closed storefronts. No light shown from the church, the service canceled with her father gone. But through the trees, the parsonage's glowing windows promised refuge and comfort. Haskell turned down their lane and drove into the open barn. Martha pushed at her hair, discovering more of it worked loose from her twisted braid than captured by it. She must look a site.

He jumped down and stood beside the wagon with his hands lifted for her, his eyes dark and churning as she imagined the sea in a storm. Her heart reached for her throat as she reached for his shoulders, and he set her lightly on the ground.

A question formed on his rugged features. "Martha, will you—"

"Oh, thank God." Her mother's voice broke with a sob as she hobbled into the barn clutching a shawl around her shoulders. "Thank God you're safe."

He groaned and quickly kissed the top of Martha's head before stepping back.

Her mother's eyes were red with weeping. Martha palmed her cheek. "Don't cry, Mama. We're safe. The Lord took fine care of us."

Her mother squeezed Haskell's forearm, then tugged her shawl closer with one hand and drew Martha with the other. "The apples can wait. Come inside and get warm and have something to eat, both of you."

"I'll tend to the horse. You go ahead."

The remark drew her mother's notice and she threw a questioning look at Martha. "Where's Dolly?" A closer inspection of the green wagon raised her brows. "And our buckboard?"

"Dolly nearly ran herself to death, Mama, but we'll tell you all about it inside." She turned from Haskell with as much detachment as she could summon. "Haskell spared her."

She understood his compassionate gesture to end Dolly's suffering, but she'd never have been able to tell her mother Haskell had shot the horse she'd raised from a filly, old though it was.

Enclosed in the barn, the wagon load of crisp, ripe fruit perfumed the air with a cidery promise.

"You certainly picked a lot today." Her mother pulled out several apples and tucked them in her shawl. "These will make a fine pie for tomorrow's dinner."

"We didn't pick them, Mama, but that's all part of the story. Come on."

By the time Haskell came in and washed for supper, they heard horses outside. Moments later, her father trudged in, dusty and tired from hard riding and harder worry. He held a hand out to Haskell and topped it with his other in a hardy grip. Then he pulled Martha into his arms. The breath caught in his chest and the sound pushed a knot to her throat.

Finally he held her back. "Thank you, Lord, and thank you, Haskell."

Haskell's features sobered and he glanced out the door glass. "My pleasure, Pastor."

Martha took her seat but kept her eyes from meeting his. She would refuse him, spare him the pain of retracting his proposal once he learned she could not give him what he longed for.

Oh, Lord, let me not bleed to death right here at the table.

They all took their seats, and hands reached out to either side for prayer. Haskell's swallowed Martha's as always and he squeezed her fingers. Her heart split like an apple beneath a boot heel.

At the *amen*, her father picked up his coffee and held it with both hands, elbows pitched on the table as if for support.

"Dolly's in the barn." His eyes latched onto his wife's. "She's in bad shape, Annie. I don't know if she'll make it through the night."

Her mother's face crumpled into a silent cry and she hid behind her hands.

He set down his cup and rubbed her shoulder. "She had a good life, sweetheart, you know that."

Her mother nodded and sniffed. Martha thanked God again that Haskell had not shot the old mare.

"And Tad Overton is behind bars."

At the news, Haskell's lips curled and he reached for the butter crock.

He had to be starving after all he'd been through. With a start, Martha remembered his ear and leaned forward to see it, catching uncertainty in his eyes. He'd sensed her withdrawal.

Grief surged through her like a fever. "Your ear. We should dress it."

Her parents both turned to Haskell, and he fingered the dried blood. "It's just a flesh wound."

"I didn't even notice, Mr. Jacobs." Mama wiped her eyes with her napkin and drew in a broken breath. "I was so glad to see the both of you, I guess I didn't look any closer. What happened?"

"Tad shot him." Martha shuddered. "At least that's what I think happened. I didn't exactly see it."

Her mother's jaw went slack.

"Is that what happened?" Her father directed his question to Haskell.

"Yes, sir. Overton had Martha in the wagon. He'd chloroformed her and I was gaining on them while he was shooting."

"Chloroform? Shooting?" Mama's voice hit a rare note and her face blanched.

Her father moved his chair closer to his wife and tucked her beneath his arm. "I think you'd better start from the beginning, son."

To hear the event retold from Haskell's perspective, he'd hardly lifted a finger. He failed to mention risking his life to save her. The more she listened, the more she loved this man so deserving of everything he dreamed of. She scooted from the table.

"Excuse me, but I'm exhausted." She faced Haskell but kept her eyes down. Maybe he would accept this parting as her refusal and be on his way. "Thank you for your assistance today. I trust you'll have a safe journey to Denver with your prisoner."

Silence hung in the room like the evening star over the mountains. She laid her napkin on her plate and went to the parlor. Tired, yes. Tired enough to sleep, no. She'd lie on the settee, put her feet up, perhaps doze. There would plenty of time to sleep later. Alone.

She closed the parlor doors behind her, and her parents' voices blurred to concerned mumbles. It didn't take much to imagine them questioning Haskell about every detail.

His deep tones answered theirs, and at times, rose with a curious urgency. What could he be discussing at such length? Surely it was time for him to leave.

She placed a cushion beneath her neck as Haskell had on that pivotal day he'd nearly trampled her in the street. The irony bit. As it turned out, he'd merely trampled her heart.

Her eyes closed against the darkness, and the muted voices drifted beyond her ears.

~

Haskell pushed the parlor doors apart, and the kitchen light spread across the room to Martha's sleeping form. He moved to her side and pulled the small stool beneath him as he had once before. Reaching for her hand, he took it in both of his, hoping, praying she'd not be frightened by his nearness, but would welcome it.

And he prayed for wisdom, for compassion. Not only had he missed the importance of her not having children, he had also misread her parents. They did not see him as a hired gun, not where Martha was concerned, but they did endorse his decision to return to Cañon City and run for sheriff.

After a trial here, and if he could prove Overton was the horse thief, Haskell figured on a month to transport his prisoner, testify in Denver, and make it back to Cañon. In that time, Pastor Hutton promised to look for a house Haskell could rent until he bought a place of his own in the country. A place of *their* own.

If she'd have him.

"Martha." His whisper brushed her ear and he smoothed her cheek with the back of his hand.

She turned her head and her eyelashes fluttered with a dream.

"Martha." He squeezed her hand. "Wake up. I need to ask you something before I leave."

She jerked and her eyes flew open, dark and wide in the dim light.

"It's me. Don't be frightened." He pressed his lips against her tightened fingers and helped her sit up.

"What happened? What's wrong?"

"Nothing is wrong. Everything is right. At least I hope so."

She withdrew her hand and buried it in her skirts. Her eyes glistened, and she looked ready to flee the room.

His conversation with her parents and what he believed to be her genuine affection for him steeled his will to continue. "I love you, Martha."

Her lips parted with a small gasp.

"Marry me. Sit on my porch swing and share what's left of this old man's life."

Crushing her brows together, she scoffed. "You are not an old man, Haskell Jacobs." Her glance flew across the room and she rolled her lips. "But…in the orchard, I was not completely truthful with you."

He knew now, and it didn't matter, but he let her say it because it mattered to her.

"I am not all that you think I am."

Clasping her hands tightly, she drew a deep breath. "There is something you should know about me that could change the way you feel."

A smile tugged his mouth "I already know about your two last names."

She choked out a halfhearted laugh but shook her head. Then she raised that defiant chin he had come to love.

"You will have no son to give your father's watch if you marry me. Nor any daughters." Her eyes pooled and her voice fell to a whisper. "I am barren."

The groan broke deep in his chest and he took her into his arms. "My sweet Martha." Gladly he'd spend the rest of his life proving she was more than enough. "I don't need a son if I have you."

A tremor rippled through her.

"You mean more to me than many sons or daughters."

She pushed back and held both hands to her mouth. Above them, soft brown eyes fixed on his.

How to convince her? He couldn't lose her now, not because of her uncertainty, not after all they'd been through.

"Do you need proof?"

She blinked and a jewel slipped from her lashes and down her face.

"What did your father say? The day of the basket social."

Her gaze faltered on a frown as she remembered.

Taking her hands, he drew from the wisdom so new to him, so fresh and full of hope. "If you cannot see the evidence of my love, then take it on faith."

She closed her eyes and shook her head.

His insides knotted. Had he misjudged her affections after all?

"Oh, Haskell." A wind whisper through the pines. He trembled at the sound. "You have more than shown me."

He pulled her close, and she wrapped her arms around him with a quivering breath. Then he lifted her chin and gently kissed the tears from her lips.

"Who knows what God has in store for us, Martha? He proved that to me the day I watched a red-haired beauty in black step from the train."

Her breathy laugh brushed his face. "Only you would see beauty where there was nothing but pain." Sitting back, she palmed her damp cheeks. "I suppose there is more than one way to fill a home with love and laughter."

"Who's to say there is not a lonely child somewhere who needs the same? More than one, or a whole house full."

Her smile spilled over him, soothing all the old scars, healing every longing.

"A porch, you say?" She slanted a teasing glance.

His heart raced. "And a swing."

She framed his face between her warm, soft hands, so full of promise and possibility.

"In that case, Haskell Tillman Jacobs, I'd like nothing better than to spend the rest of my life loving you."

~~~

Thank you for being an Inspirational Western Romance reader!

For more on the Hutton family, continue reading Book 4, *A Change of Scenery.*

I hope you enjoyed reading *The Cañon City Chronicles* as much as I enjoyed writing them. If so, I'd greatly appreciate a brief review on your favorite book websites and other social media.

Acknowledgements

My heartfelt thanks go to all who aided and supported me in telling these stories, particularly readers Jill Maple, Amanda, Lynne Schricker, and my cowboy husband, Mike. Much appreciation goes to Kim Aulerich Mahone for her expertise in the finer details of nineteenth century clothing and to my editor, Christy Distler.

About the Author

Bestselling author and winner of the **Will Rogers Gold Medallion** for Inspirational Western Fiction, **Davalynn Spencer** writes heart-tugging romance with a Western flair. Learn more about Davalynn and her books and sign up for her free newsletter at www.davalynnspencer.com

Connect online at www.davalynnspencer.com

www.facebook.com/AuthorDavalynnSpencer/

http://twitter.com/davalynnspencer

See all Davalynn's books on her Amazon Author Page: www.amazon.com/author/davalynnspencer

For the latest news, sign up for her quarterly newsletter: http://eepurl.com/xa81D

~ May all that you read be uplifting. ~

Made in the USA
Monee, IL
11 October 2024